ROOFTOP ANGELS

TIERNEY JAMES

L & D
PRESS
Owasso, OK

ISBN - 978-1-965460-06-1

DEDICATION

Dedicated to all those who protect the children of the world.

Acknowledgments

Many thanks to my editor, Kate Richards at Wizards of Publishing, for not giving up on me during this project. You made my rocky road a little smoother.

Another thanks to Jaycee DeLorenzo at Sweet 'N Spicy Designs for cover art and formatting. Your creativity and vision gave me a great deal of satisfaction.

Then there is Sharon-Kizziah Holmes of Paperback Press who is always there for me in a pinch. You continue to give hope to everyone around you on their publishing journey.

And of course, what would I be without my incredible family who continue to inspire and support me in my life as a writer? Thank you. I love you all so much.

I would also like to mention that incredible bunch of people who make up my street team. They kept after me to finish the project while passing the word about my books. You are just too awesome.

PROLOGUE

Grass Valley, California

Her husband must have forgotten to activate the security system again when he'd taken the kids to their evening activities. Tessa had noticed the lack of blinking lights on the master panel when she'd entered the house through the garage. The well-lit laundry room showed no signs of disturbance.

The mounds of dirty towels, soiled football jerseys, and lopsided white shirts needing a once-over with a steam iron remained in the same place she'd left them. The door swung open into the kitchen filled with a darkness like mud, heavy and annoying on the bottom of your best shoes. Even the night-light next to the stove offered no help. Searching for the light switch, she fumbled with her bag of groceries then dropped her briefcase.

When Tessa flipped the switch on, she stood still for a few seconds surveying the surroundings, overwhelmed by the familiar paralyzing feeling she might not be alone.

Robert called her a spook, afraid of her own shadow, of everything and everyone. A week didn't go by without him telling her to lighten up. No matter what, he promised to protect her. But her husband didn't know the secrets she carried.

Placing the groceries on the island, Tessa's eyes went to the night-light on the edge of the counter. The smashed globe raised her tension to another level. She pulled open a drawer and slipped a butcher knife out then dropped her hand to her side. The open-style kitchen spilled light into the darkened dining room and family area where table lamps on timers should have flooded the room with light.

Her common sense screamed for her to wait outside for Robert and the children. Tessa didn't want to think about her family coming home to danger. She swallowed hard as her feet took baby steps. Her eyes landed on the time flashing on the microwave. Could there have been a power surge? Tessa sighed, relieved at a logical explanation for the timers and maybe even the security system failure. An electrical problem didn't explain the smashed night-light, however.

Placing the knife on the table, she bent down to retrieve the timer from the wall socket to reset it, but tensed as she found it lying upside down on the wood floor. She'd laid the knife down on the table only a second ago. She jerked upright.

Pulling back her shoulders, she once more searched the depths of darkness in her home. The sensation of not being alone overwhelmed her just as a ribbon of light slipped through the shutters, revealing a large male form not more than ten feet from her.

He vaulted toward her. Her scream shattered the darkness as she backed into a chair preventing an immediate escape. She jerked it out to stop the intruder's advance as she swung the butcher knife at his head. He blocked it with an arm like solid steel then managed to knock it from her grasp. The split second caught him off guard long enough for her to escape toward the stairs.

Inside her nightstand rested a loaded revolver. If she could make it there, she'd kill him. Tessa had no qualms about protecting herself or her family. She knew the staircase even in darkness. The knowledge gave her an edge on the danger stalking her. An unnerving guttural chuckle reached her.

The beat of her terrified heart pounded in her ears. Halfway up the stairs, he grabbed her foot, bringing her down hard onto her knees. Tessa rotated on her hip and kicked him so hard in the jaw the intruder fell back against the railing. With a grunt, she scrambled up to the landing and raced to her bedroom.

She jammed in the lock button on the doorknob then rushed to her nightstand. She yanked out the drawer as the intruder kicked the door open. Her hands searched for the holster she'd velcroed to the upper inside of the drawer.

The sound of his heavy breathing revealed he'd stopped at the door. She wobbled as she pivoted to level the revolver at his chest.

"So, help me, I'll use this." The moonlight spilled through the open windows across her weapon and the intruder.

He appeared to be over six foot, a detail she could report later, since the dark ski mask hid his features. His body, in black clothing, looked muscular. His heavy breathing rasped as if he were winded. With disturbing calmness, the man glanced around the room then back at the weapon. The moonlight touched his demonic smile in the opening of the ski mask. His one cautious step forward drew an immediate reaction.

Tessa pulled the trigger, not once but six times. Nothing happened. As she gaped in horror at her weapon, the intruder reached in his pants pocket and took out bullets. He extended his hand to her as if offering a gift before letting them fall through his fingers to the floor. Something resembling amusement escaped his throat.

Tessa hurled the gun at his head, making contact. He stumbled sideways, opening the way for her to charge toward the door in hopes of escape. With an angry howl, the man grabbed her around the waist and dragged her toward the center of the room. He stopped several times when Tessa struggled to break free. Each time, his grip grew stronger until he shoved her against a bedpost.

Her swift kick to his shin rewarded her with another shake as he pushed his face into hers. "Stop!" he demanded.

Something snapped, taking her brain from autopilot to DEFCON 4. This would not end well if she didn't fight for her life. His size told of brute strength. How would she ever escape? Tessa scratched at his eye holes. The man captured her hands, pinning her between his body and the edge of the bed. A feeling of helplessness washed over her as his rock-hard body pressed home the power he held over her. He jerked her into his arms.

The intruder touched her long hair before sliding his hand down her face. She cringed as his fingers, smelling of tobacco and beer, rubbed across her trembling lips. When she opened her mouth to speak, the man's eyes focused on her tongue. Cocking his head, he slipped a finger inside. Her teeth sank deep into his skin. He growled and released her in one step. Once again, the thought of escape forced her heart to pound harder as he picked her up with a labored grunt. The bed groaned as her back smacked against the mattress. Tears of panic threatened to blind any hope of escape when she rolled to her knees and scrambled away.

"Stop!" he demanded again.

Rough hands with vise-grip holds locked around her ankles before jerking her legs flat against the covers. The springs creaked as she felt him climb onto the bed then swing a leg over her prone body. Before he could apply his weight, Tessa flipped over onto her back, causing him to almost pause in midair. A sinister smile appeared in the mouth opening of his ski mask. His clothes, although intact, revealed what his body wanted from her. With fierceness, he grabbed her face and shook her even as she closed her eyes.

"Look at me," he growled.

Tessa obeyed. His eyes were black which she thought matched his soul. She wanted to remember those details if she survived. He smelled of perspiration now. Maybe if she could get him to touch something besides her, the sweat might have traces of DNA. She felt nauseous at each puff of rancid breath against her face. The black clothes appeared mismatched and void of any significant details. The twisted smirk revealed crooked teeth, a sign he'd not been given the best of dental care. He sat up and reached down to unbutton her blouse.

"Easy," was all he said. When the last button came loose, he spread the cotton fabric open and leered down at her. As his hand touched her neck then trailed a descent down her chest, she doubled her fist and landed a blow on his ear.

With a shake of his head, the man grabbed his ear. A growl rose from deep in his throat. He'd pulled back his fist to return the favor when she swallowed her pride and held up her hands in surrender.

"I'm sorry. I'm sorry." She quivered. "Please. Don't hurt me. I'll do whatever you want. Please don't hurt me." The man stopped as Tessa lifted her hands over her head to rest on the pillows, inviting him to her apparent surrender. In slow motion, he pushed himself down against her again before taking a deep breath. Tessa had the impression he might be savoring the moment as his eyes searched her face.

"See? I'll be good. I promise. Please don't hurt me," she begged in small, helpless sniffs.

The man leaned above her head and captured each of Tessa's hands as his chest pressed harder against her body.

She ran her tongue along the outside of her lips then pretended to bite them. Desire sprang to his eyes. Although forced, her voice became a husky whisper. "Slow. Please." He leaned closed to enjoy a first taste. "Yes," she whispered.

His grip loosened as her mouth pressed against his. Whether he failed to notice or didn't care, he didn't react when she raised her knees, sending him off balance. She jerked her hands in a downward motion, throwing him into the headboard. Tessa flipped him off her with little effort. He tumbled off the bed into the corner of the nightstand, clipping his head on the way to the floor.

Tessa reached for the flashlight on the opposite nightstand and jumped off the bed. She circled around to where the man moaned and struggled to get to his feet. Turning on the light, she stuck the beam in his face, blinding him. He raised an arm as if to block the light as he staggered to stand. Tessa swung the foot-long flashlight at his head, but his reflexes were still better than most and he knocked it across the floor.

"Honey, we're home!" Her husband, Robert, and the kids had arrived back from evening activities.

Both Tessa and the intruder froze before looking at the door then at each other.

Pointing at the open window, she shoved at his chest with a soft fist bump. "You'd better go." Her voice turned matter-of-fact. The intruder paused a little too long. "Go. Now. Before it's too late." She walked to the window and held back the sheers.

He turned and bolted toward her. Pushing out the screen with utmost care, he took a moment to grin back at her one last time before patting her on the cheek with gentle affection.

Tessa rushed to flip the light on. The bullets were scattered near the door. She took her foot and pushed them under the dresser as she lifted the gun from the floor. With a nervous jerk, she opened her underwear drawer and shoved the gun into the back. The jewelry box her father had made her on her sixteenth birthday sat on top of the bureau. Pulling the drawers out, Tessa dumped the contents across the floor.

"Honey?"

Tessa heard Robert at the top of the stairs. A final glance at the staging before she licked her fingers then rubbed them under her eyes to make a trail of mascara helped her feel like she was in damage-control mode. Another drop of spit placed on her cheek and she sucked in her breath. When she flung the door open and ran to her husband with a breathless cry of helplessness, she wondered if God might be frowning at her, especially since she'd neglected to button her blouse. "Oh, Robert!"

He pushed her to arm's length. "What is it?" His tone revealed concern.

"A burglar!" Tessa caught her breath as Robert pulled her into his arms.

"Are you hurt?" He pushed her back again. "What happened to your blouse?"

Tessa shook her head. "No, not hurt. I was changing in the bathroom when I heard him. I locked myself inside. When I heard you come in, I rushed out to warn you. I guess it scared him off. He went out the window." Tessa fell against his chest once more to touch up her face with a quick lick on two fingers and then streaked them across her cheeks.

"What about the alarm? Didn't it go off?"

Their two boys and little daughter scampered up the stairs and stopped wide-eyed. "Turned off when I got home. I guess you forgot again," Tessa lied. God might be frowning at her lies and attempt at deception, but it needed to be done.

Robert ran his hand through his hair then rubbed his forehead. "I could have sworn I pushed 'on' when we left. I'm so sorry, Tessa. This is my fault." He pulled out his cell phone and dialed 911.

The children hugged their mother, patting her like she did them when they were hurt.

"The police are on their way, Tessa." He kissed her before walking toward the bedroom and the scene of the "robbery".

~~~
~~~

The man hopped over the fence into the neighbor's yard. He crouched for a minute to make sure no one saw him— dressing in black came from living in the shadows a number of years. With the teeth coverings removed and shoved inside his jacket, the man proceeded to move to the backdoor of the modern-style house, so unlike the one he'd invaded. He already knew the location of the spare key. The old couple who lived here were predictable; kept it under the doormat, like so many other people in the neighborhood. The woman next door had been different. It had taken him thirty minutes to find it. The security system needed to be updated, so he'd only had to pull the outside wires to disconnect it. Rather than pay a few dollars more a month to get a wireless system, they left themselves vulnerable to someone like him.

A rotating red light flashed in the darkness as a police car pulled into the drive of the house he'd escaped. He felt amused remembering the blue of the woman's eyes, the firmness of her lips, and the bite of her teeth. He stuck his wounded finger into his mouth to suck the oozing blood. He wanted to savor how she molded perfectly beneath him. If her husband had not returned home, he might still be enjoying himself. The thought occurred to him their friendship was headed toward a slippery slope.

He peeked through the door panel into a dark kitchen as he turned the key in the lock. Someone was home. Lights filled a distant living room, and the sound of the television caught his ear as he moved with the skill of a cat burglar. Voices filled with excitement as the two figures appeared and moved to the front door. He couldn't understand what they were saying but he imagined it had to do with the police car next door.

The doorbell rang as he stepped toward the refrigerator. He leaned against it, hoping the caller would not want to come in. Too many surprises in one night for his liking. Hungry and exhausted from the physical confrontation, his body also craved a very cold shower.

He heard the police ask the usual questions; had they seen anyone, heard anything, did they lock their doors, etc. He imagined the officer handing them a card with his information and number in case they thought of something. The door clicked shut, and the sound of a dead bolt being thrown made him wonder if the couple might be afraid.

The television became silent, followed by footsteps moving toward where he lurked. They spoke in soft voices until they entered the kitchen, flipping on the lights.

He felt a kind of amusement when they didn't see him at first. But they appeared to see him at the same time. Suddenly the man trembled and the woman gasped, her hand trying to cover her mouth. All three stood staring at each other in silence.

The woman stepped toward him and snatched off his ski mask with the gentleness of a grizzly bear. After tossing it onto the table, she shook a crooked finger at his nose. "What in goodness name have you done?" Hands dropped to a narrow waist.

He ran his hand across his face before opening the freezer door. He took out a package of frozen peas and laid it across his cheekbone where Tessa had managed to make contact.

"Did you hurt Tessa?" she demanded in a thick Irish accent laced with irritation. "And what about those babies? Were they home?"

"Do you have any ice cream, Martha?" Unconcerned, he dug in the freezer.

"Answer me, Chase Hunter, or I'll flog you here and now."

The old man pulled out a chair and sat down. "You'd better give us a full account or she will make your life miserable, Chase."

Pulling out the vanilla ice cream, Chase frowned as he scanned the label. "Is this all you got?" He tossed the peas back inside before shutting the door. Martha handed him a spoon and moved to the china cabinet. The moment she took out a bowl, he opened the container and ate from the carton.

"I didn't hurt her. The kids and What's His Name were gone, at least until the end of the training session." Chase leaned against the counter and scraped the last bite of ice cream from the bottom of the box. He licked the spoon and met Martha's angry expression. "She's fine.

This time she shot me." A halfhearted chuckle slipped out as a drip of ice cream slid down his chin. "Samantha did a heck of a job breaking her in. I guess we're done with the training to see if she can protect herself." He tried to smile with the spoon clenched between his teeth. "I don't know when I've had more fun."

Martha grabbed a damp dish towel and snapped it against Chase's leg, making him yelp.

"What the hell?"

"Watch your mouth in this house, young man, or I'll shoot you myself."

Chase winked at her husband. "Yes, ma'am."

The man, Francis, pointed a finger at the Enigma team leader. "I've seen how you watch Tessa. She's a married woman, Chase. Don't mess up her life."

He didn't like being told what to do or how to live his life. "I've gotta go. It's getting late." He tossed the empty ice cream carton in the trash can and laid the spoon in the sink then leaned over and kissed Martha on the cheek. "Care if I shower and change before I hit the road? The police might be at the entrance to this happy little subdivision. I don't want to fit any description Tessa gave."

They both waved him away.

As Chase left the room, he heard Francis speak to his wife in a low voice. "I don't like where this is headed."

CHAPTER 1

Foothills of the Pamir Mountains in Afghanistan

Her sense of smell forced her to wrinkle her nose at the same time her throbbing head begged her to be still. Then, as she ignored the warning, a sharp jab of pain traveled up to her hip. The floor where she sat felt like compacted dirt. Even in the dim light seeping through the ragged covering over the window, she understood this place meant danger. But where was she? How had she gotten here? Why were her hands tied with something like baling twine? Her face felt puffy as if she suffered from allergies, or had she been crying? The taste of salt coated her tongue. Dry, cracked lips needed moisture.

Who were the small people cowering along the wall near her? A small child rested her head on the edge of her shoulder. She flinched away in panic as the downward movement landed the child in her lap. The little one offered up a sleepy grin at her before snuggling back against her shoulder.

The child had light-colored eyes with skin neither tan nor white but something in between, as if she spent a great deal of time outdoors. She smelled liked boiled onions or was it cabbage? The overpowering scent of wood smoke confused her ability to piece together the events leading to this point in time.

Panic raced through her body as her heart accelerated. Even though her arms and legs felt cold, sweat beaded up across her neck and forehead. A sticky substance covered her hands. Lifting them up into the ribbons of light, she squinted to see her palms.

Blood. Her hands were covered in blood. Whose blood? Her body ached. She rubbed her hands up and down, over and over against the torn robe she wore. The fibers, rough and shaggy, pulled the blood from her hands as she worked to be free of the dried substance. The child's head grew heavy against her shoulder. She wanted to check herself for open wounds. Would she find more blood? *I need to get up and move.* She nudged the child to push her back against the wall made of mud bricks.

Standing with a grunt and the grace of an eighty-year- old woman, she staggered up. She bit her bottom lip so hard the taste of salt and blood seeped onto her parched tongue. An awkward attempt to feel her body for open wounds with tied hands helped her realize the bindings remained loose but she still couldn't wiggle free of them.

Her hands trembled against her body locating a number of bruises but no wounds. She stretched out her arms then rolled her shoulders. The movement helped her to relax. A step on weak legs propelled her forward faster than she intended. The pain now resembled stiffness rather than an injury.

Something skittered across the floor. Mice. She sucked in her breath and fell back against a table propped up by a cardboard box. It flipped over with her weight against it. She cried out as someone touched her neck. The sudden movement caused her to jerk away and lose her balance. Outstretched hands pulled her back to steady feet.

A reflex to fight kicked in, and she rammed a shoulder into the man who stood no taller than her. He looked like a young oak tree, strong and unmoving despite her attempt to escape. Instead of retaliating, the young man chuckled and grabbed her by the twine around her wrists. He pointed toward the door and added a tug indicating she needed to follow him outside. She dug in her heels to no avail. The next jerk sent her staggering into his back as he led her outside into the light of day.

The burst of brightness forced her head down. Seeing that she wore what looked like combat boots, the fleeting thought, *they're not even cute,* popped into her head. The cool wind created shivers as she cocked her head to the side to glimpse the surroundings. A scarf slipped off her head onto the ground. With the sound of excited voices of men, she stole a glance to see what had gotten them wound up. They pointed at her face then at their own eyes and hair. Their black garb and headdress told her she wasn't in Kansas anymore, as the saying went. Lumbering yaks swaying their heads and the stomp of restless horses added to the confusion as to her location.

Self-conscious, she touched her hair, and realized strands twisted free from a loose ponytail. The curls blew across her face as she pushed them back with unsteady hands. She remained clueless as to the reason her appearance caused such excitement. A fleeting thought her mascara smeared on what felt like a puffy face caused her to swipe at her cheeks. The young man who had dragged her outside wore a pillbox-like hat. He stormed up to her and cupped her chin in his hand and squeezed. She guessed he might be seventeen or eighteen, just a kid.

She took a step forward and rammed her knee into his groin. He collapsed on the ground with the rest of his sketchy friends laughing. Several others stepped forward then back, followed by mocking her actions. The young man on the ground moaned as he staggered to his feet then held himself. The defense move felt familiar, as if she'd used it a number of times. Had she done it wrong? The kid acted like she'd given him a swat on the rump.

A step back landed her against a bigger man. She spun around and stepped away. He wore a brown fur hat with flaps drooping over his ears and a stained, ragged scarf wrapped around his temples. A tattered ski mask covered his nose, but the other openings revealed almond-shaped eyes. From the large openings, it couldn't offer much warmth. His exposed mouth was wide with full, thick lips that turned down in an impatient frown.

Startled, she took another step away but tangled her foot in her robe and landed her on the ground. The man's solemn glare bore down on her as he reached to grab her by the arm and lifted with an unexpected gentleness. The strength in his hands reminded her of someone else, but she couldn't remember who. Someone tall and menacing walked through a hazy memory. That memory carried a weapon, military issued. Why she knew such a thing remained a mystery. Then the shadowy image vanished. The man in the brown hat watched her with interest, not lust, which both alarmed and comforted her. She spotted a dagger sheathed at his waist and wondered for a split second what he used it for since she noticed a smear of blood on the handle.

"Miss Melanie?" A small child peered in from the door of the shelter. Running to her, she slipped tied hands over the child's head, and pulled her into her body. "What's wrong?"

"I'm hungry, Miss Melanie. We are hungry."

Desperation in the small arms circled around her lower body. The child choked back tears. What had she called her? Melanie? *My name is Melanie?* The name evoked the dark image of another man again. An angry man in the bowels of an underground lab pushing her to give him more information than she thought she had. Darkness covered his face as the image evaporated at the chatter of more children coming to the doorway.

Five more girls appeared, dressed in dirty robes of once pale blues and greens. They pulled their head coverings across their faces when the men stared at them. Another girl, around fourteen or fifteen, stepped through the little ones to stand before her. The pale-green eyes bore the sadness of someone who had experienced too much suffering in her lifetime. Strands of brown hair peeked out from the faded red scarf tied around her head.

"The government lady is awake, Miss Melanie. She is asking for you." The teenager put her comforting hands on several of the children to guide them back inside.

She didn't feel like this *Melanie* person. What was a government lady and why would she be asking for her? The snorts of restless horses drew her attention back to the men. They appeared to be getting ready to leave. Where were they going? Maybe they should follow. It would be safer. Safer from what, she couldn't speculate.

The man in the brown hat approached and took out his dagger. She froze. The man's narrowed expression revealed little about his intention. He stopped an arm's length away as he raised the sharp weapon. Her gaze fell upon it then looked up at the man. He jerked his chin up and pointed the knife at her wrists. When she extended them, he reached out and sliced through the twine. As the constraints fell to the ground, Melanie continued to hold her hands out toward the stranger.

For the first time, he appeared to show some interest as he took in her hair then face. The closer examination reminded her of someone getting ready to purchase a horse. Being in a land dominated by males who valued livestock more than the women who bore their sons, gave her an uneasy feeling. How she knew this information succeeded in adding to an already-foggy memory.

Melanie, or so she decided to call herself, pointed to her mouth then the children inside. She rubbed her stomach then pointed toward the inside of the shack. "Food." The words came out in a tongue she didn't recognize. How did she know this word? "Food," she insisted again.

This time the man in the brown hat raised his eyebrows in surprise. With a snap of his fingers to the other men, he made his wishes known. Several of them approached with what Melanie thought might be food, but her stomach lurched at the possibilities. She took a parcel from a man whose sour expression looked like he'd been chewing on green persimmons most of his life. She mumbled what she hoped meant "thanks" before slipping into the shack.

"Miss Melanie." The children surrounded her as she handed the teenager the parcel. She tore it open to reveal stale bread smeared with something smelling like bad hummus. She refused a portion, knowing the children needed it more than her.

The government woman sat on the floor in the corner. Her face, shrouded with the dim light of the room, revealed an uncovered head of auburn hair. She stood with an awkward push then moved toward Melanie, standing a few inches taller than her. One of the girls lifted the makeshift curtain over the window, letting light spill across the bruised face of a woman she didn't recognize. The auburn hair revealed gray roots as if it had been a while since she'd gone to a salon. Were there hair salons in this place? If so, maybe she could get a pedicure. Her feet were killing her.

The government lady opened her mouth, revealing a chipped tooth and some dried blood on several others. Her clothes were splattered with blood. Melanie let her stare trail down the woman's stomach then back up to her face.

"I know. It's shocking." The woman glanced down at herself and shook her head. "Are we leaving?"

Melanie turned toward the open door and saw busy men and dust clouds caused by noisy horses. She rubbed her head for clarity.

"I see they cut you lose." The government woman spoke in a thick Boston accent. "I hope it's a good sign. Right?"

"I have no idea." Her words sounded like she'd been gargling gravel.

"Thank goodness they came along when they did." The woman slipped her arm through Melanie's and squeezed.

"I'm a little fuzzy on the details." To admit that to a total stranger who appeared to need reassurance, added yet another layer of imposed responsibility she still didn't understand.

The government woman walked back to a stool and sat down with a sigh as if it were her biggest accomplishment today. "Guess those Pashto lessons paid off for you. I forgot every single word when I saw the Taliban come down the street."

Melanie stared at her in bewilderment. She couldn't remember any Taliban. The pain in her head intensified, and she rubbed hard enough to turn it red. The children crowded at the window and door. She joined them there. These men reminded her of mountain tribesman with supplies piled on nearby yaks. A few of the children pointed, others giggled as they watched. Little girls all over the world loved horses, it seemed.

Whatever brought the tribesman to this place didn't seem to be weighing on the little urchins as much as it did on the government woman. Deep creases around her downturned mouth made her look worried.

"Children, bring me my bag." The government woman pointed to the corner. The teen hurried to retrieve a battered backpack that may have once been an expensive accessory from a shopping mall.

"Can I help, Miss Finley?" The teen, who spoke and understood English, peeked inside the bag as the woman unzipped the side pocket.

"Yes, I think you can. Here,"—the Finley woman reached in and took out a small plastic container—"take this to Miss Melanie." The teenager carried the container to Melanie as if she were one of the Three Wise Men bringing gifts to the baby Jesus.

Melanie took the container from the young girl with the perfect cherub face. "Thank you," she whispered. "What is this?" Melanie unscrewed the lid and peeked inside. "Aspirin?" Miss Finley raised eyebrows at the obvious.

"They're baby aspirin I take each day for my heart. Preventive medicine. Heart disease runs in my family. The doctor called me overly cautious. Take several. I'm afraid I loaded up, after, well you know." The woman avoided finishing the thought as she turned toward the window.

Melanie took four then resealed the container and let the girl return it to its owner. In spite of the softness of the aspirin, swallowing with a dry mouth proved difficult.

One of the men came inside, causing the little girls to run and cower behind Melanie. She didn't have time to speculate why they chose her instead of the other woman.

He grumbled some information and she expressed understanding.

"He says we need to leave with them. At least I think that's what he said. We'd better do as he says. My guess is we are miles from civilization. Maybe they'll at least feed the children."

Once again, she wondered how she could understand a language other than English.

The children gathered up a few bundles no bigger than large table napkins. The teen picked up a skinny, pale girl of about three. Was she well?

"Here, let me take her." The child reached for Melanie and hugged her neck as she wrapped her legs around her waist and laid her face against Melanie's shoulder. She couldn't resist the temptation to kiss her as the image of another little curly-headed girl popped into her head. *I have a daughter, too,* she realized with a heavy heart.

As they ushered the children toward the door, the Finley woman touched Melanie on the arm. "I never thanked you for what you did."

Melanie puzzled at the woman's downcast head. "Excuse me."

"Those men," Finley gulped. "What they attempted to do to Shirin and me."

Melanie shifted the child higher on her shoulder. She stared again at the blood on the front of Finley's clothes. "What do you think I did?"

"You killed a man. Don't you remember?"

CHAPTER 2

Her stomach lurched. Melanie handed the child to Finley then rushed to the corner to throw up. As she heaved, bringing up nothing, she wondered when she'd last eaten. Yesterday? The day before? She became aware of a man's voice hurrying the children outside. When she turned to see Finley put the smallest child down and pull her toward the door, the man in the brown hat entered. He filled up the doorway, blocking enough light to prevent anything distinguishable she might recall later.

With a cold, unemotional glare followed by a cough, she wiped her mouth. She forced herself to squint in resentment at the man who wore what looked like a lack of sympathy. The attempt at attitude gave her a little more confidence at being in control of an out-of-control situation. With a deep breath, he removed a canteen from around his neck and brought it to her. When she didn't take it, he unscrewed the cap and forced it in her face.

"Safe. Drink." In spite of a heavy accent, the man in the brown hat spoke good English.

Melanie shook her head wondering where the water came from, if it carried disease and other dangerous microbes that might kill her.

"Drink. Water good. Not hurt you."

The thirst overrode her fear of death as she grabbed the canteen and gulped down the water. Melanie drank so deep and fast, she choked. Brown Hat Man took the canteen from her then made it ready to travel. He stepped aside and jerked his head toward the door. With reluctant feet, she moved toward the open door.

The fresh air agreed with her unsettled stomach as she reflected on what the Finley woman told her. "You killed a man." *What man? I could never kill anyone.* The Ten Commandments echoed somewhere in her subconscious. She remembered going to Sunday school and listening to stories about Moses and the burning bush where God spoke to him. Every Easter, her family watched the Charleston Heston movie, The Ten Commandments. The recollection gave her peace, knowing just this part of her life remained a mystery.

"You killed a man." The words leaked out, a whisper from her lips. It now sounded like a repeating echo in her brain. Melanie raised her face up to the sun and inhaled deeply before pulling a long piece of fabric over her head. "Miss Melanie, what do we do?" The teenage girl,

Shirin, with the haunted expression plastered across her face sought guidance.

She didn't like the name Melanie. It didn't sound familiar or match up with who she felt she might be. She dared to glance at the men standing by sturdy horses with thick, unbrushed coats. The yaks, loaded with large burdens of red bundles that squeezed out from under a canvas-type material reminded her of how far she'd wandered from civilization. The lumbering giants shook their heads against the line looped through their nose rings. Grunts of impatience drew Melanie's attention back to their bundles. Were they drug runners? That was a way of life in some parts of the world.

A gust of wind blew her head scarf back and several of the men stole glances at her exposed head. Melanie felt she should not acknowledge their interest but couldn't resist being obstinate. They kept pointing to their eyes then said something like colors in their tongue. She wondered if her eyes had changed from blue to violet like they sometimes did when she got angry or were these men planning something sinister. That idea caused her heart to pound so hard she laid a hand against her breast in fear. The thought she'd killed someone from this group stirred her to further irritation. What had evoked such violence in her? She dug in her heels, unsure of what she should do next. Melanie took in her surroundings for clues.

Desolate and beautiful came to mind, as she glimpsed the distant mountains and grassy plains. The cold temperature chilled her as the wind gusted across the sparse vegetation. In spite of the briskness, she had the feeling it might be late summer or at least near fall in this part of the world. The littlest child—she remembered someone calling her Arzo earlier—came to her and caught hold of her leg. Even through her jeans, Melanie could feel the chill of the little hands. Laying a hand on the child's head, she pulled her tight against her leg. Melanie turned to see Brown Hat Man watching her.

A frown of disfavor fell on her before he shifted his gaze to his men. At a jerk of his chin upward, they moved toward the little girls, scooping them up one by one, despite their screams and cries of protest. The sour-faced man from earlier grabbed the Finley woman, but she appeared to be in a trance and unable to resist. One by one, they were tossed onto the horses then joined by a rider. Their horses pranced as if anxious to get moving. Melanie and the smallest child remained on their feet.

Brown Hat Man stormed toward her and picked her up. Every nerve ending in her body tensed as he threw her over his shoulder like a sack of feed. Even though she pounded his back, his grip remained tight until he managed to throw her onto his horse while another man held the bridle with a firm hand. The small child screamed for Miss Melanie, tears gushing down her face. Brown Hat Man went back to the child and kneeled beside her. He patted the top of her head then tickled her cheek. The child said something to him and he held his arms wide to her.

He lifted the child as if afraid she might break and handed her up to Melanie who wrapped her in her robe. The man swung into the saddle and whistled as the group moved out across the empty plain toward the mountains.

The slow, methodical bounce of the horse caused Melanie to hold tight to the man who seemed to be responsible for some kind of rescue. The other possibility meant their capture pointed them toward an unknown nightmare. She feared what lay ahead for two women and a group of children. Exhausted, she laid her cheek against his back and felt the child do the same. Dreams formed of an older man giving her advice that started her on a journey of piecing her life together.

~~~

Sacramento, California

"Dr. Ervin, what do you think of this?" Tessa brought the professor a shard found near Petra, Jordon. "This is a letter from the Hebrew alphabet."

The older man looked up from his microscope with a bland expression. She'd never impressed her mentor and apparently this discovery was no different. He pushed his glasses up on his nose, examined the shard with skeptical interest, and handed it back to her.

"Well? Is it significant?"

"Yes," he mumbled.

Tessa held up the shard to the light and examined it. "I knew it. What does it all mean?"

The professor grinned as he returned his attention to a slide of a scrap of fabric he'd found on his last dig outside Petra. "Made in China."

"What?" Tessa felt like a deflated balloon. "But…"

The professor took the shard back and pointed to the inside. "See this? Too porous. My guess it's a tourist's throwaway. Realized they'd been had and gave it a toss rather than try to get it home. Worthless."

She exhaled an exasperated sigh through puckered lips causing a fluttering sound. The professor laughed.

"Why am I here?" she asked. "I don't know anything about pottery."

"It's not so much learning about pottery as it is learning to spot fakes, whether it's a person, one of those fancy handbags Dr. Cordova carries, or"—he laid the shard down next to him—"a priceless piece of the past. Learn how to spot subtle clues leading to the truth."

"Dr. Ervin, I'm playing catch up here. I sit in a class or do research for Enigma all day and for what?" She pulled up a stool next to the professor and propped her elbows on the table, which shook. He frowned and she withdrew her elbows. "Sorry."
~~~

"You serve a grateful president." He turned to adjust the slide under the microscope. "You saved his life and now he is returning the favor."

"By sticking me behind a desk? I thought when I agreed to join Enigma I'd be a field agent, not a grad assistant to some snarky psychiatrist with a Bruce Lee complex. No. Wait a minute." Tessa rolled her eyes up and laid a finger on her chin. "No. This week he is a wise Buddhist monk who has taken to calling me grasshopper." She threw her hands in the air. "Ugh."

Dr. Ervin chuckled and leaned back to observe his newest friend. "You shouldn't speak of Dr. Wu with such disrespect. Still"—he chuckled again—"you are very funny, Tessa. It is no wonder the captain finds you so engaging."

The last comment deepened her frown. She diverted her attention to the ceiling then chewed the inside of her bottom lip. "Humph," seemed to be the most intelligent response she could muster considering the good professor watched her with growing curiosity.

The captain he mentioned was a literature professor at the University of Sacramento Science and Technology. Tessa had laughed out loud the first time she'd heard about his day job. She knew him as Captain Chase Hunter, the major pain in the neck she'd tangled with during an attempted terrorist attack at an isotope plant in Northern California. Their relationship became a complicated battle of wills during which they realized divine intervention sometimes played cruel tricks.

Their paths went in different directions for a time. When Tessa found herself intertwined with an attempt on the president's life, they were thrown together again. This time, their volatile partnership helped her to admit Captain Hunter meant more to her than she realized. She both idolized and despised him, feeling a dangerous kind of excitement. His military attitude drove her to become a reckless risk taker whose behavior often got her into trouble. But Captain Hunter would be there to catch her when she fell. Somehow, it became a partnership laced with dangerous potholes.

Even now, his words echoed in her mind and her heart. *I will always come for you if you are in trouble. I will always protect you,*

Tessa Scott.

"Tessa? Earth to Tessa." He poked a finger on her knee.

"Sorry. Thinking about what I need to get done today." She slid off the stool and patted him on the shoulder. "Why don't you and Martha come over tonight for dinner? Robert plans to grill some salmon. Interested?" Dr. and Martha Ervin were her next-door neighbors. Martha helped take care of Tessa's three children when grad school or Enigma got in the way.

"Oh. I thought your husband left town on business for a few days."

"Got back yesterday. Took today off. Dinner is at six."

Dr. Ervin offered a weak smirk. "Tessa, I know you are new with Enigma and you have a lot of questions of who we are and what we do. Trust me when I say our benefactors support us because they have lost faith in the government's ability to do the right thing. The president is trying to make our country strong again. Some things even the CIA and FBI can't do, we can."

Tessa took a deep breath and shrugged acceptance. She planted a quick kiss on his forehead. "Gotta go. I'm meeting Dr. Cordova for lunch."

Dr. Ervin raised an eyebrow in surprise. "You and Samantha becoming friends?"

Tessa laughed then spoke in a witch's voice and rubbed her hands together. "Come into my parlor said the spider to the fly."

"Play nice. She is a top agent. You can learn a great deal from her."

"So far she's taught me fifty ways to kill your lover. She must have been the inspiration for the song."

Dr. Ervin chuckled as he waved her off and turned back to his microscope.

~~~

Near Pamir Mountains, Afghanistan

Hands pulled her from the horse. She hadn't realized they'd stopped or Brown Hat Man had already dismounted. The little girl
~~~

stood on the ground looking up at her. At first, she didn't like the man's hands touching her but realized he helped her dismount. They felt hard even beneath the layers of clothing he wore. When her feet touched the ground, she stood inches from his body.

She pushed past him to scoop up the little girl into her arms. Little hands touched both of her cheeks as the child kissed her and turned her face back and forth until she laughed and swung her around. At a sharp jab of pain in her hip, she decided to place Arzo back on the ground. She watched the other men pulling food from their saddlebags and offering it to their captives.

"I'm so sore," the Finley woman complained. "I haven't ridden for thirty years or more. You look at ease riding behind the guy who seems to be in charge." She surveyed the surroundings as if she might be considering a possible vacation destination. Some of the color had come back to her face—the constant wind likely had something to do with the improvement. "Any idea where we are?"

She searched the landscape for clues as she remembered a man's voice. "Look for clues which lead to the truth," she whispered.

"Like what?" The woman put her hands on her hips and turned in a circle. "We are in the middle of nowhere. I'm cold and these guys aren't anything like the Taliban who broke in on us two, three days ago. Those are the clues. They seem harmless enough. See how they treat the children."

Without shifting her position, she shifted her eyes to the men squatting down to offer food to the little girls. The oldest girl had been approached by one of the younger riders, the same one she'd knocked to the ground earlier. He spoke to Shirin and offered her something to drink.

"Potential wives is what they see." Going to Shirin, she grabbed her hand before pulling her to the Finley woman's side. "Stay away from him," she ordered in Pashto. "He's up to no good."

Shirin glanced at the women then back at the young man who now scowled. "But why, Miss Melanie? He is kind. Rashid tries to help."

"He's a man, and in this part of the world being a young unveiled woman means you have no respect for Islam. That could be a death sentence. He's too young to afford you." She stole a glance at Brown Hat Man who led his horse to a small watering hole. "See the big guy who is in charge and bosses everyone around? Chances are good he'll sell you to some old man in the village where they're taking us. You're strong and can make babies." She took a second to take in the beautiful sky. "Why is it no matter how hard life is for a woman, all over the world, they expect romance and a knight in shining armor?" The girl bowed her head as if shamed. She reached out and lifted her chin in her palm. "Don't you hang your head down around these men. It's a sign of submissive weakness. Do you understand what I'm saying?" The girl shook her head. The young man glared and pointed his finger in her direction as he made his way over to Brown Hat Man.

The younger rider rattled on with words she couldn't understand at that speed. Brown Hat Man listened without comment. Even though he stood some twenty feet away, impatience filled his stance and glare. Only his hands moved, switching the reins from one to the other. When the young Rashid walked away to tend to his duties, Brown Hat Man continued to watch her. His head cocked a little to the side as he ran his hand down the front of his pant leg.

She'd better tread with caution in spite of not understanding what the gesture meant. She didn't believe in all the romantic crap about the strong, silent type. After all, the captain was the strong, silent type and he killed people for a living.

She jerked around as if a bee stung her. What captain? She didn't remember being in the military? "Ms. Finley?"

"Please call me Bonnie. I'm sick of the way you try to be so respectful." She lifted her chin up to catch some sun. "Makes me feel old."

"I'm having a little trouble here…Bonnie. I'm afraid I can't remember much about the last few days or how I got here." She pulled her to the side and lowered her voice. "I've got some serious gaps. Am I in the military?"

Bonnie shook her head, concern showing in her creased brow. "No. You are on loan from the State Department's Office of International Goodwill. Someone on the president's staff recommended you to come with me to a women's conference. You were to speak about being a mother and the importance of education for their daughters."

She thought about the new information for a moment. "But I'm a geographer." A lightbulb turned on in her head. "I'm a cultural geographer at a university. At least I think that's what I am."

Bonnie lowered her gaze to her with a pensive expression. "I know. I understood you had a detailed knowledge of Central Asia."

She rubbed her head. The aspirins were wearing off. "Where was the conference?"

"Kyrgyzstan, of all places."

With a new understanding of the landscape, she thought out loud. "Makes sense. Kyrgyzstan is at the crossroads of the other 'Stan' countries. There's still influence from the old Soviet power lords, but the young are going back to the ways of their ancestors. Trouble is, many of the Soviets who lived there for decades are now more Kyrgs, Kazaks, Tajiks or whatever, than they are Russian. They hang onto a past they never knew and are not sure of what to embrace now."

"And that is the reason you came along. You get it."

She frowned as she searched out the land around her one more time to gather "clues leading to the truth." The constant wind rustled with a high and low whoosh then swept across the grassy plains. It gave her a sense of liberation from civilization. The sound of wind turned her thoughts to the freedom these nomadic people must feel. "This isn't Kyrgyzstan," she mumbled.

"Then you do remember." Bonnie hugged herself against the chill in the air.

She inhaled the sweetness of fresh air. The peacefulness pushed aside the trepidation as a desire to dig for the truth welled up inside her. What had she left behind? Were her skills the reason she followed the Finley woman to the ends of the earth? Why couldn't she remember? As she deciphered pieces from her past, the haunting words of someone she cared about floated into her consciousness.

"I will find you if you are in trouble. I will always protect you, Tessa Scott."

CHAPTER 3

Sacramento, California

D irector Benjamin Clark stood at his window to observe the university campus. His hands were clasped in a tight grip behind his back. Anyone who entered the office would not have guessed he felt uneasy about his newest Enigma agent being out in the field unsupervised for the first time. An occasional nervous twitch of his index finger hinted he had second thoughts. Someone walking across the green caught his attention. Her long blonde hair reminded him of the new agent, Tessa Scott. Unlike the girl on the green, though, she was in her mid-thirties, with three kids and a husband who remained clueless to what his wife did for a living.

In spite of being a reluctant recruit, the woman had been invaluable on several occasions to prevent the United States from falling into chaos. He suspected she'd agreed to enroll in a Ph.D. program for geo-political conflict at the suggestion of his senior agent, Captain Chase Hunter. Although the two appeared to butt heads from time to time, it became obvious a volatile relationship changed how they saw the world and each other.

The director of Enigma didn't like how their friendship kept him speculating on whether it was safe for the woman to be around the captain. He trained in the art of problem solving. Tessa's gift lay in the art of making chocolate chip cookies and stumbling into turmoil. How she managed to turn a bitter warrior into a grinning idiot continued to be a mystery. She'd saved an American hero from himself. What the captain gave in return concerned him.

The director thought back to a couple of weeks earlier when he'd watched Tessa stop and stare up at the window. She'd waved with one hand while shading her eyes with the other. The director didn't return the gesture and pretended not to be amused at her carefree gesture. That was how she affected a person. A woman like her had too much to lose to work with Enigma. He wanted to kick her out of the program, but the president refused to listen. He, too, had been smitten with the head-in-the-clouds-all-is- good attitude. She'd saved President Austin's life and he would make damn sure whatever Tessa wanted, Tessa got.

Thinking back, he could almost hear her light tap at the door. He pulled his leather chair out to sit down. The door opened slower than he liked. The director expected most people to storm in with a certain amount of urgency. A problem that needed to be addressed always lurked in the halls of Enigma.

"Director Clark?" Tessa eased in and closed the door behind her. "Sorry I'm late. Sam and I had lunch. She wanted me to…"

He motioned for her to sit. Everyone knew Dr. Samantha Cordova disliked Tessa and would do anything to make her appear less than capable to the others in the Enigma group. Samantha had caused her to be late on purpose. "No matter, Tessa. How are you getting along here at Enigma? I understand your studies are going as planned. Dr. Wu says you are a great asset to his work."

The image of Tessa spluttering a retort about her watchdog had amused him at the time. "Dr. Wu is a Teenage Mutant Ninja Turtle who plays with my head. But I think you already know that." She crossed her arms in front of her as the director smirked back a chuckle.

He shuffled papers then put his small black glasses on the end of his nose. Tessa had once told him he reminded her of an American eagle. The glasses had become his way to gain some control of the serious decorum he wanted to maintain. "I hope you are not obstinate to the good doctor. You shouldn't let Captain Hunter influence you in your opinion of Dr. Wu."

He stared at her until she squirmed. "Sorry."

"Now to the business at hand. I have a small job for you which will involve travel."

Tessa leaned forward. "Back to D.C.?"

"That will be your first stop, but you'll be going to Central Asia." The director handed over a file folder. "Vernon is downloading most of the information to your phone even as we speak. He'll inform you of the password when you leave. You have two days before departure so you can get your family affairs in order and prepare a speech."

Tessa glanced over the file. "I'm going to Kyrgyzstan?" She beamed. "Are you serious? This is fantastic." She hugged the folder and stomped her feet in excitement. The director arched an eyebrow in disapproval. "Sorry. Too undignified?"

"Yes." The no-nonsense man turned his attention to a few notes.

"A women's conference in Central Asia. This is right up my alley, Ben." He peered over the edge of his glasses again at her familiarity. "I mean, Director Clark." Her unrestrained optimism returned as she opened the folder. "A speech? Who will be my audience?"

"It's all in the folder, Tessa." He sighed and removed his glasses before squeezing the bridge of his nose between his index finger and thumb. He stood and walked around the desk to loom over his newest agent. "Now, you listen to me, young lady."

"I love it when you call me young lady." She'd learned early in their relationship to circumvent his stoic demeanor by playing the innocent-sweet-airhead card. He fell for it anyway.

Director Clark knew he'd failed to demonstrate his impatience even as he frowned down at her. It remained impossible to be stoic with her. "There may be more to this than meets the eye, so you need to use some of those new skills Sam and Dr. Wu have been trying to pound into your thick head." Her brightness dimmed a bit. She straightened a little and her eyelashes batted a little faster, a sign of nerves. "By the way, you weren't my first choice."

This tidbit of news did wipe the remaining cheerfulness from her face. "Oh. Why?" Tessa's voice squeaked. "Who did you want?"

The director moved over to his small black leather sofa and sat down. He stretched his left arm along the back while loosening his tie with the right hand. "Martha Stewart."

Tessa choked on a laugh and turned in her chair to face her boss. "I guess playing second to her is still an honor."

"Don't be nosey or ask too many questions. You tend to find trouble where there is none. Stay sharp with ears open."

"For what?" She joined the director on the sofa with a kind of pensive anticipation. "What's going on?"

"There appears to be a group working in Central Asia to cripple the efforts of our troops and billions of dollars of goodwill our country has poured into stabilizing the area."

"This can't be anything new. Central Asia has fought everyone from Colonial Britain to the Russians and now us. It doesn't matter the intent. We are uninvited war mongers in their opinions. Besides, the only thing that changed is women in some areas now have a better life. This, too, will be destroyed when we leave."

"We suspect the women and children are being used as weapons against us."

"I don't understand."

"There's some indication children are being taken to force women into being mules for the opium trade. With the promise of safekeeping for their families, these women have few alternatives but to submit. Sometimes the children are spared, but other times they are sold into slavery and used in ways I'm not going to go into with you. The Taliban are vile, ruthless men who have turned the weak into vessels to carry their own warped sense of justice."

Tessa shook her head in disgust. "Director Clark, this has been going on for years. What has changed?"

He leaned closer and explained. "Someone in the US is now helping them. Every time we get close to making headway with these people, someone tips off the insurgents and we come out with egg on our face or lose soldiers. For now, this is in Afghanistan and Pakistan, but it appears to be spreading. The Uzbek government as well as Kyrgyzstan have been supportive but are feeling pressure from their people to cut ties with us. I need you to be the fresh face of the United States."

Tessa chuckled at the thought. "Maybe you should have chosen Sam. She's the drop-dead gorgeous person around here. The woman hasn't paid for a drink or meal since she turned sixteen. Men spill their guts to her. Seems to me she should go."

The fact Dr. Samantha Cordova could be the most beautiful woman he'd ever known rang true. Besides having the distinction of being one of his top agents, Sam, as they called her, embraced her dangerous and resourceful side. Tessa made no attempt at hiding her fear and admiration of the woman. His own brother, the Prime Minister of Israel, wanted to recruit her. The iceberg for a heart continued to be her fatal flaw. The woman placed her trust in physical desire and revenge, very much like Captain Hunter, and showed no signs of possessing a conscience.

"It isn't the attention of the men I want. You exude warmth and kindness. Women will be more drawn to you, maybe even confide something important."

Tessa clicked her tongue. "Guess that's why my nickname is Betty Crocker." She chuckled like the Pillsbury Doughboy, hands on her stomach.

This time the director did laugh. "Never doubt your ability to catch a man's attention, Tessa. Your kind of beauty lasts a lifetime." Her mischievous enthusiasm reappeared. "Not to mention your sense of humor. Anyone who can make Captain Hunter belly laugh has got a secret weapon none of the rest of us own."

Her expression froze whenever he mentioned the captain. He knew she'd not seen him in a month. The captain remained somewhere in Afghanistan hobnobbing with tribal elders, or so they'd told her. He wondered for the hundredth time if her glazed expression meant she was hiding something.

The director cleared his throat. Her gaze jerked back to him. "Well, anyway, be our ears, Tessa. No investigating or following a hunch."

"Got it." She offered a playful thumbs-up. "Curiosity killed the cat, I know."

The director stood then moved toward the door. "Tell Robert you're leaving very early the day after tomorrow and you'll need to stay in one of the dorm rooms here at the university. Be at your apartment by seven so the team can help you sort through things, answering questions, etc."

Tessa had been mandated to take a small apartment near campus where she could stay when coming off missions or working late. The ability to convince her husband she stayed in a dorm room or airport hotel when she left to do the president's goodwill work proved an easy enough task. The man lived in a fog of admiration for the president and his wife's serving him. Her work influenced how people looked at Robert as well. Although a good husband, the man could be a self-absorbed opportunist.

Impressed after meeting the most powerful man in the world, Robert continued to allow his wife to be away from home from time to time. Would the man be so enthusiastic if he knew the truth about Tessa's strange working arrangement?

"Thanks, Director." Tessa went to the door and stopped as he swung it open. "I won't let you down."

The director wanted to appear severe but gave her a wink instead. "Make sure you don't or I'll send you on another training mission with Sam."

Tessa wrinkled her brow in mock fear. "No pressure there, Director Clark."

As she moved through the door, he gripped her arm a little tighter than he'd intended. "Be careful and trust no one."

She patted his hand as if her doing so would vanquish his misgivings. "You know what a chicken I am. So stop worrying. You're sending me to one of the most beautiful parts of the world. I'll come back with T-shirts for everyone. Hey, do they have a Hard Rock Cafe? Heather loves the pins."

"See you tomorrow night, Tessa." He gave her a little shove and shut the door behind her.

Director Clark didn't like the feeling of impending disaster still hammering at his subconscious the day before she flew off to Central Asia. He'd second-guessed himself ever since the moment he allowed her to hug his neck in a moment of privacy before he and the other team members left her apartment. What had possessed him to think nothing would go wrong?

<p style="text-align:center">~~~</p>

Afghanistan

Captain Hunter and his partner, Nicholas Zoric, squatted beneath an outcropping of rocks, hoping the shade would give them a little relief from the afternoon sun. A breeze stirred up dust like thousands of brown ballerinas determined to attach themselves to the faces and necks of the two men. Nothing but their eyes moved as they evaluated the landscape, waiting for their contact from a tribal elder. With two hours past the prearranged time to meet, the captain expected the delay. No doubt a scout had moved ahead to check out the rendezvous spot, making sure the Americans hadn't laid a trap. Protocol dictated they arrive early for the same reason. Waiting for the Afghans to fulfill a commitment became a lesson in patience for most Americans. Time meant nothing to them. Invasion after invasion proved as much. The Afghans were masters of waiting the enemy out.

The empty hours gave Captain Hunter too much time to think about Tessa Scott. He pictured her in her little office, surrounded by the books on geography she poured over with the enthusiasm of an obsessed monk on the trail of the Holy Grail. Most days when going to the office on campus, if they didn't have a class to teach, they would take lunch together. Their chats on politics, culture, literature, and music became the highlight of his day. They argued over government policy, environmental issues, and books. They would part laughing, something he thought he'd forgotten how to do.

The image of her sitting on the top of a picnic table in a dark alley in Washington D.C., soaked to the bone, always managed to infiltrate his thoughts of her. The curly blonde hair hanging like twisted pieces of rope over her shoulder and down across her breasts drove him a little crazy at times. He'd forced her to kiss him. It had been the one time he'd crossed the line of appropriate behavior with her. In the end, it had saved both their lives. He touched his cheek and remembered the slug upside the head she'd given him mere seconds before she'd responded with passion while their lips touched for the first and last time.

Several days later, when an explosion almost killed him, Tessa whispered a promise to him if he survived. Later, she claimed the explosion created a delusional and imagined show of her real affections for him. He enjoyed bringing it up to get her red-faced and stuttering. A barrage of insults to his masculinity, intelligence, and place on the food chain would end with him laughing so hard he oftentimes felt a tear squeeze onto his cheek. Tessa couldn't resist his attempt at humor and loved to punch him in the arm as a show of strength.

The problem with their friendship continued to be staying in the safe zone. Chase didn't cross the line of being with a married woman. He also didn't want anything to do with Enigma agents. Tessa now met the criteria for double taboo. It seemed like the lives of every woman he'd ever cared about ended in disaster. His mother had died in China as he managed to escape with his sister to safety. His sister died of a drug overdose and not long after, his grandmother died in the Twin Towers on 911. Going a snail's pace with Tessa made sense if he wanted to remain friends.

Everything he ever stood for, honor, respect, and responsibility, came into question when he thought of the cute housewife from Grass Valley. A mother of three kids, she didn't need any more complications in her life. Her husband didn't abuse or ignore his family. Sometimes he wished the guy would so he could make his argument for her to leave. But he hadn't, so their relationship evolved into her giving him advice about his love life with the other women he bedded. He often wondered if her words of wisdom hid a deeper desire for him.

Washington D.C. created a past for them. They connected on a dangerous and personal level. The fact he loved her needed to be addressed and soon. His thoughts turned back to the day he'd left for Afghanistan. The night he'd invaded her home and thrown her across the bed remained fresh in his mind.

He dropped by her office to say good-bye on the way to the airport. Sadness clouded her usual happy expression as if she wanted to say something important. When she walked around her desk to stand inches away, his reflexes forced him to take a step back. He feared she might touch him, which would be a mistake in his current state of mind. She'd learned early on, Enigma agents didn't always like unsolicited shows of affection. She'd once commented it appeared everything they did had to be calculated, evaluated, and tested before touch ever occurred.

"Good luck with your studies and training." He glanced toward her desk as if by doing so she'd return to her chair.

"Good luck with your hunting and mayhem," she quipped. He struggled to remain stoic and narrowed his eyes to hide the amusement. "Oh, and by the way, if you ever sneak into my house again, I swear I'll shoot you."

"Good thing I took the bullets." He touched a bruise over his brow. "At least you gave me a good whack with the gun. Nice touch, by the way, with throwing me into the nightstand. I had a headache for two days." His defenses dropped when he pictured her beneath him again, and he didn't hide his admiration for her body as his eyes slid from head to toe. "We'll have to do it again sometime."

Tessa frowned. He'd come very close to losing control when she'd ask him not to hurt her and to go slow.

"Did you have to do that?" She stepped closer, her arms doubled across her chest as a barrier between them. "You're a despicable Neanderthal. I think you wanted some fun at my expense. It had nothing to do with training."

Captain Hunter pushed out his bottom lip to resist crumbling his defenses. "It had everything to do with training. Do you think I'm going to be around each time you get yourself in quicksand?" At the growl in his voice, she unfolded her arms and glared at him.

"Well then you wouldn't get to play the big bad hero and save the day."

"Somebody's got to do it," he mused, arching an eyebrow. "I kinda got the feeling you dug all my macho, badass stuff. Living with a man like Robbie can change a woman." He should stop doing it, but no matter how hard he attempted to conceal it, his dislike for her husband broke through every time.

She pushed her hair away from her face and dared to take a step closer. Chase didn't retreat. "His name is Robert." Another step forward and he could no longer resist a smirk, feeling he'd won a victory in some small way with her close proximity. "Why are you grinning like a mule eating briars? You are infuriating."

Chase towered over her a good six inches. He stared down his nose at her as he searched her face. "I mean it, baby. Train. Study. I don't want you to get hurt." His voice became low and sensual. "When I get back, we need to talk about a few things."

She swallowed hard and reached out to touch his forearm. "Like what?"

"Us. Sooner or later, it's going to happen." "I'm not ready."

"When I get back." He leaned over and kissed the top of her head and left.

Why couldn't he pull her into his arms and take what he wanted? It worked with other women who crossed his path. Second-guessing every move he made with her would be his undoing.

At least she didn't have to endure this hellhole. He could strategize his next move until he returned home. Maybe she used this time apart to think about him, too. He believed Robert Scott the one man standing in his way of taking what he'd wanted. The moment he laid eyes on her, he contemplated how to erase Robert from the picture.

CHAPTER 4

Don't trust anyone. An angry man standing in an office had spoken those words. Tessa wondered about his identity and his importance. Then there was someone else who was much bigger that kept walking into her head, too, with dark skin and piercing brown eyes who'd left her feeling uncomfortable. Although he appeared menacing, she felt no fear.

A horse neighed and Tessa jerked her head around to see men lifting little girls to their horses. This time, the children did not cry out for her. The government woman, Bonnie Finley, walked away and allowed one of the riders to help her onto the back of his horse. In her peripheral vision, she watched Brown Hat Man, as she now named him, storm toward her. In the process, he scooped the littlest girl she'd cradled earlier up into his arms. An excited giggle escaped the child as he handed her to another rider who already carried a young child named Pamir, Shirin's little sister. Tessa pointed in protest, shaking her head no.

Brown Hat Man walked past her, quick to catch hold of her robe and drag her toward his horse. She slapped at his grip, colorful descriptions of his manners spilling from her mouth. When they reached the horse, he grabbed her by the collar and the seat of her pants. Next, he proceeded to throw her with surprising strength onto the front of the horse. In one fluid movement, he swung up behind her.

Every part of his hard body molded against her as he took the reins and clicked his tongue at the horse. The animal pranced sideways and tossed his head then lurched forward, throwing Tessa back into her captor's embrace. She felt his chin over her shoulder and the furry flaps of his hat press against her ear. When the horse gave a last buck of resistance, he laughed deep in his throat. With the reins in one hand, he slipped his other beneath Tessa's robe and pulled her even tighter against him. When she squirmed to twist free, he moved his hand upward, causing her to freeze. Again he laughed then lowered his hand to her waist. The horse galloped forward.

She had been put in her place.

They rode onward as the sun moved across the sky. Her bottom hurt. The wind grew colder against her face, but the leader's warm body kept her comfortable. He smelled of something sweet and smoky, maybe the yak dung they burned in lieu of wood. There were no trees she could see. A few times, he'd switched the reins to his other hand then slip the free one back under her robes to hold her. He didn't try exploring again but once rubbed his thumb across her lower abdomen in an absentminded fashion. She flinched when his lips touched her ear. He, too, jerked back as if surprised by her reaction.

"Soft," he mumbled. She turned around in surprise to discover his broad smile. Afraid to spew an insult or elbow him, Tessa bristled, succeeding in making him spread out his hand against her bare skin. Several times she thought he nuzzled her ear, but she twitched away with no retribution from him.

By the time darkness fell, they had reached some rocky outcroppings surrounded by trees. The men talked to the children as they lifted them to the ground. Escorted toward the jagged rocks, Tessa spied a cave. Several men were already building a fire while others tended to the horses and yaks laden with supplies. A lighted fire soon flickered to life as the sweet smell of yak dung filled the space. Even in fall, temperatures could drop below freezing at night. Rashid and Toiluk, as she now knew them, wrapped blankets around the children in quick order before preparing the food and hot tea. The group spoke very little as they sipped tea and passed around a hard cheese Tessa guessed was kurut. She'd remembered reading about it sometime, which, like a lot of things, remained a mystery.

The children turned it over in their little hands then turned to Tessa as if she'd be able to help them. Perplexed, she took a piece, sniffed it then nibbled only to spit it back out. She stuck a finger in her mouth to rub a tooth. The men continued to munch then spoke to each other in an amused tone.

Brown Hat Man sat down cross-legged beside her. He broke off a small piece of the cheese and plopped it into his mouth. The children watched him with renewed interest as he moved the cheese from cheek to cheek, back and forth. Then he opened his mouth to push the cheese out on his tongue. Next he bit into it, showing the children it was now soft enough to eat. One by one, they followed his example. Tessa noticed how the men watched when the children giggled at their new ability to eat kurut.

Bonnie Finley sniffed at the cheese. "This is disgusting. We've got to get some real food. It smells rancid. I will die if I have to chow down on this garbage, Melanie. Can't you tell them to do something?"

Brown Hat Man handed Tessa more cheese while keeping a certain amount of attention on Bonnie. Tessa attempted to follow his example with some difficulty at first but soon mastered the technique and decided it tasted better than nothing. He showed his approval by serving her another chunk. It was time to try the tea. He handed her a tin cup with the steaming brew she'd so far been able to avoid. She choked on the first sip but noticed how the men had suspended their cups in midair to watch her reaction. Not wanting to appear ungrateful for their hospitality, Tessa lifted her cup to venture another taste. It went down warm and more pleasant than she'd expected. In spite of being an acquired taste, she enjoyed the chance to share this with these men who extended a hand of friendship. Their expressions ranged from amusement to astonishment when she held out her cup for more.

Bonnie took a sip then gagged. "What is this?" She frowned into her cup with an agonized groan.

Tessa held the cup in her hands to let the warmth permeate her fingers. "Tea."

"Doesn't taste like tea." Bonnie sniffed it again.

"I imagine it's because of the yak milk and salt." Tessa smothered a chuckle as the other woman gagged a second time. How in the world did I know that? "Bread. Eat bread." She pointed to Bonnie who wrinkled her nose at the cheese.

Brown Hat Man tilted his chin at the man who sat closest to the cave opening. He mumbled a few words and the man hopped up and disappeared outside. When he returned, he handed Bonnie a round loaf of unleavened bread the size of a small pizza. She tore into it with disregard for etiquette. The thought of sharing the bread, at least with the children, didn't appear to occur to her.

The children kept their eyes lowered, but Tessa knew they were still hungry. The cheese couldn't have been enough to satisfy growing children. The man left and returned again to give more bread to Brown Hat Man. He sniffed it with great exaggeration as he watched the little girls. He rubbed his stomach.

"Umm." The little ones covered their mouths against giggles. He tore off a large hunk of the bread then passed it to Tessa.

She understood the game so she made an effort to follow his example. But when the littlest girl stood up and edged between Brown Hat Man and her, Tessa couldn't resist any longer. She tore the bread into pieces and gave each girl a share. Brown Hat Man shared his with Arzo who climbed into his lap. Tessa hadn't bothered to save any for herself, seeing how hungry the children were, but her captor tore part of what he had left to share with her. With a whisper of what she hoped meant thanks in Pashto, she dared make eye contact with him. As he chewed the last bite, a smile spread across his mouth, making it appear too wide and thick for his half-covered face.

Silence fell again as bellies grew full and yawns appeared. Bonnie found a flat surface against one wall to lie down. She'd chosen the spot nearest the fire without much concern over the children's well-being. They grew quiet then snuggled closer to Tessa who wrapped her arms around the youngest after pulling her out of Brown Hat Man's lap. The others tilted their sleepy heads on each other's shoulders. Tessa couldn't resist planting a kiss on each forehead as it leaned toward her. With each kiss, Tessa spoke their names.

"Sweet girl, Marta." The seven-year-old could pass for a younger child.

"My favorite artist." She winked at Shirin and made it a point to speak in English to her then patted her little sister, Pamir, who waited with open arms to hug her neck. "My love," she breathed in Pashto.

"Son-Kul and Halcha." Tessa kissed her fingers before touching her heart of the two sisters, age nine and seven. "Such good girls today."

Three-year-old Arzo snuggled closer as if demanding more. Tessa laid rapid kisses on her face and neck to make her giggle. "My littlest angel who I love so much." Tessa stretched out her arms to show how much. The child relaxed and fell into a doze.

"Those children have taken a liking to you. I'm terrible with kids. Never wanted any. I wouldn't be where I am today if I'd had a family." Bonnie offered a cold frown, observing the children like they were lab rats.

Tessa let Arzo settle into her lap then lean back for an extra snuggle. "I want to take these little angels home with me." She switched to Pashto again. "My girls were so brave today. I'm very proud of them. They will be great women."

The men chuckled at her words. She shot them a warning glare and they shifted their attention to the fire. Brown Hat Man continued to stare at her as he sipped his tea. Tessa met his gaze with boldness, knowing the night could prove dangerous for her. Whatever was going to happen after everyone went to sleep would happen whether she remained obstinate or meek. She chose obstinate.

"You better watch yourself around him," Bonnie warned, diverting her eyes from the leader to her hands. "What do you think is going to happen to us?"

Tessa tore her gaze from Brown Hat Man to pull Arzo closer to her chest. "I imagine someone is searching for us." Sometime during the day she'd remembered staying at the American Embassy and that Bonnie possessed the title of the Undersecretary of State. "Wouldn't the ambassador be concerned that you didn't return?"

"You'd think so. But on the other hand I know a lot about his side business."

Tessa shifted the little girl to the crook of her arm then glanced over at Brown Hat Man who perked up as he listened to their conversation. "I'm not sure how much he understands, but he does know some English." She decided on a test as she sent him a quick glance. "I plan to pour honey on you tonight and then stuff fire ants down your pants." She displayed a brilliant smile through clenched teeth.

Brown Hat Man shifted his gaze between the women as he rubbed his forehead in what resembled confusion then settled on leering at Tessa.

"Anyway, you were saying?" Tessa took a deep breath trying to ignore Brown Hat Man's obscene observation.

"The ambassador is greedy. He might think coming after me could be bad for business."

"What kind of business?"

"Not important." She squeezed her eyes shut. "I'm the Undersecretary of State. At some point someone will miss me."

Shirin leaned over and whispered to Tessa. "Miss Melanie, we are tired. Can I spread some blankets?"

Tessa agreed as she nudged the children from her shoulders and spoke with calm to the others. Having them so close, plus the littlest one asleep in her lap, paralyzed her ability to stand up. Shirin helped the girls up and moved them a little deeper into the cave. Brown Hat Man stood up and reached for the child in Tessa's lap. When the child snuggled into his chest, a warm expression crossed his face drawing a thin grin to his mouth for a brief moment, Tessa imagined him as a father.

By the time she wobbled to her feet, Brown Hat Man had returned and flopped down next to her. She snarled down at him as he smiled. His cold demeanor now had been replaced by a kind of curious interest as he watched her dust off her bottom. Tessa took a step away from him but not before he gripped her hand. He jerked it hard enough for her to fall into his lap. At her flailing protest, he tightened his grip with more strength than she could resist.

He still wore the half mask. In the firelight, he reminded Tessa of the cover model on a romance novel she'd seen in the grocery store: mysterious, intriguing, and dangerous.

"Listen, Batman." Tessa faked a smile as she spoke through gritted teeth. "I'm cold." She hugged her body and shivered. "I'm tired and I can't wait to knee you in the balls." At her laugh, as if she'd said something sweet, his mouth turned up on one side. "Now, you listen to me. I'm going to go over there next to those little girls." She removed his hand from her hip before taking his other one and twisting until his eyes lost their friendliness and narrowed. She pointed to the line of children. "I'm going to sleep. If you get any ideas about romance, I will make it my mission in life to see you never are able to have children." He cocked his head as his eyes widened. "Understand, Batman?" Some of her words were in English, the rest in Pashto.

Brown Hat Man nodded his head. As she struggled to stand again, he placed his hand beneath her bottom and pushed her upward.

Tessa diverted her rant toward the rocky ceiling. "Thank you, Jesus."

Snuggled down with the children, Tessa leaned over to kiss the child called Arzo. "Sweet dreams." The words came out in Pashto again. How do I know how to speak those words? If the men would talk more, then maybe she could determine where they were being taken.

As Tessa stared at the shadows cast by a dying fire, the weight of the day became too heavy to combat sleep. She felt someone sit down beside her then another heavy covering fall across her. The cold disappeared and she fell into a deep sleep.

~~~

"Miss Melanie?" Shirin, the teenage girl, stirred her awake. "Miss Melanie?"

The words sounded far away, as if she were dreaming. She wanted to ignore the voice and savor the feeling of being safe. Her hand stretched across wool clothing that carried the smell of smoke. Fur pulled up around her face caused her eyelids to begin a lazy attempt at opening. She realized someone's moist breath touched the strands of hair tangled around her neck. A hard arm, under her shoulders, held her in place.

Tessa wiggled to sit up, but Brown Hat Man held her body close to his. Her head rested on his muscled shoulder. In one jerk, Tessa sat up and pushed him away as he, too, stirred awake beneath the pale mask.

Brown Hat Man spoke to her in a civil tone, his penetrating gaze locking onto her fluttering eyelids. He reached out to touch her hair and frowned when she slapped at his hand. Tessa responded the same way when he attempted to touch her again,
~~~

without success. In a sudden movement, he grabbed a handful of her hair, pulling her within inches of his face.

Any further rebuff might force his hand, but she refused to divert her look of contempt from his angry glare. Had he noticed her eyes changed from blue to violet when provoked? A subtle shift in color had made her the butt of many jokes concerning the inability to hide her emotions. To slow her racing heart she took slow breaths, and managed to reach a place where she felt in control of her future. As he released her hair, he rested one hand, partially gloved but with fingers chapped and bare, against her cheek as if it was something he'd never experienced. With the other hand, he patted his chest.

"Darya." He pointed to her then back to him. "Darya."

"Melanie." She spoke in English because the words in Pashto didn't come to her tongue. Chances were that wasn't her name since people referred to her as Tessa in her dream, but for whatever reason it seemed the name she used in that place. A moment of confusion flickered across his face then disappeared. "Mel-an-nee," she repeated.

"Melanie," he said as plain as anyone could.

Tessa's radar went up. The man spoke English better than he let on. How had he learned the language? How much English did he know? And how much Pashto did she know?

"Food. Children." Tessa glanced over at the girls who stirred and at Shirin who waited with her hands at her side. She pointed to her mouth again to say food. Darya grinned and pressed his mouth against hers. When he jerked back with an amused grin, his focus switched to her eyes as if waiting for them to change.

Tessa pushed his hand off her face. "No, numbskull, I meant food for the children. I don't want your mouth to ever touch me again." Tessa worked at making her voice even and nonthreatening before wiping her hand across her lips.

To her dismay, Darya grabbed her chin and turned her face toward several men sitting near the fire. He poked a free finger into her cheek and laughed. His grip squeezed so hard her mouth pooched like a fish's.

When Shirin spoke to Darya, he released her face and stood. After a show of stretching, he exited the cave. His men followed. Rolling to her feet, she gathered the teen in her arms as a show of thanks.

"What's his problem, Melanie?" Bonnie, who'd chosen to watch rather than assist, cleared her throat then dusted the seat of her pants. "Are you all right? Did he…I mean he slept next to you all night. I thought…"

"No. I'm fine. I think he's more concerned about me putting ideas in the girls' heads than romancing me. Then there's the way my eyes change color. I get the feeling I'm comic relief for these guys."

Bonnie put her hands on her hips then looked out of the cave opening. She sniffed back a runny nose. "I think they're trouble. We need to find help and fast. I don't know if our pilot got a distress call out or not before they crashed."

Tessa's mouth opened in shock. "Who crashed?"

Bonnie put an arm around her shoulder. "It's hard to comprehend you don't remember." She sighed. "You seemed fine until those men came in and…" She shivered as her arms came up for a self-hug. "They were horrible. The girls, they…" Bonnie took a deep breath. "But you. " She covered her face with a trembling hand. "And you don't remember anything?"

Tessa massaged her forehead in hopes of pulling something forward to memory. "No. Everything is a blank until I woke up yesterday morning. I don't know who I am, why I'm here. Sorry, Bonnie, but I don't even know how I know you." Exasperated, she paced across the small room.

Bonnie gave a relieved smile, but her pat on Tessa's back made her ill at ease for some reason she couldn't identify. "Doesn't matter. You suffered along with me and then you took action to save us. I'm grateful and so are those little girls."

A couple of men returned to the cave with bread and made tea for everyone. They didn't stick around to be sociable like the night before. Preparations were being made to leave.

"You need to catch me up to speed, Bonnie. I want to know everything. Start at the beginning." Even though trepidation engulfed her, she wanted the truth.

Spot the clues leading to the truth. Trust no one. I'll always find you.

Something about those last words made her feel hope. Who was searching for her? "And, Bonnie?" The woman tilted her head. "I think my real name is Tessa. Tessa Scott. I think I'm more than a geographer."

Bonnie's face grew serious. "I know, dear. I know."

CHAPTER 5

Airspace over Central Asia approaching Afghanistan

Bonnie Finley filled in what had happened in the missing days leading up to their capture. Some of what she heard sounded familiar enough Tessa pieced together the missing parts of her memory. Her mind wandered around until she could focus on one thing.

She heard the excited voices of women as their plane bounced on wind turbulence. The women's conference in Bishkek, Kyrgyzstan was a success according to the emails offering congratulations from the international committee. Several hundred women from all walks of life attended. The seven Stan countries were represented along with Nepal and Bhutan. India refused to come because of a conflict flare-up with Pakistan over water issues in Kashmir, an ongoing problem.

Undersecretary Bonnie Finley continued the goodwill by making sure diplomat's wives, social outreach organizers, and university instructors shared a plane with them. But when the plane hit turbulence, the excited chatter stopped. The women tightened their seat belts and Tessa's seatmate's hands gripped the armrests. The silence that prevailed gave Tessa a few moments' peace.

She evaluated the women who were the wealthy representatives of their perspective populations. It was doubtful they would venture out from their walled gardens and armed escorts to mingle among the people. Unlike the wind bouncing them, these women would not shake things up to improve the lot of others.

The ones who would make a difference had left the conference by humble means and would take days to return home. They were the ones who would carry back ideas to dream. Tessa had bonded with those women. They spoke English better than her Russian and Pashto. Even though she studied to master the simplest of terms and sentences, the language often became jumbled.

Once, while chatting with two women from Kazakhstan, Tessa had gone on and on in Russian about their embracing change. A real heart-to-heart moment came when one of the women told her in English she'd said their ideas were as bad as frozen fish pee. Horrified at the mistake, Tessa relaxed when her new friends burst into laughter.

After her workshops on teaching children to love learning and what global organizations existed to assist, Tessa found herself often talking for hours to women who wanted to know more. A few shared personal experiences of tragedy and triumph. She'd helped them set up email, Facebook, and Twitter accounts in hopes of continuing to reach out, they would become successful in obtaining a better life for their children and communities.

Several days before the three-day event, Tessa and the undersecretary had been wined and dined by the American ambassador. The Kyrgyzstan Minister of Health ad provided tours of hospitals and several elementary schools. The show impressed Bonnie, but Tessa's studies had revealed the interior of the country still lagged behind on services. Being under Soviet control for so many years created a scenario where catching up to the world became a tedious process. The Department of Tourism took pride in taking the two American women to several breathtaking parks, proud of their environmental advances compared with other Stan countries.

So when the plane shuddered, Tessa enjoyed not having to participate in idle conversation on topics that didn't include change. Bonnie Finley sat next to her and fiddled with her e-reader for a while then closed it with a sigh. She stole a glance back at some of the other passengers, waved, or gave a thumbs-up before turning to Tessa.

"You were fabulous, Melanie. It appears your small groups were well received." She elbowed her and chuckled. "I'm not into chitchat. Thanks for doing it. I'm more of a behind-the-scenes kind of person."

Tessa bit her tongue against a flippant retort. *Seems to me you are also a kiss-ass kind of person.* For someone supposed to mingle with the common people of Central Asia, Bonnie didn't appear to have a good grasp of what that entailed. Her focus remained on the wealthy women who married power.

"Glad I could help. Lots of good ideas among those women. Maybe this will be the start of something progressive."

"I hope so. Two more quick stops then we'll stay in Kabul for a few days. I have some business there."

"Kabul!" Her stomach lurched. "Is it safe for us to be there? Don't we need visas?"

Bonnie laughed. "We're not taking the scenic route, Melanie. Relax. We'll be surrounded by some of America's finest. The ambassador will see to the paperwork. While we're there, maybe you can visit the new shopping mall."

"No thanks."

"I'll see if one of the ambassador's men can take you around to some schools. Would you like that?"

"Maybe I'll catch up on some sleep." "Suit yourself."

According to Bonnie, Tessa had decided to visit some of the soldiers who had suffered superficial wounds but were slotted to return to duty after a little recovery time. After a quick shower at the American Embassy, she changed into a pair of khaki pants, short-sleeved army- green T-shirt, and combat boots slotted for the trash bin in the near future. Her black travel wear and heels didn't fit the Kabul environment. Tessa borrowed clothing that was a cross between a burka and a raincoat, before going out among the Afghan people. She didn't want to be perceived as disrespectful by showing her very white arms. While in Kyrgyzstan, she had purchased a lacy white shawl at a local market. Draped over her hair, it made a perfect head covering. One of the Marine guards became her escort and driver as they headed toward the makeshift hospital.

Some of the soldiers were well enough to sit up and play cards. Others lay on their backs recovering from a variety of either wounds or illnesses. Even a cold in this godforsaken land could set one back. The Marine stayed at her side as she moved from group to group, introducing herself as Melanie Glenn from the State Department. If pressed, she told them of the women's conference, and they appeared to like the idea and offered more ideas or their approval if it improved the future for kids. A few flirted with her, even though most of them were young enough to consider her a cougar or whatever predator fit a woman in her mid-thirties.

Several soldiers let out wolf whistles, drawing a tongue lashing from the Marine, but she smiled at the men and admitted it had been a long time since she'd heard one. She made sure not to appear as if she were flirting in return. These men had left sweethearts and wives back in the States to carry on while they fought monsters each and every day. They were tired, disillusioned, and homesick. Tessa thanked them for their service and offered to contact a loved one back home.

"Tell my folks I'm okay."

"Can you let my son know I can't wait to see his game?"

"Make sure my wife knows I miss her so much it hurts."

The Marine led Tessa back outside and told her to stand in the shade while he went to get the Jeep. She could remember a blessed Coke machine under a nearby tent awning, right next to a table. In spite of being early October, the sun grew hotter than she had experienced in Kyrgyzstan. The Coke machine helped her decide to take advantage of the shade. She dug in her pockets for change but found only a five-dollar bill. The tent sounded like a hub of activity as she stepped through the open door in search of change.

From that point on, things seemed a little fuzzy. She could remember a man's voice swearing from inside. Bonnie shrugged then admitted she didn't know anything about that.

"The Marine left you there for some reason. Minutes later, his Jeep blew up. It was a miracle you stayed behind," Bonnie said, running her hand through strands of oily hair gone straight.

"Then what happened? How did I get back? Who detained me?" Tessa felt more confused at the new layers of information which didn't seem to add up.

Bonnie shrugged and watched the tribesman as they walked out into the morning air. "Maybe we can finish this later. I'd kill for a large skinny latte."

~~~

The weather remained cooler here. Captain Hunter and Zoric had hit the trail again in search of their mountain friends who'd failed to show up several days earlier. When they doubled back to the base, they'd come under fire from the Taliban heading north, someplace usually free of this kind of trouble. Chase and Zoric managed to do some damage but were overwhelmed by their numbers. Thanks to some Rangers in the area who came to investigate the gunfire, the Taliban found themselves outgunned. In the firefight, Chase took a spray of rocks to the chest when gunfire peppered the surface in front of him. It hurt like the devil, but he managed to make it back to base without any assistance. He wasn't about to wimp out in front of a bunch of Rangers when he'd belonged to a Delta Force Team several years earlier.

Now he found himself waiting again.

"You're irritable." Zoric, a Serbian national from Chase's past, leaned back against a rock like he'd found a plush pillow and scooted down enough so not to bump his head on the low-hanging roof of their hiding place.

Chase ignored him as he lifted the binoculars to scout for trouble. He lay on his stomach, far better than trying to fit his large frame inside the small covered area.

"Why didn't you try to find Tessa?"

For the hundredth time, he asked himself the same thing. By the time he'd gotten around to calling the American Embassy, a receptionist had informed him she'd left. "I'm irritable because you keep asking me stupid questions about an Enigma agent who continues to be a pain in my ever-lovin' neck. Can you shut up about it?"

"You are irritable because you wanted to romance the honorable Mrs. Tessa Scott. You wanted to strip her of what little resistance kept you apart. You—"

Chase reached down and picked up a rock the size of a baseball and lopped it backhanded at his partner.

Zoric's chuckle sounded more like a smoker's cough. "Okay. I will mention it no more. This is your business." He stared out into the emptiness outside the cave then took a deep breath. "At least you will stop worrying about her since she is on her way to the
~~~

States."

Easier said than done. Trouble found Tessa like a heat-seeking missile. For now, he would remember their chance encounter one more time. Remembering the day when she stumbled into the first aid station still managed to remind him of the possibilities interrupted.

~~~

Military base North of Kabul

"Damn it! Get on with it. I'm not one of those crybaby SEALs you patch up!"

Chase watched a woman push inside and grow still, looking around like a lost shopper at the Mall of America. He sat hidden behind a doctor probing a shoulder wound. Another round of swearing spilled out of the doctor's mouth before Chase pointed at their guest. The doctor's continued loud and foul language drew a look of surprise from her as she took a step back.

"S-sorry. I'm lost. I, I needed change for the Coke machine. Sorry." She took another step in retreat as Chase stood up. The dim light prevented Tessa from recognizing him. As the doctor's headlamp beam smacked her in the face, she raised her hand and blinked. "I-I'm waiting for my ride. So sorry to intrude."

"Tessa?"

She shifted her attention to him standing in semi- darkness. Her body went rigid. "Chase?"

The doctor turned his pool of light toward Chase. Her gasp and hands lifting to her throat drove home his need to protect her from seeing his body, naked from the waist up, covered in blood trickling down his chest. Her attention focused on a hole just below his collarbone then dropped her gaze to the gashes and bruises patterning his abdomen. Tears pooled at the corners of her eyes as her body trembled.

"Tessa." Chase grabbed a paper gown and slipped his arms through the openings with a grunt. "I'm okay." He approached her with raised hands. "I'm okay." He stood inches from his newest agent, but she continued to stare at his covered chest. The blood
~~~

had begun to seep through the paper. He raised her chin with a bloodstained finger. "You're a sight for sore eyes."

The doctor pulled out a stool. "Maybe she should sit down."

Chase urged her down to the metal stool before pulling his own up next to her, waving the doctor off. "Give us a minute, Doc."

"We need to take care of your wounds, Captain Hunter."

Chase snarled at the doctor who huffed off to the other side of the tent. "What are you doing here?" His voice grew calm as he leaned toward Tessa. He cringed with a stab of pain, and she reached out to his unshaven face. He touched her soft hands that were such a contrast to his. "Talk to me, Tess."

"I-I." Again the stutter. Her hand slid down his cheek to his neck then tugged at the gown. She seldom touched him with such intimate gestures.

"It's not so bad. Promise. I'm okay." He lowered his head to force her attention back to his face.

He let her remove the covering and watched a trail of tears ooze down her cheek.

"What happened?" She reached to touch him again then pulled back her hand.

A Marine appeared inside the tent with concern creasing his forehead. He glanced at Tessa but shifted his attention to Chase. He straightened and lifted a hand to salute, but dropped it to his side. Soldiers didn't salute an officer out here where someone might decide to take out a leader. Chase waved him off. "Is this boy your escort?"

"Yes, sir," he snapped before Tessa could respond.

Chase patted her thigh. "I'll take it from here. She's my responsibility now."

"But, sir—"

"That will be all, son."

The Marine pivoted on his heel and exited.

The doctor strolled back over to frown at Chase. "Maybe you should wait outside." Chase resisted putting his hand to her cheek, remembering how soft her skin could feel. "I won't be long."

Tessa sighed and stood up on unsteady legs. He pointed toward the door.

Even from where he sat in the tent, he could see her sitting outside at a bistro-size table for a few minutes then stand to pace followed by easing back down at the table. Did she hear the doctor swearing? Tessa didn't like bad language so he ordered him to bite his tongue if he couldn't tone it down.

She fanned herself one minute then patted her chest the next. Maybe her thoughts raced toward a realization of what he did when not teaching Renaissance literature at the university or tracking down terrorists. She understood besides saving her life numerous times, Chase sometimes lived on the edge. Was it possible she never considered him taking part in a combat scenario? Chase had implied his work consisted of diplomatic reconnaissance for Enigma in order to keep one step ahead of whoever would do the United States harm. Now, he needed to explain a few things to her. He'd led her to believe his often cold, distant demeanor had to do with personal tragedy, hoping maybe it would bring them closer. Now she'd want to know why he was here—and wounded.

"So what are you doing here?" Chase exited the tent with his right arm in a sling, which he promptly removed after sneaking a peek back inside the tent to make sure the doctor hadn't followed.

Tessa whirled around when he spoke. She lifted her arms for only a second, as if she might want to embrace him, but he scowled hard enough to make her reconsider. She filled him in on the conference with a few sentences. "The undersecretary needed to stop here for some business."

Chase raised his chin, suspicious of anyone from the State Department. He squinted against the late afternoon sun. "What kind of business?"

Although no evidence of wounds showed through his shirt, Tessa examined his shoulder and chest with an almost casual scan. She shrugged after a few seconds. "With the ambassador, I guess. They weren't obliged to include me in their closed-door meeting." He watched Tessa slip her hands under her wrap and into her pants' pockets. "Are you really okay? Are you coming home now? I bet if I said something to the undersecretary, you could fly with us."

Chase wanted to push the lacy shawl off her head, where tangled, blond curls objected to confinement, but he resisted. "I've suffered worse. I'll be okay. My work isn't done here. A few more people I need to talk to."

"Oh." She didn't try to hide the disappointment. "Can you tell me how you got those injuries?"

"Fell down the stairs." Chase grinned. "It's a terrible idea, your being here. Why would Ben agree to this madness?"

Tessa clicked her tongue in disgust. "He didn't. It was Bonnie's idea, and I don't have a say in anything. The director informed me his first choice to be on this trip couldn't go because of her television show. None other than Martha Stewart," she laughed. "The implied meaning, I think, being I have the qualities of watching paint dry and wouldn't draw any undue attention." Her laugh always made Chase chuckle, too. "He threatened me with Sam if I screwed up."

"In other words, he told you not to be nosey or get into trouble."

She tilted her head, her expression changed from humorous to coy. "Needless to say, the threat worked like a charm. By the way, you look handsome in those camouflage fatigues. I'm glad to see my best friend."

"I'll have to remember that trick." Their silence thickened until Tessa stared at the ground. He reached for her arm and managed to pull her hand from inside her pocket. Before he could wrap his hand around hers, Tessa laced her fingers through his. "This is such a bad idea," Chase whispered in her ear.

A hot wind blew her shawl from her hair. Strands of curls fell across her nose. "I should go. But"—she surveyed her surroundings—"I don't know how to get back to the embassy."

"Guess you're going to have to depend on me, then." "I'm not sure I can trust you with such an important job."

"Maybe dinner first. I know a little place, not too fancy but very private."

"Ok. Where?" Humor returned to her mouth.

"My tent."

He continued to tease but felt wolfish having her so close. The image of Little Red Riding Hood popped into his head.

"My, what big teeth you have," she cooed, apparently thinking the same thing.

"The better to…"

A siren filled the air with its long piercing blast and people ran frantically in every direction. The doctor came outside to stand next to Tessa.

"What's going on, soldier?" Chase stopped a private crossing the yard after he noticed a plume of smoke in the distance. "Are we under attack?"

"Not sure, Captain Hunter. A car bomb is all I know. Pretty sure it was that embassy Jeep parked here today. Damn shame." Then he took off running.

Chase pivoted and grabbed Tessa who had turned a pale shade of gray. "Doc, take her to the bomb shelter until I get back. If anyone wants to know who she is, tell them…"

"To shove it up their—"

"Exactly. Now move."

Tessa's fingers dug into his arm but the doctor pulled her away. "Chase!"

He ignored her, running toward the danger.

Days later, here he hid, alone with Zoric, waiting for someone who would never show. One thing was for sure. He was done waiting for the Afghans to take a stand, for the US government to get their act together over here, and for the Taliban to be defeated once and for all. One more thing had become clear after seeing Tessa. The time to confront what they both longed to have couldn't wait. What if he'd let her leave with the Marine? How many times would fate be on his side?

CHAPTER 6

Pamir Mountains

onnie Finley wanted to stop talking about their situation and how they came to be stuck in this cold hell. She liked the beach. This place reminded her how far from a warm, sunny beach she'd strayed. Confronting a great white shark in the cool waters of the Pacific had to be better than here.

Letting her carnal desires get the better of her would be her undoing. She'd met Ambassador Jarvis in Vienna the year before at a summit. They enjoyed each other's company in the most intimate of ways. He had been an adequate lover, keeping her interested enough to stay in touch. Gossip held the ambassador might have fallen out of favor with President Austin. She didn't know why and didn't care much. But if she played her cards right, maybe she could secure an ambassadorship to add to her political accolades. The side trip to Kabul became part of her plan.

Having Melanie—or Tessa as she'd come to find out—tag along didn't sound like it would be a problem. One more do-gooder who couldn't resist sticking her nose where it could get cut off. Jarvis stood hip-deep in the opium trade with the locals. He claimed it benefited the Afghan people, but Bonnie didn't see them getting any richer. By satisfying his appetite for contraband wine in a country that forbade it, and his sexual needs, Bonnie managed to extract enough information from him to know being a part of his operation could prove very lucrative for her bank account.

The trouble with her plan, according to Jarvis, was Tessa had stumbled in on him talking to one of the most wanted Taliban in the area. She'd excused herself, but the drug lord demanded Jarvis do something about it. By the time Bonnie knew of the plan, Tessa had decided to visit the wounded soldiers at the hospital. The relief she felt at seeing her return convinced her the information would stay close to the vest. Even so, she pondered the moments which set into motion their current situation. Did Jarvis try and eliminate her, too? Men like him thought of themselves first and foremost.

Watching the Kyrgyz tribesmen make ready, she pulled up the memory of the ambassador to try and understand it all. She listened to Tessa singing "Ring Around the Rosie" with the children. They were taking great delight in the game, especially the "all fall down" part. This amused her in spite of herself as thoughts returned to what she believed to have been safer times in Kabul.

~~~

Kabul, Afghanistan

Two Marines escorted Tessa into the American Embassy foyer where dozens of personnel milled around speaking in low voices. They all turned as she rushed to the center and stopped, noting how a hush fell over the space. Disbelief expressions stared at her as she pushed through people who didn't appear capable of moving.

"Melanie." Bonnie ran down a hallway toward her. "Thank heavens you're alive." She stopped in front of her with an unexpected embrace then held her at arm's length. "We thought you'd been killed in the car bomb." She shook her head in dismay. "That poor young man. Where were you, Melanie?"

"At the base. I ran into an old friend and then got detained." She turned in a circle, surprised to see how everyone hung on her every word. "Someone else volunteered to bring me back."

The ambassador joined them. In his mid-forties, he had the appearance of a man who worked out but also spent too many hours in a tanning bed. Not much taller than Tessa, he carried himself as if he were above everyone else. "You were lucky."
~~~

Tessa had remarked something about divine intervention. A predestined meeting with Captain Hunter would have trumped any other plans. When she'd begun to weaken against his sexual prowess, another force greater than herself had intervened once more. "Yes. Very lucky, Mr. Ambassador." The other embassy personnel drifted into other parts of the building.

"You're shaking. Please. Come into my office, Ms. Glenn." He motioned down the hall. "You, too, Ms. Finley."

Both women followed him as Bonnie slipped her arm around Tessa for moral support.

"I'm glad you're okay." Bonnie gave her a friendly squeeze.

"Did you notice anyone around your vehicle while you were on base, Ms. Glenn?" The ambassador closed the double doors then motioned for them to sit in leather chairs in front of his mahogany desk. He sat on the corner nearest Bonnie.

Bonnie crossed her bare legs, her navy skirt rising over slim thighs. Tessa caught the ambassador's downward glance before he cleared his throat. Something like amusement passed between him and the undersecretary as one corner of her mouth turned up then relaxed again. It was a delicate movement that Tessa almost missed.

"No, Ambassador Jarvis. The MPs searched it before we were allowed inside the main operating area. Once on base, it was parked in a secure, guarded area."

"I see." The ambassador tapped his pencil on the desk and chewed on his bottom lip for a few seconds. He turned his attention back to Bonnie. "Any thoughts?"

Lines formed at the corners of Bonnie's eyes and mouth. "Of course not." She reached across to Tessa, laying her hand on top of her forearm which rested on the arm of the chair. "Maybe it was random. These kinds of things happen all the time in such a godless place. No telling what horrible things lie in wait for someone as innocent as Melanie." Her voice became soothing and soft. When she turned her attention back to the ambassador, Tessa thought she saw a glint of contempt. "Am I right, Ambassador Jarvis?"

"Definitely. Now"—he slipped off the corner surface then moved around the desk to face the women— "the Marines are often targets in this hell. I think the trip to the girls' orphanage should be postponed."

"Orphanage?" Tessa straightened in her chair.

Bonnie sighed. "Perhaps you're right. As much as I want those poor little things brought in, maybe picking them up can wait."

"Wait for what?" Tessa wanted a distraction from her near-death experience. The mention of orphans did the trick.

"Several wealthy benefactors from the States have made it possible for young girls to come to America to be educated for one year. The Afghan government won't allow adoption but is willing to let these children participate in the program." The ambassador loosened his tie as he stole another glance at Bonnie's legs.

"Melanie, we wanted these children to be given hope and an education. Americans are very generous," Bonnie offered as she toyed with her fingernails.

Tessa frowned. "I see. When they have to send the girls back, Americans will dedicate themselves to raising money to ensure their efforts continue. I bet the Afghan government is already planning what to do with the money. I doubt those girls will ever benefit from one dime."

"I agree, of course," Bonnie interjected. "However, I think if we work together over the next year, we can find a way for the girls to remain in the US or devise a plan where the money goes into building schools and group homes. We'll have a news team follow them for a year. Contact National Geographic, where I understand you may have some influence. It can't smell of government involvement. You, on the other hand, would be perfect to spearhead this project."

"That could work." The ambassador rubbed his chin. "What do you say, Ms. Glenn?"

Bonnie had hit Tessa where she was most vulnerable. "We are so lucky our children have safe, happy lives with access to education and health care. But here..."

"Let's do it. Can't soldiers go get them?" "Unfortunately, no. The Afghans have insisted

American soldiers not be a part of this. We suggested some international aid workers, but they are unavailable until next month. The Afghans are notorious for changing their minds. Time is not on our side. We can always try next year." The ambassador shook his head as he exhaled a deep sigh.

"If we go, will we have protection?"

Bonnie frowned. "You can't be serious, Melanie? Are you sure about this?"

The ambassador snapped his fingers like he hadn't thought of such an idea. "Yes. Of course. It isn't far by helicopter. The area has been secure for over a year now. The locals are supportive. I'll talk to the base commander and get his feeling on the matter, but I don't think there will be any objection if they've locked this car bomb incident down." He cocked his head at Bonnie. "Are you in?"

Tessa realized Bonnie would be banking on public relations gold as she gave her answer. "You bet."

~~~

Pamir Mountains

Several of the riders carrying a child behind them pushed the yaks ahead, while Darya herded the others carrying supplies. It was an orchestrated event to reach home with necessities. Tessa rode behind him, Arzo, the three-year- old in front of him. Listening to Darya explain how to keep the animals moving, even what the beasts of burden were thinking, amused the child enough she bombarded him with more questions which he answered with the patience of a patronizing parent. She caught enough of the conversation to make her chuckle. Darya grinned back over his shoulder at her, and for a moment a warm feeling replaced her contempt. He reached down to pat one of her hands gripping the sides of his clothing then turned away.

"All right, Melanie?" he asked in a nonthreatening voice.

"Yes." She didn't want to compliment the sound of his voice or the way he sang to the child.

The landscape switched from patches of forest to desolate land, heavy with rocks. The flat areas stretched forever. The jagged mountains in the distance appeared closer. All the while the altitude increased. The temperature dropped during the day as they moved up toward the mountains. The heat of Kabul disappeared. A
~~~

piercing sun morphed into a soft glow hanging in the sky. Sounds of the wind resembled voices of apparitions. Breathing would be laborious for a while, until she became accustomed to the thinner air. The sound of nothing except the grunts of yaks and the prodding of sharp whistles filled Tessa with comfort. The ripple of water rushing beneath rickety bridges tied together with rope gave her pause, but Darya didn't appear to be concerned so she laid her cheek against his back and inhaled his masculine scent.

When Darya stopped to rest the horses, he gave the children more of the cheese to munch on. While he moved from child to child, Tessa studied him. His walk exuded confidence, his movements agile for such a muscular body. Even covered in black clothing, like the other men, Darya stood out among his companions. Nearing six foot, he stood several inches taller than the men following him. In spite of having part of his face covered, his eyes revealed intelligence. His lips were thick and expressive as if God had sculpted them Himself. Even though they remained pursed most of the time, the occasional smile he'd given to the children revealed good teeth. She'd noticed the other men suffered from cavities or a missing tooth, but Darya must have practiced good dental hygiene as a child.

She admired his hair, sticking out from under his brown hat in straight dark strands. The ragged mask failed to hide his wide nose. She couldn't resist staring at his hands as he passed Bonnie Finley some bread. He didn't pay the woman much attention as he shoved it at her. Tessa liked his gracefulness as he walked the horses, checking for any problems. His kindness toward the animals paralleled his attention to the children.

These people were not monsters like the Taliban. At least, Darya appeared to be different. When he turned on his heels and leveled a fierce glare at her, she caught her breath. She hoped he couldn't detect the thoughts of admiration welling to the surface. He took the reins of his horse and walked it toward Tessa. She raised her chin in quiet defiance as his beautiful almond-shaped eyes narrowed. He swung up onto the horse then reached down for her hand.

Her heart pounding, she examined his half-hidden face for a hint of danger. She saw none. He pointed at something in the distance then extended his hand again.

Tessa grabbed hold of his leathery hand and let Darya swing her up behind him. He called to one of the other men before tapping the animal's sides with his feet. The horse jerked to life and galloped across the plain as she held on for dear life.

The horse gained speed when Darya let loose a joyful sound of freedom from deep in his throat. Tessa's grip around his waist tightened, but she couldn't contain the laughter spilling from her mouth. She felt the scarf slip down around her neck and her hair whip in the wind.

Something inside escaped in that moment. Not knowing her identity or missing pieces of her life brought her to this point in time no longer seemed to matter. She knew enough to know riding behind this man on a crazy fast horse was the closest thing to bliss that she'd probably ever know. Had she ever been so free?

When Darya jerked back on the reins, she could feel the muscles in his back flex. She tightened her arms around his neck. Darya threw the reins down before swinging his leg over the horse's neck and sliding to the ground. He reached up to pull Tessa down, and, before she could protest, his hands touched unsettling places. Once she steadied herself, he withdrew and grabbed the reins, walking the horse toward the edge of a cliff as he motioned with his head for Tessa to follow.

Uneasy at the distance from the others, Tessa imagined a number of scenarios, none of which turned out well. Yet the vastness of the surrounding land mesmerized her to distraction. The sound of silence wove a hypnotic spell around her common sense. The overwhelming taste of freedom swallowed any fear of Darya she knew should be forefront in her mind.

Her steps slowed as she stepped up next to the tribesman who appeared transfixed at the valley beneath them. Tessa sucked in her breath at its unsurpassed beauty then placed her hand on her heart. Foamy curls slammed into boulders scattered in what she imagined to be icy whitewater. The distant sounds of swift water now reached her ears as she closed her eyes. The act of breathing felt labored here. Tessa took a deep breath and held it in as long as possible before releasing it with deliberate slowness. When she dared to glance sideways at Darya, she realized he studied her with interest. Laughter sprang from deep inside her as she pointed to the land below.

"Beautiful." She wanted to divert her gaze from his, but his words kept her mesmerized.

"Beautiful," he echoed.

Were they talking about the same thing? She turned her attention back to the valley feeling an uncomfortable blush start up her neck and face. Darya stepped closer. He pointed out several things, even a snow leopard hiding in the rocks below. This took her longer to see, but she became excited at seeing such an endangered animal in the wild.

Several times their faces almost touched, but Darya made no inappropriate moves.

When he spoke in a low voice, Tessa leaned in to catch his words although she understood very little. She watched him speak, liking the way his mouth moved. His slanted eyes grew wide then narrowed to slits as he emphasized some point. Once he laughed in a light tone as if at himself. His wide mouth made Tessa happy when he showed humor. She wondered why. He reminded her of someone, someone strong who'd protected her in the past. Darya also hinted at being dangerous. Why something so sinister affected her in a positive way remained a point of concern.

The horse stomped with impatience then shied toward Tessa. She jumped out of the way but stumbled back toward the edge of the cliff where the ground crumbled under her feet. In a split second, Darya grabbed her by her clothes, yanking her into his arms. A scream escaped her throat as she clung to Darya's neck.

"Oh my gosh." Breathing fast, she peeked behind her to see rocks and earth snapping their way to the bottom of the valley. Darya stepped backwards and pulled her with him. He stroked the back of her uncovered hair while his other hand pressed her up against his chest. She eased out of his embrace.

In a timid, but grateful voice, Tessa whispered, "Thank you." She said it in Pashto then Russian, hoping he would understand.

"You welcome," he said in English. "Dangerous place. Careful." He hesitated as if searching for a word. "Please." His lips clamped together in a straight line, and she imagined his forehead creased beneath his mask considering the words sounded difficult for him.

Tessa agreed. "Yes. I'll be more careful." She stole another glance at the cliff behind her and wondered why they were here.

And why had he begun looking at her like there was something he had on his mind. His gaze spoke volumes as it roamed around her face, resting on her mouth then sliding down her neck and shoulders. Fear crept up inside her. Had she begun to trust this renegade too soon?

More words came from his mouth, deep and low, as his stare dwelled on parts of her body. Tessa didn't understand the words, but the meaning seemed to imply Darya thought she should show more gratitude.

"I guess you think I owe you a little show-and-tell because you saved me from certain death."

Darya tilted his head.

"Let me remind you your stupid horse caused me to fall in the first place. And let's get one thing straight, Batman." Tessa shoved a finger in his chest then withdrew it, frightened at the way his mouth twisted in a snarl. "I need to—"

Before she could finish her sentence, Darya scooped her up like a rag doll and tossed her onto the front of the horse. He swung up behind her and enclosed her between his arms as they rode with abandonment across the plains. His breath warmed her cheek, his scent touched her nose, and the press of his body spoke of unfulfilled desire. The days ahead would be woven with danger and treachery along with the unwanted affections of a mountain tribesman.

I will always come for you if you are in trouble. Those words once more lay bare on her mind. Would the person who said them come in time?

CHAPTER 7

Darkness fell as the group reached the river Tessa had spied while standing on the cliff hours earlier. It seemed warmer in the valley. The gurgle of the river had the children yawning as the men set about making camp. Snorts from the yaks and the horses crunching of sprigs of grass brought a quiet calm among the men and children.

Bone-tired, she longed to sleep, but the little girls clung to her one by one until she collapsed like a limber clown near the campfire to offer encouragement. She sang a lullaby which seemed to float up with the curling smoke. The men showed their pleasure at hearing her sing with clapping that involved slapping their thighs. She attempted to teach the children the song with comic results. Laughter rippled among them. Even Bonnie made the effort to sing along in spite of having remained sour faced since Tessa returned from the ride with Darya.

"Where did he take you? Are you all right? I thought he might…"

"I'm fine. He wanted to show me where we were going to be tonight." Tessa pointed to the towering cliffs and searched for the exact spot where they'd stood. "I'm not sure why he thought I needed to know." Tessa removed Arzo's head scarf and ran her fingers down the light-brown hair. She forgot herself as she sang folk songs she remembered from some other place and time. One song, in Japanese, made the children wrinkle their noses and giggle at the sounds. Tessa remembered how to sing "Silent Night" in German. The children swayed as her voice lifted into the night sky now splattered with stars.

"So what does he want? Where are we going?" Bonnie kept her questions low but her irritation couldn't be hidden. "Will they take us to the Americans?"

Tessa shrugged, not caring where they were going. "We need to take care of these children."

Bonnie huffed. "At this point, if we get a chance to go back to Kabul we need to act on it. These"—she waved toward the men—"whoever they are, can take care of the girls. Their lives will be better than what they had. At least—"

Tessa snarled. "What are you saying? I will not leave these babies to the likes of anyone but the American authorities in Kabul. Out here, they are destined to be wives at the age of fourteen, mothers by fifteen. This part of the world is rich with opium. These mountain tribesmen are Kyrgyz. Half of them become addicts out of grief for their dead children."

"How do you know that?" Bonnie's voice rose. "For someone who keeps saying she's lost her memory, you seem to have an uncommon grasp of who these people are. Have you been lying to me? This morning you said your name was Tessa."

"And you promised to tell me more about the days leading up to our departure from Kabul. Spill it."

"What are you, CIA? You seem to have a knack for being in the wrong place at the right time? And you were pretty good with a knife back there when you severed a man's spinal cord."

Tessa froze as she noticed Darya standing not more than ten feet away, listening to them argue. "Shh! Lower your voice. I think Darya understands more English than he lets on."

"Well, la-di-da. You're our ticket out of here. He keeps watching you like you're on tonight's menu." Her voice turned into a harsh whisper.

"Shut up." Tessa couldn't hide her revulsion. "What are you saying? I should sleep with him so he'll take us back?"

"Yes. Do whatever it takes. Considering how you like to slum among the natives, you'll no doubt enjoy it."

"Ms. Melanie, please don't be angry." Shirin inched closer. "They are watching us."

Tessa patted her cheek. "Sorry," she whispered. "I will be quiet. Should we sing some more?"

Darya sat down across the fire from her as food was passed out.

"What I'd give for a juicy steak. Don't these people eat meat?" Bonnie turned her nose up at the kurut again, but grabbed the bread.

"On special occasions. These yaks are part of their wealth. I'm sure when we arrive at their permanent camp, we'll find sheep. Maybe then."

After softening the kurut cheese in her mouth, Tessa chewed slowly as if by doing so might make it taste better. She made "yum" sounds to urge the children to eat more. Bread then tea followed. The young rider named Rashid kept following Shirin with his stolen glances and seemed to speak to Darya for encouragement but didn't appear to gain support. Tessa made pallets for the children from yak hides. They loved burrowing down in the soft fur. With groups of three snuggled together, she guessed they would stay warm enough. The rock outcropping deflected winds coming down from the cliffs above and formed a shelter to protect the children.

The men were bedding down for the night as well when Bonnie joined Tessa near the fire, a blanket wrapped around her shoulders. The stylish woman who had run the conference a few days earlier now resembled a homeless person. Her clothes were dirty, the reddish- brown hair stringy and thinner. With her makeup gone, Bonnie appeared older than Tessa once thought. The expensive tennis shoes she wore weren't the most practical thing you could wear on terrain like this.

The day they left Kabul, Tessa had wondered at Bonnie's wisdom in wearing snug khaki pants for a helicopter ride. A no-iron blouse in a pale shade of yellow had given her a window mannequin appearance: perfect. Tessa, on the other hand, had dressed like she planned to work at the barn with her uncle's horses. Then she'd covered her head with a shawl. Even when the air turned hot, Tessa protected her skin from being exposed. A show of respect needed to be observed even if she thought it archaic. After all, it was Afghanistan, not downtown Miami. Funny how one tidbit of information remained clear and other things blurred.

When Bonnie told her of the days leading up to her amnesia, Tessa managed to string information together. For instance, she remembered seeing Bonnie slip into the ambassador's sleeping quarters on the night before they left Kabul. The undersecretary held a bottle of some kind of wine or champagne. How in the world did she manage to get it into the country considering the culture rejected the drinking of alcohol? Tessa also became aware over the course of their travels that Bonnie enjoyed the company of influential men.

"What are you so glum about?" Bonnie mumbled as she found a twig and threw it into the fire. "Thinking about your boyfriend over there or the one you left behind in Kabul?"

Tessa jerked her head around in shock. "Boyfriend? What are you talking about?"

Bonnie smirked. "Seriously? I could tell you anything and you'd never know the truth."

Tessa wondered if the woman might have already undertaken that tactic.

"The morning after the bombing, the base commander told us the Marine left you in the care of a Delta Force captain who you found getting stitched up. Ring any bells?"

She stared into the fire to dig for answers in a clouded memory. The recall of a man in the shadows with a naked chest made her wonder if he meant something to her as Bonnie implied. "I-I don't remember."

A hiss came out of Bonnie's mouth. "One of your CIA buddies?"

"I don't work for the CIA," Tessa said in hesitation. "I'm sure of it. I'm a geographer on loan to another government agency. I serve as a goodwill liaison for children and women's issues." It sounded rehearsed, as if she were reading it from a script. "I know I work in California."

"That guy you were talking to disappeared after he loaded you up with some Rangers in an armored-plated Humvee and sent you back to us. The base commander had nothing to say on the matter. He had some reservations on letting us go get the girls but, after checking out the latest intel, he decided to let us use one of his helicopters." Bonnie released a snort. "I hate those things. Got sick as a dog, what with all their swerving and dodging tactics."

She chuckled. "You were green as grass by the time we got there."

Tessa remembered riding in helicopters with dangerous men. The image of the same shadowy man appeared in her mind as he spoke. *I will always come for you if you are in trouble.*

She couldn't remember him. Were they friends, colleagues, or lovers?

"I don't know who sent me back." Tessa pulled her robes tighter. "What does it matter? We're here now. I'm betting someone is searching for us." She took a deep breath before glancing over at Bonnie who stared into the fire. "What happened after we left Kabul?"

Bonnie's voice reminded her of a malfunctioning robot. "All hell broke loose." With each word, more of Tessa memories surged to the surface.

~~~

Kabul, Afghanistan

People moving along the congested streets like they were caught in a zombie apocalypse would be Tessa's lasting impression of Afghanistan. Centuries of destruction and violence continued to capture the Afghan people in a stranglehold. Tessa pressed her face against the bulletproof glass of the ambassador's car to observe this strange world. The beauty of the jagged white-capped mountains glowing gray blue in the distance created a sharp contrast with the rubble of the centuries-old city. Rebuilding had made resurgence in places, and Bonnie proved correct about there being a shopping mall, although Tessa puzzled over how those in such poverty could afford a toothbrush, much less a pair of boots or a jacket. She leaned back in the seat and listened to honking horns, whistles, rumbling motorcycles needing a new muffler, and an occasional jackhammer. Everything felt dirty and old. Where was the romance of the historical fiction she'd read as a girl? Where were the beautiful faces of women who struggled to become a force of change alongside men who cherished them?

Not here. War forever changed the landscape of Afghanistan. Americans continued to leave the latest bloody gash of change.
~~~

Like everything in Central Asia, soon it would scab over and heal in an unpredictable way. The scar left in its place would come back to haunt her country as it had the ones who came before. Russia would never recover from their blunder and Tessa knew America played a part as well. When the US aided the rebels against communism with billions of dollars' worth of weapons, it left a bad taste in the mouths of several American presidents. Now those arms were being used against American soldiers.

The Black Hawk helicopter waited on the runway for the women. An army colonel introduced himself to them as he shook hands with Ambassador Jarvis.

"Ready to go, ladies?" He pointed to their ride. His square jaw showed a tiny Band-Aid from shaving, and his sparse hair caught the sun for a second to glisten a deep silver. The light-brown eyes bore deep creases at the corners as he squinted against the morning light. He raised his voice to compensate for the engines of the helicopter as it rived to life. "The village is north of here, about sixty miles. Won't take this bird long to reach it. Good folks. Helped us on numerous occasions. World Cares Organization built the orphanage there. There are twelve or thirteen girls. It's been successful, but they've run out of money."

The ambassador lowered his head as the helicopter blades turned. He pressed his milquetoast hand against his tie. "I decided on these girls myself." He bobbed his head at the colonel. "Any problem with Taliban up there?"

The colonel shook his head. "None. The locals have been diligent in defending their community. We've left radios to call for help at any time. It's been over a year since we had to go in and clean a nest of those black- turban ragheads out." He tightened his jaw. "Sorry, ladies. I mean Taliban." He pointed to a soldier standing by the open door of the helicopter. "The warrant officer will need to make two trips to get everyone back. The other birds are needed elsewhere."

"Send the oldest children back first, Ms. Finley," the ambassador yelled to her. "Let Ms. Glenn stay behind for the next trip. We have unfinished business."

I'll bet, thought Tessa, seeing how he grasped Bonnie's arm and winked. She didn't like the idea of being left behind in an Afghan village without a weapon, soldier, or way to get back.

The colonel frowned. "Negative, Ambassador Jarvis. I won't leave an American woman behind without protection."

"You said it was safe."

"Nothing is safe in Afghanistan."

Tessa realized her scarf had fallen around her neck, trapping her hair. She could picture how wild that must be with the chopper blades trying to pull her strands toward chaos.

The colonel motioned for another soldier and gave orders for him to stay behind with her. "You'll be there two hours alone. A lot can happen in two hours. I'll feel better if this soldier tags along."

"Thank you, colonel." Tessa offered her hand to the soldier who waited to assist her onboard. "Yes, ma'am." He put a finger to his forehead in an offhand salute.

Tessa let the men on board buckle her in and felt trepidation as they lifted off with a sudden burst of speed.

Helicopter rides didn't agree with her. She got airsick looking at one of these birds. It reminded her of riding on the curvy roads in her home state of Tennessee. Squeezing her eyes shut helped, but she wanted to see the breathtaking landscape as they clicked off the miles to the small village. The noise of the Black Hawk prevented conversation so the women sat in silence.

The image of her children swam up to her mind as she said a prayer of protection for them and herself. What am I doing in this awful place? What if I'm kidnapped or killed? What would become of my kids? Can my husband manage?

Then her thoughts slid into dangerous territory when the image of Captain Chase Hunter loomed in her imagination. The way she idolized him continued to drag her toward dangerous territory which had nothing to do with the Taliban. His heroics, without regard for his own life, had managed to save her on several occasions. Their unusual partnership had turned into a love hate relationship. But, as of late, the complicated bond between them felt as if it led her on a path full of pitfalls.

He continued to be the most irritating yet compassionate man Tessa had ever met. His six-foot-one- inch height wore strength and power like armor which intoxicated her. The Native American features and bronze skin made him a perfect model for the cover of one of those videogames her sons loved to play. The often pouty mouth appeared too big for his face. The lips made her wonder if God chiseled them for her to kiss. There were moments when she promised herself she would enjoy it if it had to do with national security. The nose narrowed down toward his mouth then widened almost too much. She'd learned to recognize his anger when it flared. The high cheekbones tightened when she confused or teased him. He didn't understand a joke. At least not until she'd come along.

The other Enigma agents reminded her from time to time they heard him laugh for the first time the day they met. She never got tired of them telling her how stunned they were at the discovery he had a sense of humor or that he tolerated insubordination from a civilian like Tessa Scott.

Part of her loved him in spite of never acting upon it. Before God, friends, and family, she'd promised to forever belong to Robert Scott. They were happy. Three children made romance a distant memory, but something better settled in because they were a family.

Once Captain Hunter kicked in the door of her perfect life, he changed how she saw the world.

Tessa felt the helicopter descend. It hovered, tilted then sat down.

"Welcome," an Afghan man greeted them as they exited. "Welcome," he repeated. He lowered his head to both women as the soldier hopped down, armed and dangerous. He initiated the usual safety scan while cradling his weapon like an infant.

"I'm Undersecretary Finley." Bonnie shoved her hand at the man who wore his wrinkles like a man in his fifties, but in this harsh environment the number could have been an overestimation. The title didn't appear to impress the man with missing teeth, loose clothing, and pale eyes, one clouded with a possible cataract. His gray beard, streaked with the remnants of pale brown, added to the mystery of his age. He kept his hand at his side and Bonnie pulled hers back.

"This is my assistant." Bonnie glanced at Tessa who contained her surprise at the title. The less these people knew about her the better. "Are we far from the orphanage?" she asked in Pashto.

"No. No. This way. This way." The Afghan pointed toward the village not more than a hundred yards away. A few of the villagers ventured out of their homes and talked among themselves while the smaller ones pointed at the helicopter and made roaring sounds.

As they approached, the soldier spoke into his mouthpiece, requesting an update on any Taliban activity in the area. He continued to search for trouble. Tessa felt uneasy. Her steps slowed. The sight of little girls leaving a one-story building carrying bundles the size of a folded tablecloth, their young faces flushed and frightened, helped her refocus. They hurried toward them, waving. Did they feel they were about to be liberated? Tessa's heart swelled as she laughed at the simplicity of it all. Little girls wanting a better life. What a concept. So grateful for a chance to learn. Likely afraid, but ready to embrace the unknown because something deep inside them knew life could be better.

"Hello," Tessa greeted them in Pashto as a worker ran up alongside them. She held the hands of two teen girls who might be around her own son's age. "Are you ready to take a ride?" Tessa made an effort to sound excited, although she wondered if the girls would be throwing up by the time they arrived in Kabul. They giggled with excitement.

The aid worker extended her hand as the village man stood back and folded his hands in front of him like he'd just delivered a UPS package. "They're ready, all right." She laughed. "I don't think anyone slept last night."

Bonnie made a visual count and realized there were two more girls than the ambassador had originally said.

"We can't take everyone this time, but the pilot will soon return for the others. Are you going, too?" A backpack hung on the woman's shoulder. Her prematurely gray hair indicated this place may have robbed her of some youthfulness. Her skin matched the color, creases leading out from the corners of her eyes and at the edges of a thin- lipped mouth.

"Yes. This is part of the problem here. There's no money and I'm needed somewhere else in the world." She picked up the three-year-old. "This is Arzo." She was wrapped tight in her clothes, like a cocoon. Even her head covering revealed little about the hair underneath. "She is the sweetest girl in the world." Arzo hugged the woman's neck, offering a shy peek at Tessa, and pointed to her eyes then her own.

"We need to go, ma'am." The soldier took the aid worker by the arm and tugged toward the bird. "You go with the older girls. The younger six can go on the next one."

Bonnie frowned. "I planned to go this time, soldier." He continued to survey the surrounding hillsides.

"Better someone who is known among them travel with marriage-aged girls, ma'am. This woman is known around here. You are not. We don't want them or the village to get the idea we're taking them for other reasons."

The aid worker agreed. "I'm afraid he's right. These people don't always trust soldiers around their daughters. It makes no difference they have little use for these orphans. They will be glad not to have to feed them. Another reason to get them out."

A girl of about fourteen stepped forward. "Take Amena, since she is older than me. I will stay behind. My sister will be very frightened if I leave without her." She took the hand of a little girl who couldn't have been more than seven.

"This is Shirin with her little sister Pamir. She will be excellent help with the others." The aid worker moved toward the helicopter.

"Your English is very good, Shirin," Tessa complimented.

The teen beamed. "Thank you, ma'am."

With one last hug to a few of the girls the aid worker turned toward the orphanage. "Feel free to rest in our humble house."

"But—" Bonnie interrupted.

"We'll be back for you ASAP, ma'am." The soldier herded the first passengers forward.

Bonnie shaded her face as the children scrambled onto the Black Hawk. She turned to their escort. "Tell the pilot to hurry back. This place gives me the creeps."

The soldier turned away to speak in his mic.

Tessa did her best to speak to the children as she led them down the rise of the hill into the village. Bonnie made a few unflattering remarks about her dressing like a local for the trip.

"It might be a good idea to stay indoors until the helicopter returns since you chose to dress like an ad for the side of a bus." Tessa laced her words with sweetness so not to alarm the girls. Bonnie grimaced at the truth and pushed into the middle of the group of girls until they reached the orphanage. The strategy proved to be too little too late.

CHAPTER 8

The confidence of having a soldier with them helped Tessa shake off the feeling of dread. The people milling around didn't appear intimidated by a military presence. She couldn't remember a time in history when soldiers, warlords, and drug traffickers didn't wander Afghanistan. This part of the world would continue to be an open wound, festering from too much intervention by self- serving nations who didn't have a clue what they were doing. The two women ushered the children inside the place they'd called home, and the soldier backed in after them, straight-faced.

"Everything all right, corporal?" Tessa walked up beside him to peek around his body filling the doorway.

"Not sure, ma'am."

Bonnie rushed over. "What does that mean? I thought this was a safe place?"

The corporal continued to scan the outside area. "Yes, ma'am. It is."

"So what's the problem, soldier? Speak up. It's not too late to call the helicopter back." Bonnie breathed faster and her hysterical voice tipped Tessa off if things went sideways she need not count on her for support.

"No problem." He stepped back, bumping into Tessa who sidestepped like a scared rabbit. He shut the door then locked it before moving to the window.

He rolled his shoulders and straightened his back. Tessa observed how he kept touching his weapon as if to make sure he had control. When he pulled back the burlap curtain hanging on a wire, Tessa came up beside him. "Have you been here before?"

He muttered, "Yes."

Bonnie demanded information, but stopped when Tessa held out her hand then shook her head.

The children huddled together, their little faces thoughtful as they watched the new adults in their life. They lacked the mischief of American children. Her heart ached for them to be naughty, loud, or even squirm. Heads bowed, they peered up through loose strands of various shades of brown hair.

"Who will show me around this place?" Tessa clapped her hands together and regretted her sudden movement when several of the girls flinched. She squatted in front of two she guessed were between seven and nine years of age and spoke to them in Pashto. "Little girls with big dreams." She offered her biggest smile to put them at ease. "Can I see where you learn?" The girls cocked their heads. Tessa hoped she hadn't asked them if a goat climbed up their nose. "Books."

All the girls reacted to the word and grasped her hands and clothing, pulling her into another room. Shirin followed like a mother hen, letting the younger ones show the American woman their home and school.

Shirin whispered directions a couple of times to help them show with pride their box of broken pencils or a stack of tablets made from used copy paper. When Tessa picked one up, she realized they were rebound scrap paper from the States, from church bulletins, discarded stock reports, and even travel vouchers from a resort in Branson, Missouri. The front side would be blank with the back covered in whatever information destined for the recycling bin. Tessa promised when she got back to the States every one of these girls would have proper tablets, pencils, and crayons.

Shirin's little sister brought her several pieces of cardboard. A round one reminded her of a delivered pizza. Two others were like the boxes Tessa used to wrap Christmas presents. Shirin frowned as her hands took the cardboard to return it to a three-legged table.

"Please. May I see?" Tessa reached for them as her English

spilled forth. Shirin handed her the cardboard then bowed her head. Amazed at the sketches, Tessa sucked in her breath. "Shirin, these are beautiful."

They were pictures of the girls at the school. One even had the aid worker singing. Tessa's emotions threatened to spill over as she observed the tiniest details in the picture. Even the compacted dirt floor appeared lifelike. A mouse hid under the table as the children worked. A breeze lifting the mesh curtain giving the piece of art a photographic appearance.

Tessa couldn't resist giving the girl a hug. "You're an artist, Shirin. I'm going to make sure you are never without art supplies." She conveyed the promise in choppy Pashto.

The girl grinned from ear to ear as the children clapped for her. The little sister hugged the legs of the fourteen-year-old in a gesture of worship. "My sister is also talented, ma'am."

Tessa kneeled down next to the shy seven-year-old. "What is her talent?" The little urchin hid her face in Shirin's clothing.

"Sing for her, Pamir."

"Please," Tessa continued in Pashto.

In a small voice, Pamir lifted her voice in some native song. The voices of angels could not be as sweet as the little girl. Soon the others sang along. When tears trickled down Tessa's cheeks, a hush fell over them. In that moment she fell hopelessly in love with the children. Nothing would ever be the same.

"We are sorry, ma'am. We did not know our songs would hurt." Shirin shivered and gathered the girls close to her side.

Tessa laughed as she hugged each little soul before her. "You have given me a gift with your voices. Thank you so much." She was so overcome she forgot to speak in their language.

At a quick translation by Shirin, the girls giggled and reached to touch Tessa. They continued to proudly show their school followed by where they slept at night on woven mats. How fifteen children could be educated and survive in such a confined area amazed Tessa. The tour soon ended back in the first room where a rickety card table, two chairs, and a woodstove made up the furnishings. A shelf holding a few dishes and pans completed the kitchen. Tessa thought it gave new meaning to rustic as she peeked into a basket holding some rags, a bar of soap, and a first aid kit. The new bar of soap still had the wrapping on it, and Tessa wondered what agency or military patrol had donated it.

Shirin insisted the girls sit down in the corner to avoid getting in the way as they waited for the returning helicopter. She joined them after making sure their bundles rested against the front wall of the building to retrieve on their way out.

Bonnie paced with an occasional exasperated sigh then a round of hugging her arms followed by checking her watch. Several times she asked the soldier if the helicopter should be returning by now. After the fourth time, he turned his impatient glare on her and she scooted back into the middle of the room.

"He can't make it go faster. They'll be here soon." Tessa sighed with exasperation.

"Soon should have been an hour ago," she snapped. "This place smells like urine. I feel sick."

Tessa glanced over at the little girls waiting without complaint then beamed their way. "Shirin, is there any food in here? I bet the others are getting hungry."

She shook her head. "We ran out two days ago."

Tessa sucked in her breath. "You haven't eaten in two days?"

"Some of the people in the village let our teacher have bread yesterday. We are used to going without, ma'am. But the baby…" She pointed to Arzo whose hollow gaze went to Tessa. "I worry she will not make it if she does not get food soon."

The soldier frowned then reached into his pocket and pulled out some plastic bags of granola. He tossed them to Tessa. "Here. My mom sent it to me. Homemade. Code for fattening." He grinned at the children before turning back to the window.

Tessa sat down Indian style in the corner and tore open a bag of cereal. With a wink at Arzo, she motioned for her to sit in her lap. She let the three-year-old dig into the bag with a dirty hand. The other two got passed among the others. They appeared to savor each morsel as they ate in silence. Shirin offered Tessa the last few bites but she refused. Before she suggested Shirin eat the rest, Bonnie lifted the bag and sniffed.

She watched the girls staring up at her then handed it back. "Never mind. I might catch something if I put this in my mouth."

"Be nice," Tessa warned, worried Shirin might comprehend the insult. The girl lowered her head.

"It's not like they understand me, Melanie. I will make sure the ambassador makes it up to me when we get back. I should have gone back when I had a chance. This is ridiculous."

The one thing that continues to be ridiculous is your attitude, thought Tessa.

The soldier shifted his weight. A nervous kind of tension filled the room as he dropped the curtain to peek through with one eye. His serious demeanor made Tessa think something was amiss.

Tessa stood up and dusted off her bottom. Her left eye had taken on a nervous twitch as she stared at the soldier.

"Corporal, is there a problem?"

"Not sure." He frowned back at the women then the children. "It's afternoon. Where is everyone? Do people normally disappear this time of day?" The three adults turned to Shirin for an answer.

Shirin shook her head. "Not unless there is trouble."

Unfolding her arms, Bonnie's voice turned cold.

"What kind of trouble?"

"Taliban," the girl said. "Sometimes mountain tribesmen. Kyrgyz." Her voice sounded so grown up. Perhaps the girl might be trying to alleviate concerns like a mother would do for her children in a difficult time. "It is good. No Taliban for long time because they afraid of Kyrgyz. Soldiers come bring supplies for our village khan so people will not starve. But they all hide. They very scared of Americans."

"And the Kyrgyz?" Tessa hated to admit she could be intrigued at a time like this.

"They have horses. Sometimes fight Taliban. Warn to stay away from the gray-haired lady. They think the masked Kyrgyz demon."

"This gets better and better," Bonnie choked out.

"The kahn of our village has wife from the Kyrgyz tribe. She Sunni Muslim. Make Taliban angry she here."

"When were the Taliban here?" The soldier took a slow step toward the children who huddled together.

Shirin held up five fingers then five more. "This many days. They not like us, I think. Said we bad for learning." She bowed her head. "Said my pictures were bad. I should be punished. They not like the gray-haired lady, but leave her safe because the Kyrgyz say they come back and kill Taliban if harm comes to her. The masked man is very brave."

The soldier turned and radioed the chopper as Tessa stepped up next to him. All she could hear was static then a few words before it faded. "Where's the chopper, Corporal?" Tessa whispered as Bonnie's pacing turned frantic.

"Not sure." He reached in his jacket and withdrew a pistol. "A mutual friend told me you knew how to use one of these." Tessa examined the semi-automatic then slipped it under her robes. "There's a full clip." Next he pulled out a switchblade. "Do you know what this is?"

The dark menacing friend of Captain Hunter carried a similar knife. He brandished the sharp weapon like King Author's sword on many occasions. The Serbian interrogator, Nicholas Zoric, became Enigma's go-to intimidator. She'd experienced his threats firsthand during the day they met. His ability to lurk in shadows undetected and eliminate the enemy became legendary among protection agencies in D.C. He answered to no one except Captain Chase Hunter. Some compared the middle-aged Serb to a bloodthirsty vampire who took too much delight in his work. For some reason he'd taken it upon himself to be Tessa's demonic protector.

"Who gave you this?" Tessa ran her fingers along the outside, wondering how many men had felt its penetration between ribcage and heart.

"I didn't get his name." His grin hid a lie. "Maybe Dracula. Said he knew you. I was one of the Rangers who took you back to the embassy. Forgot to give it to you since we were on high alert. When I heard I'd be coming along today, I remembered to bring it."

"I'm sorry, Corporal. I don't remember seeing you." "Part of the backup team following you. You wouldn't

have noticed me. I like it that way. This guy"—he blinked at the switchblade in her hand—"wanted to make sure you had protection. Said you'd understand." He appeared to wait for a clue as to the meaning.

Tessa slipped the ugly weapon under her robes but offered no explanations. Enigma didn't like a great deal of talking about what they did. Now forced to work for them, she wondered if she might be ill equipped to handle this situation. She wondered if God and Enigma used her for comic entertainment to see how badly she could screw things up without getting killed first.

"Thank you, Corporal. Are you thinking I'm going to need these weapons?"

The soldier took his index finger to move the curtain open enough to make another evaluation of the street. "I'm thinking we need to be ready to run to the chopper when it comes." He turned back to her and leaned in closer. "You seem to have more of a level head than Cruella de Vil over there," he whispered then a smirk spread across his face. "I thought if I kept the gun much longer, I'd have to shoot her."

Tessa snickered but covered her mouth when Bonnie jerked her head up toward the two. She cleared her throat to whisper. "I promise to show restraint, Corporal."

He glanced at Bonnie standing like a statue of some investment broker. Tessa thought it must be comical to see someone like her in a place like this.

"Don't do it on my account," he whispered.

Tessa choked on a snicker then diverted her attention to the floor.

"I'm not kidding," he insisted.

As she eased away toward the children, Bonnie grabbed her arm. "What did he say?"

"Wants us to be quick about it when the helicopter gets here. I think that means run."

"Why? What does he think is going to happen?" Bonnie's frown deepened. "This is your fault. We should never have come here in the first place."

"I know. I should never have fallen for the sad story you and the ambassador waved in front of me. Now your photo op is going to turn into a fiasco which could embarrass the State Department." Tessa arched an eyebrow as she growled her response, making Bonnie take a step back. "I'm not sure what you and Jarvis are up to, but I doubt, after observing your behavior here, either of you care one iota about these children." Tessa changed her voice to a sweet, non-confrontational tone because the girls now watched with interest.

"When we get back, I'm going to have to file a report on your behavior. You'll change your obstinate attitude when President Austin hears of this." Bonnie sounded pretty sure of herself.

Tessa chuckled before walking off. "I'm sure when President

Austin hears of this; you'll be the one with a changed attitude." She didn't bother to tell Bonnie the president thought she could do no wrong and felt indebted to her. How many people could say they had the personal phone number of the most powerful man in the world? Tessa thought she heard a curse slip out of the undersecretary's mouth.

"Who are you, Melanie?"

She ignored Bonnie at the sound of an approaching helicopter. Both women joined the corporal at the window. He pushed the curtain back.

"Get ready to move," he ordered.

The girls scrambled to their feet and reached for their bundles but were ordered to leave them by the corporal. Arzo whimpered until he bent down to pat her head.

"Tell her I will replace their bundles when we get to Kabul." He spoke to Shirin so she could translate. They didn't protest further but paired up, taking one another's hands.

As the helicopter came into view, the soldier swung the door open and Tess peered over his shoulder to see an empty street. Not a good sign. Even if local adults didn't find the military activity very interesting, their children always did. So where were they?

"Okay. Melanie, start the children out after me and we'll jog at a steady clip toward the bird. Got it?" She gave him two thumbs-up.

"Right behind you," Tessa responded. Body hunched and weapon lowered, the corporal stepped out into the dusty street.

At a jerk of his chin, Tessa led the girls out, Arzo in her arms and Bonnie holding the hand of one of the other children. The soldier kept turning to check around them as they crossed the street into the grassy hillside scattered with chunks of rock. They trotted faster as the helicopter grew louder. It hovered, preparing to descend.

Then a swooshing whistle split the air followed by an explosion about thirty feet from where the helicopter would land. The Black Hawk darted upward like a dragonfly on a pond. Sounds of rapid gunfire aimed at the Black Hawk were met with a missile from the Americans. "Back! Back!" The corporal stumbled backwards, firing his weapon.

The little girls screamed and ran, arms flailing, back toward their abandoned home. Arzo's grip tightened on Tessa, wailing. Bonnie dragged the girls in her care as they neared the street. Shirin fell, trying to hurry her sister. The soldier scooped them both up then gave them a shove and they were running once more. He returned to firing his weapon. At the next explosion, everyone dropped to the ground then jumped up again to race toward the house.

Tessa turned her head in time to see the helicopter burst into flames, spiraling out of control. It disappeared behind a rocky outcropping. In seconds, another explosion shattered the already-chaotic scene.

The ability to run like a gazelle while carrying a three- year-old choking her to death amazed Tessa even more than being able to see through the flood of terrified tears gushing down her face. Every stumble brought her closer to collapse as she neared the door of the building they'd exited moments earlier. With one last burst of speed, Tessa rammed herself into the door, forcing it open with a rickety snap. Gasping and sobbing, the children hunkered down in a corner.

Tessa waited to close the door as the soldier rushed toward the orphanage while firing his weapon. Just steps away from the building, a bullet found his leg, throwing him backwards. Running outside, Tessa grabbed him by the collar and pulled with all her might. Pushing with his feet to help, the soldier got off more shots, keeping the enemy at bay until Tessa got him inside.

Bonnie slammed the door shut then latched the flimsy lock. She panted, staring in horror at the bloody leg of the soldier. Tessa's chest heaved as she bent over to touch her knees.

When she caught her breath she swallowed hard and straightened. She took stock of the girls. "Everyone okay?" Shirin shook her head like a bobble head doll then pulled her little sister close. With labored steps, Tessa moved toward the window to pull the curtain over the opening.

"Get me up," the soldier demanded. He sat up with a grunt. Tessa and Bonnie reached down to assist him into one of the few chairs in the room. "Melanie, it's going to be dark in a few hours. Tell me what you see out there."

Tessa eased back the curtain. "Smoke where the helicopter went down. Some men standing, looking over the ridge. I think they're watching it burn. Not much talking going on."

The corporal thought for a second then spoke. "Anything else?" She twisted her body to be able to see down the street. "Several men carrying guns. Long beards. Black turbans."

"Well, what does that mean?" Panic laced Bonnie's voice. The soldier shook his head. "Taliban."

CHAPTER 9

The darkness felt thicker as the fire died down. Shifting embers became smoky as the water gurgled over the sound of the occasional snort of a yak. Tessa couldn't sleep after hearing Bonnie's rendition of events leading up to whatever took her memory. She felt fear. The mere mention of the Taliban caused her heart to beat so fast, she thought she could be having a panic attack. When Bonnie trembled with a fit of uncontrolled tears, the conversation stopped until another time. The woman calmed down after Tessa silently slipped an arm around her shoulders.

After Bonnie fell into deep breathing on her pallet, Tessa edged away then stood, pulling her furry blanket around her. The temperature had dropped, but she continued to enjoy the crisp, clean air. She inhaled the sweetness in hopes of purging the memories Bonnie stirred to life inside her. She moved away from the camp to where the horses were tied. They shuffled their hooves then tossed their heads with nervous recognition.

Darya, deep in conversation with the other men, hadn't showed any interest in sleeping next to her this time. The others had eventually meandered off to find a good spot to sleep and Darya had rolled out his bedding near the fire.

"Shh," she whispered, reaching out to pat the neck of Darya's white horse with gray speckles. The pat turned into a rub as she realized it felt therapeutic to do such a simple task. The troubling story Bonnie told unsettled her ability to conjure up a rational thought. As she laid her face against the horse's neck, his smell made her sneeze. A soft laugh escaped her as the horse jerked his head up. "I know. I know." The horse calmed down quickly enough when Tessa pivoted to return to camp.

She slammed into a wiry body. As a hand came across her face and dragged her deeper into the darkness, Tessa realized it wasn't one of the Kyrgyz tribesmen.

His thin body kept Tessa from fighting. In spite of their similar heights, she couldn't connect her wild punches to the scruffy face that rubbed against the back of her neck. As he jerked her around, she caught her hand in his beard and flailed her arms to protect herself. He threw her on the ground and jumped on top of her, knocking the wind from her lungs and preventing her from calling for help. He jammed a rag in her mouth and she gasped for breath. The sound of his snarl against her ear reminded her of someone else who forced her into submission for the sake of training.

She grew still even though her chest rose and fell with heavy breathing. His grip on her wrist left room for her to move her arms on the ground where he pinned them above her head. As he leaned forward, Tessa whimpered a submissive croak to calm down when his beard touched her throat. It smelled sour as she jerked her restrained hands to her side then pulled up her knees, a tactic that felt familiar. The sudden movement toppled the man to the ground on his face. As he flipped over, Tessa aimed her elbow where she thought his Adam's apple would be, but he dodged in time for her to make contact with his shoulder.

With one swift movement, he jumped up. One second later he'd jerked Tessa to her feet and raised his fist back to pound her face, but something caught his fist in midair then twisted it so hard he spun around to face Darya.

The next thing Tessa knew, the attacker stumbled backwards with Darya still gripping the man's fist. In one swift movement, Darya dislocated the man's arm. Before he could scream, the Kyrgyz landed a punch to his head, knocking the intruder out.

As the man collapsed to the ground, Darya turned in slow motion to Tessa with his brooding eyes now uncovered. She managed to remove the rag from her mouth and sniffed back any tears of weakness. The light of the fire glowed in the distance behind him, causing his image to cast a foreboding image.

"Darya," she whispered, taking a step toward him. Although he no longer wore his mask, she couldn't make out any distinct features in the darkness. "Thank you." In a split second, Tessa sensed she remained in danger but wanted to believe Darya, the lesser of two evils. "Who is he? Why would he come here?" She stumbled over her Pashto words but felt confident she'd communicated her meaning.

Darya reached out to touch her hair. Tessa dodged his hand, but he grabbed it anyway. She froze but he didn't seem to want to hurt her when he pulled on her long blonde strands. He seemed to want to feel it between his fingers.

"Man is Taliban, a scout for others who track us. Your hair glows in the dark. He wanted you."

"Yes. But you saved me, Darya."

With one quick jerk, he folded her into his muscled arms. "I save you for me. Not for Taliban."

Tessa made a halfhearted effort to push away. "No. I- I…" She knew at some point the fear she exhibited needed to be controlled. "I belong to no man."

The moon had risen and now made enough light for Tessa to see Darya smile so wide his teeth shone. "Not to worry. I marry you when we reach my home."

With one burst of strength, she managed to pull free. "No. You don't understand. I didn't mean I belong to no man so you'd marry me. I meant you can't have me."

Darya turned his head as several of his men came rushing up. "You talk much for a woman." He gave some orders for his men concerning the attacker then scooped Tessa up in his arms. He marched back to camp and set her down next to three of the little girls. "Sleep now. We take care of Taliban. Leave early. You and children safe with us. No worries. All good."

Then he disappeared into the night.

It didn't take long for Tessa to shiver at the possibilities facing her. What if Darya hadn't shown up? What am I going to do? She snuggled under the covers with the little girls. Soon one of them molded her backside into Tessa. The added warmth made the ground feel less uncomfortable.

The memory of being powerless in Darya's arms added another layer of uneasiness with the knowledge she enjoyed it. She tossed and turned to block out the memory of his earthy smell when his warm embrace foretold a message of desire with his declaration of marriage.

As she succumbed to sleep, another larger-than-life shadow of a man moved back and forth through her dreams. His dark stare spoke of some ethnic diversity. He called her name. Sometimes he laughed low in his throat.

There were flashes of his entire face but then they disappeared as he turned away. A dark alley in some city, rain pouring down over her as he forced his mouth on hers then a gunshot shattered the scene.

Another one sprang up to replace it. A man in her bedroom wearing a smirk as she held a gun pointed at his chest. Another gunshot. The intruder wore a mask like Darya but also a uniform. He did not frighten her like Darya.

I will find you if you are in trouble, always concluded the dreams. He remained a mystery. Bonnie mentioned someone from the military base in Kabul being the reason she stayed behind the day the Marine's car exploded.

When the light of day spilled across her face, Tessa had a headache. She touched the bump on her head from a couple of days ago. How did she get it? Why couldn't she remember? Could it be she suffered from a psychological trauma?

Something inside her clicked. Scales of blindness fell from her memory. The day the Taliban kicked in the door, her safe, sheltered world had shattered into a million pieces. Everything she ever believed about herself turned to a fiery inferno of anger. "Vengeance is mind, saith the Lord," now meant kill or be killed. There were no other options.

The scenario played in her head like a horror movie.

~~~

The corporal reloaded his weapon. Sweat poured down his face. Tessa removed a first aid kit from her backpack then rushed to the soldier's side. She kneeled beside him.

"Ma'am, I don't have time for your fussin'."

"Corporal, you're no good to us like this. It will take a minute."

He agreed, but continued to make himself ready. "It's gonna get
~~~

ugly, ma'am." Tessa ripped his pant leg where the wound continued to bleed. "These guys don't respect human life, so don't think you can sweet-talk them." He cringed as she poured something into the wound then applied a bandage. "Don't make eye contact."

She listened to him and realized for the first time he should be home playing football or taking his best girl to the movies.

"Keep yourself covered. Be submissive." She trembled until he laid his free hand on her shoulder. "I'll do what I can. When they breach this place…"

"When?" Tessa whispered in horror.

"Yes. When. I'll be the first target. You need her"— he jerked his head toward Bonnie who stared at them with both her fists up against her mouth—"and the children to be quiet, respectful."

Tessa put her hands on each of his thighs. There would be no happy ending here. "Thank you, Corporal." She paused. "For everything."

"Now help me over to the window. Maybe I can hold them off for a while. With any luck, the chopper got off a distress call before they crashed."

It took both women to pull him up on stiff legs. He did one hop then walked forward, dragging the wounded leg. No complaints. No sign of pain, but an abundance of determination.

The soldier lifted the curtain with his finger. Tessa came up behind him.

"They're close," he whispered. "Can you block the door with the furniture?"

Tessa and Bonnie piled the rickety furniture in front of the door. It wouldn't take much for men bent on entering to force the barricade aside. But it would be something to prolong the inevitable.

Voices grew closer. They heard gunfire but none seemed directed toward their hiding place.

"What's happening?" Bonnie's voice grew frantic as she retreated to the corner where the children were, collapsing on the floor next to them.

"Shooting up in the air. Intimidation. Crazy hajis." The soldier's voice showed no increased level of concern, but Tessa imagined it had peaked about an hour earlier.

"What's a haji?" Bonnie moaned as if she were about to hear more bad news.

"Soldiers call the Afghans hajis. Haj means they've gone to Mecca so they call all of them hajis," she explained in a whisper before turning back to the corporal. "How many?"

Tessa remained at his side in case he needed assistance. In this situation, she could offer nothing more than moral support. Her feet remained planted behind him.

"Maybe ten. That's all I can see. Doesn't mean there aren't more nearby. They're in no hurry. Probably hoping someone will come to rescue us and they'll get another shot at taking one of the big birds down." He turned his head to evaluate her. "I'm not sure how long we can hold out if they decide to come in."

Tessa shivered. Her throat constricted so she couldn't swallow without making a large gulp. "What will happen to us?"

"If they don't kill me first, they'll use me as a bargaining chip for something they want. I think I'd rather die than survive under their imprisonment. You guys…" He pointed toward the children with his weapon, holding his breath. As he released it, the corporal turned back to the window. "Use the gun if you have to. You've got nothing to lose. You're a worthless female infidel who came here to corrupt the Afghan women. Keep quiet. Save your weapons until absolutely necessary. They won't search you if you pretend to be terrified."

"No problem there." "Get ready."

Slipping over to the basket she'd seen earlier, Tessa pulled the rags out and found one the size of a small tablecloth. She tossed it to Bonnie. "Wrap this around your head and face." She found a dirty long-sleeved shirt which looked like it had been a uniform shirt in another life. "Put this on over your blouse." Next she dug in her backpack and found a pair of socks. "Cover your feet."

"My feet?" Bonnie wrinkled her nose and appeared to inspect the shirt for bugs before slipping it over her head.

"No skin showing. See the girls?" Tessa pointed at the little ones so Bonnie would notice except for the upper part of their faces, they resembled cocoons. The earlier decision to wear extra layers to hide her body in order to show respect proved to be a good decision.

"You. Inside. Come out with rifle over your head." A man's

voice spoke in broken English.

Silence hung like soaked blankets. "No one is coming for you."

Tessa peered past the soldier. The man talking held his rifle on his shoulder, like a squirrel hunter from the hills of Tennessee. Her uncle had carried his gun the same way. Determining the man's age at this distance proved futile. His black turban appeared to be smashed on his head like a rotting squash. A black patch covered his left eye, reminding Tessa of a pirate.

"I am Massoud. You know me?"

The corporal glanced at Tessa. "The guy is in charge of some heavy drug trade. Didn't know he lived in these parts." His voice lowered to a whisper. "Compared to him, the other Taliban might be Boy Scouts."

"Great. Now what?" Tessa breathed.

Massoud laughed loudly as he twisted his body around, motioning at his men. "You come to take our children. I think I will stop you." He paused, and when they did not respond, continued, "The government woman." He extended his hand outward, palm up toward the little house. "Maybe I will take her."

A cry squeaked out of Bonnie as she cowered farther into the corner.

With a quick pull of the trigger, the corporal shot several of the Taliban. Massoud managed to jump behind a rusted-out truck maybe used for target practice by a drone. Tessa let a scream slip out then retreated to the corner where the others covered their heads. Their crying created more chaos as Tessa squatted down next to them and placed her hands over her ears.

When return fire began, the American soldier sprayed bullets as well. Shells clinked against each other as they flew up into the air, leaving the smell of gun powder. He reloaded faster than Tessa thought possible in such circumstances. She heard groans when other Taliban caught a bullet. She wondered at their training. Did they believe they were invincible?

Sudden silence unsettled her. Then the soldier slammed backward to the floor. Tessa screamed as she fell forward into the girls, their little hands pulling her closer. She struggled to roll over. Seeing the soldier lying on his back, blood pooling on his chest, Tessa pushed up with clumsy determination. She stumbled to his side and squatted next to him.

Peering at his shattered shoulder, he pointed toward the door. "They're coming in."

CHAPTER 10

The sound of splintering wood and unfamiliar voices in a tongue she couldn't understand had Tessa taking the soldier's hand in hers. He shook his head then pulled free. "No. Get over there with the others. I don't want you hurt because of me."

Tessa's hands shook, silent tears creating trails down her face as she stood.

"Go. Now," he croaked.

The door split around the hinges. Grunts and yelling continued as the furniture slid across the floor. The door fell in against the pile of worthless pieces forming a barrier. The reprieve lasted a couple of minutes before a man's face appeared in the window.

The women and children screamed once more as he climbed in through the opening. Peering at the soldier incapacitated on the floor, their attacker shouted something to his fellow Taliban and pushed through the window. As his feet hit the dirt floor, the soldier grabbed up his gun, firing into his chest and jerking him around. Once he fell, the soldier fired toward the door.

Tessa had no way of knowing if the soldier's action was buying them more time. She could only hope for such a miracle. Another Taliban pointed a rifle through the window and fired at the soldier on the floor.

The soldier became still. This time, the Taliban pushed through the flimsy barricade without interruption. Without acknowledging the females in the room, they slammed the broken furniture into walls and threw it across the room, clearing the space in front of the door. The bearded men propped the door, now hanging by one hinge, open and stood back.

Massoud entered and took a casual glance at the soldier on the ground then spat a stream of words at his followers. Tessa watched in horror as two of the brutes grabbed the limp soldier by his arms and dragged him outside. A hero deserved better, even in death. Paralyzed with fear, Tessa couldn't force out a protest. Just as well. It would be a shame if the corporal died in vain because she got them all killed with her insolence.

Massoud dressed better than the others or maybe his white shirt created a sharper contrast. His brown hair poked out from under his turban in a couple of spots. Taking into consideration this land could take a twenty- year-old and make him look forty, Tessa gauged him to be in his late thirties. Afghanistan sucked youth out of people almost from the time they were born. His beard showed no signs of gray like the others, though. The black patch succeeded in creating an impression of evil. The other eye reminded Tessa of a rat's on an unremarkable face pocked with scars. He stood an inch or so taller than Tessa, yet he cast a much larger persona.

"Hello." Massoud's voice carried a slight British accent. "Which of you is the government woman?"

Tessa dropped her gaze to her hands.

When his silence drew her intimidated glance, he squatted in front of her. She could smell his body odor. "Is it you?" She lowered her gaze again, but his hand snaked out to grab her chin. As he jerked her head up Tessa felt compelled to stare back into the speckled green of his eye. "So is it you?"

Shirin's little sister, Pamir, pointed to Bonnie then cocooned herself again.

Massoud turned his head toward Bonnie but kept his hand on Tessa's chin. "And why would you not speak up for blue eyes?" He turned his gaze back on Tessa. "Who are you? Do not try and trick me with words. You can tell I speak very good English. Now. Who are you?"

She pulled back as Massoud withdrew his hand, but remained squatted in front of her. His thin lips puckered.

"These little girls were coming back to Kabul. The orphanage here could no longer support them. The village is poor and they were a burden. There are people in Kabul who can take care of their needs."

"Do you mean the American military?"

Tessa made sure her head scarf covered her mouth as she spoke. "They came to help us take them back. I'm here so the girls would have a chaperone. It would not be fitting for them to travel alone with the soldiers." Massoud raised his chin to stare down his nose at her. "There are aid groups helping Afghan women and children during this war between us."

"These girls would be educated?"

Tessa imagined the mental slippery slope looming ahead of her. "They would learn to take care of themselves for the future."

He turned his head to the side as he reached out to jerk Tessa's scarf from around her face. Startled, she flinched back, trying to readjust the scarf, but Massoud caught her hand. He turned it over in his before laying his other hand over her palm. Tessa grimaced when he moved to push the scarf to the back of her neck.

"Look at me, woman." His voice sounded serious, controlled, and confident. His grip tightened. "Now."

She couldn't resist opening her eyes wider when Massoud moved his face inches from hers.

"You should not have come. Are you afraid?"

"Yes." She hoped the simple answer would have a positive effect on this man's macho ego. "We are all scared."

Massoud turned to his men standing near the door then tilted his head back at Tessa. Her Pashto was poor, but when he spoke slowly she comprehended a few words that sounded like, "Safe. I take this one." With quick, jerky movements Massoud pulled her scarf back onto her head then across her mouth. His quick inhale as he stood made Tessa dare to glance up at him.

"The soldier. What will you do with him?" Tessa knew better than to speak but couldn't resist.

He shrugged. "He will die soon. He killed several of my men protecting you. Now I must take revenge first on him then on them." He extended his hand toward the rest of the girls. "Education is not good for women. You are an excellent example of that. It clouded your judgment when you come here. No place for an American woman. Afghan women know their place." He turned to go.

"Serve the men. Yes, I know," Tessa mumbled then sucked in her breath in horror.

Massoud turned back to her. "It is good you know this. It does not give me pleasure to discipline." His voice showed no emotion, but Tessa imagined below the calm exterior beat the heart of a monster. She remembered hearing those words before, someplace.

When he turned toward her with his good eye showing, Tessa knew he'd been in the embassy the day they arrived. There had been loud voices coming from the ambassador's office. With the door cracked open, she'd caught a glimpse of a man with slicked-backed hair the color of mud. He wore a suit with a long robe hanging around his shoulder much like the president of Afghanistan. Compared to the ambassador, Massoud appeared short, but intimidating nonetheless.

"It does not give me pleasure to discipline," were the same words Tessa had heard at the embassy.

Massoud shifted his attention to the other woman. "You come here." Bonnie's eyes were the size of saucers. "Now," he demanded.

Tessa stood and pulled her to her feet. She helped her over the children before squeezing her hand as a warning.

He told his men to leave the building. They complied in quick order before Massoud turned back to Bonnie with a scowl. "You work for the ambassador." She denied it with a shake of her head. "Liar." His whisper reminded Tessa of a warning from a rattlesnake. "I saw you with him."

Tessa sucked in her breath at the revelation. "American women sleep their way to the top. Is that right Undersecretary Finley?"

Tears poured down the woman's face as her body shook against an attempt to hold tight the sobs in her heaving chest.

"Bonnie, what is he talking about?" Tessa spoke from the corner of her mouth. "What's going on?"

"Tell her, Bon-nie." The name sounded slow, like pouring water into a sink. He took two steps toward the undersecretary and yanked the dirty scarf off her head. "It seems the ambassador has a small drug problem. The man does enjoy his heroin."

"I didn't know," Bonnie insisted. "Of course not," he mocked.

Tessa noticed the children stand and stretch their frail bodies.

She lifted Arzo into her arms. Several others buried themselves against her. Even Shirin stood close.

Massoud observed the teen with his one good eye then spoke to her in Pashto. The words Tessa understood when Shirin mumbled were "help, good, song." He grunted at her words then rubbed his chin as he frowned at Tessa. "You teach these children songs?"

"Yes," she responded a little quicker than she intended. "They were frightened. I want them to feel safe. I care for them very much." Tessa shifted Arzo to her other hip. "They are hungry. Do you have food?"

Massoud yelled something to the men outside before turning back to Bonnie. "You want to take these children to Kabul then to America."

Bonnie shook her head no as she backed against the wall.

"Yes." Tessa made her voice flat. Why lie when he already knew the truth. "They were to get an education then return in a year. I think, because your country won't allow adoptions, their host families will send thousands, maybe millions of dollars to this country in order to keep them safe, continue their schooling, and prepare them to make a difference."

Massoud glared at her as his forehead pinched in confusion. "Then why let them go in the first place? They are Afghans. Exposure to the West will turn them into whores."

Tessa kissed little Arzo then touched the top of Pamir's head. "I believe the Afghan government thinks the money will roll in and they will line their pockets. They are corrupt."

This made Massoud choke then laugh like a growling pit bull. "An honest woman. Why would you tell me this?"

Taking a deep breath, Tessa met his one eye with hers. "Because you already knew the truth." She wanted to take the focus off Bonnie, realizing the woman pushed back into the mud bricks as if hoping to become invisible.

"Yes. The government is corrupt, as you say. Not any different than the Taliban when it comes to being ruthless. Your country pretends when they leave, all will be as it should be."

Tessa set Arzo down. "I know. They try to change things, make life better but…"

Massoud's expression revealed contempt. "But we are a backward people. Sheep following whoever has bigger guns."

Tessa agreed. "Sheep living in constant fear and poverty. You want to be left alone."

"That is not the fault of the Taliban."

"According to the Koran, it is the place of every Muslim to protect the innocent, the weak, and those who can't fend for themselves."

Massoud arched an eyebrow at the remark. She wondered if he understood he'd just been chastised. She didn't avert her eyes this time. If his plans involved torture or killing her, then these girls would know one woman had stood strong against the Taliban.

"Are you a Christian?"

"I am." She raised her chin to show pride. "Both our religions share the same great leader Abraham and the one true God. My faith demands I help others, as does yours."

"What do you know of Islam?"

"I know one of the Five Pillars of Islam is you give alms to the poor. Charity is good works." Tessa bowed her head to appear humble although her hands trembled.

"I don't care what the government does with the money. I care about these children."

Massoud turned his attention back to Bonnie. "And you? What do you care about, government woman? Are you getting"—he paused—"kickback from the ambassador?"

"No. Never."

Massoud leaned in to Tessa and stage-whispered. "Every week after the ambassador has his meeting with the base commanders of the area, he lets me know the safest route to take my opium. In return, I pay him a fee and provide a few samples. I think he has become quite wealthy. It works for both of us. She lies when she says she is not involved." He shrugged. "The ambassador did not want a partner, I think." His amused expression fell on Bonnie.

"Then why have you come here? Do you plan to hurt us? These children are innocent. I beg you to take them someplace safe."

"The government lady discovered the ambassador's little secret. She wanted in or threatened to turn him over to the military." He flaunted a crooked smirk toward Bonnie. "It was always about the money. The ambassador made deals with the Afghan government, too."

"Bonnie, is this true?" Tessa grew irritated. "You made deals with the Taliban to get drug money?"

"It wasn't like that," Bonnie insisted.

"Then tell me the truth," Tessa snapped.

"The woman is a liar," Massoud whispered as he pushed away Tessa's head covering again. He touched the blonde curls falling around her shoulders. "I said I would not deal with a woman." His voice grew serious as Tessa shied away from his touch. "You understand. She is an infidel. The ambassador got skittish. I said I would handle it. Then someone else walked in on us. He promised to handle you." His mouth widened as he coiled a curl around his finger and inspected the lock.

Bonnie sucked in her breath. Tessa could see the gravity of knowing the ambassador set this whole thing up, sink in on her as she chewed her bottom lip. He'd also gotten a Marine killed.

"I must tell you." He continued to smirk at Bonnie while holding Tessa's hair in his hand. "He did not hesitate to give you up."

Tessa cringed as Bonnie lost any remnants of common sense and unloaded a barrage of insults concerning Ambassador Jarvis. She raised her hands toward the ceiling as the curses kept coming. Her professional, lady- like demeanor vanished.

Massoud pulled Tessa's scarf over her head as his men returned with small portions of food. He pointed toward the children. The food was dispersed, the children finding spots on the floor to nibble their meager scraps. When Arzo offered Tessa part of hers, she refused. Shirin pulled off half of hers for Bonnie who snatched it. Massoud grabbed it away from her and returned it to Shirin.

"You are a vile woman," he snarled at Bonnie before turning back to Shirin. "How old are you?" She dropped her head, trembling. "Speak!"

"Fourteen."

"My brother is almost thirty. You will be his wife."

"No!" Tessa blurted before she could cover her mouth. "I mean, please, no. She is only a child."

"Many girls this age already have children."

"She has a gift. Please." Tessa found the drawings on the shelf and brought them to him. "See? If she goes to Kabul, maybe even the United States, she will bring honor to the Afghan people with the beauty she creates."

"Education makes women think too much." He glanced from the pictures to the children. "They start to get ideas and think for themselves."

Tessa bit her tongue so hard she thought it would bleed. "You are educated. I can tell by your speech."

"I am a man." Massoud waved his men out. "It is getting dark. I will decide your fate before I return." He pointed at Bonnie and grinned. "Yours has been decided." A terrified sob escaped her mouth. He dropped Shirin's drawings in the dirt and stomped on them. "Such a waste of time."

"Do you take pleasure in being a monster?" Tessa asked in a serious voice.

He had been on his way out the door but paused to rub his chin. Standing in the dim light of a candle one of his men left behind, Massoud chuckled. "You will soon know how I take my pleasure."

"He's going to kill you," Tessa warned. "Who?" Massoud challenged.

"Captain Chase Hunter. He's coming for me."

"I will be ready."

"It won't be enough." Tessa turned away and sat down next to the girls. "You'll never see him coming."

Massoud shifted his feet then rushed to leave. Tessa heard him giving orders again. She took a small amount of pleasure knowing she'd managed to unnerve the scariest man in Afghanistan. She prayed the threat would come true.

CHAPTER 11

The children grew tired as the night deepened. Cool breezes flowed down from the mountains and in through the windows and open door. Even though they didn't complain, Tessa knew they were cold. She had them bunch up together before taking some of the broken furniture to the small wood stove sitting in the middle of the room with a stove pipe straight up through the ceiling. Part of her wished the building would catch on fire so they could avoid what might lay ahead for them. Since the rebels had not searched her bag, Tessa still had a pack of matches she'd gotten at the hotel in Kyrgyzstan to ignite the fire. Some kerosene oil in a lamp made a good accelerant. A man came to the door to check on them but didn't object to Tessa's attempt to warm the room. The fire burned hot for a while until the wood crumbled to burning embers.

Tessa sat down by Shirin with a few sheets of paper the size of large index cards. The young girl sat with bowed head as if knowing her fate would soon destroy any dreams she carried in her heart of being an artist. Tessa handed the sheets to the soon-to-be teen wife along with a dull pencil she'd found on the shelf. Even in the dim light of the candle burning on the floor, she could see the fear in her, creasing the lines on her forehead.

"I know this is hard, Shirin." The girl lifted her eyes with such deep sadness Tessa pulled her into her arms and rocked back and forth. "Don't cry. We've got to stay strong, no matter what." The girl laid her head on Tessa's shoulder. She patted the girl's cheek. "I need you to do something for me."

"I will try."

Tessa handed her the paper and pencil. "I need you to draw a picture of me and Ms. Finley." Shirin appeared bewildered but agreed. "Then I need you to draw a picture of Massoud, the man in charge. Can you do that?"

"I will be in trouble if he finds out. It is against Islam, Ms. Melanie. That is why he destroyed my other pictures. I was bad." The fear in her voice was understandable.

"I know, Shirin. But Allah has given you a gift to save your little sisters here. Bonnie and I are not Muslim, so maybe Allah will understand that I forced you to do this. We will hide the pictures on the shelf. When someone comes for the helicopter, the soldiers will find it. They will know we are alive and who has taken us. Then we can be rescued."

Shirin took the supplies and went to work with enthusiasm. "It won't take long, Ms. Melanie. I'll do it for you."

Tessa hugged her. "Do it for all of us, Shirin. You are my hero."

The girl did not appear to hear the last comment as she hurried to complete the task set before her.

Cries of anguish reached the women several times. Tessa dared slip to the window to see one of the houses on fire. A family stood in the street crying while a crippled man begged to reason with the men with guns. A gunshot toppled the man to the ground and drove Tessa back to safety.

The men stationed outside their house spoke in loud voices. Even so, Tessa felt too terrified to try and understand the ruckus going on among them. Intuition told her she and Bonnie were in for a long night. Several times, men peered in through the window or came to the door carrying a rifle.

After Shirin finished the drawings, Tessa folded them before sticking them into a broken teacup. When she turned to join the others, two men slipped inside. At first they were silent then they pointed at Bonnie and Shirin.

Tessa froze. She knew what their plans were by just looking at their nervous movements around the room. A hysterical Bonnie pushed herself up off the floor as if by doing so she'd be safe. One of the men no more than twenty years old, grabbed her by the arm then jerked her forward so hard she fell facedown.

The second man appeared older than Massoud. He motioned for Shirin to stand. She did so with head bowed, but her sobs could be heard over the sniffles of the other little girls who reached up to her. Like a lamb to slaughter, Shirin stepped towards the man who pulled at her head scarf as he dragged her toward the door.

The man with Bonnie fell on her back with a hyena laugh, closing his hands around her neck.

"No!" Tessa screamed as her hand went under her robe to extract the switchblade hidden in her jeans' pocket. The robe parted when her arm came forward. She pushed the button that clicked the blade open. "Stop!" she screamed.

But they didn't.

Shirin flailed, but her actions managed to encourage the aggressive behavior of the older man.

With a blinding rage, Tessa propelled herself at the back of the man wrestling with Shirin. For one split second, he paused. In that split second, Tessa rammed the knife into the base of his skull, severing his spinal cord.

As he dropped to the floor, Tessa whirled around to see the man on Bonnie's back spring to his feet in one swift movement. Before he had a chance to retaliate, Tessa slammed herself into him, her heavier weight throwing him off-balance as he staggered back against the stove. He flung his hand behind him and shrieked as he contacted the red-hot stove. With an unrestrained cry of rage, he propelled back toward her. Tessa jumped to the side and stuck out her foot which caused him to sprawl onto the floor.

Fury loomed on his face as he crawled to a hunched stance. His ragged breathing lasted a split second before he lunged at Tessa with his full weight, slamming her against the broken table. Somehow she reached the gun hidden in her back pants' pocket. But the movement caused him to get the upper hand as he slapped her with such force her head snapped back against a shelf. He stepped back to take another swing at her.

Tessa felt the weapon in her grasp as she struggled to bring it forward. As his fist swung downward she lifted the gun and pulled the trigger three times. The gun dropped out of her hand as the blast startled her into realizing what she'd done. The sound of crying and Bonnie moaning, "Oh my god," over and over paralyzed Tessa with fear.

The man appeared to curse her as he felt his stomach and groin where she'd shot him. His screams brought the other men pouring into the house.

Tessa sucked in her breath at seeing the dead man on the floor with a knife sticking out of his neck. Then, without her turning her head, she shifted her attention back to the younger man pointing down at his groin, screaming. Instead of regretting her actions, the desire to finish him off surfaced in her muddled brain. A great deal of pointing, shouting, and confusion ensued until Massoud strode in with a rifle strapped across his chest.

Everyone grew quiet while Massoud surveyed the mayhem Tessa created. There were a few quick inquiries of the wounded man. Between the attacker's sniveling replies, Massoud developed a dark glare resembling a belching volcano. He reached in his pocket then withdrew a thin piece of rope.

"Did you do this?" Massoud yelled so loud in her face his breath moved her hair. When she trembled, tears squeezed from the corners of her eyes. He lowered his voice. "Did you do this?"

Tessa whimpered a yes. She could feel her nose run as salty tears ran across her lips.

Massoud grabbed her hands and tied them before pushing her to the floor.

Bonnie crawled back to a corner, sucking air with sobs of terror. Shirin ran to her little sister for comfort.

The younger man pointed at the handgun lying on the floor then bent over in agony.

After a couple of questions, Massoud nodded then pointed to the gun for another man to fetch it for him.

"It gives me no pleasure to discipline. Have I not told you this?" He pointed the gun at Tessa as she cowered back against the wall then he turned the gun toward the wounded rebel and pulled the trigger.

His last cries of pain drowned out the screams of the women and children.

Massoud handed the gun to one of his men and motioned for the bodies to be removed. "See what you forced me to do? He would have died anyway. I saved him from further misery."

Gunfire echoed outside, filling the night with rapid flashes of light. Excited voices yelled orders as some battle took place under the stars. The men ran outside. One of the Taliban was visible just outside the window as he fell back then slid down, out of sight. Sounds of retreat echoed off the mountains until silence covered the tracks of the Taliban.

The sounds of galloping horses, more voices of men, and the promise of violence returned. By now the women and children were so traumatized their bodies formed balls of self-preservation against the new evil promising to rain down upon them.

Tessa could hear sounds of men going door to door as if they were on the hunt for the Taliban who scattered from their presence Were they searching for Taliban? They weren't American soldiers or she would have heard English. She didn't understand what they were saying and Shirin silently hugged her knees and rocked back and forth. They were getting closer. Finally two men stopped outside their house and entered with caution. Holding their weapons gingerly, they walked back and forth before the children. One of them called out to others in the street. Tessa noticed the children stopped their crying. The men dressed in dark clothing appeared to be more Asian than Afghan by the fold of their eyes and high cheekbones. Were these the men the girls said protected the orphanage from the Taliban?

In seconds, a well-armed Kyrgyz tribesman wearing a tattered mask walked into the room. There were traces of blood on the dagger in his hand and a rip in his sleeve. He surveyed them from a distance then approached and came to a sudden halt. He stood with his legs apart and his arms crossed his chest. Earflaps moved on his rounded fur hat as he twisted around to examine the surroundings. The mask wrapped his face like an Arabian knight of old. Large holes were cut out for him to see. He stepped toward Tessa. He caught hold of her bindings and gave a hard tug, dragging her to unsteady feet. He examined her hands speckled with blood. He pointed. "Hurt?"

"No," she whispered, darkness swirling up around her. The feel of strong hands catching her was the last thing she remembered.

~~~
~~~

Kunar Province – Northeast of Kabul

Squinting against the midday sun, his loose clothing moving in the wind, reminded him how hot this godforsaken land could be. He peered over the ridge into the valley below. A river snaked through the area known as Death Becomes You, or at least Delta Force called it that, among other things. Captain Hunter knew from experience the river stayed shallow for at least another month then it would dry up until the spring snow melt gushed down from the mountains. Rebels hid here due to the shallow caves dotting the hillsides. Word leaked out Massoud was spotted in the area and he hoped he might return this way. The land, inhospitable to most humans, created a perfect channel of hiding places for one of Afghanistan's most notorious Taliban leaders.

The captain knew his own appearance played a part in his ability to blend in with the rebels. There had been a few close calls where American soldiers mistook him for a member of one of the rebel factions. If it weren't for his obvious Native American looks, he would have been shot by a US sniper long ago. He resembled some of the Uzbeks or Kyrgyz tribesmen. Some of them were friends to the Americans. It would not be wise to kill one of them. From his concealed position, he could soak up the raw beauty of Afghanistan. Something about the emptiness bathed him in a peace. Although when the wind roared, it deafened a man to other distractions, and he found himself lost in the rugged landscape. The air smelled clean. No garbage or human waste here, just the occasional whiff of dust or wild goat. Even the emptiness filled the captain with a sense of belonging.

He sat so still, if someone had come upon him he would have blended with the rock formations around him. The thought of being invisible pleased him. The practice had begun as a child in China with his missionary parents. Avoiding bullies in the villages or the Red Guard became a survival skill. Even when his parents would pack him off to be with his diplomat grandfather for several months every year, he learned to stay out of the way. Hiding became a game to frighten aids or other staff left to care for him. As he grew older and bigger, he had to learn new tricks to become invisible. He'd learned much this way; a gift of languages, secrets of powerful men, how to charm a woman and, most important, how to make sure she never forgot you.

But his favorite part had always been being alone to think or to read. There were many times, growing up in the villages of China, that his best friend was a book. His grandfather never tired of forcing the boy to learn, to think about the world around him. Whether it was in Honduras or Zimbabwe, everything became an educational experience. The boy would be made to think and evaluate at the end of each day for his grandfather.

The time to think and evaluate again lay before him.

His eyes were the only thing which moved. They fell on the man propped against a rock next to him, asleep. With his paler skin, dark hair, and beard, Zoric could pass for a Taliban instead of a Serbian. He wore a tattered turban and some loose clothing covered by a brown suede vest. His wiry body remained lean well into his forties. His covered arms hid the colorful tattoos trailing down his forearms. The captain and Zoric had often talked about the designs.

"It's no wonder people are terrified of you, Zoric. That ink looks like the apocalypse is playing out on your arms."

Zoric would shrug, followed by a rude comment about the Chinese characters on Chase's upper arms. "I am not as big as you, my friend. I need to make an immediate impression."

"Trust me when I say the tat of an opened artery will do it."

Chase and the Serb shared a shadowy past Enigma dared not approach. In some circles, Zoric was known as the Vampire because of his hollow gaze, narrow face, and bloodshot eyes. Most people at Enigma could not imagine him being an accomplished artist before the war between the Serbs and the Bosnians. When a bomb killed his family, a monster evolved inside him. He often said drinking the blood of his enemy would give him great pleasure.

He continued to be at his best friend's side to do the work of Enigma.

"How did you feel when you saw her again?" Zoric mumbled.

"Uncomfortable."

"Did you tell her how you felt?"

For the first time in over an hour, Chase turned his head toward the Serb. "I don't feel anything. She's an Enigma agent. Married. Poison."

Zoric waited before venturing into more conversation. "Are you ever going to tell her?"

"Shut the hell up." The words sounded like a rehearsed chant, one he'd said many times. Calm, controlled, and indifferent formed Captain Chase Hunter's persona. "Give it a rest, will ya?"

"I'm in love with her," Zoric declared without emotion.

"Good for you. Better make your will out because she's a death sentence waiting to happen. I would have thought you knew that by now," Chase's voice whispered, hoping his voice would not carry on the wind. He dropped his fist low enough to punch it into the ribs of the Serb.

A grin toyed with Zoric's thin lips. "Whether you know it or not, my friend, Tessa Scott has managed to be the one who has ever come close to making you show emotion. When she walks into a room you morph into a human." He smothered a chuckle with the back of his hand. "I know this irritates you for me to say it. Is it her innocent view of the world that sets you off-balance or that she is easy on the eyes?"

Chase pretended he didn't want her to do field work because she was a civilian. Several members of the team, even Samantha, mentioned how much harder he made it on her to be successful. Keeping her from field work guaranteed she remained safe and be waiting for him each time he returned home.

"She's…" Zoric continued.

"Married." Chase's voice grew cold.

For a few seconds Zoric pretended to be deep in thought. "I can fix this problem. It would be child's play to make the husband have an accident. Then you could swoop in to be the hero." He adjusted his position to be more comfortable. "I think she likes it when you save her."

"If I had known you were going to be a gossipy old woman, I would never have brought you along." Chase lifted a pair of binoculars to hint the conversation had ended. "Interesting. Looks like a Kyrgyz tribesman."

Zoric rolled over onto his knees before lifting his own binoculars. "Kind of far from home."

They both continued to watch the Kyrgyz man walk his horse along the bank of the river.

"Not in any hurry," Zoric observed. "What's he carrying tied to the horse?"

Both men continued to peer through their binoculars for another ten minutes when the horseman stopped to pull up a canteen. He unscrewed the top before twisting around to offer water to someone.

"Whoever it is, they're in bad shape. See the blood on the guy's leg?" Chase commented with interest. "Someone beat the crap out of him, too." He adjusted the binoculars. "Zoric?"

"I see it, my friend. An American soldier is on the back of the horse."

CHAPTER 12

It took several hours to maneuver themselves to a position where Chase and Zoric could cut off the progress of the tribesman moving through the valley below. They discovered another hiding place to wait. As luck would have it, the Kyrgyz headed toward them so they could intercept him. At first, they'd worried the Kyrgyz slipped away until they heard the crunch of rolling pebbles.

They watched from a distance to evaluate the target. "He's Kyrgyz, all right," Chase mumbled as he lowered the binoculars. He pointed with an upraised chin. Zoric took the field glasses again. "See the head covering? It's more of a scarf than a turban wrapped tight around the skull. The Mongol-shaped eyes, dressed head to toe in black…he has tribesman written all over him." He glanced over at Zoric to make sure he listened. The Kyrgyz now rode the horse instead of walking alongside.

"He put the reins of the horse in his mouth to reach back and adjust the soldier."

"Kyrgyz, all right. Those guys can run their horse full speed like that while throwing around a headless goat. Called Buzkashi or kid grabbing. It's a national sport in Afghanistan. Sometimes they even carry a whip in their mouth. Tough SOBs." Chase took back the binoculars.

"What's on the soldier's head? Not government issue." The soldier sat lopsided behind the Kyrgyz. He appeared to be tied to the tribesman for safety.

"Some of the men wear those pillbox-shaped hats. I'm not sure how they're decorated with bright colors, but I'm guessing it's embroidery. Not much color in your life when you live on the rooftop of the world."

"Trying to make the soldier appear Kyrgyz, maybe." Zoric checked his weapon.

"Let's go." Chase felt his body demand to stretch his tall form after being scrunched in such a small space but decided to also check his weapon.

The two slipped off their perch to hide behind a boulder until the Kyrgyz rounded the bend of the trail. Zoric circled back behind the rider to ward off a sudden retreat. If the tribesman pulled a gun on Chase, he wanted to neutralize the threat.

When Chase stepped onto the path, leveling his AR- 47 at the tribesman, the horse spooked then shied causing the man to tighten the reins. When the horse settled down, the tribesman stared down at Chase with no emotion. He evaluated Chase through eyes that resembled slits. His head turned when Zoric came up from behind. All three remained quiet at first until the soldier moaned.

"American soldier." Chase spoke in Pashto now. The Kyrgyz pursed his lips in silence. "What are you doing with him?"

The Kyrgyz stared up in the rocks. He dug his heels into the animal's side, causing the horse to buck at Zoric who managed to jump back so fast he fell to the ground.

This time the Kyrgyz took on an amused expression then turned his attention back to Chase.

"Zoric, you all right?"

Zoric grunted a few colorful descriptions of the rider and joined Chase but raised his rifle at the tribesman. "Captain Chase Hunter. American."

"Look like Taliban," uttered the Kyrgyz as he jerked his chin toward Zoric.

"The American soldier is hurt. Where are you taking him?" The captain ignored the reference to Zoric.

"Try and find help."

Chase and Zoric lowered their weapons. Zoric took the bridle of the horse in his hand as Chase walked around to the soldier.

"What happened?"

The Kyrgyz turned toward the soldier as Chase untied the belt holding him against his back. "Taliban go to village where he hides. They shoot down helicopter."

Zoric and Chase exchanged concerned looks. "Helicopter? When?"

"Two days ago. We run them off so not hurt women and children."

Chase pulled the soldier down into his arms. "Are the men on board the helicopter dead?"

The Kyrgyz shrugged then admitted they were all dead. "No one came to help so we shoot the Taliban. Found this one."

"Thank you. He's been shot, Zoric. Go up on the ridge and call for help. This boy is in bad shape. I'm not sure how long he's got without immediate attention." Even before Chase finished the sentence, Zoric headed to climb the rocky outcropping to use his radio. "How far is the village?" Chase continued.

"My horse takes one day with extra weight of man with me. Faster to go back."

"Are the Kyrgyz still there?"

Chase understood the tribesman protected his friends by not offering an answer.

"I would like to thank them. What can I do to help you and your people?"

The man shifted in his saddle. "The khan wants a road. Can you build us a road to the mountains?"

"No. Your country must build a road."

"Then you cannot help us." He jerked the reins of the horse to turn and galloped off back in the direction from which he came.

It was absurd to try and call him back so he didn't try. He sat down on the ground to cradle the soldier in his arms to evaluate his injuries. He might lose the leg. Gunshot wounds on several parts of his body where the bulletproof vest didn't cover left him lifeless. His black- and-blue face, showed signs of a beating with one eye swollen shut and blood matted at his hairline.

"Corporal, what the hell were you doing in the village when the bird went down?"

~~~
~~~

The helicopter came in quick. A medic jumped out even before the rotors stopped. They would grab the soldier and head back to base as soon as possible.

Even though Chase had trained as a medic in the Rangers, his skills were rusty after spending several years with Delta Force. Besides, he had nothing to alleviate the suffering of the corporal. The soldier was loaded onto the bird with the same care they'd give a newborn.

"Another bird ten minutes out, Captain Hunter. They'll pick you up. Lucky you came across this guy. We couldn't find the downed chopper. We had them in a different quarter. Ambassador Jarvis sent the second crew out to pick up some aid worker. The crew headed out on their second swipe when they didn't call in."

"Couldn't the aid worker help?"

"Negative. The ambassador took her to the hospital after she arrived. Complained of chest pains. Died two hours later. She brought in some teen girls slotted to go to the States. They are already on their way with several chaperones. They're safe for now."

"Jarvis didn't know where they were?"

"Negative," he yelled over the sound of the helicopter. "Another politician who couldn't find his way out of a paper bag. Either way, they'll bring back those guys now we have some idea where they might be. Don't worry."

Chase remained silent then ran back a safe distance while the helicopter took off. In minutes, the second one arrived to pick them up. Soon they were flying over areas very much like the villages he'd lived in with other groups of clans who always treated him well. Sometimes he caved in to becoming one of them until duty dragged him back into the fight. They were good people caught in a lawless land.

"There!" Chase almost missed it but then he spotted something long sticking up out of a pile of boulders. "I think I saw a rotor blade." The helicopter swung around and went back. "I see it," he called out. "Still smoldering."

"Got it, Captain. I'll set us down over there. Looks like it isn't the first time a bird landed there." The pilot cocked his head toward the spot.

Once on the ground, the soldiers onboard made haste to get to the downed helicopter. Zoric and Chase stood guard, uneasy with the village some one hundred feet away, downhill. The rise could be a problem if you had to run up the slope. They carried their weapons ready.

Moving forward they saw the village men come out of their shacks. As the two soldiers approached, the villagers backed inside their dwellings but peeked out windows or doors.

"I don't see any women and children, Chase." Zoric continued the safety scan.

"I'm guessing they have them hidden away in case the Taliban are watching." Chase searched around him. It wouldn't be hard to hide on a rooftop or in the low, rolling hills circling the village, void of much vegetation. "Maybe they can tell us what happened."

One of the soldiers ran back. "Three dead. Recovery now. Then we blow the bird. Don't want anyone getting some sensitive electronics. We won't be long, Captain."

"Care if we go down and check things out? Might find out what happened."

"My guess is a stinger, sir. No mystery there."

Chase tilted his head to survey the surrounding area again. "Why did those guys come back? I thought they got the aid worker and the girls."

"No, sir. There were more children. Couldn't take them all the first time. Came back for the rest. Orphanage, I think. The word I got, they came for two more women from Kabul who came out to assist in the transfer. Can't verify for sure since the commander left for Pakistan to smooth some ruffled feathers soon after. I understood them to be Afghans, but the ambassador seemed more than a little vague about who our guys dropped off. Truth be told, we got caught up in finding our guys and didn't think twice about any Afghans. We got your call and took off."

Chase headed toward the village. "We won't be long."

"Yes, sir."

Zoric walked beside Chase with caution, evaluating his surroundings as if his life depended on it…which it did. They entered the street. A slow walk, turn this way then back around, check the roofs, down streets, and in the windows for a pointed gun. Even a barking dog looking away from them could mean trouble.

A woman covered in a blue burqa stepped out of her doorway and pointed to a house ten feet from where Chase and Zoric stood. Then a man reached out and jerked her back indoors.

The door had been busted in. Smears of blood streaked down the wall below the window. Piles of horse manure were evident in this area but not down the street. Shell casings lay scattered everywhere they looked. A couple of discarded weapons and a variety of footprints, both animal and man blended together to show chaos. The Kyrgyz must have had their horses here when they made a stand, Chase surmised. The two stepped over debris into the dim room.

The smell of woodsmoke and urine reached his nose. Splintered furniture had either been burned or just pushed aside in a hurry. Either way it was a mess.

"Looks like it could have been used to block the door." Zoric moved objects with his foot. "This must have been the orphanage."

Chase agreed. They inspected both rooms before the task of picking it apart. Lifting some drawings off the floor, Chase examined them. "You don't see people drawing in this part of the country. Taliban frown on such frivolous activities. This must have been where the children were, all right." He dropped the drawing as something caught his attention on a shelf hanging lopsided on the wall. "What the hell?"

Both men moved toward it.

"Don't you have a knife like this, Zoric?"

"Not anymore." Zoric pulled it out from some debris as his suspicions grew. "This is dried blood, my friend."

The shelf fell to the floor sending up several pieces of paper into the air which Chase caught.

"What is it?"

Chase turned one of them around. "This one is Massoud." Then he stared at the last one before handing it to Zoric. "Tessa."

CHAPTER 13

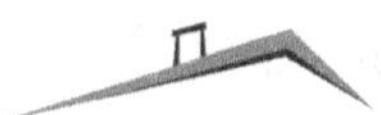

Inside Badakshan Province

Now here she stood, remembering the nightmare. How long ago? Yesterday or the day before? When did the Kyrgyz save them? Tessa staggered forward and leaned against one of the horses. It neighed in protest. Without hesitation, she laid a gentle hand against his neck, adding several strokes. Then she rested her forehead against the animal in hopes of taking a normal breath. The explosive realization she had indeed killed a man, paralyzed her with incredible grief.

Kyrgyz tribesmen went about the process of breaking camp as children milled around. Tessa could hear their laughter. Even Bonnie appeared to be more relaxed, or maybe she'd lost her fear of the men. Tessa listened to her teach the girls "London Bridge is Falling Down." But Tessa didn't care. She felt as if someone had kicked her in the stomach.

After slipping between the horses and avoiding the yaks, Tessa came to the shallow end of the river's edge. Large smooth stones jutted out creating a kind of dam backing up the water into deep pools reflecting the blue of the sky. The gurgle of the stream, pushing between the stones managed to calm Tessa.

She dropped her robe on the ground then removed her scarf. With slow steps, Tessa walked out onto the flat stones, letting the sounds of nature refresh her. The temperature must have been close to fifty, Tessa guessed. The breeze brought goose bumps to her arms as she rolled up her sleeves and untucked the blouse from her jeans. She squatted down to scoop icy drops into her hands. Splashing it on her face, Tessa felt refreshed or at least embraced the attitude she survived and so did the children. Being thankful kept her from throwing up.

Something moved in the deep pool, causing her to leap to her feet. A man rose up out of the depths with a roar. The sound bounced off the nearby cliffs, a flock of birds taking flight, combined to startle her. With a scream, Tessa realized Darya jumped up from the deep pool in front of her. He stood naked in the icy stream up to his navel. He shook his dark hair like a dog then slapped the water with his hands, splashing her.

"Oh my gosh. Oh my gosh." Tessa turned to hurry back across the rock formations. She could see Darya approaching in her peripheral vision. The closer he got, the faster she scampered. When her ankle twisted, her weight shifted and threw her sideways. Her arms went up as her body went down.

Darya rushed forward and caught her in mid-flight like she weighed as little as a child. Tessa found herself staring into the unmasked face of the mountain tribesman who'd rescued her from the Taliban, not once, but twice. Not handsome but ruggedly beautiful. His narrow eyes were light-hazel brown with a few specks of green. A wide nose led down to his thick lips. It made his eyes narrow until they appeared to be no more than slits. The icy water dripped from his hair and ran down over his bare chest, soaking into Tessa's clothing. The press of his hard body against hers told Tessa Darya might be as strong as one of the yaks he herded.

He moved forward to put her feet on the rocks then backed up so the water covered him again. Tessa lowered her head but couldn't resist stealing a glance at him sideways one last time as she escaped toward the riverbank. The splash of water warned her Darya moved toward the riverbank. She wanted to acknowledge him but tried to put more space between them. In her haste, her feet hit some gravel which sent her sprawling on her stomach then down the slope into the deep end of the river. She went under, feeling her clothes weigh her down. When she stopped splashing like a beached whale, Tessa could hear

Darya's laughter. She lumbered out of the water before falling on her knees. She didn't care if he was naked. He didn't have any business scaring her. Whirling around she noticed Darya tying a belt around the top of his trousers but his chest remained bare. He stood glistening in the morning sun. Tessa couldn't resist gazing at him. She experienced a reckless feeling as her need to gaze at his chest then his arms increased. The tattoo on his upper arm of a Chinese character and a dragon created a strange sensation. It reminded her of someone else with a tattoo on his arm. When Darya slipped his shirt over his head, Tessa's trance broke.

Darya walked up to her. "You need wash now."

"What? No. I'm not stripping in front of you to take a bath." Tessa turned to walk away, but Darya grabbed her up in his arms. She kicked and punched her way toward freedom. "Stop," she demanded as he moved to the water's edge. "Put me down."

Darya stopped and chuckled. Were her eyes violet? "Put down?" he asked as if he understood.

"Yes. Do it now."

Darya tossed her out into the deep water and laughter erupted from deep in his chest. The thought occurred to her he also needed to be taught a lesson so she held her breath until her lungs felt as if they'd burst. Breaking the surface of the water, she saw he had jumped in and frantically searched for her. She crawled out onto the bank, watching with amusement as he scanned the bottom. "Mel-E! Mel-E!"

"Looking for me?" Tessa wobbled to her feet and put her hands on her hips in a show of victory.

Darya slapped the water then flailed his arms about and growled words she didn't want to interrupt. Tessa gasped. He grabbed her from behind, lifting her off the ground before swinging her around to march back to the water. She did her best to escape but found herself being thrown back into the water. She grabbed him by the shirt, pulling him in after her. In seconds, they were both laughing.

When Tessa's teeth chattered, Darya led her out of the water. He grabbed her robe then her hands to lead her back up to the camp. The children and Bonnie were standing on the incline watching the whole escapade. Little girls covered their giggles with small hands while Bonnie crossed her arms with a lemon-sucking expression.

Since she hadn't been able to bring any extra clothes with her, Tessa felt grateful for the black Kyrgyz pants and shirt Darya pulled from his saddlebags. His fellow tribesman pieced together a change of clothes for him. Even her boots got tied together with their laces and thrown over one of the yaks replaced by a pair of warm boots being taken back to someone in their village. Their furry inside went a long way toward returning warmth to her body.

"You need to grow up, Melanie, or Tessa, or whoever you are," Bonnie scolded. "What do you think you're doing flirting with that throwback to the Stone Age?"

Tessa continued to lace up her shirt then slipped the robe speckled with blood back onto her shoulders. She glanced over at Darya who readied his horse. His gaze met hers, followed by an amused lift of one side of his mouth before he walked away to check on the yaks.

She sighed, becoming aware of Bonnie's pale face. "I thought you said I needed to get on his good side so he'd take us back?"

"I said have sex with him, not lead him on." Bonnie grabbed her arm and squeezed. "You're getting him all hot and bothered. He gets us to their village or wherever they're taking us and it's all over. The children will be farmed out and Shirin will be married to the testosterone- crazed boy over there who keeps tripping over his own tongue. And who knows what he'll do with us. Is that what you want?" Before Tessa could respond, Bonnie tightened her grip. "Time is running out for us. We don't even know if the Taliban is on our trail or if the military is coming for us."

Tessa failed to tell her about the Taliban scout coming into camp during the night. She also decided not to reveal the point Darya made about keeping her for himself. "There's something off about him," she admitted as she remembered the tattoo.

"Hmm. Well I'm not sure what you're talking about but I saw him coming out of the water and trust me there is nothing off about that guy." Bonnie's voice held a husky tone.

Tessa threw up her hands as she turned away toward the children and motioned for them to come closer. "I'm talking about his teeth." She tied scarves on little heads then added a kiss for good measure. They responded by hugging her around the waist then scampered off to whatever rider was assigned to them. They no longer showed hesitation.

Bonnie huffed impatience. "Teeth? That's it? Teeth? The fact he has teeth is amazing."

"No. I mean he has straight teeth. They're whiter than the others. Have you seen him smile?"

"Mostly I've seen him watch you like he wants to rip your clothes off. You act like he's a nice guy who plans to ride off into the sunset with us," she hissed. "He is not so different from the Taliban. You didn't see what they did to those murderous savages after they caught them. You chose to pass out on us. I'm here to tell you they were vicious." She rubbed her back then neck before starting to stretch. "Got anything else besides 'teeth'?"

Tessa pretended to glance around to make sure none of the tribesman stood close enough to hear. "He had a tattoo of a Chinese character and a dragon down his arm."

"So?"

"Kyrgyz don't tattoo."

"More information you learned in CIA school?" Bonnie watched the tribesmen walk their horses around then mount.

"I'm not a spook, Bonnie."

"For somebody who claims to have lost her memory, you're pretty confident about that."

Tessa picked up Arzo in her arms to give her a kiss on the cheek. "I remember you and the ambassador got us into all this trouble. I remember you wanted a piece of the heroin trade which made Massoud come after you. I also remember you thought more about yourself than these kids." Her voice took on a low tone as she glanced around to see if anyone listened.

Bonnie crossed her arms on her chest. "Do you remember snapping a man's spiral cord when you ran a switchblade into his skull?"

Her bitter tone made Tessa's stomach lurch. "I remember. I also remember shooting the guy hell-bent on destroying any self-respect you had left."

Bonnie's arms dropped and she stormed off toward the tribesman who waited to help her onto his horse.

Something inside Tessa made her think this ability to stand up to people might be a new phenomenon. It didn't feel right. Searching to find Darya and feeling her heart almost leap out of her chest didn't feel right either. He stood there like some ancient Asian god summoning her to him with his smoldering expression.

He possessed no shyness in showing what he desired. He examined her with lust while mounting his horse. He pranced the beast around her as she stood still enjoying the dance of intent he displayed on her behalf. Yet, a nagging voice deep inside her said stop. Even though she couldn't quite remember why, Tessa knew she belonged to someone else, someone who loved her. Could it belong to the shadow of a man walking through her dreams?

Tessa felt the necklace with the charm of a Christian cross. She didn't understand why it was so special to her except it had been a gift. With a tug, it came loose from the magnetic clasp. On the back it read a grateful president. As the group of tribesman, children, and animals moved toward the water, Tessa hung her necklace on the end of a branch so it dangled in the wind. She remembered once again the words I will always come for you. Was removing the necklace a cry for rescue or an act of leaving her old world behind?

~~~

Sacramento, California

Director Benjamin Clark stared at the phone in his hand. If he had been in a science fiction movie, the glare would have melted the phone and burned a hole in the desk surface. His teeth clenched over and over as his mind raced at hearing the news. One of his agents had disappeared in Afghanistan.

"Sir?" Vernon Kemp, a member of Captain Hunter's team, stood before him. Some at Enigma claimed if you searched for "genius" in the dictionary, a picture of Vernon would be next to the word. In spite of being the youngest of the team, Vernon was the master of artificial intelligence, spyware, and infringing on anyone's personal cyberspace.

The director cut his harsh glare to Vernon with one arched brow.

"Chase and Zoric are searching. The chopper dropped them off near the entrance to Kyrgyz territory. They'll be dark now. It might
~~~

be a couple of days before we hear back. No cell service most of the time, but their radios should work. In higher altitudes, the Enigma phone should kick in."

"Chase still got connections with local clans?"

"As far as anyone knows. He's pretty guarded about those guys."

The director frowned at Vernon. The kid continued to flaunt the hippy-like appearance of one who spent his time surfing. When not in the field, he wore a Hawaiian shirt, faded jeans with holes in the knees, and a pair of flip- flops. But with one cross word Benjamin had his ability to whither the kid to a stuttering imbecile.

"And Massoud? What of him?"

"Chase got a few of the villagers to talk. He figures Massoud might be planning to retaliate against the Kyrgyz."

The black leather chair creaked under Ben's stout body when he sat down. "My guess, too. Massoud is an educated terrorist. They're the worst kind. He'll have his revenge no matter how long it takes. Did the villagers say anything about Mrs. Scott?"

Vernon couldn't hide the grim expression. "She may be in even more danger with the Kyrgyz. The leader who ran the Taliban off didn't spare his brand of brutality with the ones he caught. He took Tessa with him." He handed Ben a black file folder then stepped back as the director placed it on the desk.

Opening up the folder, a flush of heat filled his face. He thumbed through a few pages. "Do Chase and Zoric have this information?"

"No. Can't get it to them, either."

Benjamin ran his hands across his face, imagining what might be happening to an innocent woman like Tessa Scott. This should not have happened. All the woman needed to do was give a couple of speeches. Now she was God knows where with the Undersecretary of State and a bunch of little kids. He shuddered to think about her being carried off against her will by a Kyrgyz tribesman. They could disappear into the mountains and not be seen again until spring. How could one person be such a magnet for trouble?

"So this Kyrgyz tribesman is a rogue military intelligence agent?" Ben picked up the picture of a man who didn't fit the description of Asian or Caucasian but a combination of both.

"Who is he?"

Vernon shrugged. "Locals call him Darya. Disappeared five years ago undercover. Never came back.

The military reported him MIA but believed he'd died until the CIA ran across him. Guess he's quite a character. His appearance had changed to the extent they first thought him just another local. One thing they did say." Vernon swallowed hard. "You wouldn't want to cross him. Even the Taliban avoid him."

"Tell Dr. Wu I want him on a plane to Kabul tonight." Vernon fidgeted. Dr. Wu enjoyed messing with everyone's head. Being a psychiatrist gave him liberties with such things, except with Captain Hunter. They locked horns every time Dr. Wu evaluated the captain's state of mind after a mission. It would always end up with the doctor complaining about the lack of respect or filing a report about the captain being a walking time bomb. "Mrs. Scott, provided we find her in time, is going to need someone to talk her through this. I imagine she's terrified about now. Probably thinks she'll never be found. God knows what she's been through."

"Director, her husband has been calling to find out when she's scheduled to return. He's concerned he hasn't heard from her."

"I'll call Robert."

"Are you going to tell him the truth?" Vernon reached for the doorknob.

"Of course not."

CHAPTER 14

Badakshan Border

Darkness had fallen like a heavy blanket by the time Chase and Zoric stopped for the night. They found refuge under an outcropping of rocks where they'd spotted a shallow cave they could rest in until daylight. The days in Kabul had been reaching close to eighty degrees when they left, but up here in the mountains, the temperatures could drop to freezing at night. The higher they climbed, the colder it would get. If the monsoons reached them at higher altitudes then snow would become an issue. In this part of Afghanistan, the weather was yet another mortal danger. Maybe if they didn't have to skirt any Taliban they'd reach an encampment of Kyrgyz bringing their animals down to graze on the lower south side of the mountain valleys for the fall season. This might be the one thing going for them.

"You haven't said more than ten words since they dropped us off up here. We've been walking for hours," Zoric whispered. Taliban could be in the vicinity, after all.

Chase pretended to sleep. Zoric elbowed him. "Take it."

Chase opened one eye and grabbed the half candy bar Zoric offered. He shoved the whole thing in his mouth. "Say something." Zoric took small bites of his half.

"Shut up," Chase mumbled through the melting candy.

"I know you're worried, old friend. I am, too. We'll get her back." Chase remained silent. His brooding added to the fire burning inside him. Questions had begun to avalanche in his head from the moment he realized Tessa was at the orphanage when the Taliban entered the village. Between the blood on the floor, broken furniture, and the locals' version of the Taliban shooting the helicopter down, Chase wondered what shape she might be in.

"She is so damn naive," he whispered. "Believes God is always protecting her."

Zoric chuckled. "I hope she's right. This is not her first brush with trouble. Everything worked out and, statistically speaking, it should have blown up in all our faces." Chase turned his head toward him, watching Zoric dig in his pack. "Okay, so it did blow up the last time. But it worked out." He referred to a mission in Washington D.C. when an assassination attempt on the president came close to being a reality. He withdrew his hand from the pack.

"We both know this is not going to end well. Who knows what the Taliban did to her and the undersecretary, not to mention those little girls." Chase swore under his breath.

"Why do you think the Kyrgyz took them? You know them better than anybody. Doesn't make sense. Why not leave them?"

"Death rate among children is pretty high up there on the rooftop of the world. If they make it to five, it's a freakin' miracle. You come across a bunch of little girls no one wants and suddenly you got children for grieving mothers, not to mention new blood for future wives. They marry young up there." Chase tried to refocus but the image of Tessa loomed in his mind. "As to the women..." He paused. "Ransom. Maybe to taunt the Taliban. Or..."

Zoric cocked his head, his brow arched. "Or what?"

"One of the elders in the village said the leader took Tessa with him. The undersecretary was in the care of others. Why not take someone more valuable? Tessa is a nobody."

Zoric sobered. "He took her because he wanted her for himself."

Chase moved to get more comfortable but failed. The thing irritating him couldn't be soothed. "I'm betting he never saw hair and eyes like hers. Even when she's been through the wringer, Tessa is a striking woman." He remembered how she'd felt the few times he'd protected her from harm: the press of softness in her body, the smell of her hair, and the sweetness in her mouth when he forced a kiss on her moving lips. He remembered her not as a skinny, model type but a woman who abounded in curves.

He grinned. "Well, maybe she'll talk them to death."

Zoric grinned, too, but it faded as he prepped for sleep. "You need to prepare yourself, my friend. Bad things happen up here. She has been missing now several days. Tessa is not the kind of woman who knows how to cope with the lawlessness of Afghanistan. She is a babe in the woods."

The silence thickened as a light sleep fell upon them.

Zoric muttered in his sleep as he often did, of the wife and children he lost in Serbia to a bomb. Chase had heard it many times. He battled demons of his own, the men he'd killed and the ones he planned to kill to save Tessa Scott.

~~~

Giggles from little girls were contagious even among hardened men who had little to be happy about in a desolate land that takes more than it gives. But the tribesmen appeared to enjoy the children as they continued the Ring Around the Rosie game Tessa taught them. A rag ball appeared from one of the riders and another game began, resembling soccer without rules. Even Shirin played, forgetting to play mother to her little sister. Arzo attempted to get in the thick of it but kept falling until she covered her face with little hands to cry.

Darya marched into the foray to scoop her up in his arms. He scolded the other girls in Pashto then swung her up onto his shoulders. In seconds, they were playing again and Arzo, arms wrapped around the top of Darya's head, beamed as if she'd won the ultimate prize. With reins in hand, he led his horse to the small stream near where they'd stopped to rest the animals.

Standing together at a distance from the women, Darya talked to the horse then to the three-year-old to instruct her on something. She listened intently before hugging him so tight he pretended to be annoyed. But a smile spread across his thick lips, making them appear thinner. The mask no longer covered his face. Tessa could at last observe his interesting face, not handsome in a Hollywood style but begging one to use their fingertips to explore the folds of his eyes and the stretch of his lips when they parted. After
~~~

he'd removed his brown hat, dark hair fell down his forehead with a few strands slipping across his face. The occasional gust of wind moved his black clothes against his body, outlining what lay beneath. An elbow jabbed into Tessa's side, making her jump. "Stop gawking at him," demanded Bonnie. "We're in enough trouble as it is. I'm going to talk to him."

"And say what? You think you can order these guys around? You're in Afghanistan. Women are property. They aren't seen or heard."

"Here he comes. Wipe that ridiculous grin off your face. Interpret for me." Bonnie blocked Darya's path as he swung Arzo to the ground. His eyes narrowed in contempt.

"Tell him I work for the American government. I'm worth a lot of money. The military will pay for my safe return. He will be a hero."

Tessa stumbled over the words at first but managed to convey the meaning. "What are you planning to do with us? It is important we return immediately." Bonnie hit one fist in the palm of her hand to emphasize her meaning.

Before Tessa could translate, Darya held up his hand. "I know your words."

"Good." Bonnie faked an expression of gratitude, with little success then shifted her weight to one foot. "Good. So when can you take us back?" He stepped to the side to walk off, but Bonnie cut him off again making him bump into her. "It's important Tessa and I leave right away." She glared at him. "Do you understand?"

"Understand." He tilted his head toward Tessa. His visual examination ran over her as a frown formed on his lips. "Name not Mel-E?"

"No. My name is Tessa." She took his hand and placed it on the back of her head where a knot remained. "Hit my head. I forgot my name. Now I remember, Darya. Taliban wanted to hurt us and I..." Tessa froze remembering how she'd killed another human being even though he hadn't acted like one. Her lips trembled and tears threatened to spill. She sucked them back as her chin jerked up in mock bravery. "My name is Tessa."

"I punish Taliban." His attention went back to Bonnie. "Taliban follow. They want revenge. We need to keep moving."

"No," Bonnie insisted. "I have to go back. I am important. You must understand."

Darya put his hand in the middle of Bonnie's chest then shoved her to the ground. She let out an exasperated gasp. When Tessa rushed to help her, Darya caught her by the robe and pulled her back with such force if he hadn't been standing there she would have fallen.

Whirling around on unsteady legs, Tessa shoved him with as much force as she could muster. "Don't ever do that again. I'm not your property, you overgrown pile of yak dung."

For a few seconds, he pretended to be confused then the corners of his mouth turned up. He pointed to her face. "Eyes turn color. I like." He puckered his lips in approval. "Yak dung make good fire for you and me when we…" He seemed to search for a word. "When you my wife."

"Wife," Bonnie groaned. "You'd better do something," she yelled at Tessa.

Tessa bobbed her head between Bonnie and Darya. Nothing could stop the flood of tears now. They burst forth so fast, she spun around and pushed several men aside then dashed around the children before heading toward the stream. Several of the yaks lumbered out of her way. A tree standing alone on the plain stood like a lone sentinel in the opposite direction from the one they'd been headed. Something inside her thought if she could reach such a small destination, it would be a step toward returning to her old life, the life where she hadn't killed a man.

When she reached the tree, her heart raced, sweat ran down the back of her neck, and salty tears trailed down her face. Her heart broke. She imagined the incredible sadness drowning the remaining of her self-respect. At the images of three children, two boys and a girl, calling her, she crumpled against the tree, a moan of despair on her lips. She buried her face in her hands and sobbed.

A distant sound of a bell around a yak's neck lifted on the wind. Tessa dared to turn around. Her vision blurred at first. She wiped her sleeve across her face then saw the tribesmen had left and were moving ever closer to the mountains. She would die all alone, next to the tree. Her American family, as vague as the memory was, would never know what a monster she'd become.

Then she saw him. Darya. He sat in the grass some fifty feet from her. His horse grazed a little farther away. Whatever he stared at in the distance made him appear a great deal more peaceful than she felt. Tessa staggered to her feet and leaned against the trunk. She sucked air deep into her lungs. The air had grown thinner with each passing mile. The altitude robbed her of strength. Darya stood and meandered casually toward her. He held a blade of grass between his teeth.

"Darya fool. Scare you." He dropped the blade of grass. "You are brave. Fight Taliban like a Kyrgyz. Save girls. They tell me what you did. Proud."

Tessa pressed her back against the tree and covered her face with her hands. The sobs returned. "I hate myself."

The next thing she knew Darya moved within inches of her body. "Tes-sa." He reached out and pulled her hands into his. "You good. I like you. Other woman not so much." Darya made talking signs with his hands then rolled his eyes. "Not trust her."

"Darya." Tessa stepped forward, believing he was all she had as Darya wrapped his arms around her and held her tight. She felt both lost and comforted in his embrace. "I'll have to carry this awful secret forever."

"Darya have secrets, too, Tes-sa." He pushed her to arm's length and lowered his head to stare at her. "Tell you soon. Okay?" His hand went to the back of her head where the knot still jutted out. "We marry when reach my people." Darya whistled for his horse. "I protect you."

"I can't marry you, Darya," Tessa insisted as the horse halted in front of them. "I belong to someone else."

Darya lifted her to the front of the horse then swung up behind her. "He not here. I want wife. We share secrets together. I save you so now you belong to me." His body molded against her, he slipped his hand under her robe to pull her close. He clicked his tongue and the horse moved at a slow walk toward the other riders.

He talked in a low voice. Since he spoke in Pashto, Tessa caught a few words. They sounded like poetry, soothing her broken heart, and soon she found herself relaxing into Darya's hold on her. Several times he kissed her ear and she turned her face just enough so he would do the same on her jaw, which he took full advantage of. His touch sparked life into her dead emotions. Maybe a life here would make her forget the terrible thing she'd done. The family she left behind, whoever they were, could remember a person of character, not this person who had taken the life of another.

They continued to ride some distance behind the others. Darya pointed at things along the way, murmuring in Pashto. At times he rested his face against hers as he spoke. She would bob her head in spite of not understanding, but enjoyed the way his voice sounded along with the movement of his mouth against her ear. She couldn't resist touching his cheek for mere seconds to let him know she was grateful. Once he kissed her fingers then laughed softly against her hair.

Darya pulled up short when Toiluk, one of his men, turned the pack animals around and herded them back in their direction. Tessa felt Darya let his horse have his head as the animal picked up speed. He pulled up short when he neared Toiluk who ventured away from the group.

Tessa managed to understand most of the conversation. "Why turn back?" Darya sounded concerned and scanned the land behind them. Her first thoughts were that the Taliban had found them. The true meaning scared her far worse.

"Children very sick," Toiluk said twisting in his saddle to glance at the approaching menagerie.

Tessa stiffened thinking of little Arzo.

"We must go back for a few days." Darya squeezed Tessa around her waist. "Altitude sickness. We rest. Girls get well."

Both men moved their horses to join the others. Several of the girls whimpered when Tessa neared them. Arzo rode in front of one of the older men, leaning back, her body frail and listless. The rider handed her off to Tessa. She felt like a rag doll in her arms. Tessa kissed her head and gathered her close.

"Darya." Desperation held her captive. "I want to check the children. Please."

He dismounted and reached up for Arzo. Tessa threw her leg over the horse's neck and jumped to the ground.

Toiluk assisted Bonnie off the horse she shared with another tribesman. She appeared a little green as well. She rubbed her head then patted her chest as if she couldn't breathe.

"What is happening?" Rubbing her temples, Bonnie sounded a litany of complaints. "My head is killing me. Shut those kids up."

"They're hurting, too, woman," Darya snarled then brushed past her. He assisted Toiluk and Rashid with gathering the children together before attending to the animals.

"We rest for few hours, and then go back to the river for two days." Darya carried Pamir in his arms and Shirin walked alongside them, patting her sister's leg with concern. Although pale, Shirin didn't appear to be suffering from altitude sickness. Tessa passed Arzo to Shirin. The men handed a couple of blankets to her which she spread on the cold ground for the children to rest on. Marta lay down, drawing up her legs as she grabbed her stomach and cried. Halcha and Son-Kul seemed in better shape but held their foreheads and swayed.

Darya sent a couple of the men ahead to set up a camp where they could get out of the weather, herding the animals before them. The night would be cold again, and the children would be susceptible to other medical problems if the altitude sickness ate away at their ability to fight infection. Darya spoke to the tribesman and they all bent to check their weapons.

"Everything all right, Darya?" Tessa watched him as he stood on the edge of the blanket.

Before he could answer, Bonnie chimed in. "No. Things are not all right. We're all sick as dogs. Except you. Why is that?" She frowned up at their protector. "Maybe you poisoned us so we'd be out of the way for you to do whatever you plan to do to Tessa."

"Bonnie! That is enough. Don't insult the very man who saved us." Tessa couldn't hide her outrage. "What is wrong with you?" She drew Arzo closer.

Darya glared down at the undersecretary. "She is right, Tes-sa."

Bonnie gasped.

"I put yak pee in her tea. Thought it make her shut the hell up, as you Americans say." His voice came out so even Tessa had to inspect him closer to make sure he was taunting Bonnie. "Tonight I bed her with one of my men to see if this work better. They beg me not to." He shrugged. "So what do you say, government woman with heart of stone? More yak pee, or—

"You made your point, Darya." Bonnie rubbed at her forehead again. "No need to be rude."

Darya pooched out his lips and squatted down by the little girls. "What she mean 'rude'?" He pretended to be confused as he crossed his eyes for the girls, causing them to give a weak snicker.

"Darya good man." He cocked his head over at Tessa who rewarded him with a warm gaze. Reaching out, he patted her knee. "Tes-sa good woman. Good mother."

"Humph." Bonnie turned away. "Now I know what made me sick. It's the savage attempt at romance with Tessa." Bonnie pretended to gag. "Do whatever you want with her. But take me back to Kabul. The State Department will reward you with enough money to feed your people for a year."

"Enough, Bonnie," Tessa warned, feeling embarrassed and betrayed at the same time.

"And these girls?" Darya pointed to each one and offered a fake smile to the girls. Except for Shirin, they couldn't understand English.

"Just take me back. The longer you delay, the greater the chances you will get nothing."

Pamir and Marta pulled him down to a squatting position next to them as he stole a glance at Tessa. "I have all I need or want right here." He planted a kiss on the top of Pamir's head. "Tes-sa will need someone to help her with the children when we marry."

"Marry! You can't be serious." Bonnie's pinched expression made her appear ready to vomit. "Are you listening to this?"

Tessa grinned and unfolded her legs to kick Darya so he would fall back on his butt, which only caused him to chuckle. "He's pushing your buttons. If you stop talking, then he will, too." She lowered her voice so the children could rest.

~~~

Walking alongside Toiluk's horse, Darya held the reins loose as he took a moment to watch her twisting and turning in the saddle to observe everything around her.

From time to time she would sigh as if something profound crushed her heart at the same time placing a hand across her chest. Sometimes she would lean forward and offer a compliment on such a beautiful landscape. The Hindu Kush with its breathtaking scenery and dangerous trails helped Tessa's mood improve.

"How much farther?" She leaned forward in the saddle and patted the horse's neck when they topped a ridge. Darya stopped to sip some water from his canteen then handed it to her.
~~~

"Not far. One kilometer I think." He stared into the distance. "Feel better?"

When Darya had suggested the two of them leave for Ishkashim District to restock supplies Tessa's heartbeat had accelerated. A headache surfaced, too. She couldn't hide her shortness of breath or the fear of being alone with Darya.

"I need to stay with the children." They'd gotten them settled near a gurgling stream. "It's not like we're going to wander off. Take Rashid or Toiluk." She spoke Pashto out of respect for Darya's men. Her speech and understanding got better with each passing day. The men mumbled their objections to Darya immediately. "I don't understand."

"Toiluk and I are well-known in these parts. The poppy business has people from many districts as well as countries like Tajikistan and Uzbekistan, not to mention the Afghan Taliban. It is a blend of Sunni and Shia. Most of the time we all get along. When the Taliban arrive for extended periods problems arise for Kyrgyz." He busied himself with readying the horse. "The Taliban are searching for us. They will not come to the Wakhan because they are not strong like us. But they know where we go for supplies. So they will wait."

"What if they are there now?" Tessa knew she sounded like a nervous Nellie.

"They are there," Darya said so nonchalant she thought she misunderstood. Her silence drew his attention. "They don't know this horse or believe I would travel with a woman." He reached to touch her long braid falling over her shoulder. "I dress you like good Taliban Muslim woman when we get closer. I change, too. No problem."

"I'm not sure what line of gibberish he's feeding you, Tessa, but don't go with him." Bonnie pulled her away from listening to Darya. The woman had given up on understanding Pashto. "You'll be all alone. He could trade you for God knows what." Bonnie turned her back on Darya. She lowered her voice. "I know I've been difficult. I'm not like you. I don't find any of this fascinating or romantic. And you're right. I'm scared and think of myself first. But that doesn't mean I want anything to happen to you." Bonnie reached for Tessa and grasped her arms. "Darya's right, too. You are a good person. These kids need you here. I don't have a clue of what to do."

Tessa's lips narrowed at an attempt of bravery, but didn't erase Bonnie's terrified expression. "What choice do I have? We're running out of supplies. The children need nourishment. We can't go any higher until everyone has adjusted. Maybe I can get some medicine. A couple of days should do the trick."

"What about Arzo's fever? I still have some baby aspirin."

Was leaving the children insane? "Good lord, don't give her aspirin. It will kill her. You don't give kids that."

"Geez. I'm glad you told me. Tell me what to do for her." Bonnie followed Tessa's observation of Darya as he lifted Arzo in his arms and laid his cheek against hers. "Damn, I think he loves the kid."

"Yes." Tessa warmed at seeing him kiss the little girl. "I think he does. That's why I'm willing to go wherever it is we need to go for supplies." She shrugged, letting her imagination embrace every inch of him and realized she longed for something forbidden. "You want to go home don't you?"

Bonnie turned to Tessa as she continued to watch Darya's imposing form carry Arzo inside the cave. "God help us if you don't come back."

CHAPTER 15

Ishkashim District, Eastern Afghanistan

If my mother saw this place, she'd make me come home, thought Tessa as she browsed the market stalls and poverty of the Afghan people. She couldn't visualize her mother very well but felt sure of the sentiment. She walked humbly alongside the horse Darya now rode, covered head to toe in a blue burqa with a small screen in her head covering to peer through. She wanted to throw it off and run with abandonment to show the few women moving along the outside of the market stalls how an American woman shopped.

But that would mean certain death. Darya had warned her as he helped her with the burqa after the town appeared on the horizon. Then he changed to look more like the Taliban, although with his Central Asian looks there was no mistaking him as a Kyrgyz tribesman. He explained that his clothing gave the appearance of someone who followed the letter of the Islamic Law, at least in the warped Taliban version.

"Do not speak. I will do all the talking for you. Understand?"

Dread had seeped up inside her. She'd seen the documentaries of women being beaten for appearing in public without a male escort or making the mistake of revealing the skin on their wrist when reaching for a wayward child. Now here she stood with even her hands covered in blue fabric.

Darya dismounted after finding the market stalls he spoke of along the way. He told the man what he wanted and where to bring the items. Tessa spotted some earrings and reached to see them. The seller screeched at her and she realized the end of one of the fingers had a small rip, revealing white skin. Before she could withdraw her hand, Darya slapped her so hard she fell to the ground. When he yelled insults at her, Tessa cowered in fear. He reached down and yanked her to unsteady feet then shoved her forward. Grabbing her from behind, he shook her.

He continued the onslaught of insults while he led his horse to a building serving as a hotel. A young boy took the animal, and Darya dragged Tessa inside with such force she tripped several times on her burqa. Once, when she sniffed back tears, Darya came unglued on her in the lobby, calling her everything but human. He paid the man at the desk some Afghani money then shoved her up the stairs to their room on the second floor.

Tessa's vision blurred through the flood of silent tears gushing from her eyes as Darya swung the door open. With another jerk, he threw her into the room. Her feet tangled in the burqa causing her to tumble to the floor. He barred the door and stormed toward the open windows. A curtain drooped over the opening until he jerked it closed with such force Tessa believed it might rip off the rod made from a branch.

Now she feared the oncoming attack. How long would it last and how many times could she endure such savage treatment? By now, he knew she could fight and could circumvent her ability to defend herself. She quaked on the dusty floor, watching his feet move through an open doorway. The sound of running water reached her. In seconds, the feet appeared again in front of her then Darya kneeled down beside her. Tessa cringed, expecting the first wave of abuse. She had nothing to lose so the decision to fight swam to her braver side.

Darya remained still as a mouse hoping not to be discovered. "Tes-sa." His voice, now calm, encouraged her to lift her head enough to see him through the peephole in her head covering. He reached out and pulled her forward as she swung her fist at him. "Tes-sa," he whispered. "Come to me. I not hurt." His English replaced his Pashto for a second then he switched back. "Come to me, I said. Now." Even though he commanded her, the tone continued to be nonthreatening.

Tessa pushed herself up to look at him. Darya reached out and slowly removed her head covering as if she would spook like his horse. "Tes-sa," he whispered. "Come to me," he encouraged. "Tes-sa," he said again and again.

She snarled at him and he reached to touch her cheek.

When she fell back, he edged closer.

"Come to me, Tes-sa. I won't hurt you. I had to do those things to you to show I was Taliban. Very sorry, my Tes-sa. Please forgive me." He tilted his head to the side then took the wet cloth in his hand and cleaned her face. "Understand? My Tes-sa." He pulled her closer and finished wiping her face then removed her blue gloves. Without warning he removed her burqa. "There. You brave again. Taliban can kill you for showing any skin. I don't want anything to hurt you."

Tessa shoved at his chest without him budging. Instead, he wrapped his arms around her. "You did hurt me." She pointed to her heart. "Here, Darya."

"I know. It hurt me here, too." He pointed to his own heart.

They were both on their knees now, so close a whisper sounded too loud. "You pretended to teach me a lesson?"

His lips touched hers as he spoke. "Yes. Pretend. And I would do it again if you did something so stupid. If I not there, it would be much worse." He stroked the red imprint where he had hit her then went to her hair as he pulled her tight against his chest with his free hand.

"Tes-sa, it is time." Darya caressed the back of her entire body with one slide of his hand.

She felt nervous and excited all in the same flood of emotion. "Time?"

"Soon we will marry. It is time you stop trying to bring back your past. It is no good. We will make a life here in the Hindu Kush. Together. No one is looking for you. I make sure." His fingers slid down her neck, his lips resting against hers. "I will wait until you are ready for me. But I am getting impatient to make you my wife. Do you understand my meaning, Tes-sa?"

With his body pressing against hers it didn't take a genius to know exactly what he meant. "And if I refuse?" she asked in hopes of sounding shy and submissive.

Darya chuckled as he got to his feet and pulled her up. "You will not." His confidence showed through his grin. "I can be very persuasive."

She touched her cheek and stepped back, remembering the hideous anger flooding his face in the market. He'd become a monster without warning. "Let's get this done and get back to the children. That's what I care about." He moved toward the door. "Where are you going? Are you leaving me here alone?" A number of scenarios chiseled away at her renewed self-confidence.

"Bolt the door. Let no one in but me. No matter who comes to this door, keep it bolted. No matter what anyone tells you, do not let them in. Understand?" When she didn't answer, he sobered and followed with a snarl. "Do. You. Understand, Tes-sa?" He motioned for her to stand behind the door and demonstrated the bolt. She finally shook her head with an anxious acceptance and he disappeared.

~~~

Captain Hunter realized he stood a head taller than anyone else meandering through the street market that showed signs of closing for the day. Both he and Zoric dressed the part of other locals, and he felt confident they wouldn't draw unwanted attention. Even here in Satan's hellhole, people would avoid walking too close to Zoric. Both men scanned rooftops and alleys as they made their way to several stalls. An old man asked a few questions concerning their business or destination, but the captain gave as little information as possible at first. Zoric appeared as if he might explode into a murderous rage.

"I am searching for a group of Kyrgyz traveling with children toward the Wakhan. They are friends." The captain had rehearsed the words until they sounded right. He asked once or twice, knowing the word would travel fast enough and come back with answers if there were any.

After inquiring about a place to stay and finding out there was nothing available, the two men accepted an offer of staying in a Tajik's home with his wife and three children. Although he never saw the man's wife, he did watch a delicate handshake out from behind a ragged curtain with a plate of food for the guests. The
~~~

Tajik lifted his hands over his head in resignation, saying Allah had blessed him with an ugly wife who could cook and three daughters who made life worthwhile in such a harsh land.

"No. No. Nothing of the Kyrgyz in a while. They are overdue. They are good for business. Buy from us. When the poppies bloom, they are here many days." He laughed revealing his front teeth barely hanging on.

"Anyone new in town besides us? Maybe they have seen them."

The Tajik rubbed his chin as if lost in thought then slapped his hands together. "Yes. A Taliban." The man spat on the floor. "He come then beat his wife for all to see. He thinks she disrespected him." He shrugged. "Who knows? Maybe she did. Then he left. He wanted a large amount of supplies."

Chase glanced at Zoric to see if he, too, thought the information curious. "Unusual?"

The Tajik waved him off. "No. Said he was taking it back to his men and their families. They are making their way south for the winter. It will be very cold here in a few months. They want more and more of our opium. Dogs. All of them. They want to profit at our expense. Sometimes we accommodate." Again the shrug. "Sometimes not so much."

"So this Taliban, the one with the wife, did he want more opium?"

The Tajik laughed. "No. He wants to trade his opium for food and supplies. He must be rich with the poppy to trade with us. They often very greedy." He scrunched up his face. "He didn't look much like Taliban now that I think of it. But I'm not sure. He was not close."

"Where is this man now?"

"I will find out for you. Taliban not a friend to local Kyrgyz. If he saw these Kyrgyz you speak of, they are dead."

"Thank you. May Allah bless this house," Chase proclaimed.

"Now we have tea."

~~~

Tessa sat on a bed not much wider than a cot. The mattress felt lumpy but didn't appear to be infested with anything wanting a piece of her skin. Because a sheet and pillowcase would have been
~~~

a luxury, she sat on the burqa with her back up against the wall. Twice a male voice spoke at the door, the first informing her that her husband requested her to come downstairs and a second, who banged on the door, also referred to her husband. She shivered with fear and from the cold. The headache returned. They were in an even higher altitude than where they'd left the children. She hoped they fared better than her.

Another bang on the door. "Open up!" demanded a voice with a British accent. "You. Come here. Your husband needs you."

Tessa cowered at the end of the bed then she heard a weak voice. "Tes-sa. For the sake of Arzo, open the door." Then a fit of coughing.

She ran to unbolt the door, but stood behind it as she pulled it open. As soon as the two men came inside, she slammed it shut and secured the bolt. When she turned around, Tessa saw a man leading Darya to the bed. Blood trickled from a cut on his forehead and he held his side.

"Darya." She rushed to his side and kneeled on the floor next to him. "What happened?" She forgot herself and spoke in English.

"Mother of the Almighty, Darya. This is your wife?" The man spoke English as clearly as she did. "And a pretty one, too."

Tessa frowned up at the man who resembled one of the Afghans instead of a Brit. "Who are you? British Intelligence?"

This caused the man to burst into deep laughter. "Did ya hear that, Darya? Me. British Intelligence." He laughed again. "Not anymore. Darya and I work together from time to time. Try to get the best product for the least amount of money." He plopped down next to Darya and scooted back against the wall.

Tessa shifted her glare from the man to Darya in the realization her protector made his living by drug smuggling. "Darya? What is he talking about?" When he didn't answer, she hurried to the bathroom to get the same wet cloth he'd used on her face earlier. She dabbed at the gash. He winced and jerked away then took the rag to do it himself. "Are you a smuggler?"

"He's the king of smugglers, lady. And if I'm right, you aren't his wife. You're one of those Americans the hotshots in Kabul are turning over every stone to rescue." He arched his thick eyebrows and revealed a toothy grin. The man, big boned and square shouldered bore an angular face, weathered from too much sun. A strand of sandy hair hung down on his forehead. His beard and mustache matched the color with a few twisted hairs of gray throughout. The close-set eyes grew round and expressive over a nose too large for such a narrow face.

Tessa waited for Darya to offer an explanation then asked, "What happened?"

"Just guy stuff. A little name calling led to some posturing then 'I can whip your ass' kind of talk. Seemed to be a dispute over parentage as well." The man laughed again slapping Darya on the back which drew a groan of pain. "Oh, I'm Mick Cavanaugh by way of South Africa. And you are?"

"Tessa Scott."

"Hmm. I think I need to take you back to the Americans. Maybe I'll even get a reward." He scooted to the end of the bed and pushed himself up. "What'a ya say?"

Darya shook his head. "Do not go with him. You will be in danger."

Another laugh from Mick. He lowered his voice and spoke from the side of his mouth as if chewing on the words. "The supplies are ready. I'll get his horse. My horse is already out back. He's going nowhere like this. Probably busted a couple of ribs. That eye is goin' swell shut here pretty quick. He can't take care of you. I can."

Tessa felt torn. Everything she knew to be familiar matched with Mick. He would take her to safety. Then she could return for the children. But what if she couldn't? Arzo. That baby needed food and medicine.

"I need to take those supplies to the children."

"No, Tes-sa. He can't protect you. I can."

The image of him knocking her to the ground then throwing her inside the room still flashed to mind. Darya struggled to his feet and something fell out of the folds of his jacket. Tessa reached down and picked up the earrings she'd seen earlier in the market. Holding them in her hand, she made her decision.

~~~

"You guys stick out like a sore thumb." Mick engaged the two men sitting outside drinking tea at the old Tajik's house. "You CIA?"
~~~

He continued to speak in a mix of English and Pashto.

Chase and Zoric drank their tea as if they didn't hear him. The common practice of ex-patriots taking advantage of the chaos in a war-torn country to make their fortunes flourished in this part of Afghanistan. Mick didn't try to hide his British heritage. Everyone knew him and the business he practiced.

"Okay. Maybe military intelligence or some of those badass Special Forces. Am I right?" Mick pulled up an empty five-gallon bucket and flipped it over for a chair. "So who are you? Not seen you around here before?"

Chase spoke in Pashto. "Are you a deserter or common scumbag?"

Mick chuckled, letting his laugh float on the cold night air. "I like to think of myself as an entrepreneur."

Chase dug in his pocket and handed Mick a picture of the woman he'd just left in the hotel room. "She's traveling with some Kyrgyz tribesman. I'm thinking maybe we need to talk to them about an important matter."

Mick examined the picture and whistled. "I'd remember if I ran into this bird. Not many blondes in this part of the world. Heard there were some American women lost up here. Who is she?" He handed the picture back.

"A friend," Chase growled.

Mick stood and stretched. "Nope. Can't help ya. But if I run into her, I'll let her know you want a visit."

Chase shoved the photo in his pocket. "There's a reward."

"How much?"

"Enough to be comfortably away from this godforsaken place."

"All the more reason I'll keep my radar up." Mick grinned and strolled away into the darkness.

~~~

Tessa followed Darya along the trail leading through a narrow mountain pass. The sun had risen an hour earlier, in time for them to navigate the treacherous path. One side of the trail was formed of jagged rocks and the other a thousand-foot drop. Soon, they decided to take a break.

Darya's eye didn't quite swell closed and the gash remained
~~~

hidden under the dark hair he pulled down across his forehead. Tessa continued to worry about the ribs, but he assured her they were okay. It was good to have a woman concerned about him again. She appeared to struggle with breathing due to altitude and the constant walking. This made the trip slower than he would have liked. He wanted as much distance between them and the Ishkashim District as possible. She peered over the edge at the perilous fall awaiting her with one awkward stumble and laid a hand over her heart more than once. She drew his attention as she rubbed her forehead but didn't complain of a headache. The undersecretary could have never made this trip in her current shape.

"Good thing Mick alerted us," Tessa said between deep breaths as they exited the pass and took a break. "Scared me to death his banging on the door before dawn."

Darya agreed as he scanned the nearby rock formations. It would be a good place for a trap. "Yes. Taliban like to go door to door and scare villagers when they are not ready to meet the day. It gives them an advantage."

Darya thought about the two men Mick met the previous evening. He used the Taliban story to get Tessa moving, knowing if the strangers were Americans; it wouldn't take long to locate them. Wondering who they were and why one of them had a picture of Tessa concerned him. The sooner they reached the Wakhan, the sooner she would be out of reach.

"I'd love a cup of coffee," Tessa whispered as she drank in the beauty of the landscape. "I could stand here all day and take this in." She tensed as something moved high on the rocks. "Darya." She pointed, seeing it move again. The two horses shied and neighed.

Slipping his binoculars out of one of the saddlebags, he zeroed in on the movement and handed them off to Tessa. "See. A mother snow leopard and her cub. It is a good sign."

She smiled as Darya took advantage of the moment. He slipped his arm around her waist and pulled her in front of him so her back rested against his chest. She didn't resist, continuing to watch the big cats move with stealthy precision across the mountain.

When his face pressed against her cheek, she lowered the binoculars and stared straight ahead. The thought she might push away at this show of intimate affection clawed its way into his desire to take more of what was inevitable. Instead of retreating, she snuggled back against him and brought his arms tighter around her body. They stood locked in an embrace, staring at the nothingness of the Hindu Kush until the sun warmed the air.

A great deal of excitement arose when they rejoined the others at their temporary camp. Even Bonnie clapped her hands at seeing them. Once again, Arzo could walk and laugh like the other children. Tessa made a quick soup of some dried vegetables and lamb. Everyone got a dose of acetaminophen for their low grade fevers and body aches. Even though the bottle had expired two years earlier, she remained confident it would be good enough for the children. Even though they didn't seem to want to play, the color had returned to their cheeks and they rested on blankets near the fire.

By noon they were on the move again toward the Wakhan Corridor and its promised protection from the Taliban. Darya kept an eye on Bonnie who slumped against the rider she'd been paired with earlier. Something told him the woman would not last an entire winter up here. The children had already suffered altitude sickness, and they were still climbing. Even though Darya stopped every hour or so for the girls to rest, he wondered if it would be enough.

This time Darya kept Arzo in front of him and sang to her. The supplies were moved from the extra horse Darya bought in the village to one of the yaks so Tessa could ride alone. They stopped early and made camp. More medicine and soup and everyone seemed to be adjusting, including Bonnie.

By the time they herded the animals near the gathering of yurts that made up their clan encampment the next day, the sun tilted toward the tops of the mountains. The plain, round yurts appeared like giant snowballs set against land which appeared to stretch to eternity and back. A rocky wall extended out some twenty-five feet to form a crude corral. All along the top were piles of yak dung drying in the dry air. Young girls dressed in bright red moved about the corral to milk the goats and yaks.

Men dismounted as women came out of yurts, some carrying babies, others with toddlers at their sides. The youngest rider, Rashid, greeted an older man and woman who appeared relieved to see him. They spoke then turned their attention to Shirin who dismounted and stumbled two steps before straightening her back. She stared at the ground then to Tessa for support.

Darya's horse stomped its hooves. He watched the older man with Rashid take in the unexpected guests. He greeted them as Rashid took both reins in his hands. With a quick dismount, he removed Arzo and placed her with Tessa then walked her horse around the camp, giving Tessa a quick visual tour. Others were pointing at them now, and speaking in low whispers.

~~~

Wakhan Valley

"What is wrong, Darya?"

"It is an old custom, one we don't use much anymore. The government does not like it, but sometimes it is necessary."

"I don't understand. What custom?"

"We call it 'bride kidnapping.' They think I have taken a bride."

An uneasy feeling made Tessa a little sick to her stomach. "Darya, we need to talk about this. I can't marry you."

"If not me, then someone else will want you. These people are very wealthy. Any man here can pay the bride price to me if I choose."

Tessa observed the poverty of these Kyrgyz people. Besides their yurts and animals, she saw no show of wealth. "How much am I worth?"

"One hundred sheep."

She clicked her tongue then offered a grin to her future husband. "Seems reasonable. Guess by bride napping you won't have to pay one sheep."

"I will still have to pay kahn to respect you. But if I sell you, I will be richest man here," he spoke straight-faced until Tessa shuddered. "I married once."

Tessa turned her head toward him in surprise. "Is she here?" She remembered some Muslims took more than one wife.

Darya pulled Tessa down to the ground, and Arzo reached for
~~~

him with fragile arms. "She died. Baby, too. This place hard on families." No emotion crossed his face. Death was a fact of life up here. "I ready for wife number two. You be good wife." He tickled Arzo's cheek. "Good mother, too."

Taking stock of the Kyrgyz girls milking animals and grown women doing other odd jobs around the compound, Tessa realized she needed a way out and fast. "I'm in serious need of a caramel latte, Darya. Whipped cream, please. That should tell you all you need to know about whether or not I'd make a good Kyrgyz wife."

The statement somehow made him chuckle. She wondered if the word "latte" meant something else in his language. Maybe "I can't wait to make a baby with you. I talk to Kahn. You help children."

Before she could add a retort about not being very good at taking orders, Darya strode away, leading his horse.

Bonnie limped up beside her, rubbing her butt. "I hate horses. I will never walk in a dignified way again." The two women watched Darya approach another man who examined Tessa from head to toe in one glance. He grinned at Darya and puffed on his pipe. "What's going on?" Bonnie tensed.

"I think it's my wedding day."

~~~

Badakshan Province

Chase squatted on the ground to examine the remains of a campfire. He held his hand over the ashes but felt nothing. He squinted as he surveyed the abandoned camp. The Kyrgyz had broken camp a short time ago. The gurgle of the nearby stream beckoned him. He squatted once more to observe the area before venturing out into the open. He could already see the heavy indentions of hooves made by yaks, horses, and maybe a few sheep or goats. The narrow stream revealed a ramp of mud where animals had exited the water.

Chase stood silent for several minutes before pivoting back toward the remains of the camp. Something swung back and forth, glistening in the afternoon sun. He stared at it, willing it to stop
~~~

moving. He swiped the necklace from the branch then closed his hand around it. He didn't need to check for an inscription. The necklace belonged to Tessa Scott. President Buck Austin had it made for her after she'd saved his life. She never took it off.

"Reminds me how lucky I am to be alive," she'd once told him. "When I wear this, I know God is protecting me and his Enigma angels have my back." Then she laughed the way only she could and talked about her kids, worms in the garden, or her husband Robert's golf game—things which made her light up with uncompromised joy.

He took long strides back to find Zoric entering the camp area. "I think they caught a Taliban sneaking around. Appears his neck was snapped with a few important body parts missing, if you get my drift. Not a pretty sight." Coming from him, the information showed brutality since he'd committed similar acts of violence on deserving men in the past. Holding out the necklace, Zoric stared at it for mere seconds before meeting his partner's stern face.

"Alive. She's letting us know."

He buttoned the necklace into a pocket for safekeeping. "I'd say they're four days ahead of us. The animals and a bunch of kids will slow them down. Problem is we'll be in the open now."

"The dead Taliban guy I found must have been a scout. He's been left as a warning I think."

Chase agreed. "I doubt they followed. Air gets thinner and Massoud knows the Kyrgyz will come back down to trade. Time is on their side. Our problem is they trade about four times a year. It'll be months before they come back this way."

Zoric took a deep breath. "Too long. By the time—" Zoric bit off his words.

He touched the pocket where he'd secured the necklace. "I promised Tessa I wouldn't let anything happen to her. What if I'm too late?" He stared down at his feet then up at the sky, wanting to confront God. "I'm getting tired of being tested."

~~~

The Kyrgyz women were a contrast to their men. Bright- red skirts billowed, layered with even redder tunics. When the women walked, the adornments fastened to their blouses tinkled softly in
~~~

the breeze. Brass trinkets no bigger than a thimble, tiny bells, and multicolored ribbons with beads, decorated the front of their clothing. The young, unmarried girls wore long red head scarves draped down to their waists. Married women wore white scarves in the same fashion. One of the older women came forward and was quick to point out the differences, but it wasn't hard considering the age gap between the two. Some wore multiple bracelets or watches. Boots peeked out from under the hems of their skirts.

"They're beautiful," Tessa whispered as the little girls clung to her legs or leaned into her body.

They were shy, now, in this strange place dotted with rocks and scattered grasses without a tree in sight. Hundreds of animals dotted the land. Bactrian camels moved into a huddle as afternoon light faded. The darkness brought a cold, demanding warmth, and routine drove them together. Their disgruntled call of disrespect caused several of the older women to fuss at them with waving arms.

"Miss Melanie." The children still didn't know her by any other name—"when can we go home? I'm scared." Pamir peered up at Tessa, eyes round with fear.

"I don't know, Pamir. I will try and find out." Pamir put an arm around Tessa's waist and leaned into her body for comfort. She rubbed the little girl's cheek.

"Will we stay together tonight in those?" Shirin came to stand next to her sister then pointed toward the yurts.

Bonnie snorted. "Yes, Melanie," she said in a sarcastic voice. "Will we sleep together tonight, or do you have other plans?"

Tessa shot a snarl of contempt to her before trying to reassure Shirin. "I hope so, Shirin. Are you okay?"

The teen pointed to several girls, who looked to be about her own age, working with the yaks. "I do not want to marry a man from here. This place is cold. The women look hard. There is no school."

"No. There is no school, Shirin."

"I want to go to school, Miss Melanie. Please."

Her pleas tugged at Tessa's heartstrings. "I want that, too." Tessa extended her arm so Shirin could slip under it next to Pamir. "I'm not sure what I'm going to have to do to make those plans happen," she said, sucking in her breath.

Several of the women urged the guests to follow them to their yurts. Although colorless on the outside, the kaleidoscope of color inside was shocking. Not an inch of the ceiling and walls lacked vivid splashes of reds, yellows, and blues. The cooking fire burned low in the middle of the space. A tea kettle sat atop with a trail of steam seeping out from the spout.

The Kyrgyz women settled them on the rug-covered floor and gave them cups of steaming tea, murmuring soft words. Patting the shoulders of the children brought timid smiles to their cherub faces. Besides the sweet smell of burning yak dung, there rose up the tantalizing aroma of food. Tessa couldn't identify what the boiled meat could be, but at this point she didn't care. Never one to eat much meat, she found herself craving it.

Several other women came into the yurt and spoke to the hostess as they pointed to Tessa. Surprised chatter, followed by a number of bobbing heads, put up Tessa's radar. The wedding was happening. It might as well have been a shotgun wedding in the hills of Tennessee. The excitement created a kind of electricity among the women. For those who lived bland lives 365 days of the year, this might be the Super Bowl of the Kyrgyz.

Without hesitation, the four women pulled Tessa to her feet then pushed her gently toward an upside down metal can that reminded her of the five-gallon popcorn tins she sometimes bought at Christmas. Her knees popped as one old woman shoved her down to sit. Their giggles sounded girl-like. A quick pull of her scarf made her long blonde curls fall in disarray around her shoulders. They clicked their tongues. A comb appeared. Soon the duty of making her curls appear more like yellow silk proceeded. After the job was completed, they braided her hair into two long plaits falling across her shoulders.

Bonnie stood with arms folded across her chest. A contemptible smirk formed on her lips. The little girls came to sit in front of Tessa, beaming up at her. Shirin stood next to Bonnie. Her arms hung at her side and a pensive concern filled her eyes.

"Miss Melanie?"

Tessa cringed as one of the women pinched her cheek. "Ouch!" She jerked away. "Yes, Shirin?"

"What is happening? Why are they doing this to you?" Her

voice quivered.

"Yes, Melanie. Pray tell," Bonnie cooed with flippant disregard for the teen's nervousness.

Tessa ignored the jab. "I seem to remember reading that among the Kyrgyz; one of the things a bride does is have her hair braided by her aunts. These women have taken it upon themselves to be my aunts, it seems."

"You will marry Darya?"

"It appears I don't have a choice."

"I do not understand. I always hear American women do as they please, whenever they please." Tessa sighed but remained quiet as Shirin continued. "I think he is a good man, Miss Melanie. He helps the children. The other men ask him many questions." She took a deep breath before speaking again. "Do you want this?"

Tessa wanted to avoid Bonnie's uptight opinions by focusing on the teen. "No. But I need Darya to take us back. Take you back so Miss Finley can make sure you get to America. Right, Miss Finley?"

With an arched eyebrow and thinning lips, Bonnie bared her teeth. "It's what I live for."

The response reminded her a great deal of Ursula from The Little Mermaid movie.

Shirin lowered her voice and sounded respectful as she commented, "I am very grateful, Miss Finley." She pointed at the others. "We are grateful."

Bonnie put her hands on her hips. "I'm begging you to stop this, Tessa." For once, her voice held genuine concern. "He's smitten with you now, while you're young, pretty, and able to have children." She pointed at the women working on Tessa. "Look at them. Not one has a mouth full of teeth. Their skin resembles dried apples. I can't believe you want this. Darya will tire of you as soon as this rooftop hell makes an old woman out of you. For all we know, these women are younger than you. Chew on that. If you marry him, he'll tire of you anyway and just set you aside for a younger version. Seduce him, promise him the moon, and be done with it."

The Kyrgyz women pulled Tessa to her feet and shooed the girls outside, along with Bonnie. The clothes tinkled as they closed the door behind the children. When they whirled around, it sounded like blurs of music filling the yurt. They pointed at her clothes and shook their heads in disapproval.

~~~

Darya inhaled the smell of lamb cooking on the stove in the khan's yurt. His wife stirred the pot while giving orders to her husband to carry the food outside to the night fires burning in the summer camp. Makeshift tables were being set up for the big night. It was unusual to celebrate a wedding this late in the season and at night, but the khan listened to Darya out of respect.

"You bring these Americans here. Trouble will follow." The khan smoked opium to ease the pain in his back. It had been a hard life. He'd said many times he'd given up hope of having medical help for such things.

"The Taliban killed your sister's husband. They would have killed the children and made the women beg for death. This is not our way. Massoud brought this trouble to our land."

The khan puffed on his pipe. "You kidnapped these people."

"The Taliban were close. I waited. The Americans did not come for them or for the helicopter. We had to leave. The Taliban would have come back with more men and more guns. They would have taken our animals and supplies and killed us."

"I should say these people are now under my protection. You say you want to take this American woman for your wife."

"I can protect her."

"It is good for you to not be alone. Too long you grieve."

Darya waited before speaking. "I can pay you ninety sheep for the woman."

"One hundred ten sheep plus one camel." The khan squinted and pointed his pipe toward the grazing animals outside the open door.

"One hundred sheep and two horses," Darya countered. "She is not worth more. The woman is headstrong. My life will be hard for some time."

The khan grinned so big Darya could see his bottom front teeth were missing. "Agreed." He gave a satisfied wink. "And the children? What of them? We will make them one of us. It will be good."
~~~

Darya shook his head vehemently. "They would die. The air is too thin for them where we live. Even here they struggle. I must take them back with the government woman. If we do not, it could be trouble for us."

"But she is strong. Take her as a helper for your wife."

"They do not get along."

The khan moaned with understanding. "Will there be a reward?"

"I will ask for a road." Darya knew this would mean everything to the Kyrgyz. The khan dreamed of a car. "This would please the khan?" Darya already knew the answer. The elder's favorite topic involved retelling the story about his trip to Mecca. His second favorite involved a road and a car. The khan claimed to understand the ways of the world. The Kyrgyz numbered a little over a thousand. Without medical care, his people would not last another twenty years. Their way of life grew more endangered each day they remained on the rooftop of the world.

"And will your wife want to return to Kabul with the government woman?"

"I hope to make my wife very happy under the yak skins."

The old khan laughed, something he did on rare occasions. After losing six children to the harsh life at the top of the world, little remained to make a man happy. "I will take your sheep and horses. Tonight, we celebrate, since you are in such a hurry to have a wife. Bride kidnapping is old-fashioned, even for us."

Darya shrugged. "I think maybe it is something we should consider in the future." He chuckled. "I go now to prepare myself for my new wife."

"Some of the women have put your yurt in order. It is their gift. Our young girls will be sad they cannot have you."

Darya stood. "Thank you, my Khan."

He squinted through the opium smoke at Darya with seriousness in his voice. "Will you stay in Kabul with the woman?" When Darya did not answer, the khan struggled to his feet. "You are of two worlds, Darya. Sooner or later, you will leave us."

"This is my home."

"Yes. But you are an American."

CHAPTER 16

From their hidden position, Chase and Zoric observed the camp of Massoud. Five men sat around a fire with a sixth patrolling the perimeter. Several parked Jeeps with a good twenty years on them, formed arc on the edge of camp. An argument between the men, with exaggerated hand movements followed by a great deal of posturing caused a satisfied grin on Chase's face.

"These guys are in a twist about something." Chase handed off the binoculars to Zoric. "I can't understand what they're saying. Talking too fast."

"We're a little too high up to get much." Zoric adjusted the binoculars.

Chase frowned. "At least we know Tessa and the kids aren't with them. Any sign of the Finley woman?" He sat up and checked his weapons. By slipping on his night vision goggles, he hoped to get a better idea of what lurked in the dark.

Zoric lowered the glasses then lifted them again. "No. But that Kyrgyz who brought in the soldier is down there.

He's not in good shape." He handed the binoculars back to Chase.

"Any sign of Massoud?" Chase scanned the area but saw no sign of the man at first. "Where are you?" He lowered them to take up his rifle.

"I thought we were to bring him in." Zoric readied his rifle scope.

"Accidents happen," Chase spoke through clenched teeth. "But I would like to know for myself what those guys wanted to accomplish before the Kyrgyz ran them off. How did Massoud know about the kids being picked up? Did they know a state department person would be there? A ransom deal or something more?"

"Then what?"

Chase caressed his weapon as he lifted the scope to his eye. "Then we kill him. Slow. One inch at a time. Give him a little taste of American justice for the boys he took down in the chopper."

The voices of the Taliban grew quiet as someone came to stand on the edge of the camp. A match flared then a curl of smoke from a cigarette. The man remained in the shadows.

"I see him," Chase spoke up before Zoric could alert him. "Come out, you worthless bag of yak dung. Show your miserable face."

~~~

"Stop your arguing like a bunch of women," the voice from the darkness called out. "Do you want someone to hear you? The Americans are everywhere searching for us." The men silenced. If Special Forces were on their trail, it would be a death sentence. No one could exact revenge like the ghost men of the American military.

Massoud strolled over to the Kyrgyz tribesman, careful not to come out in the open. The man rested on his knees with his hands tied behind his back. His naked torso revealed cigarette burns placed in no particular pattern across his chest. Massoud cocked his head to inspect him with his one good eye. Taking one last puff off his cigarette, he dropped it then ground out the light with the toe of his leather boot.

With one hand, he caught hold of the tribesman's black hair and yanked back his head. It didn't take much scrutiny to know the man appeared more Asian than the Taliban throughout Afghanistan. Around the Kyrgyz's slanted eyes were bruises. The left cheekbone swelled with a nasty laceration. Without medical treatment, it would be a matter of time before infection set in.
~~~

"This is your last chance. Tell me which way they are headed and I'll end this right now. If not then, in the morning, my men will do it their way. Trust me when I say my way is much better."

The Kyrgyz man stared straight ahead, drool seeping out of his mouth. He recited something from the Koran. Massoud stormed off toward one of the Jeeps.

"Now or never, Chase." Zoric took a deep breath as his finger slipped over the trigger.

"I'll take two on the right then the Jeep. You take the other three." Chase inhaled then exhaled as slowly as his body permitted. "Now."

The first two men fell over into the fire causing the remaining four to jump up in panic. Massoud's retreat appeared to accelerate as he ran then slid into the driver's seat of the open Jeep. Chase and Zoric both made their kill shots of the Taliban around the fire. The sound of the engine lifted into the air as it backed farther into the darkness.

Chase let off a series of shots. Each one sounded like it ricocheted off the front end of the vehicle. The Jeep careened out of control then flipped over, throwing Massoud out into the night.

Chase and Zoric picked their way down the hillside between boulders and over loose rock which made them lose their footing. Once on the ground they waited as they scanned the area with their night vision goggles. With their weapons raised they searched the perimeter then worked their way in until Chase split off and ran into the darkness for Massoud.

A small explosion under the back end of the Jeep threw him to the ground just as he reached it. He dropped his rifle, a bullet zipping by his ear just as the sound of a startled horse caught his attention. The flash of fire from the explosion blinded him momentarily. Throwing off the night goggles, he saw Massoud race off on the back of a horse. Chase managed to pull his Glock from inside his clothing. He rapid-fired into the darkness, although it could be a waste of ammunition and would more likely hit the horse than Massoud.

With a new kind of urgency, he replaced the goggles, grabbed the rifle, and headed out into the darkness at a dead run. After trailing Massoud for fifteen minutes, he turned back toward the camp. He could no longer keep up with a running horse and lost the trail.

After Chase returned to camp, he watched as Zoric released the tribesman who now sat Indian style on the ground. Clothes were removed from one of the dead men for him. After some first aid, the Kyrgyz man accepted some food and water. Zoric moved on to go through the belongings of the Taliban.

"Anything?"

Zoric shook his head.

Chase kicked dirt onto the dying embers of the fire. Soon the darkness closed around them. They took any weapons, ammo, and food they found and they piled it in the back of the remaining Jeep. Chase jumped in but found the key missing, so he hotwired the vehicle in seconds and he concealed it in a pile of dead brush.

Together, Zoric and Chase helped the tribesman to a covered area near the Jeep where they could spend the remainder of the night. With one last trip back to the camp, the two men lined up the dead Taliban side by side with their arms crossed over their chests. An artist when he wasn't torturing terrorists, Zoric drew a helicopter in the dirt next to them then a line through it. At the feet of each dead man, he drew a laughing skull.

"You're morbid, you know that?" Chase growled. "They used to say those things about Salvador Dali and Goya."

"Are you sure you want to keep that kind of company?" Chase nudged his friend toward the darkness where the tribesman waited.

"I am redeeming myself by painting angels now." They sat down on each side of the Kyrgyz man.

"Some of those angels are a little hellish, too."

"Except for one."

"Except for one," Chase repeated, pulling up the image of Tessa.

Zoric had all but abandoned his painting until he met Tessa Scott. Something about her drove him to create again. The paintings were large, violent, and told a story. They involved demonic forces of the world battling for the good of mankind. A warrior angel always resembled the Grass Valley woman. It irritated Chase that his image appeared in some of the art. The warrior angel always seemed to be saving the soldier, not the other way around. Whatever the reasons for the Serbian to return to his work, the art critics loved to hate him. But the art world couldn't get enough of them. Like his work, Zoric stayed elusive and indifferent to the world around him.

Chase spoke to the Kyrgyz tribesman in his own tongue. "What is your name?"

"Abdul." He stared straight ahead as if half-expecting to be tortured again. "My horse?"

"Massoud took it. What did they want?" He turned his eyes toward the camp of dead bodies.

The tribesman spit some blood then touched his lips to remove a drip. "To know where we took the women and children."

"Did you tell them anything?" Chase continued. The Kyrgyz frowned at him with a smoldering rage. "Stupid question. Do they want them for ransom or just to get their pride back?"

The man stretched out his legs then pulled them back up and circled his knees with his arms. "To kill us. We shame them. I hear they want the government woman because she knows a secret."

Chase translated for Zoric who ran his hand over his face in concern. "Do you know what the secret is?"

Abdul shook his head then blinked as if saying no. He waited a few seconds to speak, touching the cut on his cheek. "They do not want her to leave alive. The blue-eyed woman."

"Yes?"

"She know secret, too. Not sure if little girls know. Kyrgyz take supplies to camp in Wakhan Valley on south side of mountains. Animals have plenty of food for season. Women and children safe there. Will move soon for rest of season. One more trade trip before winter."

Chase cocked his head with suspicion. "Anyone hurt?"

The tribesman stared at Chase for a few seconds before answering. "Blue eyes hurt." He touched his head. "Here, I think."

An uncontrollable feeling of panic gripped Chase as he translated for Zoric then asked the tribesman. "Was she shot?"

Abdul's forehead creased. "Covered with Taliban blood."

Chase jumped to his feet as if he'd sprouted springs. He ran his hand across his face then stared out into the darkness. "I'm going to torture Massoud a hundred different ways before I kill him." Several different scenarios raced through his mind as he envisioned Tessa Scott confronting Taliban monsters. He stared down at Abdul to try and calm himself. "So it wasn't her blood."

"She fighter." His lips turned up in amusement. "Hurt Kyrgyz with knee." Abdul pointed to his knee and made a jabbing motion. "Stand up to us. Afraid but brave."

A wave of relief washed over Chase as he sat back down. "Why did you take them?"

"Taliban might come back when we leave. We need children." He continued to look amused. "My friend need wife. He like blue eyes. Maybe she is already wife."

Zoric frowned. "This keeps getting better and better. The woman is either a threat to national security or our best hope in defeating the enemy." When Chase raised his head toward the sky, Zoric asked. "Are you praying?"

~~~

Massoud hunkered down in a cave after riding for several hours, unsure if his injuries were severe. He hurt all over, even his head. After bringing the horse inside with him, he piled some rocks up, blocking the entrance the best he could to keep the animal from wandering out if he fell asleep. After patting himself down, he decided nothing appeared to be broken. Relief washed over him as he leaned against the wall of the cave. The cold kept him from feeling more pain than he did. After a few hours of rest, he could escape to places where he would be welcomed and nursed back to health. The scrapes and bruises would heal, provided he kept them clean. For now, he needed to stay hidden from the ghost warriors. How had they managed to find their camp? Were they overheard during their conversations about the government woman? Could the men who attacked understand Pashto?
~~~

CHAPTER 17

The low light in the small yurt came from the cooking fire in the center of the room. Twin curls of smoke lifted up to the smoke hole in the center of the ceiling. The warmth inside contrasted with the air temperature outside that dipped low enough to see your breath.

Each time she pushed herself to remember life in the States with a husband and children, it was always replaced with the image of a man dragging Shirin screaming for help. The memory of a knife in hand, how it felt before she rammed it into the man's neck, kept pushing aside the faces of those she must love. The sound of a man wounded by her gunshot, mixed with the image of a hysterical Bonnie Finley, all came together to prevent her from forgiving herself. Without those actions where would they be today?

Her thoughts turned to the last few hours. The Kyrgyz people didn't show a great deal of joy. The dances they performed would never catch on in other parts of the world, considering they consisted of moving around in slow motion with a slight wave of the hands, but Tessa thought them beautiful nonetheless. Their voices sounded soft on the breezes sweeping down from the jagged peaks of the Pamir Mountains. The sight of all the orphan girls now dressed in red like their Kyrgyz hostesses gave Tessa something to dwell on with fondness. Bonnie, on the other hand, remained in the same clothes she'd worn for days. How long had it been? She couldn't even remember.

What she did know concerned the man who'd chased away the Taliban and saved them from a horrible death. It struck her for the first time how rugged and handsome he could be in his clean black clothes, wide embroidered belt, and pill-box style hat. He'd even danced with the men at one point. Not once did he steal a glance at her in her beautiful red dress and white head dressing. No declaration of love or flowery words to make her swoon. Nothing to reassure her everything would be okay and or that he planned to make her happy beyond reason. It was not the Kyrgyz way.

Now, here she stood, alone in the marriage yurt which would be her home unless she could escape. But where would she go? Every direction showed no detail to use as a compass toward Kabul. Only the sun could provide those details. Even then, without horses, supplies, and protection, it would be impossible to run with little girls.

The thick rug door opened. Darya stood there a few seconds, searching her out before letting the door fall behind him. She noticed he had to duck his head a little to keep from hitting it on the top of the door frame. His height, although average in America, remained remarkable here. Several steps brought Darya near to the fire where he stopped.

Tessa eased against the wall, reaching back to flatten her hands against the canvas-like material. She wondered if snow leopards watched their prey in the same way

Darya watched her. Moving to the side, deeper into darkness, gave her a sense of becoming invisible.

"Come." His words sounded more like a request than a command. She froze in place.

Darya removed his hat then tossed it on the stack of yak hides. The belt came off next and it, too, landed on the bedding. She remained silent as the man who considered himself her husband put his hands on his hips as his legs parted in an irritated stance.

"Come." This time his voice deepened and sounded more like a command. When Tessa remained rooted in the dark recesses of the room, Darya lunged forward and caught hold of her arm, pulling her toward the light of the stove. "I want to see you. Not hurt Tessa."

Tessa shuddered with fear. She stared down at her feet. Somewhere she'd read if you're ever kidnapped, don't make eye contact. Be submissive. Don't challenge them. It all seemed a wise thing to do at this moment.

He reached out and touched her head covering, causing her to flinch away. His hand paused in midair. "I want to remove your covering."

Tessa stood still as he used both his hands to remove the long white scarf from her head. He laid it on a nearby table then returned to her side. This time, he stepped into her personal space. At her step back, he reached out and took both her arms. Tessa sucked in her breath and lifted her gaze to meet his.

"Tes-sa." Darya's eyes roamed her face. "You are beautiful wife."

Without knowing why, Tessa couldn't prevent the corners of her mouth turning up in a moment of relief. "Thank you, Darya. You are beautiful as well." He chuckled.

"Talk first or…"

"Talk. Definitely talk." Her words were hurried. She hoped he understood.

"Tea?"

Tessa moved toward the table. She placed her hand on his arm after he came up beside her. "Let me. Please. You sit." At least, off his feet, he wouldn't be leading her to the bed piled with yak skins.

After she fixed the tea and joined Darya on the rug, they sipped in silence. Her hands shook a little and a few drops splashed on her hands, burning her skin. She sucked in her breath at the pain. He relieved her of the cup she grasped like a holy chalice.

He stood and retrieved a small jar the size of a shot glass from a saddlebag. He dipped two fingers inside a red-colored gel then took her hand. With the utmost care, he massaged the gel into her palm and between her fingers, over and over until it disappeared. The burning evaporated and her skin felt soothed once more. She held up her hand to examine then touched it to her face.

"Better?" he asked as he set the jar aside.

"Yes. Thank you, Darya." She wondered if her voice sounded submissive and appreciative enough.

"Tessa have husband in America?" He tilted his head, his forehead pinched as if trying to understand.

"Yes."

"Why he let you come here? Kyrgyz men do not let their women go about on their own. Stupid."

Tessa couldn't agree more at this point. "Women in America don't like to be told what to do by a man."

He blinked several times as his forehead creased in what may have been confusion. "Do you miss this husband?"

Tessa turned her head to stare at the embers in the stove. "I. I don't know. I can't remember much about him."

Darya touched the back of her head. She flinched, still feeling a little pain where she'd hit it. "This make you forget husband, who you are, and the place you left."

His hand on her head somehow gave her comfort. "I guess so. I'm starting to remember a few things. I have children."

Darya withdrew his hand from her head. "I had son three years ago. Would be size of Arzo. He died."

Something inside Tessa snapped and she laid a hand on his arm. Pain showed in his voice and face. "And his mother?"

Darya turned an icy stare into the fire. "I killed her." Tessa snatched her hand back, catching her breath.

Darya sat like a statue as he spoke. "I run away. These people take me in and I marry a girl very young. Seventeen, maybe. Too young for man like me. I…" Darya turned his attention to Tessa and continued to speak in Pashto. "I loved her. Life hard here. We were happy about a child. I wanted to take her to Kabul where there were doctors, but she afraid they would find me. She died when my son born and he died two days later. My fault."

Tessa reached around him and held tight. "I'm sorry, Darya."

"I thought when I saw you…" Darya stopped and pushed her back and let his eyes trail across her face and hair. "You are older. Not have children. We could live in another place, not so high. We keep Arzo for our child."

"Arzo needs to go back to Kabul. This is no life for her. The other girls want to go to school. You must take them, Darya."

"No." He stood up and carried the cups to the table.

Tessa stood as well, but it felt awkward in long clothes. She thought about threats then considered a tantrum, but guessed men like Darya had a way of dealing with discipline issues like every other harsh thing in life.

"Who were you running from, Darya?" Tessa wanted to keep the conversation going to put off the marriage bed as long as possible.

"You like to talk." Darya's eyebrows lifted as he untucked his shirt and moved toward Tessa. She backed up. "It will be good to have someone to talk to again." He pulled his black shirt over his head, revealing a well- muscled chest. Two scars trailed at an angle from his shoulder to his waist. They drew her eyes in curiosity. She hadn't noticed them when he'd grabbed her in the water. Something else had caught her attention on that day.

Like a snake striking at a victim, Darya reached out and captured Tessa in his arms. "Stand still while I help you out of this."

With a shove, Tessa jumped away to escape, but he easily pulled her back by catching her hand. "I will not be your wife. You can force yourself on me all you want…"

"Thank you." He switched to English. "I would much rather you participate with your free will."

Then it dawned on her Darya spoke with very little broken English. She stared at him as he took his time undoing the clasps on the front of her shirt. "Darya?"

He stopped. His stare traveled over her face as he reached the top of her braids then slid his hands down to the tips where they rested above Tessa's breasts. "Yes, Tes-sa?" His next movement tugged her braids pulling her against his chest.

"Who are you?"

Darya lowered his mouth to her neck and kissed her firmly. "I used to be American military intelligence. Now I'm your husband."

This time when Tessa shoved him, she added an elbow to his side, making him cringe. "Get away from me," she fumed.

He stood with his feet apart, his arms crossed on his chest. Tessa wondered for a split second if he joked about her predicament, but signs of amusement didn't register on his face. The emotion on his face continued to be unreadable. "I'm Kyrgyz now. This is my home. You don't remember your home, so I give you mine."

"Stop with the humble mountain tribesman routine. I'm not buying it. To think I fell for that story you told about a wife and child." Tessa watched as the mask of apathy morphed into anger.

"That was true. I became so disillusioned with this war, one step forward and three steps back. People dying on all sides and for what? When told I had to shoot a kid if I suspected he was wired with explosives…You cannot change a tribal society. I'd had enough. So, one day I didn't go back. I came here to my mother's people." He glared at Tessa who stood rigid.

"Tell me the truth. All of it, Darya." Her voice softened in hopes he'd reveal more of his character. She took a step toward him and he dropped his arms.

"My mother was Kyrgyz. My father Russian. He, too, ran away seeing the war going nowhere. I was born here among these people. But my father wanted a better life for my mother and me so, when I turned seven, he took us across the mountains. He found an American CIA agent. With his help, we made it to America. It came with a price, of course. For our citizenship, my father worked for the CIA.

Tessa moved closer. She stood less than two feet away. The anger drained from his face and it became unreadable again, his features classic Asian, but she could see now the Russian influence. The broad shoulders, the height, and the lips that appeared a little thicker than the other Kyrgyz now made sense.

"Did you ever come back here after you became an American?" Tessa's voice turned to a whisper. "You seem more Kyrgyz than…"

"American?" he interjected. "My mother grieved for this harsh place. She always talked about the beautiful land and mountains. I'm glad my father didn't take us to Russia. It is tradition with the Kyrgyz for the bride to go to the husband's family." His eyes searched her face inch by inch, focusing on minute details. "We lived on a ranch in Montana. My father bought sheep to please my mother." He smirked. "He even found an old yak from a bankrupt zoo in Canada. It made her cry."

Tessa also felt amused at the story. "She raised you like a good Kyrgyz."

Darya stepped closer, a breath away from her. "Yes. I hated it. I wanted to wear cowboy boots, rope calves, and play football. But she never let me forget I was also a Kyrgyz. I never spoke English at home. Pashto and Russian only. My parents said I needed to work hard because I would help America and this place someday."

"Your father continued to work for the CIA?"

"Yes. Because of his service, the government made sure I got into West Point. They had plans for me. My parents died in a plane crash coming to my graduation."

Tessa stepped into him, wrapping her arms around him. His chest felt warm against her body as did his shoulder against her cheek. "Such sadness in your life."

Darya pushed her back. "No. My parents gave me a path back to this place. When I couldn't keep going, these people saved me. My wife gave me something I never had. Do not be sad for me. I am not." His voice grew stronger.

"Why do you want me for your wife? You don't even know me." Tessa couldn't decide if she wanted flowery words or the truth.

The glowing embers of light faded around them. "I don't need to know you. We have a lot of time up here." His accent came and went. "My English is rusty. Sorry."

His confession warmed her heart. "I love it."

Darya's gaze narrowed to slits and his mouth widened in a grin. "I saw you and first thought you were trouble. Then the little girls." He paused, his fingers touching her cheek. "They like you. You protect them. Want a better life for them. Good qualities." He let his stroke trail down her throat. "I decided I wanted you. That is how it works up here."

"Darya." Tessa reached for his hand on her throat. "You are an American. I am an American. This is not the way to win me."

He smirked as his hand slipped up to her hair and pushed at a rebellious curl. "I don't need to win you. I already have you." He captured her mouth with his. His kiss, hard and powerful, unleashed his passion, which had been restrained for too long. Tessa sank her teeth into his lip with a vicious bite. Darya jerked free to rub the back of his hand over his mouth.

Tessa backed away. "I'll make a deal with you." Her fingers touched her lips, already puffy from the press of his mouth.

"Kyrgyz men don't make deals with their brides." He grabbed her by the arm but didn't pull her back. "I paid one hundred sheep and two horses for you. The khan granted me this."

"Okay. Okay." Darya, although raised in the States, was about as mom and apple pie as Osama bin Laden.

"How about this." Darya looked amused, tugging on her arm. "You take us back to Kabul. I help Bonnie get the girls on a plane to America so they can go to school. Then I come back here with you."

Darya stopped his physical domination. "You'll stay here with me?"

"Only if I get those girls back safe and sound to Kabul. But until then, this"—Tessa waved a hand between herself and Darya—"this is not going to happen. When our business is completed, I'll…" She took a big breath. "I'll be your wife in every way, Darya. I want those girls to have a chance. Please."

Darya scooped her up in his arms and carried her to the yak-skin bed. He dropped her and she scampered to the other side. He grabbed her by the foot and dragged her back. "Get all these clothes off. I know you are wearing other things under them. By morning, you'll be burning up." Before she could kick him, Darya pulled off her shoes and threw them across the room. In one swift move, he pulled the long red shirt over her head. His eyes caressed every part of her in the delicate chemise she wore underneath.

"Now the skirt."

Tessa sat paralyzed under his penetrating gawking. When she didn't move, he proceeded to remove the skirt. She wore black leggings, but Darya didn't try to remove them. He reached out and appeared to take pleasure in stroking the texture back and forth.

"It's a deal." Darya folded back the yak skin and motioned for her to get under. The heat inside the yurt cooled as the fire died. "I'll take the girls back and you will then be my wife."

"Really?" She climbed under the covers. "No funny stuff from you. Understand?"

Darya stripped off the rest of his clothes then got under the covers, too, much to Tessa's dismay. She scooted away, but he pulled her back to rest in the crook of his arm. "I'll behave but, I will"—he rolled her to face him and buried his lips in her neck—"make you change your mind."

She squirmed away, but this seemed to excite an already out-of-control situation. "Don't count on it," she fumed. Releasing her, he propped himself up on his elbow and gazed down into her face. Shivers raced up her spine along with fading willpower. What would be so bad about letting this man make love to her?

"Is there anyone else searching for you I should be concerned about, Tes-sa?"

"Like who?" Tessa sucked in her breath at the touch of his naked skin against hers. His hand trailed down her side and hip.

"CIA. I heard Bonnie talking about you being CIA. They want me. I am not their favorite person. I've caused a lot of trouble for them."

Tessa let herself drown as she gazed upon his face that was as mysterious and dangerous as Central Asia itself. It would be such a simple thing to cave to her longing, to enjoy being safe and loved. Why couldn't she remember her husband? What about the man who kept whispering the words, *I will always come for you*?

"No one is coming for me. I don't work for the CIA. I work for someone named Enigma."

"Who is Enigma?" Darya moved his hand to Tessa's back. He nuzzled her cheek and corner of her mouth.

"I have no idea." Resistance melted away as she chose to surrender to the sensations of Darya's touch. She wanted to keep the conversation going, but his mouth pressed passionately against hers and silenced further talk.

<h1 style="text-align:center">CHAPTER 18</h1>

Darya stood in the open doorway of his yurt watching the activity in the summer camp. He held a cup of steaming tea in one hand while propping the other against the doorframe. The morning grew late. Being a newlywed had caused him to sleep later than usual. Having a beautiful woman in his bed could force a man to forget loneliness. A fellow Kyrgyz man walked by holding a cell phone about the time Tessa came up behind him. He felt her arms go around his waist. He turned his head enough to kiss her temple and smile. Darya yelled for his friend to use his cell phone camera to take their picture.

"What's he doing?" Tessa asked as Darya pulled her forward to his side. He rested his chin on the top of her head. The cell phone camera clicked.

"Wedding picture." He grinned. "We don't have phone reception up here. Cell phones are used for games or taking pictures. Kyrgyz love their cell phones. We carry solar batteries to charge lots of things. We trade for them. A cell phone costs one sheep. A yak can cost ten sheep. A wife"—he frowned down at her in mock contempt— "can go for one hundred sheep. I paid more for you."

Tessa eased back behind him. "I'd say you got a bargain because I'm worth twice that."

Darya spotted Bonnie Finley staring at him with disgust. He narrowed his eyes at her, but continued to speak to Tessa as she stared up at him. "We will soon see, Tessa. It would be a shame to ask for a refund." Tessa landed a playful jab in his side causing him to spill his tea. He chuckled as he turned his attention back to Bonnie who watched them. Turning to go back inside the yurt, he made a show of jerking the rug door closed. As Tessa walked back to the fire, Darya grabbed her up and tossed her on the bed.

"Not good to have bare feet here." He ran his hands down her ankles and feet.

"Stop it." She jerked away. "I'm ticklish."

Darya leaned in close to her face. "Good." He ran his fingers up and down the bottom of her feet. Tessa squealed with laughter, losing her breath at times as she fought to kick free. He stopped when she closed her eyes and moaned his name. Tessa fell back on the bed as she took a deep breath. He climbed on top of her kissing her on every available bare spot he could find.

"That's not fair," she complained, pushing him aside. "You weakened me on purpose so I couldn't resist."

"Maybe I should start with tickling tonight." He put his hands behind his head, grinning. "Talk. Talk. Talk. You wanted to talk all night instead of…"

"Not true," Tessa said, rolling to rest her head against his chest. "I want to know you better before we—you know."

"I think we had a good start last night." Darya brought one hand down to stroke the side of her face. "Someday you will love me. I promise."

"You want me even knowing what I did?"

"Tessa." He sat up and pushed her down so he could level a hard glare. "All I want is for you to kiss me like I'm the only one in the world." He pulled her up into his arms. "I will protect you from anyone who tries to harm you. There is me and you now. No one else. If you want me to take the girls back, I will. But I keep you."

"No," she whispered as her lips crushed against his mouth. "We keep each other."

Darya pushed her away then brought her the boots and socks she'd worn the night before. He took great care to help her into them when she swung her legs over the side of their bed. Sitting down beside her, Darya slipped an arm around her shoulders and pulled her into him.

Tessa drank in the power of his magnetic Asian face and how it affected her common sense. Part of her still remained breathless. Even though they had spent hours talking the night before, Darya would not be put off exploring the possibilities of her flesh. So far, he held to his promise of not consummating their marriage until the girls were returned to Kabul. Part of her wished he hadn't made the promise.

"Shouldn't we go out to check on the girls?"

"Can't let the others think I am an unfit husband who can't perform his duties to his wife." His expression grew wicked as Tessa shoved him, collapsing him on the bed. "Besides, the government woman stared like an angry yak at me when you stood for a picture. She doesn't like Kyrgyz."

"Darya, I need to tell you something." Tessa watched him sit up then pushed her braids to her back. "It's about Bonnie and what she's done."

Tessa told as much of the story as she could without having to revisit killing the Taliban, but it became part of the story anyway. When she gave an involuntary shudder, Darya drew her close into his arms. "She's the reason we are in such trouble. I'm afraid they'll still come after us. I'm frightened, Darya. The sooner we leave, the safer your people will be."

Darya remained silent as he rested his cheek against Tessa's hair which curled out of its confining braids. "I will talk to the khan. I still own a couple of horses and donkeys. If…"

Shocked, Tessa grabbed his hand. "Did you give the khan your entire fortune for me, Darya?" She gasped, pressing her hands to each side of his face.

"Yes. Of course." Darya hopped off the bed and pulled her after him. "But I had to keep a few horses for us. I will trade for what we need later. Don't worry." He patted her cheek with one leathery hand. "I will be able to care for you. We don't need much up here."

"Darya," she whispered. "You should not have given so much."

He grew stern faced. "Why? Because you plan to trick me once we are in Kabul and run away to America?"

She swallowed hard. "You could come with me, Darya."

"No." It sounded final. No need to talk about something so ridiculous at this point. "You and I have a deal. Are you breaking it?"

With crossed fingers, Tessa shook her head. "A deal is a deal."

Darya cupped her chin, forcing her eyes up to meet his. "I bought you. I saved you from Taliban. I take girls back like I promised. I keep my promise. Do you?"

Tessa couldn't resist searching the face of the man she'd thrown her fate to. "Yes. I, too, will keep my promise."

Darya's hand squeezed her chin. "You're a terrible liar, Tessa." He released her and walked out.

You're a terrible liar, Tessa. I hope the enemy never captures you for interrogation.

Those words rambled in her head. Who said them?

Had she made a habit of lying?

~~~

The Jeep bounced along the open plain. The two Americans and Abdul, the Kyrgyz tribesman, made their own road as the land opened up. Some stretches were easy to navigate and others places they would have been better if they'd been on foot. Their progress slowed to a crawl at times.

Massoud remained hidden. With any luck, he'd died from injuries, but Chase doubted it. "I'm hoping I shot the SOB and he's lying in some hole bleeding to death."

Zoric drove with caution over the landscape. "The man has nine lives."

"I'd say he has one left. I intend to take it," Chase yelled above the whine of the engine. Several times it stopped as if no amount of coaxing could fix the problem. After reconnecting the coil wire, they were on their way again. Two five-gallon cans of gas were tied onto the back bumper.

Abdul held on for dear life in the backseat. He claimed to feel better, but cried out at the constant jarring several times. Chase glanced back at him in concern, but the Kyrgyz always showed perseverance with a stiff body posture. He even gave a thumbs-up.

The three men took a break to refuel at a narrow stream near one solitary tree on the steppe. Chase hoped they would have enough to make it to the camp where Tessa might be hiding. Abdul warned them the Kyrgyz didn't like to be surprised with a visit.
~~~

They needed to approach with respect.

Chase took in the desolate plain resembling infinity of nothing. He wondered how these remarkable people could survive such harsh environment. Tough as nails, he guessed. The few Kyrgyz he'd run across were never gregarious, but thought nothing of sticking their hand in your pockets to see what kind of trinkets or tools you might be carrying. He wondered if he'd ever seen one show amusement and realized he hadn't. Abdul fit the stereotype. Chase wondered if the reserved manner hid their intentions.

His thoughts raced to Tessa as they'd done for days now. He needed to know about her safety. These Kyrgyz made no bones about their hatred for the Taliban. Their intervention in the small village proved they didn't fear them. When asked why, Abdul shrugged. Chase continued to pepper the man with questions without success.

"Give it up, Chase," Zoric demanded. "He knows nothing. This man's job was to return the American soldier. The others went on without him. He has no idea what shape the children or Tessa are in."

Chase narrowed his glare at the Kyrgyz as Zoric spoke, knowing the words were true. "We are to rendezvous with the Black Hawks in four days to take everyone back to Kabul. Let's get moving." Chase attempted once again to engage Abdul. "How much farther?"

"Tonight." A man of few words, but at least this good news helped him hope he'd find Tessa unharmed.

The three made good time across the steppe. Mountains loomed like angry gods frowning down on potential victims who refused to prepare for the harsh life ahead of them. The land now rose up sharply, revealing more rocks than grass. Chase felt overwhelmed with the immensity of the emptiness in this unforgiving land. The beauty of it overshadowed the fear lurking inside him. He glared up at the majestic peaks and grazing lands sneaking up to the base as if the rawness should be revered.

"A good place to live." Abdul broke the silence for his new friends who stared awestruck at his home. They'd made good time; the Jeep had not broken down in several hours, the gas mileage was decent, and the passageway had been well-traveled by horses, yaks, donkeys, and sheep for decades.

They hadn't expected to reach Abdul's camp until after dark. Now, the Jeep idled, echoing off the peaks which offered shelter. The Kyrgyz moved their herds into an area of the canyon where they would be protected from predators and the cold wind dropping below freezing even this time of year.

"I think this is moving day, Abdul." Zoric turned off the engine to save gas before opening the door. He stood up on the edge of the frame, propping himself over the top of the door. Bringing the binoculars up he continued to speak. "Will they set up yurts for the night?"

Abdul got out of the Jeep and walked toward his kinsmen.

"I think he said they'd have a few covered areas for the women and children. This narrow pass will protect them from cold mountain winds." Chase walked around the front of the Jeep, watching the Kyrgyz strode off toward his people. "Is she there?"

Zoric tossed him the glasses. "Hard to say. The women are covered head to toe in red."

Chase took the binoculars. "Abdul is talking to someone. I think maybe he likes this pile of junk we're driving. Grinning ear to ear. Maybe we've got a negotiation point." Chase got back inside. "Come on. Abdul is waving us in."

The Kyrgyz women huddled behind the men, sneaking excited peeks over their shoulders. The sound of bleating sheep and large brass bells on yaks burdened with the tasks of moving entire households greeted Zoric and Chase as they pulled up a few feet from Abdul and a man who appeared to be in charge. Chase noticed a couple of others taking pictures of the Jeep with their cell phones.

"This is the khan." Abdul made the introductions then stood straight and silent.

Chase addressed the man in charge with respect. "Forgive us for intruding on your camp. We have come a long way."

The khan walked past them to the Jeep. He ran his hand along the front bumper then the rusty hood. Peering in the window, his face beamed with satisfaction. In seconds he had jerked the driver side door open and slid inside behind the wheel. He grasped the steering wheel as if manhandling an ill-tempered Bactrian camel. Jumping back out of the vehicle, he evaluated every inch as if were horse flesh. Upon completion of the inspection, the khan rubbed the thin beard on his chin as he returned to confront the two Americans.

"Abdul has told me how you saved him from Massoud. We are grateful." The khan's hand spread out toward his people then came to rest on his heart. "His mother and I are grateful."

Chase raised his chin in acceptance, but did not speak. He wanted to make sure he understood every word. His Pashto didn't get enough practice of late.

"You will eat and drink tea with us tonight. This land is not safe for you."

"We are searching for two American women and some children from a village your son"— he shifted his eyes toward Abdul— "visited a few days ago. We've come to take them back so they will not be a burden to you any longer."

"American women and children?" The khan tried to curl his pencil-thin mustache around his fingers.

So, they had entered the game of discovery and barter. It would open with ignorance of the truth followed by navigation toward a price for what was desired. Chase informed the khan of the government woman's importance and if she didn't return to Kabul soon, the big helicopters would bring soldiers to find her.

The khan grinned mischievously. "Let them come. We could use some help. Would they help us build a road?"

"No. They would frighten your animals away. We will trade for the women and children, Khan, if you will let us see them. They are of no use to you. Your men saved them and my government will be generous."

The khan continued to rub his chin and walked around the Jeep again. "I want a car."

Chase paused for effect before speaking. "Would the Khan be pleased with my car?"

The Khan threw up his hands. "We eat and drink tea first before we trade."

"I need to see the women." Chase's voice had turned cold.

The Khan frowned. "And I need a road. It appears neither of us will get what we want so fast." He turned away and motioned toward the women. "First. Food."

Zoric muttered, "He's stalling."

"I've got a bad feeling about this," Chase mumbled as he

followed Abdul to a campfire.

CHAPTER 19

It had become more than a habit, the constant evaluation of his surroundings. Every rock tumble, wind shift, or animal grunt meant change. Some changes in life were considered therapeutic, but here change could spell death. Being observant had served Chase Hunter well over the years. Never one to tempt fate, he'd managed to dodge a bullet several times after taking note of his environment, or maybe the changes in it.

The tribesmen sat around the fire. Several smoked opium. This harsh land bestowed almost no reward, offered tremendous pain, and a constant struggle to stay alive. He guessed the opium took the edge off the crippling arthritis he noticed in some of the older ones. The younger men didn't appear to partake but stared into the fire or carried on a mumbled conversation with others who sat nearby. Their stolen glances darted to him, and Zoric followed by rapid speculation and even a few grins. Those gestures concerned Chase. Trying to determine if the delay meant being detained in order to hide Tessa and the others kept him shifting his weight where he sat.

"Khan, we need to talk trade now. I want to see the women and children your men brought here." Chase snuck a glance at the other women who whispered to each other shyly. Their slightest move made light tinkling sounds lift from their clothing. Since the younger girls wore red scarves over their heads, he surmised the white head coverings denoted a married woman. The sight of small children going to them for care reinforced the thought.

The khan puffed on his pipe. Chase didn't care if the opium cloud floating around the leader's head delayed the trade. He inhaled the pungent smell, wishing it affected his expectations in a positive way.

"I first will tell you a story about the Kyrgyz."

Chase wanted to groan with impatience, but knew to show respect for the khan's words as if they moved heaven and earth. He didn't catch a lot of it. They were stories about the past, history mixed with embellishments of truth. At certain points, some of the men appeared to make light of the story, and at other times the khan would argue with them over the truth.

Whether because of Chase's rigid posture, flaring nostrils or jaw which clenched over and over, the khan decided to get down to business.

"You have the face and hands of Kyrgyz." The khan pointed to the Mongol shape of Chase's dark eyes.

"I'm a Native American. Cherokee Tribe."

The khan bobbed his head in approval. "I do not know this tribe, but it is good. And do the Americans treat your tribe as the Afghan treat the Kyrgyz?"

"The government took our land and made my people walk the Trail of Tears in winter. Many died trying to go. Some stayed and fought. My family fought and won."

The khan grunted an approval as did the other men. "I like this story. We are poor living up here on the roof of the world. But we are free to do as we please. This makes us rich." He turned toward the women for a few seconds before continuing. "But our children die young without medicine. When my father took me to Mecca, I prayed for a road to bring a doctor for us. We could have a teacher and the things men have in other parts of the world. But I think this would only bring men who want to take us away."

Chase knew it had already happened. Some of the Kyrgyz had already been relocated to public housing in Turkey. Their children played rap music, watched TV, and played video games instead of working to make life cohesive for their families.

"The khan is wise. Be careful what you wish for."

"I like your words. Now." He set his pipe down and called for one of the men. A man in his late twenties tossed the khan his phone. "We get down to business."

"Where are the American women and the children? I do not see them."

"We trade. I want your car and the gasoline to run it. I give you two horses."

"I want the women and children." Chase shook his head. "I must see them before I trade anything. I want to see for myself they are well."

"They were welcomed into our homes."

Chase looked around him. "Then where are they?" "The car for the women. I give you two horses. Long way back to Kabul."

"No deal. I don't believe you have them. I am done talking."

The khan pushed some buttons on the phone. "Here are some pictures of the American women and the children." He handed the phone to Chase.

The first picture showed little girls dressed in their drab Afghan clothing. They were dirty and appeared frightened and shy on the phone camera. The next picture of the girls, in their new red dresses, couldn't hide their transformation into happy children. Chase saw two who looked as if they were laughing. The color agreed with them.

The next picture showed Bonnie Finley sitting on the ground, eating with several. Her clothes were plain. The camera had snapped the image through firelight so it couldn't reveal her physical condition. He could tell by the frown her temperament bordered on miserable.

The last picture of a muscular man standing in the doorway of a yurt gave him pause. His black shirt had not been laced up, and his jagged dark hair must have been chopped by an ax. His features were Kyrgyz-like except he stood taller and bigger than these guys. Chase brought the camera up for closer inspection at seeing the woman standing next to him. Her gaze up into his face startled him. Wearing a long red tunic over a red skirt didn't hide her bare feet. The white head scarf slid to the back of her neck. He felt his lungs empty of air as he noticed her hands were on his side and abdomen in a personal fashion. The man stared down at her the way he often had when she wasn't watching. It bordered on worship.

"Tessa," he whispered.

Zoric grabbed the phone from Chase's hand. "Mother of God, what have they done to her?"

Chase could feel his pulse increase. What had they forced her to do? Who stood holding her in the doorway?

Zoric handed the phone back to the khan. "Who is the man with the American woman?"

The khan took the phone and pretended to see the picture for the first time. "Her husband. He saved her from the Taliban and she very grateful. I made him pay one hundred sheep and two horses for her." The khan chuckled as did the other men. "I think he would have paid more. But…" The khan shrugged. "But I have a soft spot for him. His mother was my sister, so I take the sheep and horses."

"Where are they now?" Chase made an effort to keep his voice calm as if he didn't care and understood the art of a deal.

"Gone. They leave yesterday. Take children and government woman back to Kabul."

"And what about the other woman, the one in the picture with the man who bought her? Is she with them?"

"Yes, of course. Kyrgyz men do not leave their women behind to run about. This is stupid. Besides, I think he likes being married."

"The Jeep is yours with all the gasoline. There's an extra car battery in the backseat. We'll also leave a spare tire. In return, I want two horses, supplies, and directions on how to reach them.

"And why should I do this? I could take the car." His devilish smirk faded to a straight line.

Chase took a deep breath. He felt the khan wanted to sound in charge rather than appear threatening. The old man liked the art of negotiation. "Because you are an honorable man who has shared his home with strangers. I believe the Taliban will try and attack them. Your son can explain. I want to leave at first light. Will this be possible?"

The khan pulled the pipe away from his lips as a cloud of opium smoke circled his head. "I agree to the terms. I will send two of my men to lead the way. My nephew took a secret way to be safer for children. Once you find them, you can take charge of the government woman and the girls. Then my men can return." Chase didn't mention Tessa would in no way return to the camp.

The khan pointed his pipe at Chase then narrowed his eyes. "The woman with gold hair is Kyrgyz now. You cannot change this. Her husband will fight to the death to keep her. It is best you not try and stop him. He is not as reasonable as me."

Chase clenched his jaw tight so not to say something he would regret.

"He kills many Taliban. You? Not a big problem. Besides, I think the woman likes us." The khan turned to his people and laughed.

Chase stood. "I understand, Khan. My friend and I will rest now. Our journey is long."

"So be it." The khan waved them off toward a yurt where they could spend the night.

~~~

Darya had pushed the children so hard, they were exhausted, irritable, and difficult to manage. Even the horses grew unresponsive so it became unsafe to have the children ride. Three friends of Darya volunteered to tag along: Rashid, the young man who made his intentions known concerning Shirin, Toiluk, and another villager.

Tessa and Bonnie each rode her own horse. Each adult carried one child except Darya who transported little Arzo and Pamir. Shirin rode behind Tessa by choice. She'd become afraid of the young man who offered her more attention than she'd ever had from a man. The harsh land he wanted to share with her had removed any romantic notions she once carried.

Horseback riding drew complaints from Bonnie. She demanded to stop so she could rest but Darya ignored her. After her face became etched with pain, Tessa came alongside Darya to request some time.

"We are near shelter." He tugged on the reins of his horse which caused it to prance impatiently. Arzo squealed and Pamir buried her face in his back. Tessa caught him slipping his arm around the littlest child to hold her tight. With the reins in his teeth, he reached back to make sure Pamir remained secure. "Just another kilometer or so." He spoke through clenched teeth. "We cross the
~~~

river. There will be a large cave for us to spend the night. We have come down several thousand meters, so it will not be as cold."

"Thank you, Darya." Tessa offered him a warm gaze as he moved away.

The river meandered in a peaceful flow where the group stopped to cross. The sounds of rapids nearby spoke of peril if they weren't careful. Although not very wide, it proved deep enough the horses needed to swim. She hoped they weren't too tired. The little girls swung their feet out to keep them dry. Tessa waited for Bonnie to follow Darya's two friends before urging her horse into the icy waters. The mare rebelled to go back, but Tessa kept her going forward with a strong hand. She could see Darya move his animal into the water without the problems she experienced.

As Tessa neared the point of no return, the horse started to struggle. The mare's ears lay back and her head thrashed. When an otter jumped off a nearby rock, creating a splash, the horse reared up, throwing Shirin into the icy water.

Tessa maneuvered the horse toward her but managed to create more chaos. "I'm coming, Shirin. Keep your head up." She reached down to catch Shirin's hand. In a panic, Shirin pulled her into the water. Both of them floated downstream toward rapids.

Shirin shrieked and grabbed Tessa by the neck, and they sank under the surface.

When their heads bobbed back up, Tessa sucked in so much air she choked. "Shirin, turn me loose so I can help you." After being pushed under again, she broke the surface and spat mouthfuls of water. "Stop!"

Tessa struggled against the pull of accelerating water, the roar of the rapids deafening her. She missed hearing the splash of horses as a tunnel of swift water collided against boulders ahead of them. Then the young man who fancied Shirin appeared, the water up over the belly of his horse. He reached down as easily as a trick rider in a circus and grabbed the girl. Tessa gulped more water and sank under again, but an arm circled her neck and was towed back toward shore until her feet touched bottom.

She crawled out onto the rocky shore with determined assistance from Darya's strong hands. He staggered then fell on his knees next to her as she rolled over onto her back. The little girls rushed to her side and fell upon her with open arms, crying.

Tessa chuckled between spits of water. "I'm okay." She patted each of them. "I'm okay." She even managed to kiss Arzo, who cried like a baby. The three-year-old released Tessa to steal a look at Darya. He offered a half grin then motioned for her to come to him. When the mountain tribesman gathered Arzo into his warrior arms, something inside Tessa lurched. The sight of such a man comforting the most helpless touched her in a way she hadn't expected.

"Miss Melanie." Shirin rushed to her side and fell down beside her. When she threw her weight against her in an embrace, Tessa fell backwards. "You should not have come to save me. I almost killed you. I'm so sorry, Miss Melanie. I do not know how to swim." Shirin bestowed a grateful look of admiration up at the young man who still held the reins of his horse in hand. He appeared to be shaken, too. "He saved me, Miss Melanie."

Darya stood then reached down to pull Tessa to her feet and into his arms. "I had to put the girls on land before I come for you. You all right?" He rested his lips against her forehead. It felt natural. It felt right.

Tessa sniffed like one of the little girls, trying to hold back tears of relief that would only frighten the children further. Darya rocked her in his arms and pulled her tighter to his chest. When he did, Tessa caught sight of Bonnie standing several feet from the fray with her weight shifted to one hip and her hands clutching at her heart. The creases on the once-classic face made her appear older. Tessa couldn't decide if being soaking wet caused her to shiver or if it was the look of apathy on Bonnie's face. The realization Bonnie Finley cared more about being able to escape than Tessa's survival made her feel a sense of caution.

They gathered around a small fire in the cave opening as darkness fell. Tessa told the girls about what school might be like in America. They wanted her to sing but Darya had warned against it, saying the Taliban might have a scout. The little girls understood, as they always seemed to, and fell asleep in each other's arms under coarse woolen blankets. After kissing them each goodnight, Tessa returned to the fire.

Bonnie edged closer to her after throwing some twigs on the low blaze. "Where's your husband?" The tone sounded condescending. "Run to the market for milk?"

Tessa stole a glance out the opening of the cave to see the four Kyrgyz men talking in whispers among themselves. "If you've got something to say, Bonnie, now is the time." Her body ached and she didn't have the strength for verbal combat.

"First, let me say, good job on taking one for the team, Tessa." Her clenched teeth appeared through a forced smile, exhibiting evil in the glow of the firelight. "I didn't think Darya could be so easily persuaded. That must have been some wedding night."

Tessa didn't trust the woman enough to tell her the truth. She peered over her shoulder at the children who were already breathing deep with sleep.

"So, what did you do to get him to take us back?" Bonnie smirked. "Guess you're not the Goody-Two-Shoes I first thought. Clearly, he is smitten with you. He dove in after you like a crazy man this afternoon." Bonnie sighed. "Heaven knows what would have happened to us if you drowned."

Tessa leveled an incredulous frown at Bonnie. "You mean to you. I'm sure the girls are the least of your concern. All you want is to get back to take revenge on the ambassador." Bonnie curled a lip in a snarl. "You need to work on your people skills and make better choices in the men you sleep with."

"Maybe you can let me in on your kinky techniques as to how I get a renegade Kyrgyz to bend to my every wish. Now that's something I could use," she hissed. "Don't act all holier-than-thou with me, Tessa. You're nothing but an adulteress. You sold your self-respect to rescue these kids who won't even remember you two weeks after we're gone."

"You act like I had a choice," she snapped loud enough for the four men to turn and peer inside. When they turned away, Tessa continued. "I made the best of a bad situation." She felt guilty about deceiving Darya but not Bonnie. "I'm not proud of what I've done."

"So, what is going to happen when we get back to Kabul?" Bonnie whispered maliciously into her ear. "Are you going to stab him or shoot him?"

Tessa jerked her head around to find Bonnie's nose inches from her own. "I beg you to never mention what I did again. Whatever you think of what I've done to get us this far, I'm the one who will have to live with those acts of violence the rest of my life."

Bonnie tossed another twig on the fire. "Okay. I owe you that. Your secret will always be safe with me. But, in return, you never reveal the reasons the Taliban came after me. They were all lies, but they would be hard to live down."

"I bet," Tessa growled. "I need some air." She stood and walked to the opening of the cave.

Darya joined her as his friends separated to different tasks. He cocked his head toward Bonnie getting ready to bed down for the night. "Problem?"

"No," Tessa whispered. "I needed some air."

Darya pulled her in front of him so her back rested against his chest. His arms went around her. "You shouldn't keep things from your husband, Tessa. The woman in there is evil. She has wounded you. Tell me." His accent had sounded less evident now that she knew the truth. His constant practice of English was also helping them to communicate. "Tell me," he repeated as his hold tightened around her.

"She thinks I'm tricking you into taking us back by sleeping with you. I didn't tell her the truth."

Darya rested his lips against her ear. "I doubt you've told me the truth about everything. For instance, sometimes you act as if you're waiting for someone. It's like you expect to find a familiar face."

Tessa took a deep breath. "I am."

Darya turned her around to pull her even closer. "Who?" She shook her head, gazing up into Darya's face.

"I don't know. There's an image of a man which keeps appearing in my head, my dreams. I can't shake it."

"A lover?" Darya spoke through gritted teeth, and Tessa could feel his muscles tense.

With a chuckle Tessa reached up to take his jacket between her fingers. "No. I'm sure of it." She thought a second longer. "I think a friend, like a big brother maybe, someone who I know through my work. I think he is in Kabul. Bonnie told me I visited someone the day before I went to get the girls." She shook her head. "I want to remember, to make sense of my life, but it clouds up in my head."

Darya pulled her in so tight her head lay on his shoulder. "I will get you and the girls back. Then we see what to do?"

Tessa pushed back. "Are you thinking of my offer to come to the US?"

"Yes."

CHAPTER 20

Massoud watched them, calculating the best way to attack the Kyrgyz men who guarded their position. He studied them with concern mixed with curiosity. Why would some mountain tribesmen wander away from their protected environment to come this way? Were they going to market to trade? Since before dawn, he'd observed the men coming and going from the river to fetch water. A thin ribbon of smoke twisted out the front of the cave, he guessed from the remains of a fire. He didn't recognize the men watering the horses.

Others waited for the Taliban leader at a camp less than a half kilometer away. A young boy from the group of families living nearby had been searching for a lost lamb when he'd spotted the fire in the cave and rushed back to tell Massoud. The boy had received a pistol as a reward. No matter it hadn't been cleaned in months and misfired more times than not.

Still in possession of the horse which aided in his escape several nights earlier, Massoud went to see for himself. His men followed on foot then waited for Massoud to return with further orders. He thought ten men would be enough to attack four Kyrgyz all alone with five horses. He motioned several of his men who tagged along with him, to come closer to observe in case he missed something. He lifted his field glasses at an unexpected movement at the mouth of the cave.

A disgruntled choke escaped his throat when he recognized the masked Kyrgyz who attacked him in the village who had been ruthless in his attack on his men, killing four and wounding others. His banshee yell still made the hairs stand up on the back of his neck. The man stood within striking distance. A chill ran down his spine as the Kyrgyz adjusted his mask over his nose. A moment sooner and Massoud would have caught a glimpse of his entire face. The dead calm in the man's relaxed body warned Massoud to tread lightly. Where the man in the mask traveled, so did trouble.

The original plan to move in on the Kyrgyz, kill them, and then take their horses changed when the bare-chested man in the mask appeared. Massoud admitted to himself he feared the masked brute. His reputation of cold- blooded disregard for the Taliban created unrealistic stories about his ability to murder them in their sleep, take their children, and steal their opium. There were even stories he would cut the heart out of a Taliban fighter and eat pieces of it. In spite of his skepticism, the one-eyed Taliban admitted the growing legend gave him pause.

"Do they have weapons?" he whispered to his follower, not trusting his vision enough to speculate. After all, this one Kyrgyz always seemed to have the best weapons, plenty of ammunition, and the cunning of a lynx to outmaneuver any threat the Taliban attempted. If he didn't know better, he would suspect the American Special Forces trained him. But the thought evaporated as a ridiculous notion.

"Don't see guns." The toothless man squatting next to Massoud passed back the glasses.

"Go back and get the others. Come quiet. The Kyrgyz have sharp ears. Don't take chances. I'll stay and watch." The man slipped away as Massoud lifted the glasses to scrutinize the options.

He watched the large Kyrgyz turn back into the cave, returning moments later, fully clothed. He tensed when a little girl ran past the legendary tribesman only to be scooped up in his arms and scolded before he set her feet on the ground. The little girl leaned against his legs as he patted the top of her head. Something made the legend turn his head back over his shoulder when a woman stepped outside the cave carrying two bandoliers. He crisscrossed the bullet belts across his chest as the woman stepped beside him.

Massoud recognized the woman with the startling blue eyes. Her yellow hair swirled around her face in the morning breeze as she pulled a white scarf up over the tangled curls. The masked man leaned into her ear to speak, bringing a smile to the woman's lips. Whatever he said appeared to give him license to touch the woman in a personal manner, one which she did not rebuff.

"I will now be able to get even with that filthy Kyrgyz," Massoud whispered to himself.

~~~

Darya felt Tessa's arm slip around his back as he squinted at the surrounding rocks and foliage. The touch of a woman softened his senses. The urge to shake her off conflicted with his rising desire to force the enviable contract to completion. Even standing here, he could smell her skin. A stray curl brushed against his cheek in the morning breeze.

Her body had felt almost hot against his skin when he'd slipped beneath the blankets after his night watch. She'd cried out several times during the night, perhaps from nightmares. He'd managed to comfort her by rocking her in his arms then whispering Pashto words of devotion against her mouth. Salty tears ran across his lips as she quivered, digging her fingers into his naked back until she fell into a fitful sleep.

"Last night…" Tessa stopped.

Darya broke his focus from his safety scan of the surrounding area.

"Thank you. I know I've put you in an awful position." She stared out at the river while Shirin slipped outside the cave and moved to talk to the young Kyrgyz who lit up when she approached.

Darya leaned down to Tessa's ear. "Awful position? Not how I would put it." He pulled her arm down from his back then lifted her hand to his lips and kissed her palm. "Soon I will show you how much you mean to me. And you will do the same." Tessa kissed the corner of his mouth and slid her hand down his backside before turning to gather up the children.

An urgency to conclude this trip created an impatient Darya. He whistled to his men who led the horses closer to the mouth of the cave. Shirin came, too, blushing as she moved past Darya. He
~~~

turned his stern attention on the young man. "Until we get to Kabul, you keep your eyes and ears open. Stay away from the girl. Do you understand?"

"Yes, Darya. B-but." The boy took a timid step closer. Darya turned to see Shirin in the edge of darkness, gathering up their things. "This girl is going to America, to school. You have nothing to offer her except a hard life on the rooftop of the world."

The young man patted the neck of his horse. "I think, if the woman comes back with you Shirin will, too."

Darya didn't like the implication. "If? My wife goes where I go," he snapped. "As to the girl, we will see. Now do your job. Keep watch. We will prepare the horses."

The young man led his horse away then took up a position to keep watch.

~~~

Chase experienced another night of fitful sleep. The sun was not yet up when he prepared to leave. Zoric and the two Kyrgyz mumbled a complaint, rubbed their backsides while taking their tea before tying their bedrolls on their horses. By the time everyone had mounted, Chase had already exited the camp without them. He trotted the horse knowing the others would catch up. He just wanted a few minutes to pull his thoughts together. The rhythm of man and beast working together gave him a sense of calm. Once he gained some peace concerning Tessa, he slowed the animal to a walk.

His thoughts returned to her. Envisioning the traumatic events which engulfed her in recent days fueled the images of the woman he'd come to admire being destroyed. Contact with the Taliban, watching the Black Hawk go down followed by the beating of a soldier sent to protect her would terrify a hardened warrior much less a PTA president from Grass Valley, California. Memories of her optimistic attitude and musical laughter played on the recesses of his mind. Would she still possess those things he cherished about her or would a mental darkness suppress the brightness she brought to the lives around her?

Gunfire pulled Chase up short. Zoric and the two Kyrgyz joined him.
~~~

Chase turned to his guides. "Weapons?" They pulled out their rifles.

"We are close, my friend. Do you hear water?" Zoric stood up in the stirrups, squinting his eyes toward the distant horizon.

The two tribesmen informed Chase of a place on the riverbank where they often stopped for the night. "Go upstream to cross. With no packs, we can get out fast and circle back. Shallow cave. Women and children there." The tribesman pointed ahead of them as another shot rolled across the steppe.

Chase found it difficult to understand the Pashto, but he caught the gist of the conversation. The tribesmen clicked their tongues as the horses were given their head to run unrestrained. They didn't wait to see if Chase and Zoric could keep up. It appeared their own private priorities had kicked in, leaving them to fend for themselves. Something now drove the Kyrgyz headlong toward danger as they rode low in their saddles toward a river which appeared not to be as shallow as expected. The five men plunged their horses into the icy waters, ever mindful of the possibilities awaiting them on the other side.

~~~

The children were mounted behind their riders. This time Shirin and Pamir rode behind her young man, Rashid, and seven-year-old Marta clutched the back of Tessa's robe. The horse danced around at first, but Tessa managed to get it under control as she rode up alongside Darya. He carried Arzo behind him this time, explaining to put her in front would make her an easy target if they came upon the Taliban.

Bonnie used a small boulder to climb onto her horse as Toiluk held the reins. She grunted once she'd fallen into the hard saddle. After making a show of straightening her clothes, she grabbed the reins from the man who stood on the ground, unaffected by her display of impatience. She failed to offer a thank you, sorry I made you wait, or appreciation of any kind. "I can't wait to be shed of these animals," she fumed at Tessa as Toiluk lifted another little girl to ride behind her. "I think I'm getting saddle sores."

Tessa winked at the child, Son-Kul, who stuck out her lip in disappointment at her riding partner. "Want Miss Melanie," she
~~~

whined. "Please, Miss Melanie."

The Kyrgyz glanced from the child to Tessa who agreed to the request. Snatched from Bonnie's horse then tossed up in front of Tessa, Son-Kul wiggled with pleasure. Although seven years old, her small statue hinted at malnutrition. She bounced with joy as she leaned back against Tessa who kissed her cheek then whispered, "I love you."

"You spoil them." Darya faked a frown at the two little girls.

Tessa straightened her back before patting the leg of the child behind her. "And what of Arzo." She pointed at the youngest hanging on for dear life to Darya's back. "Do you not melt at the slightest sound of her voice?"

Darya twisted in his saddle to level a stern frown back at Arzo who offered a giggle. "I would feed her to my yak if she were a big enough bite," he proclaimed with exaggeration. Arzo sucked in her breath in fear, making Darya chuckle at her reaction. He patted her leg then turned his focus to Tessa. He switched to English. "Be her mother, Tessa. We need a child."

The deep emotion in his narrow eyes could not be covered by the mask he wore. Tessa felt like a hostage under his penetrating gaze. He brought his horse up so close so that their legs touched then reached out to stroke her cheek. "Maybe we stay in the lowlands when this is over."

Tessa laid her hand on his fingers. "You can't go into Kabul with me. Someone might find out who you are." Darya withdrew before turning his head to scan the area around him. "The government woman does not know who I am."

"You don't trust me, do you?" Tessa leaned toward him. "You think I'll run."

Darya let his attention return to her. His thick lips twisted in disgust. "I know a lot about running. It is in your eyes. I feel your passion spilling toward me every night, but something holds you back or you would have already given yourself fully."

"You must know how I care for you. I am very grateful for your protection and help, Darya." She could sense an anger building inside him.

"It is not your gratitude I want." He tapped the sides of his horse to move away from her.

The group funneled through a boulder-lined path away from the protection of their cave camp. Sun ribbons split through puffy clouds floating across the sky. Hawks screeching above replaced the tranquil sounds of rushing waters as the Kyrgyz led the group out onto a path through brush and skinny trees starved for nourishment. The horses' slow progress moved over the uneven trail as it curved upward to a ridge.

Darya's horse shied abruptly, causing Arzo to cry out as she slipped sideways off the horse. He caught her with one hand as she dangled over a ledge. With one swift movement, he jerked her up in front of him. Tears flowed down her hollow cheeks as the others stopped. He placed a hand over Arzo's mouth, using a thumb to wipe away the wet streaks. She stopped her crying and, sitting sideways in the saddle, Arzo buried her face into Darya's chest for safety. He held the back of her head with reassurance. His lips touched her head scarf.

He nudged his horse forward with more insistence this time. The entire group moved away from the ledge with a degree of caution. As they neared the top, a shot rang out, bouncing off a rock near Tessa. A startled scream escaped as she struggled to settle the spooked horse. But he continued the dance of impatience, threatening to back over the ledge with Tessa and the two girls. Darya jumped from his horse, bringing Arzo down with him. He reached Tessa's mount in short order, grabbing the bridle with a jerk followed by comforting words as he led the mare under a ledge. The others dismounted then hustled the children and Bonnie to the same area.

"We are almost to the top," Darya spoke to his friends. He pointed at a narrow trail that forked from the one they traveled. "Take the women and children up there. They'll be protected."

He spoke in rapid Pashto now. Tessa struggled to understand his rapid speech as he instructed Rashid to get them to a nearby village if they didn't make it out of the coming fight. "It is not far, Rashid. They are friendly to us." Darya shot an expression of regret to Tessa. He fished a small pistol from his saddlebag then passed it to her. "Can you use this?"

Tessa stared down at it as if she'd never seen one before, but she recognized it as the one the soldier had given her days earlier to defend herself. "Yes," she whispered as a sob threatened to choke her. "Don't die, Darya." Tessa's voice quivered. "Please."

Darya gave a signal to Rashid to get moving.

As they disappeared around the bend to safety, Tessa heard a voice that would haunt her the rest of her life.

"I see you have brought my hostages back," came a loud declaration from above. "I am Massoud." Darya did not respond but inched his way upward toward the voice. "You killed my men and now I must kill you. I see now you are not a ghost and bleed like the rest of us or you would not be hiding from my rifles. Release the women to me and you can keep the girls. They are worthless to me." A volley of gunfire rained down around Darya, his friend Toiluk, and Akbar. They scrambled to take cover behind some boulders.

"We will come after you then the women and children."
Silence.

The Kyrgyz resumed their climb, agile as a mountain goat. They reached the top then took cover behind a rock outcropping. They readied their rifles before aiming at the men ahead. The Taliban scrutinized the area where Darya escaped. With an upward jerk of Darya's chin to the others, the Kyrgyz unloaded their weapons at the Taliban.

CHAPTER 21

Massoud fell to his knees when the gunshot took out the man next to him. Once again, he'd underestimated the Kyrgyz ghost known as part mountain goat, part demonic killer. His men rallied by turning their weapons toward the tribesmen, firing at will so as to pen them down. The smell of gunpowder filled the air as the bullets ricocheted off stone barricades. The Taliban ducked and covered when the sounds of gunfire created echoes, an impression of many fighters surrounding them.

The one-eyed Taliban encouraged his fighters to take a chance and two of them were picked off in short order. Massoud, despite having only one eye, soon realized they were being held down by three Kyrgyz. He yelled out the information causing a false sense of courage to surge as they began taking chances and closed in on the tribesmen.

~~~

Each Kyrgyz would reload a weapon, alternating with another that held the Taliban in place. The sight of the Taliban venturing out into the open suggested they were about to be overwhelmed. In one last effort, the Kyrgyz jumped up, unloading their weapons as the Taliban rushed forward. The Taliban were soon mowed down, sacrificed to draw the tribesmen out into the open.
~~~

Enemy guns stopped momentarily as if they might be regrouping. The Kyrgyz took the lull as an opportunity to charge Massoud's cover. Massoud's remaining six men rose up with startled expressions as the tribesmen jumped off rocks into their midst, knives drawn in one hand, pistols in the other. The Taliban fired, missed then threw their decrepit weapons aside to attack. It was two on one now with two of the rebels knocking Toiluk to the ground as he continued to fight. Akbar fought on as well. Massoud shoved one of his men forward, edging his way closer to the masked Kyrgyz.

Darya remained on his feet, wheeling his knife that managed to connect with one man's throat, spewing blood across Darya's chest. Another Taliban took his place, ramming his head into Darya's body. The force slammed him back onto his butt. He rolled as the man fired his gun and missed then took aim again. As Darya crabbed crawled backwards, the man jerked forward and pitched facedown into the dirt, displaying a gunshot wound in his back.

Two unexpected Kyrgyz from his village jumped into the fray. Two other unfamiliar men joined them in the fighting. Darya didn't have time to identify who they were or if they were Afghans but felt grateful for reinforcements. The bigger of the two leveled his weapon at the enemy, ready to sink his blade into the chest of Toiluk.

Now the Taliban were evenly matched, but suffered injuries. One tried to jump onto a rock, missed, and fell over the side of the ridge into the churning waters below. They continued to fight until the new Kyrgyz emptied their guns into their bodies.

Darya whirled around, searching for Massoud. Once again, he had escaped, leaving only a dust cloud to track him by.

He met the gaze of the large man who didn't look so different from him, but from his ability to fight, he must be Special Forces. "Horse!"

The stranger pointed toward where they'd left the animals. Darya sprinted over rocks toward the untethered horses. He jumped onto the back of the smallest one then took out after Massoud, not knowing whether the Taliban leader had any weapons that might bring him down. Beast and man became one as he followed the dust trail. The hard beat of his horse's hooves almost made Darya miss the sound of another up ahead. He rounded a bend to see Massoud sneaking worried glances over his shoulder. The one-eyed man's horse slowed through a narrow, rocky passage filled with rock indentions, big enough for a man to hide and ambush an unsuspecting traveler.

Darya slid off his horse then scampered up the hillside, knowing from earlier trips, the trail curved back toward where he could intersect the one-eyed leader. As he came up over the boulder next to the trail, Massoud eased by on his horse. Darya jumped into him, slamming him, gasping, to the ground.

As Massoud attempted to stand, Darya gave into temptation and punched him in the stomach, flattening him to the ground once again. Darya grabbed him up once more by the throat as if he were a ragdoll and squeezed so hard Massoud's one good eye bulged. As his ferocious struggles slowed, Darya released him only to add another blow to the cheek and dropped him.

"Get it over with, you worthless pile of yak dung." Massoud spit blood onto the ground.

Darya reached down and yanked him to his feet then slammed him against a boulder. He didn't let the one-eyed man bait him into speaking. He'd won. The horse Massoud stolen from Abdul stood nearby. It wouldn't be difficult now taking one of the most wanted men in Afghanistan back to Kabul.

~~~

Chase watched the tribesmen clean up their handiwork. After digging through their pockets and saddlebags, he noticed they secured a few trophies as well as boots that seemed to have fewer holes than the ones they wore. The Kyrgyz worked in silence as if they were cleaning up a pile of garbage. Soon no trace of the fight existed. Even the bullet casing had been retrieved.

"Bullet casings?" Zoric asked. "What the hell would they want with those?"

Chase shrugged. "I'm guessing they don't want anyone to know they were here. Something I'd do. These guys fight like some of my Delta Force buddies, SEALS, maybe. Look at them. They're always scanning. Always ready."

"Ask them about the big Kyrgyz who took out on the horse. He
~~~

seems a little out of place next to these guys. He's not as big as you but compared to these men he's a giant," Zoric observed.

"The man who left, who is he?" Chase wiped his forehead with his sleeve.

They frowned at him as if they didn't understand his Pashto.

"The women and children," he said, pointing at Toiluk who had bent down to pick up his knife. "Government woman. Where is she?"

He cocked his head to listen to the men he brought along and filled Toiluk in on the last couple of days including the rescue of the khan's son, Abdul.

"The government woman? Where is she?" Chase repeated with impatience.

Toiluk left and returned with his horse. Chase waited, rooted in the same spot, hands slightly out from his side, a nine-millimeter in one hand and an M16 in the other.

"My friend returns. Talk to him." Toiluk spoke the words slowly in Pashto.

Zoric returned his 44 Magnum to its holster then closed his switchblade. "These guys don't say much, Chase. But I think they know plenty."

"We'll soon find out." A rider approached leading the one-eyed Taliban on another horse.

Toiluk assisted the returning men with the horses. From the Kyrgyz's size, Chase speculated he must be the man in the picture with Tessa the khan flaunted to him. The man stood right at six foot, broad shouldered and more muscled than the other Kyrgyz. He couldn't explain why he impressed him as being a threat. A brown fur hat with ear flaps tied up on the top, a ragged mask covering part of his face, black clothing and a wool vest couldn't hide the fact this man was more than a tribesman from the Wakhan Valley.

Chase cut his eyes to Massoud who lifted his gaze resembling apathy more than fear.

He called out to them. "These barbarians plan to kill me."

Although he was slumped over, beaten and bloody and unable to do anything about his present predicament, Chase knew better than to underestimate the Taliban leader.

Massoud spat blood on the ground. "Who are you?"

The other man slid off his horse then turned to land a blow to the Taliban's leg. The man howled and the horse shied away, but Toiluk's firm grip on the bridle kept it in place.

Chase moved toward them with determination, careful not to surprise the big Kyrgyz. He and Massoud locked glares like two male markhors, ready to do battle. "Captain Chase Hunter." He forced his voice to go flat, his Pashto void of any emotion or respect. "And you are?" "He is a butcher," Massoud hissed, earning another blow to his leg. "He moves about these mountains like a demon then slits the throats of innocent women and children."

With those words, the big Kyrgyz reached up to drag the one-eyed rebel off his horse then tossed him into a dead spiny bush. In one step, he reached the man, caught him by the ankle then pulled him flat on his back where he hit his head. He kicked some rocks in the Taliban's face then stormed off.

"Bit of a hothead." Zoric arched an eyebrow. "That Kyrgyz is in charge here. Make nice, Chase, if we plan to find Tessa."

Chase squatted down next to Massoud, who had managed to sit up. He was surprised at the man's small size, considering his big reputation. The American military had underestimated the man's cunning.

"American dogs." Massoud grinned.

Chase's gaze remained fixed on the Taliban rebel; his lips pooched out in contemplation. His head cocked to the left. When Massoud squirmed under the examination, Chase stood up to tower over the man. As if in slow motion, he raised his foot then planted it on Massoud's chest, forcing the rebel back to the ground. As the pressure increased, Massoud gasped for breath.

"This American dog," Chase growled, "is going to rip you apart. You killed some good men in that helicopter. They were on a rescue mission not a threat to the Taliban. If I find out you harmed one hair on any of those kids or American women, I will carve you up piece by piece. Then I will leave a trail of your body parts for any other Taliban to find as my warning. Are we clear?"

Massoud shoved at the foot on his chest. Chase reached down to yank him to his feet. As he wheezed, Chase turned him around to secure his hands behind his back.

"You and that Kyrgyz devil they call Darya are cut from the same filthy rag. I can't ride like this," Massoud complained. "Do you want me to fall?"

Chase leaned in to his ear. "Yes."

He turned to see Darya had slipped up behind him. Making a mental note of this ability caused Chase to speculate further about the Kyrgyz man. The realization it would be a mistake to underestimate him put Chase on guard.

When Chase reached inside his jacket pocket, the other Kyrgyz cocked their weapons then pointed them at him. He froze his hand as he evaluated the group.

Massoud laughed. "I told you they were animals. You cannot trust them." He now spoke in English. "Let me go and I will go for help. I hate these sons of yaks."

"Easy," Zoric whispered to his friend. "Nice and easy."

In Pashto, Chase explained what he wanted to do. The big Kyrgyz called Darya did not point a weapon at his chest but continued to glare at him through the large holes of his tattered mask.

"I want to show you a picture."

Darya looked over at his buddies then back to Chase before raising his chin, indicating he should proceed.

Careful not to move too fast and startle the men, Chase withdrew the government ID photo of Bonnie Finley. One of the guys on the helicopter who had dropped them off to continue the hunt for the State Department representative had given it to him. He kept the personal one of Tessa inside his vest so not to tip his hand. The thought of a jealous tribesman knocking out any competition to secure the release of his new bride was not a pleasant one.

Chase offered the picture to Darya, but he didn't take it. Toiluk walked up and snatched it from Chase then held it in front of the other man.

Darya stuck out his thick lips. His narrowed scowl lifted to Chase then ran over him like a steamroller.

"Bonnie Finley. Works for the Americans. They want her back. The khan said you had her." Chase managed to get the whole thing out in Pashto. He needed to practice the language more. It had been a while since he'd used it this much. "Bonnie Finley," he repeated.

Darya waved off Toiluk.

"We take you to her." Toiluk spoke void of emotion. "Go now."

Everyone turned to go to their horses except Darya and Chase. They stood facing each other without a word, evaluating the next move and each other.

Zoric called out. "Chase, let's go." He led a horse to him.

Chase took the bridle without taking his focus off of the dangerous Kyrgyz leader.

"Can he ride enough to keep up?" Darya spoke to the two men who had tagged along with Chase and Zoric from the summer camp.

Chase swung up into the saddle and pulled on the reins. He didn't wait for the men to answer. "I'm an American Indian. I can ride."

Darya continued to evaluate the American and smirked as if he planned to find out for himself.

Although he expected to be tested by the Kyrgyz leader, nothing out of the ordinary occurred. The group moved across an open area at a rather smooth trot, with Darya leading the horse which carried Massoud. In spite of the Taliban's earlier concern, he didn't struggle with riding hands free. Chase guessed him to be an excellent Buzkashi player by the way he leaned in the saddle from time to time. There were no further complaints from him while they rode.

A small village materialized on the horizon. The horses picked up speed as they grew closer. When the mud huts were less than a hundred yards away, Darya threw the reins of Massoud's horse to Toiluk then kicked his horse's sides.

"What's got into him?" Zoric snarled. A group of people came out to the edge of the village.

Chase kicked his horse, too, as did Zoric. In moments they were close enough to see two women, a group of children, and another Kyrgyz, standing guard. The Kyrgyz leader rode like poetry in motion.

Even before the horse came to a complete stop, Darya threw his leg over the saddle and jumped to the ground. Chase managed to snap a picture of him with his phone while everyone was cheering the leader's arrival.

He then turned his attention back to the women and children.

Darya took long strides toward them as if determined to greet them with some kind of victory.

Shocked to see the shorter woman run toward the tribesman, he watched her white head scarf blow to the ground as she reached him. Her blonde hair had been braided into two pigtails but curls escaped near the crown of her head.

With little effort, Darya caught her up in his arms in a bear hug and swung her around in a circle. As her feet touched the ground again, she frantically opened his shirt and ran her hands over his skin. The leader grabbed her hands and said something in a low, soothing tone. His arm went around her waist and she fell against him. As Chase and Zoric rode up, Darya leveled a warning glare at them.

The laughter of children followed as they ran toward the woman and Kyrgyz. He scooped the littlest one up in his arms. She hugged his neck so tight the man faked a choke. Several other little girls encircled him, crowding close. He patted them all on the head. The oldest of the children held back to walk alongside a young man not much older than her. Their faces reflected happiness at the reunion until Darya held out his arm toward her. She fell into his embrace, resting her head on his shoulder.

Chase sent their coordinates for a helicopter pickup. Next he sent the picture of the Kyrgyz leader through the handheld computer to the director at Enigma. His phone, part cell part radio, vibrated in his hand a few short minutes later. He stared at the screen then lifted his attention to stare at Darya who glared back at him. Zoric took the phone from him and stared at the info beneath the photo Enigma sent.

"I'd say, instead of one prisoner, we might be taking two." Zoric shifted his gaze back to Darya.

Without responding, Chase dismounted and walked toward the group. He focused on Tessa who now beamed a smile down at the children. She lifted her gaze to him and stumbled backward.

The confusion he experienced caught him off guard. Why doesn't she run to me? She's scared out of her wits. Something is wrong with her. Any other time she would be smothering him with her gratefulness and insults at waiting so long for rescue.

Chase brushed past Bonnie, as Tessa turned and ran. "Tessa!" he yelled as he continued marching toward her.

She stopped and turned around; her brow furrowed. Chase halted and extended his hand. This time his voice grew quiet. "Tessa."

Darya stepped in front of her. His arms crossed on his chest; his feet separated in a defiant stance.

Tessa placed her hands on his arms to peek around his body. "You know me?"

"Know you?" Chase grabbed the picture from his pocket. In it, she stood with him and the President of the United States. He extended his hand, not quite sure what to make of her confusion. "Here."

She stepped around Darya and reached for the picture. "Tessa, you and I…" He shifted his momentary focus to Darya who had taken on a murderous expression. "We are good friends. We work together." He pointed to Zoric. "It's Zoric. Don't you remember us?"

"Do you know these men, Tessa?" Darya spoke to her in Pashto.

Tessa examined the picture then Chase. She then turned to Darya, blinking rapidly. "No. I've never seen them before."

"They know you." Chase took note of the irritation in Darya's voice. "Do not lie to me," he growled. "You said someone would be looking for you. Is this the man?"

"This picture says I do. I don't remember. Please, Darya." She squeezed his arm. "Maybe they can help us with the girls. That's all I care about now."

Chase sidestepped Darya to face her head on. Troubled she could speak Pashto like a native, he decided to confront the man. "What the hell have you done to her?" He spoke in English. Even if the man couldn't understand the meaning he would recognize the tone. Chase reached to take Tessa. Darya shoved his hand aside as he put his body between them.

"Tessa," Chase said with as much calm as he could to reassure her, "I am here to take you home. I've sent for helicopters. By tonight, maybe tomorrow, you can be sleeping in a bed, have some hot food, take a shower, and do all the things you love to do. I'll even get a call in to your family."

Tessa stepped up beside Darya and let her gaze ping-pong between Zoric and Chase. "My family?"

"We are her family now," Darya said in English. "Arzo!" The littlest girl came running to him. He lifted her up then passed her to Tessa. "Tell him, Tessa."

Her lips quivered. "I will always come for you," Tessa recited.

"Yes." Chase took a deep breath. "I told you that a long time ago. No matter where you are or what trouble finds you, I'll always come for you. A promise I intend to keep." He focused on Darya for a second before switching back to Tessa. "What have they done to you, Tessa?"

Bonnie Finley walked up, leading another girl by the hand. Her disgusted tone drew Chase's attention. "Well, if it isn't the mighty Captain Hunter. I take it you're the cavalry. It's about damn time." She pointed toward Darya. "In his defense, he kept the Taliban from making us their hostages. Heaven only knows how that would have ended. He's treated us well, protected the children, and was trying to get us back to Kabul." She sent a mocking smirk to Tessa. Chase caught the condescension. "Tessa got a bump on the head when the Taliban came in. I guess with all the things going on she managed to get amnesia." Bonnie spoke to herself. "I should be so lucky." She took a deep breath. "As you can see, our fearless leader"—she raised an eyebrow at Darya—"has taken quite a liking to Melanie or Tessa or whoever she is and thinks he has some claim on her." Darya grabbed Tessa's hand and pulled her after him. "Done talking."

"Like hell we are!" Chase followed and, this time, he stepped in front of Darya. "I know who you are, Darya. The mask doesn't fool me. You're AWOL and have been for five years. Military Intelligence has been looking for you. I'm taking you in with Massoud."

"You are not taking me anywhere." They were nose to nose. "I told Tessa I would get these girls and her"—he tilted his head at Bonnie—"to Kabul so they can go to the US. I intend to keep that promise. Then I'm going back to the Wakhan Valley."

"At this point I don't care where you go after you talk to your CO. You've got some explaining to do."

Their voices reached a fever pitch.

"And how do you think you're going to take me back? From where I stand, you are a little outnumbered." Darya shoved Chase's chest but barely budged him.

Tessa pushed in between the two men, facing Darya. "Listen to me. You caught Massoud. This is your ticket to freedom, Darya. You saved a State Department employee. All that will go a long way on your behalf. Bonnie will tell them. You've got to face whoever you're running from. Do you want to keep hiding the rest of your life?"

"Is this what you want?" he whispered, his mask covering any emotion that might tip his hand to Chase.

"Yes, Darya." She stroked his arm. "Freedom."

Before he could respond, screaming came from near one of the buildings. Chase and Darya both took off at top speed, their guns drawn. They rounded the mud brick building to find several Kyrgyz wrestling Massoud to the ground. A couple of horses stomped nervously then shied away revealing a young man lying on the ground.

CHAPTER 22

Catching up with the men, Tessa saw Shirin kneeling on the ground next to Rashid. His chest, covered in blood, hinted at what lay ahead. The young girl cried, inconsolable sobs racking her body. She kept repeating the boy's name over and over.

Tessa fell to her knees beside her, gathering the girl in her arms. "Bonnie, keep the children back. Don't let them see this." Bonnie herded the little girls away from the young man they'd come to trust.

Massoud struggled against the two men holding him. He shouted insults at Darya and continued to twist against his restraints.

"What happened?" Darya joined Tessa as the young man struggled to roll toward him.

Toiluk shook Massoud violently before speaking. "Rashid helped Massoud from the horse. The son of a dog managed to slip out of his ties. He took Rashid's knife from his belt then grabbed the girl. Rashid rushed in to save her and…" Toiluk frowned down at the boy. "We tried to stop Massoud, but he stabbed our young Rashid before we could get to him."

Shirin turned back to Rashid, slipping her arm under his head. "Don't leave me, Rashid," she demanded through her sobs.

He reached up and touched her cheek then looked to Darya. "Take Shirin to school," he choked.

Darya placed his hand on Rashid's head and agreed to his wishes.

Tessa remembered the grim-faced Chase. "Do something," she demanded. "You're a medic. Help him." Tears pooled in the corners of her eyes.

Chase got down next to the boy and opened his shirt. With every pulse, blood poured out. He shook his head at Darya with the verdict. In seconds, the boy took his last breath. Darya squeezed his eyes shut as if he were the grieving father. Shirin became hysterical and Tessa had to pull her away. She led her around the edge of the building where the other little girls waited. Together they cried, holding on to one another. Even the hardhearted Bonnie let tears trickle down her face as she picked up Arzo who struggled to run to find Darya.

"Dear God in Heaven," she whispered. "He was a kid." Bonnie shook her head.

"Let's move the children away from here, Bonnie." Tessa motioned for the children to move toward the empty house they'd been given by one of the men in the small village of six mud houses. Bonnie led the way. Arzo wrapped her arms around Bonnie's neck but followed Tessa's every move. She spoke a few words of comfort to the little girl, hoping she would settle down for Bonnie.

By the time the men came to the house, darkness blanketed the land. Leading their horses to a lean-to attached to the back of the house, the Kyrgyz took care of their horses before coming inside. Even Chase and Zoric remained with the tribesmen to help with the animals. A woman dressed in Kyrgyz attire came to the hut to start a fire and put on a pot of something which smelled like stew. A dozen tin cups of various sizes were brought by another woman along with some unleavened bread and wooden spoons. Tessa didn't care at this point how clean they were. The food smelled too good to her rumbling stomach. When the woman left, Tessa dipped up cups of food for the children, Bonnie had them sit down against the wall.

"How do you know Captain Hunter," Bonnie said with caution as she passed out the food. "Is he the man you visited the day before we left Kabul?"

Tessa shrugged. "I'm not sure. He is so familiar." She walked over to Shirin to hand her some food before turning back to Bonnie. "I think I know both of them."

Bonnie whispered with a smirk, "Captain Hunter is quite the good time. Am I right?"

It sounded more like a probe than a question. "Good time?"

"Come on," she coaxed. "Captain Hunter has a reputation with the ladies falling at his feet." Her grin widened. "I'll have to say I've had the pleasure of his company a time or two." Her glance went to the door. "Married or not, you can't tell me you wouldn't want to be all over that. Besides"—she leaned in to Tessa's ear—"we both know you have a taste for roughness or you wouldn't have taken up with a mountain Neanderthal."

With a frown, Tessa took a step back. "Everything is not about sex, Bonnie. Maybe if you'd remembered that we wouldn't be in this mess."

Bonnie chuckled satanically. "Touché, Mrs. Darya." She cocked her head as she offered a flippant gaze at Tessa. "And how are you going to wiggle out of this? Are you going to let the captain save you from the brute?"

"Stop it," Tessa snapped. "Darya isn't a brute. How can you be so insulting after seeing the way he treats these girls?"

"You aren't exactly a little girl, now, are you, Tessa?" Bonnie scooped herself up a cup of food then sniffed it. She took the edge of her shirt and wiped along the rim of the cup before taking a sip. "I think you really care for him. Granted, he is easy on the eyes when he isn't hell-bent on killing people." She took another swallow then examined Tessa a little closer. She set the cup down and moved toward her. Although she tried to step away, Bonnie grasped her arm. "Listen to me, Tessa. I'm not sure what you promised Darya to get us back, but all bets are off once we get to Kabul. You don't have to do anything you don't want to do. You're an American citizen and, as strange as it sounds, he may be, too. You can't be bought and sold like cattle. I appreciate what you've done here but…"

"But what I did, Bonnie." Tessa knew she sounded helpless.

"What you did saved Shirin and me from being raped and tortured. I will never tell anyone, just like you asked. I will always owe you. Whatever you did with Darya is your own business. If it doesn't give you nightmares, who am I to complain. We both have secrets. Remember?"

Tessa dropped her eyes to stare at the dirt floor.

Bonnie reached out to raise Tessa's chin. "We've got to protect each other. Nobody gives a fig about a couple of dead Taliban. Your biggest problem is getting away from Darya. With any luck, the military will throw his hide in jail until after we leave."

"You've got to protect him, Bonnie."

"Not until I'm in airspace over the Pacific Ocean. Then I'll call the State Department and one of the joint chiefs I know. Don't worry. Your rooftop-of-the-world Romeo won't go to jail for long. I'll see to it. Promise. But I need you to keep your mouth shut about me and the ambassador. Agreed?"

"How are you going to keep Massoud quiet about the ambassador?"

"No one is going to believe him. When headquarters get finished with him, he'll be crying like a baby for a deal. He'll spill his guts about every terrorist group from here to Islamabad. Then they'll pack him off to Gitmo if he's lucky. If not, then he'll be vulture bait."

Tessa shook her head. "You've got it all worked out, don't you?"

"Don't take that tone with me. Not only do you have some poor sap back home waiting with the kids for his little sweetie to return to domestic bliss, but you managed to marry a renegade military intelligence officer and maybe even have an affair with one of the sexiest men in Delta Force." She clicked her tongue. "Trust me. I know what I'm talking about when I speak of Captain Hunter." Bonnie bowed her head and cooed. "You are the master."

The sudden urge came over Tessa to knock Bonnie to the ground, but Captain Hunter, Zoric, and Darya pushed the half curtain door aside to walk inside. Tessa grabbed another cup to fetch Darya some food. He showed his appreciation by offering her a pat on her back.

Tessa met his gaze as he removed the mask then handed it to her. The rough world he chose made his body beautiful. His stealth movement resembled the snow leopards roaming the mountains. She reached up to touch the dark-brown hair falling over his ears. He removed the brown hat and black scarf. She reached for it as he snatched it back with a tease. This made her chuckle as he handed it to her again. In Pashto he asked her to sit with him against the wall. For a split second she stole a glimpse at the other two Americans.

"Get them food, Bonnie Finley," Darya ordered with his eyes narrowed to slits. She hurried to obey, but not without mumbling a few insults. "We sit." He walked to the wall and slid down to a sitting position.

Tessa joined him but kept her attention on the captain. "How did you know he was a medic?"

Tessa shrugged. "I'm starting to remember him. I do work for him. I'm not sure what exactly I do." She turned to Darya who watched her with mistrust. "He's protective."

"He your lover?" Darya could've been asking about the weather with such a nonchalant tone.

She didn't know for sure but decided to take the high road. "No," Tessa. "I never cheated on my husband."

Darya smirked. "Which one? Me or the first one?"

Tessa opened her mouth to speak but nothing came out. She felt mortified. Then Darya smothered a chuckle as he leaned over and kissed her cheek. Relief washed over her as she jabbed him in the side with her fist.

"How is Shirin?" He waved toward the teenager who sat with her knees drawn up under her chin. "We buried him outside the village. It needed to be done right away."

Arzo moved toward Tessa then flopped down in her lap. Darya accepted her kiss then offered her a bite of his food. When she held up her bread he took a large bite from the edge. He laughed at her surprised giggle.

Soon the little girl snuggled against Tessa, before drifting off to sleep. Darya set his cup down before removing the blanket from his shoulders to cover the three of them. He, too, soon fell asleep. She understood his leathery hand lay atop her thigh to mark his territory.

~~~

Chase and Zoric had taken the first watch along with one of the men who had been their guide. The Kyrgyz waited outside for his replacement so they could go inside for some sleep. Zoric found a
~~~

spot along the wall and stretched out his legs. Chase moved toward Darya and paused to loom over him until his anger quieted. He kicked the boot of Darya.

"After midnight." Chase kept his voice to a low growl, a trait known all too well to his team members. It meant a slow burn fired deep inside him. "Still quiet."

The moonlight coming through the window highlighted Darya's face as the mask of sleep fell away. It reminded him of the intensity of a hungry leopard. Even his movements reflected the animal as he rose, dropping the blanket back down on Tessa and Arzo. Chase blocked his way, but Darya slammed into the captain's shoulder to push past him.

Chase followed him, noticing Toiluk had already joined the other Kyrgyz outside. "Darya."

Darya turned his head but continued to walk.

The night sky sparkled with stars. He came alongside Darya. "We need to talk."

Darya came to an abrupt stop. "About what?" "Tessa."

"What about her?" In the moonlight, the cold determination etched on Darya's face sent a message of an obstinate man used to getting his own way. Not all that different from himself.

"Why can't she remember? What happened to her? It has to be more than a bump on the head. Something traumatic has affected her." Darya glared at him. "Is it because you did something to her or something else?"

"Something else."

"What?" Chase swallowed hard. He shuddered at the thought of what the Taliban may have done to her. "Did the Taliban…"

"No. I got there in time." Darya turned to leave, but Chase closed his hand around his arm, hard enough to spin him around. He spit out the words. "Why did you come here? To find Bonnie or Tessa?"

"Both. I wouldn't have even known she was here if I hadn't stumbled across Abdul taking the soldier back, another thing in your favor."

Darya jerked free. "How do you know these women?"

"Bonnie works for the State Department. We've crossed paths in D.C. Not all that trustworthy, as I remember. Tessa works at a university in California as a geography analyst for an independent group working for the government wanting a safer America. I'm not sure how she got to Afghanistan. She has a husband and three kids who love and need her." Chase paused to let the information sink in.

"The husband?"

"What about him?" Chase hated making Tessa's husband out to be some kind of hero.

"Do you know him?"

"Met him. He's an okay guy. Don't like him."

"Why?" Darya's voice showed interest.

Chase shrugged. "Hard to say."

Darya raised his chin in defiance. "She told me you were like a big brother, always protective."

Chase chewed his bottom lip. "She's a bull in a china shop. Trouble follows her everywhere."

"So, which is it? Big brother or something else?"

Chase leaned in close with a snarl. "Something else."

He gave Darya a warning shove and turned on his heel.

CHAPTER 23

Chase didn't know how long he stood in the doorway watching Tessa. Moonlight spilling through the window highlighted the wide-open eyes staring back at him. Several times her gaze strayed to one of the children, but it always came back to him.

With quiet steps, he moved toward her, careful not to appear threatening. She seemed frozen except for the startling blue scrutiny following his movements. The toe of his boots touched the heel of her foot beneath the blanket. She pulled up her legs without a word.

"Can I sit down? Here? With you?" Chase pointed to where her feet had rested. When she didn't protest, he squatted in front of her. "Tessa." He whispered her name loving how it lingered on his tongue. "Are you all right?"

Silence. She nodded, pulling the blanket to cover her mouth.

"I'm taking you home." The absence of emotion on her face ruptured his heart. Tessa had always worn her feelings on her sleeve. She cried at the drop of a hat and loved to spout Christian philosophy at him when he broke the rules of civilized people. She'd made him feel human, given him laughter, and branded him her hero even if she couldn't bring herself to admit it. He'd experienced her gratitude on more than one occasion along with her devotion and friendship. Tessa was the girl next door in the house he'd never own in his lifetime. Her very existence kept him from falling off into the abyss of depression and rage.

Something had broken inside her. Darya had taken over as her protector. She allowed him to get physically closer than Chase ever dared. The Kyrgyz created a family unit with Arzo for the three of them. Tessa loved her own kids beyond reason. Darya must have sensed a yearning in her as she connected with these girls.

Tessa laid Arzo against Shirin, propped against the wall with her little sister Pamir in her lap then crawled forward to Chase and rested on her knees.

"I remember you. Chase," she whispered. Chase fought the urge to touch the tangled hair and smudged face.

He wanted to reassure himself she existed in front of him instead of spinning in his dreams. "What do you remember, baby?"

"You sometimes call me baby. But I don't know why."

Chase edged closer, his gaze exploring her face now cloaked in shadows. "I never told you why. I call you baby because you are special to me."

Tessa wrinkled her nose in confusion. "Are we lovers?" He smiled at her.

"No. We are not lovers. But we are very close friends, Tessa." Chase sighed. "You have a husband back home who loves you very much."

"What's his name?"

"Robert Scott. He's a good man."

The corners of her mouth turned up slightly. "I know." She moved forward on her knees. "What else? I have children. I know I have children."

"Yes." Chase reached toward her face, but, when she jerked back, he held his hand suspended in air. "Three. Two rowdy boys and a little girl who is almost identical to you. Her hair is brownish red, but curly like yours."

Tessa leaned back on her heels and chuckled in her throat. "I remember. I miss them."

"I'm taking you home, Tessa. Do you understand what I mean?"

She rose up on her knees and leaned toward him. The sound of panic rose in her voice. "No. I made a promise. I have to keep my promise first."

"To who, Tessa?"

"To me," came a disgruntled response from the door. Darya stood in the doorway with his rifle at his side.

~~~

Massoud rested under the lean-to with the horses. He could smell their waste mixed with the stale hay he managed to drag up with his feet to make a nest. His hands were bound with leather and secured to a three- foot-long piece of iron chain attached to the wall. There remained enough give for him to sit rather than stand for hours.

His face hurt. Leaning into his bound hands, he managed to touch the dried blood around his nose. To see out of his one good eye remained difficult, which frightened him more than the Kyrgyz. What good would a blind Taliban leader be to the cause? His power would be stripped from him without a second thought. The image of becoming a burden or, worse, a beggar on the streets of Kabul, threatened his confidence. He thought back to earlier in the evening when the woman from the American government brought him food.

"Guess you should have been doing less talking and more listening." Bonnie Finley set the cup of broth in front of him. She understood, maybe better than Massoud, his value lay in volunteering vital information. There was always the hope he would die at the hands of the crazy tribesman, Darya, who reminded her of a devil when dealing with the Taliban.

"Will you help me with the cup?"

Bonnie smirked. "No." She put it in his bound hands. The sight of you struggling to sip from a cup gives me great pleasure. Not so tough now, huh, Massoud?"

Even then, he worked to manipulate the situation. "We can help each other."

Bonnie sniffed. "I doubt it. But, go ahead. Enlighten me."

"Why should the ambassador get such a large cut? I can eliminate him and you would take his share."

Bonnie started for the door. "With you out of the way, I can take care of that little detail myself. Give my regards to Gitmo."

"Wait." He turned his head to get a better glimpse of her from his good eye. "I will tell the Americans the ambassador is dirty and
~~~

you are involved."

She paused and faced him, a forced laugh passing through her thin lips. "You are a desperate man. There is nothing to tie you to me."

"The children know. The other woman knows. They both heard the words I spoke."

Bonnie's face turned hard. "Shirin is the only one who can speak and understand English to any degree. Do you think after you killed her young man, she'll say anything on your behalf?"

Massoud frowned.

"And, as for my friend, she's lucky to remember her name, thanks to your oversexed goat herders."

"That should also be of interest to the military."

Bonnie walked over and kicked the cup of hot juices onto his face. He let out a cry. "Not one word, Massoud, or I will make sure you become a test dummy for an accidental dose of the Ebola virus." She kicked some manure into his lap. "Get used to that, too."

Massoud fought shadows in his rage to get free for an attack on the woman. He heard her laughter as she strode away into the dark. Bucking up and down several times, he removed the manure chunks from his lap. A searing pain showed the punches he'd taken from the masked devil they called Darya may have busted a few ribs. His gut hurt, too. Remembering the big American standing by with cold unconcern gave him a moment to be grateful he wasn't the one who landed the blows.

His breathing came fast with irritation at the government woman. He decided to focus on the American brute dressed like an Afghan. Why go to so much trouble? How had he found them? Did he search because of the government woman or maybe the children? Massoud hadn't thought any of them important enough, but the Americans. They never seemed to tire of rescuing stray dogs who could someday turn and bite the hand feeding them. Understanding such emotion remained out of reach for him.

None of it mattered. Soon his men would come for him. Then the impertinent female would be put in her place.

~~~
~~~

Darya watched Captain Hunter stand then straighten to his full height. His sitting so close to Tessa angered him. She remained on her knees until Darya hurried to her side to help her stand.

"Get the girls together," the man called Zoric shouted then began to shake them awake himself.

"What is it?" Chase grabbed his rifle.

"We've got movement about three hundred yards out, on the edge of the tree line."

Darya switched his focus from Chase to Tessa. The terror on her face made him pull her to his side. "Listen to me." He put his hands on each side of Tessa's face. "I won't let them get close, but you must protect yourself."

"Darya," she whispered. "I'm not sure I can." Her hands went to each side of his waist.

He rested his forehead against hers. "Just keep the girls quiet. We will do what we can."

Chase pulled out a Walther P-90 handgun then extended it to Tessa. Her brow creased. "Take it. Remember what I taught you."

Tessa gingerly lifted it from his fingers then turned toward him.

"We practiced three times a week during your training," Chase snapped. "Get a grip. I need to know if you can get the job done. You're not helpless, so whatever is eating at you, get over it. We all have crap to deal with. Those kids need you to be on your game." Tessa racked the slide of the weapon then lowered her hand to her side. "I got this." Tessa pulled back her shoulders. "I got this," she repeated.

Chase turned toward the door. "Well, it's about freakin' time," he growled.

Darya followed the man's movements with eyes narrowed to slits. Did Tessa's new posture, the determination on her face, indicate her memory had returned?

<div style="text-align: center;">~~~</div>

Tessa threw off her poncho-like robe and motioned for Bonnie to follow her to the children who were sitting up and rubbing their eyes. "Help me get them all together in the corner."

Bonnie lifted sleepy children as instructed. In minutes, they were all together. "Miss Melanie!" Pointing at the gun with alarm,

Shirin cringed. "What is wrong?"

Tessa went down on one knee. "Taliban." A gasp escaped the child's mouth as she cowered against the other girls. "We'll be fine, Shirin. The helicopters will be here at first light. If we can hold out until then, we'll be on our way to Kabul." She reached out to stroke the girl's cheek. "Can you help us with the little ones?"

Shirin jerked her head up and down nervously then swallowed a loud gulp.

"Bonnie and I will be right here, sweetheart."

"Yes, Miss Melanie. I do it for you because you are brave like Darya and my Rashid." Her words, although weak, reassured Tessa there would be an extra set of hands if needed.

The backdoor opened and Toiluk strode in, dragging Massoud by the collar. The bandit twisted his body in resistance as his feet pushed up clouds of dust from the floor. Toiluk, in spite of being a little taller than Tessa, jerked the man to his feet then shoved him against a wall where he toppled to the floor onto his side. As Massoud let loose a barrage of loud insults, Toiluk took a filthy rag from the floor then motioned him to open his mouth. Massoud responded by spitting at the Kyrgyz. In one swift movement, Toiluk stomped down on the man's leg. A cry of pain opened his mouth wide enough for Toiluk to shove in the rag.

The man shook his head, trying to spit it free. Toiluk took out a knitted ski mask. After pulling Massoud to a sitting position, he put his boot on the man's groin. The man instantly stopped squirming. With one quick movement, he pulled the mask over Massoud's face. By this time, the Taliban leader's chest rose and fell as if he couldn't breathe. The Kyrgyz withdrew his foot then strolled away.

The children fell back to sleep in minutes. Only Shirin remained vigilant. Bonnie covered them with the few blankets they'd brought before turning to Tessa.

"I want a gun, too." She gestured to Massoud glaring at her through the openings of his ski mask. "If those goat herders come in, we may not be able to fend them off until the military gets here."

Tessa grabbed her arm and pulled her aside. "Shush! You might wake Shirin and the others. I don't want her to hear you. She's been through enough. Do you even know how to use a gun?"

Bonnie rolled her eyes. "That's what I thought."

"So why did Chase get in your face?"

"I believe I tend to push his angry buttons more times than not. If I remember right, we don't always get along. He wants to tell me what to do. I promise to follow orders then try to find a way out of it."

Bonnie sniffed. "Well, if I'd thought I'd get that kind of attention from him in D.C., I would've been a lot more uncooperative." She shifted her interested gaze to admire

Chase's backside. "If you know what I mean," she whispered. "But the two of you aren't…"

"No. I'm married." Tessa bristled.

"Yes, I know. Two men and counting. Interesting dilemma." The women stood watching the men standing at the windows. "So, is your memory still fuzzy, or are you good?"

"What do you care?" Before Bonnie could answer, Tessa moved toward Darya standing at the door.

He used the field glasses but at Tessa's approach, he backed inside. She slipped her hands around his waist. He dropped one hand on hers then pulled her tight against him. He turned to glance over his shoulder at her. Her heart beat faster as she pressed against him.

"Tes-sa." He said her name in the way that made it sound like music. "Tessa," he breathed into her face then turned back to stare through a pair of field glasses. "A couple of hours before light. I think they'll wait. They fear we hide in places they can't see."

"Darya," she murmured in his ear. "The captain and I work together. Nothing else." She felt his shoulders tighten. "I wanted to remember who I was. What I was. Seeing him helps me remember. Things are so much clearer now. I need you to understand."

The tribesman who had literally ridden in on a white horse and saved her took a large breath, but remained silent. As Tessa pulled away, she let her hand trail down Darya's hip and realized she wanted to make him happy. Maybe she felt a sense of obligation mixed with gratitude. But the warm affection she once carried for him had morphed into a burning turbulence.

The promise would be kept if they could make it back to Kabul.

CHAPTER 24

"I think they've hunkered down til first light." Chase stood next to Darya. "Zoric and I can slip out the rear entrance, circle back around them. Pick 'em off one by one. There's plenty of cover. Increase our chances." He didn't like not being in charge. His temperament, stretched to the limit, now threatened to boil over.

Tessa joined the tribesman, whispered in his ear, and walked away. Darya flashed him a broad smile. Chase wanted to rip something apart, the tribesman being at the top of the list.

Darya sobered, but held his gaze. Chase realized his intimidation tactics of invading a man's personal space had little effect on the solemn-faced Kyrgyz. "No." Darya's voice sounded flat. "Too risky. If you are captured, then we come up short on firepower."

"The risk is worth it." Chase rolled his shoulders, feeling a tightness in his neck. "I don't need your permission."

Darya nodded then motioned outside.

Chase followed him through the doorway.

"Take two of the horses. You'll get there faster." Darya gave him directions as to how to circle back without being spotted. "I don't like it. Massoud trains his men. They are smarter than most Taliban. Do not underestimate them." As he turned to go back inside, he pointed toward the horses. "Go ready yourself." Chase grabbed his arm. "Tessa needs to return to the States. This is no place for a woman like her."

Darya jerked away.

"She already has a family. They want her back." Chase stepped into his personal space again until their noses nearly touched. "If anything happens to her, I'm coming for you. Understand?"

Darya's eyes narrowed to slits. "If anything happens to her, it will be because you didn't do your job and I am dead."

Darya stared at him a second longer before turning slowly to return inside.

~~~

Stealth can't be achieved when riding nervous horses toward a Taliban encampment. Tying the reins to a clump of dead bushes, Chase and Zoric moved farther into humid darkness. The night air managed to cool their skin as sweat evaporated around their necks. They'd blackened their faces with soot then wrapped their heads with ragged scarves, and trickles of anticipation trailed down the backs of their necks and under their arms. To move over unfamiliar terrain, the black night lit by millions of stars, grew tedious, if not treacherous.

Over the years, Chase had relied on night vision goggles to assist in these kinds of situations. Having given his to the Kahn in Darya's village, he let Zoric take the lead. The Serbian moved like a ghost through air void of any breeze. A rolling, misplaced pebble could sound like an explosion to an enemy anticipating trouble.

The smell of woodsmoke and burnt meat wafted to the two men hunkered down behind a rock not much bigger than themselves. After surveying the camp, Zoric handed Chase the goggles and he peered into the ebony curtain before first light.

"I see three at the fire," Chase whispered.

The Serbian pointed to four bundles the length of a man around the fire. Chase held up seven fingers. The Taliban basked in the slumber both men wished they'd had before attempting this mission.

The standing guards stood rigid, holding rifles. Chase gave the sign for neutralizing them first. A few more signals and they had decided which sleeping and waking target each would take. Three quiet pops from their silencers and the Taliban fell into the fire
~~~

then burst into flames. With knives unsheathed, they rushed toward the camp. Chase and Zoric froze on the perimeter. The lack of screams from the burning men put them on alert. They dropped to the ground to see if the sleeping men would react. No twisting or moaning to alert the others. Something was wrong but they had to keep going.

"Ready?" Chase mouthed the words to Zoric and both jumped to their feet and attacked the nearest men on the ground.

Their knives plunged deep several times before they moved to the next. After each stabbed two, they retreated to the cover of the rocks. Winded at the sudden escape, both men pressed their backs against a boulder while continuing to do a security scan of the area.

Chase gulped a breath. "Decoys."

That explained the silent men falling into the fire. He guessed they created a makeshift cross with clothes draped around the exterior. The flames consumed them too fast. The rifles most likely were something left over from the Russian years. The bundles on the ground were nothing but stuffed grain sacks.

"Where are they?" Zoric stole a glance over the rock then hunkered back down, his shoulder touching Chase who readied his weapon.

"My guess is they've moved in on the village. They anticipated we might attack them during a vulnerable time. I see no signs of horses so they're probably on foot."

"If we reach the top of the ridge, we would have a clear signal to get those birds to light a fire under Massoud's men." Zoric's voice still remained a whisper in case someone remained behind to make trouble.

Chase transferred the radio earwig to Zoric. The eastern sky lightened. "I hope they're on their way. Warn them there could be trouble. I'll head back. Give me some time then follow. No use both of us going in blind."

Gravel rolled down from somewhere above them. Both men ducked then gave a signal to separate and seek out the source of the noise. They moved akin to a hunting lion.

Taking the lead since he wore the night vision goggles, Chase saw the Afghan first. He peered over a ledge not more than ten feet above the camp. The nervous back and forth of his head indicated he searched to find whoever entered the camp. The fire blazed high enough to light the entire area. Zoric crept up behind him and slipped his six-inch blade under the man's throat.

"Quiet," Chase ordered, arriving at Zoric's side. With a raspy intake of breath, the man trembled. Chase relieved him of his M16 and patted him down for any other weapons. "He's clean." He questioned the Afghan. "Are you alone?" Even though Chase spoke adequate Pashto, sometimes the dialect left a lot to be desired. He repeated. "Alone?"

The Afghan's nervous nod resembled one of those bobble head toys at ballparks in the States. Zoric let his knife puncture the skin enough to force a whimper then let him fall backwards into the loose gravel. Chase jammed his boot into the man's chest, which forced a gush of air from the man's mouth. He tilted his head at Zoric who squatted next to him and gave a primal growl in his throat before licking his lips. The man's eyes bulged as Zoric leaned in.

Zoric kept a small vile of red gel food coloring for moments needing a little more encouragement. He'd been called a vampire more times than he cared to remember. Times like these, it paid off. When Chase flashed his pen light at his partner's face, red syrupy gel oozed from his mouth. The Afghan cried out and grabbed his heart.

"Where are the others?" Chase pressed his boot a little harder.

The Afghan whimpered louder as Zoric hopped closer on his bent legs. He let the red syrup drip onto the man's chin then ran his finger through it, followed by sucking it off the Afghan's face. The Serbian shook his head back and forth, moaning. Zoric fingered the man's ears and neck, pinching at times then laughed deep in his throat.

"Easy, Zoric." Chase reached down and rubbed his partner's head like a beloved dog. "If he doesn't talk, I will let you have him." Chase removed his foot from the Afghan's chest. The man pushed himself up to a sitting position and kicked at the gravel to back away, but Zoric followed on his hands and knees until he breathed into the man's face.

"I talk!"

Chase towered over him with his gun pointed at the man's crotch. "I'm not a patient man. Don't make me use follow-up questions." Zoric sucked in exaggerated gulps of air as he licked the syrup spilling into his own beard. Then he lunged at the Afghan, growling viciously. Chase grabbed Zoric by the collar and threw him back. "Talk."

"Yes. Yes. I'm the one left behind. I was told to shoot in the air if someone came. They left one, two hours ago. They're waiting to move in first light. They were afraid to make accident and shoot Massoud."

"What's the plan?" Chase watched Zoric edge closer and jab his gun into the man's crotch. The Afghan yelped. "The plan."

"Rescue Massoud. Kill the men. Take the women and children if possible, especially the government woman. She is worth money. Sell the others. Massoud wanted the other for himself. She killed one of our men with knife. Shot another..."

Zoric jumped to his feet and met Chase's expression in alarm. "Killed a man?"

"Yes. All I know. I was not there. Massoud very angry. Wants to teach woman a lesson."

Chase raised his chin in a quick jerk toward Zoric as he left him with the Afghan. "I'll leave you the other horse. Be careful."

CHAPTER 25

"You scared even me this time, Zoric." Chase handed Zoric the night vision goggles as he brought his horse alongside. "Glad I had Tessa's crucifix in my pocket."

Zoric shrugged. "You shouldn't encourage me if I'm not to be your monster."

"I'm just saying maybe tone it back a little next time. Don't do anything around the kids." The first morning breeze brushed his face. "I'm assuming you secured him."

Zoric grinned as he tucked the goggles inside his jacket. "He decided to hang around."

Chase stole a glance back into the darkness even though there would be no sign of the prisoner. "You need to talk to Dr. Wu when we get back. I thought you were making progress."

"I am. He is still in one piece." Zoric shrugged. "Shouldn't have messed with little girls or…" His voice froze into silence as he squinted against the lifting darkness toward the village. "Those aren't Kyrgyz, Chase." His horse stamped with impatience.

"Massoud's men are already there."

~~~

"You are kidding yourself, tribesman, if you think you can protect yourself against my men." Massoud refused to use Darya's name.

He sat against the wall with knees drawn up as he attempted to
~~~

loosen his hands secured behind his back. Toiluk had tightened the twine until he winced in pain. This forced a chuckle from the square-shouldered tribesman as he shoved him onto an already-sore hip.

"Where is the big man? The one with the devil at his side?"

Darya continued to use the night vision goggles. "Tribesman." Massoud shifted his attention to the women and children. "You." Massoud whistled at them as if he were calling a dog. "The one with the blue eyes. Where is the big man? Are those two Americans? Tell me and I will spare you when my men come." He squirmed to comfort his aching body. "My men come for you and the girls. I can protect you now."

Darya whirled around to glare at Massoud. He crossed the room in two steps with such quickness, the Taliban leader cowered back farther into the crumbling wall. In one swift movement, Darya reached down and jerked him to his feet. He tried to pull away but the tribesman drove his breath from him with a punch to his stomach. When his mouth opened, Darya shoved his tattered mask, into Massoud's mouth then swept his foot against the back of his knees. He collapsed back onto the dirt floor.

Darya wanted to continue the beating until he saw Tessa rocking Arzo back and forth with two other little ones clinging to her. She shook her head in protest and began to sing a lullaby which quieted the children as well as the turmoil brewing inside him.

Would the American helicopters arrive in time? Did Captain Hunter find the Taliban camp and eliminate the possibility of an attack? Or could he have been taken prisoner? No shots echoed across the land between the dense cover and the village. He glanced at his men posted at the two windows and rickety doors before going to Tessa.

"Little one." He kneeled down to touch Arzo's head. "Darya will protect his little girl." Arzo pushed away from Tessa to wrap her arms around the tribesman's neck. He stood, loving the way the child clung to him. Extending his hand toward Tessa, he felt her take his hand. The two other girls scrambled up to wrap their arms around their protector, too, as Darya pulled Tessa to her feet.

Tessa patted Arzo's short legs before lifting her face to him. She didn't resist his pulling her into his embrace, her head tucked beneath his chin. In English, he whispered into her ear, "Thank you for giving me these days, Tessa. Whatever happens today, know you have my heart. Know, if I die today, you made me happy." She tightened her arms around him. If there had been more time for them to get acquainted, maybe she would not have looked at the American captain.

"And if I die today, I will meet you in paradise, Darya." She stroked his back. "I'm sorry I've caused you so much trouble. You've given up everything for us to return. If I could change one thing, it would be to keep you safe with your people in the Wakhan Valley."

"I am doing what is right, Tessa. I have no regrets." Her smirk brought a chuckle from his throat. "Well, maybe one regret."

Tessa's forehead creased. She reached up to touch his face. "Is it the bride price you gave for me?"

"No. It was not taking my rights as your husband on our wedding night." His grin made Tessa land a light punch to his side. He kissed her forehead. "But, if we do survive, I will hold you to your promise."

"Then you better get us out of here."

Darya felt surprise at seeing warmth instead of dread or fear in her face. She focused on his mouth and neck. Arzo reached for Tessa who welcomed the child into her arms.

Darya patted the two girls hugging each of his legs. "Go with your mother." He had heard the children call her mother several days earlier. Whether she understood the Pashto word was irrelevant. She'd taken the orphans in like a guardian angel. He remembered seeing a picture on a calendar once where two small children crossed a dangerous bridge. An angel followed them with outstretched arms to catch them if they should fall. Tessa had reminded him of the picture from the moment he watched her defend the children and especially when he discovered what she'd done to protect Shirin from the Taliban.

Tessa ushered the girls back to join the others along the wall. Darya watched her for seconds longer before turning back to his companions. He came alongside Toiluk who stared out the window from the corner, so as not to be a target.

"They are coming." Toiluk glanced at him. "The Americans may be dead." His voice, now a whisper, continued with an unemotional evaluation of the situation. "We are outnumbered. Hand to hand, we can defeat the dogs. If they carry any weapons taken from the downed helicopter, we could be in trouble. Our ammunition is low." Toiluk glanced back at the women and children. "We need to decide right now, Darya, what you want to do if we are overwhelmed. Those women and children will die a thousand deaths if the Taliban take them."

Darya resisted looking over at his new weakness. "I will do it, if it comes to that."

Toiluk reached back and put his leathery hand on his friend's shoulder. "Let me do this for you. No man should have to kill his family to save them."

"Blindfold Massoud." Darya nodded to one of the other Kyrgyz. The man retrieved Massoud and pulled the stocking cap from his head then forced him to face Darya. When Massoud continued to resist, Darya shoved him back against the wall then pressed his foot against his chest. As he quieted, Darya kneeled beside him. "If I let you go, will you take your men back into the hills?" He jerked the cloth from Massoud's mouth.

"My men are coming to kill you." His tone showed no fear. "I do not need you to free me."

"When your men get within ten feet of the village, I will kill you, Massoud."

"And if the American helicopter comes to save you and the women? What will you use as a bargaining chip to keep them from throwing you in jail?" Massoud smiled so big his crooked teeth became visible. "Yes. I know who you are and why you have been in these mountains so long. I am your get-out-of-jail-free card as the Americans like to say."

"I didn't desert. I made it appear as if I did. All this time, I've been searching for you and anyone helping from the inside. I intend to take care of the ambassador on my own."

"So, you free me and then what? What makes you think you can trust me?"

Darya rose to stand. "You are right. I should never trust a rabid dog." He strode away as Massoud laughed deep in his throat.

~~~
~~~

Bonnie Finley nudged Tessa. "What do you think those two are up to? Maybe Darya is working for him."

Tessa shifted her attention from Arzo playing patty cake with Shirin to the man who consumed her common sense. Darya. What would she do if she made it back to safety? Chase made it pretty clear he meant to take her home to her real life family. Imagines of her husband, Robert, and their history grew clearer by the hour. The emptiness she experienced when imagining him confused her, although she felt she must have loved him.

But what of Darya? Although their marriage wouldn't be recognized in the United States, he was her husband, too. Without him, she would not be alive, nor would the orphan daughters she'd grown to love. Her responsibility to him when this nightmare ended remained a problem she'd deal with later. When memories rolled over her like an unpredicted tsunami, other emotions returned.

Some of those emotions involved Captain Chase Hunter. Just good friends? Somehow, his claim didn't feel right either. Tessa shook her head to clear the confusion.

"Darya hates Massoud and what he stands for. Don't be ridiculous." Tessa sniffed a retort at Bonnie as she felt for her gun.

Bonnie arched an eyebrow. "Or maybe love is blind." She shrugged as she stared across the room at Massoud. "We need to bargain out of this."

"And how do you propose we do that? Make a deal with Massoud and turn our backs on these people who have risked everything for us? No thanks."

"Time is running out. If those helicopters don't get here soon, we're dead. The captain and his ghoul…"

"Don't you dare call him that." The viciousness in her voice took Bonnie aback.

"Okay. The captain and his sidekick. Happy? Anyway, they've been gone a long time. Chances are they aren't coming back. They're either dead or captured, which, with the Taliban is kind of the same thing."

Tessa didn't want to believe the captain and Zoric could be dead.

"They'll be back."

Bonnie got to her feet then went through some awkward

stretches to loosen up. She stepped over a child who had fallen back asleep then moved to the center of the room. Tessa didn't trust the woman. When Bonnie moved closer to Massoud, Tessa thought it curious but became distracted as Arzo jumped into her lap and kissed her on the cheeks. By the time she'd settled the child, Bonnie had wandered away.

~~~

Chase and Zoric followed the Taliban at a distance until forced to veer off to avoid detection. They led the calm horses into the village at the opposite end. Sunrise flooded the land with dabbled light as they passed several shacks. A woman peeked out a window then pulled the rag of a curtain, to block out a view to the inside. One old man came and stood in the door holding a brew with curls of steam escaping around the lip of the cup. He held it in midair as if trying to decide whether or not to take a drink. His clothes, ragged and soiled, blended the Afghan and Kyrgyz style. He dropped his hand to his side and nonchalantly pointed an arthritic finger to a nearby building before holding out two more fingers. After taking a sip of his brew, the old man backed inside and shut the door.

They stopped along the side of one of the buildings, their ears tuned to any sudden movement or noise. The horses bobbed their heads but settled down with a pat to their necks with reassurance.

The door swung open in front of them as they rounded the corner which revealed three Afghans who swung their rifles up at hearing the horses. But they reacted too slowly. Chase and Zoric fired the instant the men raised their weapons, dropping them where they stood. An avalanche of gunfire ensued, from rooftops, behind overturned carts, and through darkened windows.

They faced more than the fighters they'd followed. Chase could see the house down at the end of the street where he'd left the Kyrgyz fighters. They fired their weapons, aiming at a group of Taliban swarming in from several directions. Chase and Zoric managed to duck into an abandoned house, jerking the bridles of their horses to follow. Once inside they took up positions at unadorned windows to pick off the hidden Taliban.

They took turns, shouting.
~~~

"Roof. Your two o'clock." Chase knew Zoric could make the shot.

"Doorway across the street."

"Two behind the overturned truck."

"Back window. Don't shoot the horses!" Zoric continued to shoot as he shouted.

"I'm almost out of ammo!"

<h1 align="center">CHAPTER 26</h1>

"Here they come!" shouted Darya as he took aim with his rifle. The weapon spit bullets with deadly accuracy as the building filled with the smell of gunpowder and the screams of children scrambling to cower into the corner with Tessa.

Bonnie fell on top of Shirin as a bullet landed above her head. Her cry faded into the chaos of the rapid fire of weapons and the hail of casings being expelled. She covered her head with her hands as if doing so would protect her. When she looked toward the backdoor a man appeared with a gun pointed at the backs of the Kyrgyz. She screamed more in terror than as a warning. Her cries diverted his attention long enough for Darya to swing around and shoot him two times in the chest.

Tessa pushed Arzo into Shirin's lap then pried the little hands of the others off her body the quickest way she could. "Stay down, children!"

She hunched over to drag a table, flipped on its side, in front of them. There were several wooden crates used as stools the night before which she carried to stack up in front of the table. A bullet pierced a metal bucket making it fly back and hit Tessa in the side of the head. Shirin scrambled up to help her as she set the children aside.

"I'm fine! Stay down, Shirin!"

The sun now shone through the windows, making it easier for

231

the Kyrgyz to pick off the Taliban who ran out in the open. Clouds of dust and gunpowder choked Tessa as she crawled back to the children. As she got to one knee, something took hold of her foot and yanked her down on her stomach. In one fluid motion, she rolled to her back to see Massoud bending over her.

For someone who had been beaten, the one-eyed Taliban moved with remarkable speed as he pounced on Tessa, forcing all the air from her lungs. In one swift move he jumped up then jerked her to an unsteady standing position. He circled her neck with his arm. In his free hand, he held a glass shard pressed against her throat. "Darya," screamed Shirin as she stood in slow motion.

"Darya!"

This time he turned his head to where the young girl pointed. He gave an order for the men to stop firing and they, too, turned toward Massoud backing toward the door with Tessa.

Bullets continued to hit the building from outside.

Massoud gave a contemptuous smirk. "It seems the situation has changed, huh, Kyrgyz? I will kill her if you come closer." Massoud jerked her up against him. Tessa whined in fear. Her expression pleaded with Darya to save her.

"Then you will be dead as well," he said, holding his tone level. "What is the point in killing her? You have nothing but a sharp piece of glass, and we both know this will not protect you from me or my men. Let her go and I will return you to your herd of swine myself."

Massoud's amused expression continued. "I think I will take her with me. I do not trust the words of a man who burns yak dung for warmth or compares Allah's faithful to swine."

Darya avoided checking further on Tessa. It would make him indecisive. "I'm going to kill you whether you take the woman or not. Maybe not today, but soon."

"I think not. You need me alive if you ever want to return to the West with these pitiful orphans." He continued to sidestep toward the door. "This woman has made you weak. You think you can barter with me for forgiveness with the Americans. They are less trustworthy than me."

Tessa took advantage of Massoud's obsession with Darya to jerk sideways enough to drop her fist so hard into his crotch, he dropped his arm from around her neck. Before he could slice her throat, she fell to the floor. As she rolled to her back, Tessa pulled out her gun and aimed it up at Massoud. Without hesitation she squeezed the trigger.

Nothing happened.

In the next split second, she saw Massoud take a step forward. At the same time, Darya's legs straddled her head. He grabbed the Walther from her raised hands, causing Massoud to lose his smug expression and run to the door. She cringed at the report, covering her ears with her hands. Two hot casings landed on her throat where Massoud had held the shard seconds before. The one-eyed terror of Afghanistan grabbed hold of a shelf, bringing it down on him as he hit the floor.

Darya stepped aside so he could reach down and pull Tessa to her feet. The men at the door and windows commenced firing their weapons again, not giving Massoud further attention.

Tessa panted so hard she felt as if she'd been out for a run. Darya forced the Walther back into her hand. "It works better if you take the safety off."

She managed to inhale deeply in acknowledgment before he returned to fight with his men. She dared to stare at the man sprawled on the floor, a dark blotch growing on the front of his shirt. Massoud continued to breathe. Tessa hunkered back down behind the table. Bonnie cowered there, as well, with knees drawn up tight and a blanket pulled across her midsection and mouth. The little ones covered their ears until Tessa joined them. As she settled on the floor, the children scrambled to cover her with trembling arms and legs. To reassure them, Tessa whispered in their ears one by one, hoping they could hear over the shouts of the Kyrgyz and gunfire.

A sudden realization washed over her. The deafening noise had halted to complete silence. Men stood rigid at the windows and door, staring out into the light washing over the dusty street and uneven land beyond. Another sweeter sound, occurred, the whump, whump of rotary blades from helicopters.

With Arzo in her arms around her neck, Tessa struggled to her feet. She grabbed the hands of two of the children. She passed Arzo to Bonnie as she helped the other children.

The woman frowned at Arzo. "I'm not carrying this child. She'll slow me down!" She put the little legs on the floor then took

Arzo's hand. "She can run faster than me anyway."

Tessa dropped down to face Arzo. "Can you run, daughter? I need you to run like Darya's horse. Yes?"

Arzo's head bobbed up and down with her promise. "I can!"

"Good girl." Tessa kissed her cheek.

The room clattered with the noise of making ready to leave. She eased from behind the overturned table when Darya motioned for them. When she reached him, he slipped a satchel over his head, along with a canteen. He checked both revolvers and slung his rifle over one shoulder. "Toiluk makes the horses ready," he informed her.

Outside the window, the Taliban had turned their guns on the helicopters. A machine gun plowed up the ground through an open door of the Black Hawk. The confusion of Taliban screams mixed with gunfire gave the Kyrgyz time to escape.

"We're going to make it." Darya extended his hand to rest on her shoulder. "My friends and I will ride out, and you will run behind them. We can hold off any Taliban who escape."

"Are your friends coming with us?"

"No. That would leave their horses to the Taliban. These animals are part of their wealth. They will ride home, after we lift off."

Tessa grabbed the front of Darya's shirt. "You listen to me. Go with your friends. If the military catch you, you'll go to prison."

Darya's eyes twinkled as he slipped a hand to the back of her neck and pulled her mouth to his where he forced a long, hard kiss. "Some things are worth going to prison for. Wait for us to swing around the front. We're bigger targets. We can form a wall of protection for you and the children." Small hands tugged at his pant leg. Arzo wrinkled her nose up at him as she gave a sniff. He scooped her up in his arms then planted a kiss on her forehead. "Can you show me how fast you can run, my sweet Arzo?"

"Scared."

"What?" Darya landed his free fist on his chest with a thud. "How can you be scared with me as your protector?" He frowned and touched her nose with his. She took both her hands and patted each side of his face then hugged his neck so tight Darya faked a choke. "Do not shame me, daughter. Run like the wind when your mother says to go."

"This is madness." Bonnie bristled then put her hands on her hips. "Let's wait for the soldiers to come get us."

"Those helicopters are going to blast this place apart in ten minutes. If Captain Hunter made it to the ridge, he called for more help. He marked this building before he took off."

Tessa jerked her chin up in a show of disbelief. "Then he must be alive since there are three birds."

Darya shoved past Bonnie. "Stay or go. I don't care. But my wife and children will do as I say." He stopped at the back door and turned to scowl at the State Department woman. "Do not let anything happen to Arzo. You do not want me as your enemy."

Tessa heard Bonnie's usual disapproving huff as she came up beside her. She continued to stare out the window when a moan from the other side of the room drew both women's attention. The wounded Massoud, now covered in his own blood, coughed as if he were taking his last breath.

"What are you doing?" Tessa asked as Bonnie moved toward Massoud and let out a cackling laugh.

"If you don't want to be incinerated, you'd better get out." She watched him open his feverish eye then nod. In a quick retreat, Bonnie returned to Tessa's side.

"Are you thinking he can somehow help you down the road if he lives? You're unbelievable."

"I don't have the luxury of having two American badasses at my beck and call like you." Tessa rolled her eyes to the sudden dust cloud sweeping their way.

"You go first, Tessa." Bonnie peeked around her as the thunder of hooves reached their ears. "Someone is going to pay for putting me in this kind of danger." Her voice resembled the scratching on a blackboard. "I will make…"

"Shut up, Bonnie," Tessa bit out. "Not another word. This is your fault. If you hadn't made a pact with the ambassador for a piece of the drug market, Massoud wouldn't even know about us. It's not hard to figure out the ambassador wanted you out of the picture."

A piercing whistle drew Tessa's attention to horses prancing outside their door. Darya motioned for them to follow as the sounds of gunfire continued from the helicopters and Taliban in the distance. She lifted the scarf over her head but shed the wrap. Her exposed jeans revealed some rips and holes absent days earlier or had it been weeks? The white tunic hung lopsided over one shoulder.

Moving outside from the safety of the shack, Tessa felt a morning breeze, raw with the hint of an early fall, brush against her exposed neck and shoulder. Shivering, she noticed two more horses thundering down the street toward them— Captain Hunter and Zoric. The captain pulled back on the reins, making the horse rear a few feet from her. The bottom part of his face, wrapped in a blue rag, created the appearance of an outlaw from the old West. His horse continued to prance as he pulled down the covering and glared at her.

In that moment, Tessa realized where her alliances lay. All the confusion, fear, and fog surrounding her for so many days became clear as the streams flowing through the Wakhan Valley. This man had promised to always protect her, find her then drag her kicking and screaming from any trouble she'd gotten herself into. He'd done it on several occasions. Her heart raced as he danced his horse in circles like some mating ritual. This man also meant peril. Even though he tore his dark eyes from her after a few seconds, Captain Hunter was as dangerous as Darya. She'd have to consider her propensity for such men later.

The horses lunged forward as the Kyrgyz and Americans shot at the Taliban as they ventured back into view. This gave two of the Black Hawks enough time to land. Soldiers jumped free and took up positions to protect their passengers trying to run toward them.

Later, Tessa would remember the children did not call out in fear or cry. They ran toward their future with determination. When they fell, they bounded back to their feet. They turned loose of the adult's hands, and even Shirin could not keep her sister confined.

Bonnie cried out as her ankle turned against a rock. Even so, she picked up speed, letting Arzo's hand go free. The little girl fell with Bonnie but missed hopping up like the others. Blood poured from scratches on her face and arms. The child opened her mouth as if to cry, but nothing came out but puffs of white vapor on the morning breeze. She stood alone, looking at her hands while gunfire pounded the ground all around her.

The soldiers tossed the children one by one into the helicopter where they were caught by other sure hands. Bonnie shoved one of the soldiers aside as she plowed into the opening, landing on her stomach. Someone pulled her the rest of the way inside.

"Where's Arzo!" Tessa screamed at Bonnie over the sounds of the blades of the helicopters. Bonnie pointed out into the field.

Tessa whirled around to see the orphan confused, lost, and alone. She took a step toward rescue when one of the soldiers grabbed her arm. "We'll get her. Time to leave!"

"No." Tessa jerked free, knowing the first helicopter would lift off without her. She ran toward Arzo, calling her name and waving for her to run.

The Taliban continued to fight, but their attention shifted from the helicopters to the tribesmen on the ground. One bird remained in the air and fired a missile exploding the shack where a few Taliban escaped for cover then aimed at the shack where Massoud lay bleeding. Tessa shoved Arzo to the ground and covered her body against flying debris. She rose up when someone yanked her to her feet. A Taliban shook her violently. His sour breath filled her face as he spun her around.

Tessa had become the man's human shield.

"Arzo. Run!" She screamed the command over and over until she saw the child get up and stumble toward the remaining helicopter. Before she could run more than ten feet another Taliban scooped her up and pressed her to his chest with one arm. Arzo squirmed but received a smack upside the head for the effort.

Sinking her teeth into the arm around the neck, Tessa heard the man yelp as he stepped back. His next movement pulled a club from his belt. Lifting it over his head with both hands he growled undistinguishable words. As the club fell, Tessa dropped to the ground.

CHAPTER 27

Darya carried the reins of his horse between his teeth as he rode, firing his weapon. The beast moved beneath the press of his knees whenever Darya indicated to turn and pull up short. On one such turn, he saw Arzo had not made it to the helicopter lifting off with the other children. He watched Tessa run toward the child with several Taliban in hot pursuit. The whoosh of the released missile followed by an explosion caused his horse to rear then bolt toward safety. Reining the animal in took a great deal of strength and balance since he decided to try and buck his rider to the ground.

After gaining control once again, Darya watched Tessa crab crawl backwards away from a Taliban fighter prepared to club her into paradise. His heart leaped into his throat as Arzo's screams paralyzed his reasoning processes. In a split second he watched the child get a severe smack from her captor as he swung her under his arm. Darya fired off a shot at the Taliban's shoulder.

When he dropped Arzo, she hopped up like a jackrabbit and raced back toward Tessa.

Darya put the reins back between his teeth and squeezed his knees into the sides of his horse. The animal lunged forward. Tessa's attacker swung the club, but she rolled away in time. The man overbalanced, staggering forward. He regained some control before rushing Tessa again, this time getting closer and aiming his club. Darya could hear the man's yell of victory as he reared back once more. Arzo had covered a lot of ground and was within yards of Tessa when she turned to see the child.

He slowed the horse, but Darya could only raise his gun enough to try and shoot the Taliban somewhere that would halt him long enough for Tessa to escape. He didn't want to miss his target and make her the casualty. Someone grabbed the bridle, dragging horse and Darya to the ground as a Taliban fighter pushed his rifle into the horse's head then pulled the trigger. The animal died instantly, pinning Darya beneath the bulk. The Taliban fighter jumped back as Darya yelled out in grief, knowing he'd failed another wife and child. He managed to catch an awkward hold of the fighter's pant leg, the man laughing as he shoved the barrel of the rifle in Darya's chest.

A shot rang out and blood squirted from the Taliban's neck, toppling him across the head of the horse. Captain Hunter thundered his horse past. He leaned forward in the saddle with his rifle raised, much like a Kyrgyz defending what he loved. Tessa. The captain might get to her in time. He could ponder why the captain saved his life later.

<div style="text-align:center">~~~</div>

This time, Tessa couldn't outmaneuver the man with the club. He landed his boot on her leg, causing her to cry out in pain. Yet, she wiggled to free herself, using her elbows to push herself away. From the corner of her eye, she could see Arzo trying to reach her. The last thing the orphan needed to see was a Taliban fighter clubbing her second mother to death.

Please, God! Save Arzo from seeing what's about to happen.

Another shot echoed, throwing the Taliban back as he dropped the club on her stomach. He held up his bloody fist at the stampeding horse barreling toward him. Tessa caught a gasp in her throat as the muscled power of the beast mowed him down to the ground.

Tessa jumped up as Chase positioned the horse between her and the fighter. Without another thought for her safety, she ran toward Arzo. As she scooped up the girl into her arms, another shot rang out from Chase's rifle. Turning back, she could see her attacker lying on the ground beneath Chase's horse. The sound of rotary blades of the second helicopter turned her attention to escape. She spotted Darya's downed horse, fearing the worst. A sob caught in her throat, knowing she must choose between saving Darya or Arzo.

The third helicopter appeared to be herding the Taliban away from them. Tessa hobbled forward when she heard the sound of a galloping horse once more. Chase stopped his horse next to her and extended his hand. When she handed Arzo up first, Chase placed her in front of him. The next time his arm extended, he leaned out from the saddle.

"Let's go." His warm gaze embraced her soul. When she hesitated, he leaned even farther out and touched her face with a chapped hand. "I'm taking you home."

Tessa grabbed his arm and let him swing her up behind him. As his horse pranced under the added weight, she turned her attention to Darya's horse lying lifeless on the ground. Zoric stood on the backside of the downed animal, pulling at something. When Darya stood, he searched for her. Zoric pointed toward them before urging the tribesman to mount up with him.

The two horses stopped some twenty-five feet away neighing with protest and fear of the helicopters. Toiluk remained mounted, waiting for his friend to join him and return to the freedom of the Wakhan.

Darya slid to the ground and grabbed the bridle of Zoric's horse so he could dismount without being thrown. He walked the animal over to Chase's. Tessa carried Arzo to the helicopter and handed her off before returning to the men.

She arrived in time to hear Chase and Darya talking. "Get on the horse and disappear, Darya." Chase's words sounded more like an order than a suggestion. "We both know what will happen if you go back. They will never understand what you did to protect these women and children."

"He is right, Darya." Tessa wanted to sound tough. "Let us try and sort this out so you can come home." Her voice softened. "If you still want to come home."

Toiluk's horse stamped impatient hooves. "Listen to them, Darya." He probably understood the hand gestures but not the words.

Darya took the reins of the two horses and handed them back to

Toiluk. "These were the last of my stock. They are now yours. Go. Join the others before the Taliban return."

Toiluk frowned at Tessa. He bowed his head in somber agreement and trotted off, leading his animals.

"Darya." Tessa got in his face. "You got us this far. That is enough. The captain can see this through. Please."

"We have an agreement. I take the children all the way and then you can fulfill your end of the bargain." He looked over her head at the captain. "Thank you, Captain Hunter. You saved my life."

Chase's nostrils flared as his jaw tightened and released. "It seemed like a good idea at the time."

This brought a smirk to Darya's lips as he shifted his attention to Tessa and spoke in Pashto. "Arzo is waiting. This will be the last day of fear for our daughter."

~~~

Military base outside Kabul

A great many people waited for them as their helicopter landed near the one which had left with Bonnie and the other children. Many hands appeared to assist with the little ones. Tessa felt such gratitude toward warriors who could be so gentle with God's most precious creations.

Chase and Zoric exited the bird first, extending a hand to several military officers. Tessa knew you couldn't salute a superior for fear the enemy would pick him off at the first opportunity. She wondered in for a moment if such information would ever be important when she attended the neighborhood book club meeting back home.

A soldier took Tessa's hand as she stepped down out of the helicopter. When she turned to check on Arzo, she saw Darya standing in the open door, one hand resting on a safety strap, the other holding the little girl close to his chest. She'd fallen asleep on his shoulder during the flight.

His expression narrowed as his eyes scanned the area. She wondered if the noise confused his ability to think straight. Having been in the Wakhan for a short time, listening to the indescribable
~~~

silence cloaking the land, Tessa understood the complexity of returning to civilization. The smell of diesel, garbage, and port-a-potties overwhelmed the senses having just left the sweet smell of smoke and yak tea.

Darya appeared confused until Tessa extended a hand to him. The pain in his expression couldn't be hidden. He released his hold on the overhead strap and hopped down with Arzo secured against him. Together the three of them stood like a family. The other little girls spotted them, escaping their new protectors.

"My girls," Tessa laughed. "We made it." The children jabbered all at the same time. Her Pashto had improved by leaps and bounds, but, with everyone talking at once, she understood none of what they were saying. She shrugged at Darya, hoping for help.

For the first time, he grinned at the little girls. "They are glad we are all together again." He patted each one on the head, reassuring them with praise and bragging on their bravery.

A man who appeared to be in charge ignored Chase's protest about something and sidestepped him, followed by two MPs. He walked up to Darya, showing contempt.

"Lieutenant Roman Darya Petrov?"

Darya's bottom lip shot out. He refused to answer as he handed Arzo over to Tessa.

"Are you Lieutenant Petrov?"

Chase came around to step between Darya and the colonel. "Don't do this here. These children see him as a father figure. Probably the only one they've ever had. He has done everything in his power to protect them so this woman"—he lifted a hand toward Tessa—"could bring them here and then on to the States for an education."

The colonel took a step closer but Chase straightened to his full six-foot-one height and blocked his path. Zoric stood shoulder to shoulder with his friend.

The colonel's lips thinned. His twisted snarl intensified as the captain continued to protect the tribesman.

"Stand back, Colonel." Bonnie, with a soldier at her elbow, pushed into the fray. "I'm Bonnie Finley, Undersecretary of State. Do whatever you're going to do later after these children are settled. I'm sure Darya can be trusted to turn himself over to you at the appropriate time."

"But—"

Tessa was a little proud of Bonnie when she held up her hand for silence. "Captain Hunter, please escort these children to the mess hall. They haven't eaten any decent food since early yesterday."

"Yes, ma'am." Chase turned to the group. "Follow me, please."

Tessa watched the colonel pivot, leaving an angry retort with Bonnie. "If he bolts, I'll have your head." He snapped at the stoic guard. "Follow them, soldier."

The children reached out to touch Tessa and Darya. One of the girls grabbed the hem of Bonnie's jacket when she couldn't edge closer to the others. She leaned in when Bonnie's hand came down on the top of her head.

"Tell the children to go with the captain, Tessa, before the colonel changes his mind."

Tessa shifted Arzo to her other shoulder as the little girl's legs circled her torso. She leaned into Darya when his hand came up to touch her back, moving her forward.

"We go. Safe here." He spoke with a quiet reserve, following Captain Hunter.

The girls stumbled several times, gawking at all the activity on the military base. New sounds startled them, but laughter would ensue very much like children being frightened on Halloween. With a pat on the head from Darya or a comforting word from Tessa, the children entered a mess tent like herded cattle. A few soldiers sat conversing with several women in surgical scrubs. They switched their focus to the children, joining the group with friendly faces and soft words. Captain Hunter filled them in and suggested medical exams after the children had a chance to fill their bellies.

Darya's rigid, solemn presence drew sideway glances from the medical team. His open, penetrating examination of their figures hinted at disdain rather than admiration. The captain introduced Tessa and explained the circumstances of her native dress and caring for a ragtag bunch of orphans. They greeted her with more than a little admiration in their expressions. Darya was introduced as Lieutenant Roman Petrov. Rather than reply, he turned and took Arzo, who had begun to squirm, from Tessa's arms.

Food and bottled water arrived for the children who sat shoulder to shoulder around a table with benches for seats. They watched Tessa and Darya for guidance before hungrily attacking their meal. The captain sat down across from Tessa between two of the girls. He made an effort to speak Pashto and managed to make them giggle.

Wiping her mouth on a paper napkin, she knew it was only a matter of time before he shifted his attention to her. In spite of her disheveled appearance, the captain offered a comforting, warm gaze.

"Tessa, I need to debrief you. Finish up and we'll head out."

"No," Darya snapped with such force the children stopped munching on their bread and cheese. "This is not proper."

Tessa slipped an arm around Darya's back. "I'll be all right. I need to do this so you'll be cleared."

"No." His voice grew flat and void of emotion. "Stay with children." Darya swung his legs around to the back of the bench before standing up. Several MPs from the doorway took a step forward, but the captain held up his hand for them to stop. "I will go with the captain. He wants to know about me."

Tessa reached out to take Darya's hand in fear. The two men glared at each other like battling lions trying to win a pride of females. She understood that it was her life binding them like cement to the military base.

"Have it your way, Lieutenant." He waved the approaching MPs off. "There's no need for that. Right, Lieutenant?"

Darya's chin came up in agreement.

Before Darya could take another step Arzo climbed up on the bench, standing as tall as her little body would go. She motioned Darya closer. This act brought a wide grin to his generous mouth as he let her circle his neck with her arms. He lifted her up into a tight hug. She patted his face then shoulders and whispered in his ear. Tessa felt her heart break seeing them together.

"I love you, too, Arzo. Be good for your mother. Do as you're told."

"Let's go." The captain's voice, now rich with impatience, brought yet another smirk to Darya's lips. When the tribesman rubbed the back of his hand on Tessa's face, she caught an inflamed glare from the captain. She imagined the next few hours would not be pleasant for her Kyrgyz tribesman.

would not be pleasant for her Kyrgyz tribesman.

CHAPTER 28

Pacing in a large tent heavy with the smell of sweat, dust, and shaving cream, Tessa glanced again at the clock sitting precariously on the edge of a makeshift desk created from two sawhorses and a piece of warped plywood. A discarded water bottle, a pad of paper, and various tools related to auto mechanics spread across the surface in disarray. Duct tape crisscrossed the clear plastic cover over a computer of the kind she'd had as a kid when she'd played Frogger. She spotted a rolled-up power strip with no way to plug it in, making her question whether or not soldiers ever made contact with their families. Another memory surfaced of Robert, her husband, kissing her good-bye as she headed out the door of their home. Should she call him?

Cots held napping children who'd filled their bellies, followed with exams by a female army doctor then been given what appeared to be their first shower. Their giggles of surprise and delight forced Tessa to laugh at their enjoyment for a short time. Bonnie Finley arrived with clean clothes both for the girls and her. She waited as Tessa slipped into the shower to wash grime and fear away.

"Thank you, Bonnie."

Tessa felt appreciation mixed with skepticism knowing the woman held enough information about Darya and herself to use blackmail like a Samurai sword. The ambassador, mired deep into the Afghan drug trade, might make it difficult to transport the children to the states. Would Bonnie confess to her lover someone else knew way too much about his thriving business? The continued danger to her life weighed on her ability to process her current situation.

The flap door of the tent pushed back without warning as Bonnie once more appeared with a man following her like a devoted puppy. She recognized him straightaway as Dr. Wu, the Enigma psychiatrist who fancied himself as some Buddhist master of all things true in the world. A fleeting thought of how she'd complained about his constant life lessons surfaced at the same time as the realization those same teachings enabled her to survive the last few weeks.

"Dr. Wu." It didn't occur to her to hide the pleasure in her voice.

Dressed in army fatigues, he stood a little taller than her. His hands folded in front of him suggested he might fall down in prayer at any moment. A simple greeting caused his chin-length black hair to swing a little forward, revealing the stripe of gray which trailed from his crown down to his ear. As she stared him down, amusement toyed at the corners of his mouth.

"Undersecretary Finley will stay with the girls while we take a walk, Mrs. Scott." The emphasis on Tessa's marital status felt like a slap in the face. He stepped sideways with a hand outstretched toward the exit. "Shall we?"

The disguised request was, in reality, an order. Tired of taking orders from domineering men, she considered refusing, except he wore the unconcerned expression of a man who knew how to pound patience into his patients. A huff of disgust pushed through her lips as she brushed past him and out the door.

"We have nothing to talk about, so whatever you want to know, get on with it. I don't want the girls to wake up and see I'm gone."

"Miss Finley is well-known to the children. I'm sure they will be fine. And we have much to talk about, Mrs. Scott. Lose the attitude and we can move this along much faster." He moved beside her but continued to stare straight ahead.

Tessa halted, raising a small cloud of dust around her feet. The doctor walked away from her in a nonchalant manner. "Remember. A single conversation with a wise man is better than ten years of study."

"Do not use a hatchet to remove a fly from a friend's forehead," she mocked. The doctor stopped in his tracks then lowered his head to steal an unconcerned glance back at her with an arched eyebrow.

"You remember your lessons well. Do you also remember what name I call you when we are alone?"

She felt a kind of hope he would help with the darkness inside her head. "Yes. You called me Grasshopper after some Kung Fu show from the 1970s. I thought it pretty ridiculous at the time."

"And now?" He waited like a patient monk.

"I'm drowning, Dr. Wu." Her voice cracked, but she recovered by pulling back her shoulders in a show of bravery. "Can you help me?"

He motioned for her to continue walking with him. "To get through the hardest journey, we need to take one step at a time, but we keep moving."

"That's it?" She spat the words.

"Better to light a candle than to curse the darkness." He held his head high and spoke with such confidence; Tessa followed him without further comment.

~~~

Chase strode across the compound, determined to confront Tessa about the days spent in the care of Darya Petrov turned Kyrgyz tribesman. The man had CIA written all over him. Was he a deserter or embedded with the Kyrgyz so he appeared to be a rogue agent? Had the Taliban been a threat to Tessa in the village? It seemed a little too convenient he chose then to make an appearance. Stories about the Kyrgyz being a part of the drug trade running rampant in Afghanistan could put him in bed with the CIA.

Answers to these questions remained elusive even after Chase threatened his manhood. Darya showed his amusement with a smirk and a casual evaluation of the room where he waited for interrogation. He appeared to take a visual inventory of possible solutions to his confinement. Even the appearance of Zoric failed to shake his confidence. However, when Tessa's name came up, Darya refocused his attention on the matter at hand.
~~~

"If I find out you harmed her in any way, I'll kill you." Chase's stance put Darya on alert as the tribesman eyed his opponent. "Why didn't she remember me?"

"Maybe you weren't worth remembering." Darya's low, condescending tone drawing Chase a step closer.

"Why did you take her?"

Darya shifted his attention to Zoric who made a show of examining the six-inch blade of his stained knife. "It is curious you are more concerned with the woman than what I've been up to for the last five years. Why is that?" He backed up to an unsteady table in the middle of the room and rested part of his hip on the edge. "Why not ask her?"

"I intend to. This is just a friendly conversation between soldiers. She works for," Chase hesitated, "the State Department. It's my job to make sure nothing happens to her."

"And yet you were not so concerned about the Finley woman who is the Undersecretary of State." A smirk toyed at the corners of Darya's mouth. "Tessa says she works with you. That doesn't sound like the State Department to me. You have the look of an ops guy. Trust me I know what that looks like."

"She's a low-level analyst working at a California university. Tessa has an uncanny ability to see things in geography the rest of us seem to miss."

Darya tilted his head in acceptance of the explanation. "You plan to take her back." His focus intensified toward Chase's with a hint of confrontation.

"She has a husband and kids to get back to."

"And you, I suspect." Darya stuck out his bottom lip.

Chase didn't respond at first. "You're wrong."

"Am I?" Darya grinned with amusement. "Whatever was between you two has been forgotten. She can't or doesn't want to remember the husband left behind in California. Now she loves me and I married her. She plans to stay here if I am freed."

Without thinking, Chase lunged at him with a doubled fist, knocking him backwards over the table. Before he could grab him for another punch, Darya jumped up and returned the blow to Chase's cheek, forcing him back against the table which collapsed under his weight. The tribesman jumped on top of the captain, landing several blows. The two men rolled several times across the floor, punching sensitive areas. Both men emitted sounds of pain and sprays of blood, yet neither stopped.

Darya managed to stagger to his feet only to fall back against the mud brick wall with a gasp. He sucked up his strength and propelled himself forward at the beast of a man rising from the floor. Landing a kick to his chest, Chase felt a rib crack. As he went back down on the floor, Zoric stepped up with his bloodstained knife, jabbing the tip against the tribesman's throat.

"I'm more of a man of action than my friend here. All this grunting, punching, and rolling around the floor like a couple of schoolboys is a waste of time. I much prefer to do the job and get it over with." Zoric applied enough pressure so a trickle of blood oozed from Darya's skin. He took a step back from the Serbian and leaned against the wall, his chest heaving.

After Chase splashed water on his face, he applied a bandage to the small cut on his cheek. When he confronted Tessa, he didn't want her to start asking too many questions as to how he received a bruised eyelid and several cuts.

Darya hadn't fared any better than him. He had to hand it to the tribesman, he could give as good as he got. The man managed to bait him into a fight, with Chase realizing too late, if Tessa got wind of the beating, she'd take her rescuer's side.

"Chase." Dr. Wu's raised voice drew him back to the present. The doctor marched up to him. "Chase. Tessa is in my quarters."

"Is she okay?" Chase turned toward the doctor's tent. "Traumatized." Dr. Wu stopped and squinted up at the captain. "She killed a man up there in those mountains."

Chase stared down at his boots for a long time before speaking. "One of the Taliban said as much, but I thought I misunderstood."

"No. She wouldn't tell me why. She didn't even appear to care she'd done it."

Chase lifted his head and couldn't hide his surprise. "This is not the Tessa we knew. Whatever happened up there scarred her to her very soul. You must be careful when you speak to her." Dr. Wu stepped in front of Chase as he took a step toward the tent. "She is not like us. Her coping skills are different. Although she may not feel remorse for her actions, in her mind, she has sinned against God and is unworthy to return home to her old life. If I am to help her, I need to know everything. You need to convince her to talk to me."

The darkening sky made Chase wonder about evil in the world and wonder why God allowed bad things to happen to good people. "What makes you think she'll tell me? Our relationship was…" He stopped himself because he didn't understand their relationship. Before he left her in the States, he'd promised to discuss things when he returned. When she showed up in Afghanistan and found him being stitched up, he'd planned his seduction of the honorable Mrs. Scott. He needed to get her out of his head once and for all.

"Yes. Your relationship is suspect at best. I don't know what is going on between the two of you, but I do know she listens to you more than anyone. To confess your interest in a romantic relationship would confuse the already-dangerous ideas filling her head." Dr. Wu took a deep breath. "There's a good chance she had to compromise her self-respect with the man she calls Darya. I believe she is suffering from Stockholm syndrome, Chase."

"Did he rape her?" Chase glared toward the tent where Tessa waited.

"I'm sure it doesn't seem like that now to her. But I don't know. Don't belittle him or confess what you've already attempted to do to him." Dr. Wu pointed to his bruises. "She'll defend him and threaten you."

"It wouldn't be the first time."

"This time is different. I promised her I'd get the children some dinner. Her concern borders on hysteria when it comes to those girls. Remember"—Dr. Wu stepped aside—"tread lightly if you want the old Tessa back."

"So, you want me to lie."

"Whatever it takes to move forward."

Even before he opened the flap of the tent, Chase planned to use his own methods to reach the woman he admired.

<h1 style="text-align:center">CHAPTER 29</h1>

The doctor occupied the tent reserved for US Congressmen and other visiting dignitaries. With a wave of a piece of paper bearing an important signature of the Secretary of Homeland Security, the base commander decided the doctor would be spared roughing it along with everyone else. A netted screen window on each side allowed the late afternoon sunlight to filter through. The interior, compared to everything else on the base, resembled a room at the Holiday Inn. Even the door, fitted with a doorknob and push-in lock, seemed luxurious in such a wasteland.

Chase ducked his head in the low doorway and spotted Tessa sitting on a folding chair next to a cot dressed to appear as if it were a twin bed instead of an army-issue piece of equipment. He removed his helmet and stuck it under his arm before shifting his weight to the less-painful hip. Nightfall would engulf the land soon, drenching them in breathless darkness, the kind that scared the hell out of you and forced you to keep a weapon under whatever you used for a pillow.

Tessa rose to her feet in slow motion, their cautious gazes locked. Her eyelids didn't flutter, a detail he'd learned meant her fear level peaked.

"Let's get some more light in here." Chase dropped his helmet into a folding chair suited more for a Hollywood director than a tent in Afghanistan. Spotting an LED lantern the size of a large flashlight, he turned it on before setting it on a small table holding a variety of toiletries.

"I need to get back to the girls." Tessa's voice showed impatience as her arms crossed across her chest.

The camo fatigues hugged her body a little tighter than the loose garb she'd worn when he'd found her in the mountains. She'd lost weight and in all the right places. His heart hammered with such intensity he rubbed a spot on his chest. She dropped her hands to her sides. "You're rubbing that spot again." Tessa cocked her head and frowned. "Did you ever go to the doctor about the pain?"

She remembered. "Yeah. Said I was a mean SOB with a guilty conscience." One corner of his mouth turned up in hope she'd note the humor in his voice. But the moment evaporated.

"I want to go back to the girls. Now."

"We need to talk, first, Tessa."

"I don't have anything to say to you either. I told Dr.Wu the same thing."

He could never remember her sounding so snarky. "Apparently you told him something. He's very concerned about you."

"I imagine he's concerned I'm damaged goods and no longer any use to Enigma." She took a deep breath as she reached over to a wooden table and fingered a metal cup stuffed with tea bags. When Chase didn't comment, she cut a wounded-animal glare to him, iced with contempt. "Nothing to say? I'm sure your mind bender doctor has already updated my file as to my mental state."

"Rumor has it you've been breaking commandments again." It was cruel, but a risk Chase wanted to take.

Tessa chewed her bottom lip, her body turned rigid. "Commandments?"

Chase dared take a step closer, forcing her to take one back, her retreat stopped by a plastic dresser. "Commandments. You married another man. Adultery." He ran his hand across his face, feeling the throbbing on his bruises. "Thou shalt not kill." He lowered his voice in hopes she would feel comforted rather than threatened. "The Taliban said you killed someone." Tessa spread out both her arms to brace against the dresser.

She snarled like a cornered feline facing a pit bull. "Yes," she snapped. "I killed a man. Maybe two. I shot the second one, but Massoud may have finished him off. I don't know. I hit my head."

He blinked at her callous disregard for her actions. "I'm sure you had a good reason. Care to share what happened with me?" He resisted the temptation to gather her in his arms to comfort and reassure her the pain would pass.

"The Taliban are vile, evil men."

"I know, Tessa." He kept his voice calm even though he feared hearing her story might destroy the last bit of sanity he owned. "We fight them for that very reason. What did they do?"

She fidgeted, staring past him into the darkness. "He was going to rape Shirin. She's a little girl. A little girl!" she yelled. "I sank the knife Zoric gave me into the back of his neck." She shifted her gaze back to him. Did she expect him to be outraged, repulsed, or sorry for her?

When he said nothing she diverted her eyes and spoke softly. "I couldn't let that happen."

"And the other man?"

"The soldier gave me a gun. When Massoud's man went after Bonnie, I shot him. They'd beaten and shot the poor soldier who tried to help us. They dragged him away." Her voice turned melancholy. "He was so young."

"Tessa, the soldier is alive." At least Chase could give her some good news. "The Kyrgyz must have gotten there in time to save him. One of Darya's men was helping to get him back to the Americans. That's how I found out you were missing. We ran into him while on patrol. He's in Germany, being well taken care of. He has a long road ahead of him, but he's going to make it."

"Darya never told me." Her eyes widened as she spoke with a little more of the old Tessa showing through. "Thanks for telling me."

He'd managed to give Darya a set of wings and a halo. He wanted to steer the conversation back to the subject at hand. "Tessa, what you did saved a young girl from a brutal attack. The other children saw how you stood up against some of the worse scum of the Earth. In a way you saved their lives, too." He made a conscious effort to sound respectful. "I know what that feels like." Her eyes lifted to him in suspicion. "You saved me, too, you know."

"Ha! You're the poster boy for some apocalyptic soldier saving the world. When did I save you?"

Chase took a deep breath. "You save me every time you walk through the damn door, Tess. I thought you knew that."

She pushed away from the dresser and covered her face. An anguished howl of pain escaped from deep in her throat and tears burst forth. When her knees buckled, Chase scooped her up in his arms, pulling her tight against his body. The fight dissipated as she circled his neck with her arms, sobbing. With one hand, he rubbed her back from top to bottom, but remained quiet until her tears abated.

Holding her so close evoked a sense of guilt because he craved this moment of intimacy, albeit at the expense of her deep pain. Her hands touched the back of his head then slid to his stumbled jaw. Pushing her back, he could see the raw pain in her bloodshot eyes. A ghost of a genuine smile spread across the delicate mouth he dreamed of in the middle of the night.

"Come on." He took her hand and led her to the cot. Motioning for her to sit, he pulled up the chair to join her. Chase reached for her hands. As her breathing returned to normal, he rubbed his thumbs across the back of her knuckles before lifting one hand to remove a damp curl from her forehead.

"Tell me everything. From the beginning. I, of all people, have no right to judge you for anything you did to survive. You know me. You know about my demons. I will understand."

"Okay," she sighed raising her face to him. Chase braced himself against hearing about events which forever changed the woman who owned his heart. It was useless to deny it any longer. He loved her. Whatever happened between her and Darya could be forgotten as long as she continued to exist.

<center>~~~</center>

Darkness allowed Chase to take Tessa's hand as he led her across the compound to her tent where the children waited. Shadows skittering across the ground forced her to step closer to him. She searched the depths of darkness with nervousness as they stopped.

The doctor waited outside her quarters. "Dr. Wu, I owe you an apology." Tessa released Chase's hand. "I was rude and uncooperative."

Dr. Wu's eyebrows rose as he glanced to Chase. "To begin a

treacherous journey is never easy."

Zoric, half hidden in darkness, waited, too, without acknowledging her. She'd feared him once but knew without his knife, saving Shirin would have been impossible. Tessa stepped toward him, noticing his face remained void of emotion. He had practiced a lack of empathy for so many years that it was hard to know if he even had a heartbeat. Most people found it difficult to confront him in the light, much less at night. Yet Tessa moved closer to him. The Serbian's face grew void of interest or emotion. She knew of his demons that remained unconquered, yet he survived.

"Zoric," she whispered as he shifted his gaze to her. They hadn't spoken since he and Chase found her. He quickly glanced away as if losing interest. The Zoric she remembered would not avoid eye contact. She moved to push past him to enter the tent when he reached out to lift the door flap. When she flinched, he withdrew his hand and stood rock still. She turned to him and remembered all the nightmarish atrocities he'd committed to those who would do the weak and innocent harm. Did he suffer as she did? Was he showing her that even he could feel the uncertainty of moving on with your life?

"Zoric," she breathed again. When she took a step toward him, his eyes turned cold and sterile. She searched his face with a new kind of understanding. "I'm happy to see you. Thank you for coming for me."

Zoric blinked then bobbed his head in acceptance. He appeared to hold his breath as she once again stepped closer. With a gentle embrace she wrapped her arms around the man she knew to be a coldhearted killer and felt him stiffen. "I've missed you. Maybe Chase can tell you how your gift saved my life."

As she backed away, Zoric circled her waist and pulled her body to his chest so his rough face rubbed against hers. He smelled of cigarette smoke and his hair felt damp. He stepped back and released his touch without a word and opened the door once more for her.

Joyful voices cried, "Miss Melanie" or "Mother" when she appeared inside. Tessa scooped Arzo up in her arms as the others scampered up from the floor where they played games with two female soldiers. It appeared they were playing something like Old

Maid or maybe Go Fish. They giggled and talked all at once, sometimes pointing at the two women or the cards on the floor. Shirin stood patiently until Tessa stretched out her one free arm toward the girl. She moved under it and leaned in as it came down around her narrow shoulders. Tessa kissed her on the temple.

The rest of the evening remained lighthearted for the children's sake, Tessa careful not to mention Darya or where he might be, even though her concern grew with each passing hour. She hadn't noticed at first the bruises on Chase's face or the cut on his cheek. Now as he sat on the floor with the girls, letting them win at cards, she imagined the probable source of those injuries. Darya didn't compare in size to Chase but his strength matched the ex-Delta Force captain's.

"Time for bed, girls." Tessa's Pashto came so easily now she found herself thinking in the language. What little English the girls knew, they used with Chase although he spoke their tongue. He made funny faces at them and pretended to be clueless to their mischief. "You have them all stirred up, Chase. Go outside until I get them settled. We can say goodnight then."

Chase stretched one leg then the other, and became solemn faced. "I'm staying in here. Zoric will be by the door all night."

Tessa felt a wave of concern wash over her as the girls climbed onto their cots. "Are we in danger?"

Chase helped cover one of the little girls who had a case of the giggles. He wrinkled his nose and stuck out his tongue at her. This made the entire group burst into laughter.

"They didn't find Massoud's body when the helicopter went back for it."

Tessa covered her mouth in horror. "Someone stole his body."

"Or he got out in time. Could he have done that?"

"Darya shot him, but it wasn't a kill shot. He wanted Massoud to suffer and know his death would be imminent. I'm sure he was still alive when we left." Tessa covered Arzo then kissed her cheek. "Why would he come here? There are so many soldiers and weapons."

"Pride." Chase moved toward the door. "I'll be back in a few minutes. Zoric will be outside if you need anything."

"Chase?" Tessa followed him to the door. "Where is Darya?" She whispered so not to alarm the girls. "I want to see him."

"No." He turned his back to her and strode out into the darkness.

~~~

Bonnie Finley gazed on Darya in what the base used as a makeshift jail. The mud walls took on a grayish tint in the dappled light given off by an LED lantern hanging from a hook outside the room. Inside his cell, the size of a walk- in closet, a cot held his outstretched body. It took up half the enclosure. His head rested on an arm tucked behind his head. Staring at the ceiling, the tribesman appeared to be lost in thought until he spoke.

"Come to gloat?" He continued to stare at the ceiling.

Bonnie grasped the bars and grinned. "Doesn't seem like you have much of an accent anymore, Darya, or whatever your name is. You fooled me with all that 'Me Tarzan, you Jane' routine. Turns out you're an embedded operational officer for military intelligence."

Except for the rhythmic rise and fall of his chest, she couldn't make out any movement. He remained in his tribal garb which in some ways flattered his sinewy body. Remembering his rise out of the stream to grab Tessa as she fled brought back the image of his naked body. No wonder Little Miss Perfect didn't protest much at having to marry the rogue agent. Combine Russian with Kyrgyz DNA and Bonnie could imagine the sparks flying on their wedding night.

Taking a deep, impatient breath, she continued, "You can pretend you don't hear me, but I won't be silenced. You kidnapped the Undersecretary of State, a close personal friend of the ambassador. I'm sure you were very persuasive getting information from Tessa about my extra-curricular activities with the ambassador and"—she paused as he turned his head toward her—"as I was saying, perhaps I can help you."

Darya swung his legs to the floor then took one step to the bars. The mask of silence remained on his face. It reminded Bonnie of the ragged covering he'd worn the day of her rescue.

"You're in a lot of trouble. Tessa and I know the risk you took rescuing all of us then taking out Massoud." As an afterthought, she added, "At this point, we're not sure if he survived. His body is missing. Any chance he could have survived the gunshot
~~~

wound?"

A look of pleasure formed on Darya's thick lips, drawing Bonnie's eyes, yet he remained silent.

"This place is pretty much on high alert because you didn't finish him off. If my information is correct, he'll probably come after me and your precious wife." Arching an eyebrow, Bonnie offered a cynical tilt of her head. "By the way, Captain Hunter is with Tessa this very minute. I believe he plans to keep her safe by staying in her tent tonight."

In the time it took to exhale, Darya lunged at the bars, grabbing Bonnie by her shirt then jerking her against the metal. She cried out, drawing the unwanted attention of the outside guard who rushed in to pull her free. The guard rammed his billy club between the bars, but Darya jumped back before he made impact. Rushing forward again, he grabbed the club and twisted it from the soldier's hand followed by landing a karate move on his forearm. The young guard jerked his arm away and staggered back, surprise filling his eyes. Darya let the weapon drop outside the bars at Bonnie's feet. The tribesman held up one hand in surrender and stepped back.

Bonnie told the guard to leave and that it was a misunderstanding. She shouldn't have gotten so close to the bars. The young soldier picked up his baton and slammed it against the bars without causing so much as a flinch on Darya's face. He backed out, color rising in his face.

Straightening her shirt and tan camo jacket, she took a step closer to the bars. "Don't be so stupid. You're not running with the wild bunch anymore. You'll be expected to show a little civility if you want out of here. I can help you."

"Where's Tessa?" he asked in a flat voice.

"Not to worry. The children are with her. Chase's ghoul is standing guard outside. The captain isn't about to let anything happen to your bride." She let go a soft laugh. "You know, of course, she is already married to some lawyer in California. I think that trumps whatever mumbo jumbo was spoken over the two of you in the Pamirs." She sighed with dramatic flair. "It was entertaining, though. I don't think I've ever seen a more beautiful bride."

Darya took a step forward before touching the bars with

caution. His face continued to be solemn, but the hooded eyes filled with rage. "She wants to be with me so stop your taunts."

"Ahh, Darya. She wanted to be with you when she didn't know about her real life. Every minute you're locked up in here, she reverts more to the old Tessa. With Dr. Wu and Chase prying out every tiny bit of information from her and reassuring her who she really is, Tessa will be her old self in no time. Dr. Wu is a miracle worker, they say. Chase, on the other hand, is no stranger to"—she put her hand over her heart—"winning over the ladies, if you get my drift. In Tessa's weakened mental state, who knows what he can convince her of? Maybe the fact you're a drug-dealing outlaw who committed treason against the US." She put her finger on her cheek and rolled her eyes to the ceiling. "He'll send her back to her real hubby. Chase waits for her to decide hubby is not very exciting. He's in and you're out."

"They work together. Nothing more." His words held the slightest edge of disbelief.

She couldn't contain her laugh this time. "Oh, honey, there's more to it. We both know an operative doesn't break protocol. The captain sure as hell didn't come after me. He's in as much trouble as you are. But he's in a much better place than you. You know what they say. Out of sight, out of mind." Again, the cackling laugh. "Do you want my help or not?"

"Get me out of here and I'll make sure your secrets remain that way."

Bonnie turned to leave. "I knew you would be reasonable. Oh. And there's a little matter of dealing with Ambassador Jarvis."

CHAPTER 30

The early morning sounds of dawn that fell across the base confused Tessa at first. She waited to hear the hollow tinkle of a yak's bell, the neigh of ponies, or the bawl of a goat. No longer did the deep cold of morning force her to bury beneath scratchy blankets. The winds of the Pamirs failed to push against the yurt like giant lungs. The smell of boiling food mixed with the smoke of burning yak dung no longer teased her nose. Kaleidoscopes of colorful designs created by the Kyrgyz women were missing on the ceiling and walls. Now the dull colors of camo tan and olive were the fashionable décor. As the cobwebs of sleep vanished she remembered she'd left the Wakhan Valley.

Turning her head to the side, she saw Chase asleep in a canvas chair with his chin dropped against the bottom of his throat. He'd refused to leave the evening before as lights extinguished.

"I'm not taking any more chances with your safety, Tessa. When I know you and the children are on a plane and out of here, I'll relax. Not until then will I let you out of my sight. Understand?"

Zoric curled up in a blanket just inside the door. If anyone came through, they'd have to cross him. The girls were frightened at first so he waited until they were all asleep.

She took a deep breath and stretched her arms up before feeling a tickle on the bottom of her foot sticking out from the soft blanket. Jerking herself upright, she found Darya sitting at the end of her cot with an amused expression. He held his finger to his lips as he pointed toward the sleeping captain.

Tessa eased off the cot to stand before the man who had changed her world. A year ago, she'd believed only Captain Hunter possessed that talent. Squatting down, she drank him in, longing to feel his embrace.

"Darya," she whispered with pleasure. She reached out and touched the injuries to his jaw. "They let you go?" Her optimism couldn't be restrained.

Closing his eyes, he placed his hand on hers. "Not exactly." Her hand slid to his hair. "When do you leave for the States?"

Tessa blinked. This life would soon be over for her. "Tomorrow. Will you be coming with us?"

A click of a readied weapon drew her attention to Chase who eased out of his chair with his Glock pointed at Darya. "The answer to that is no." His voice sounded methodical and slow.

The tribesman lifted his hands to clasp behind the back of his head, continuing to stare at Tessa with an unemotional expression. He rolled to his knees. She jumped to her feet as Chase grasped Darya's collar and jerked him to his feet.

"Tessa, find Zoric."

She maneuvered around cots until she reached the door. Zoric lay on the ground, gagged, with his hands zip- tied behind his back. A welt the size of a quarter protruded from his forehead.

"Zoric," she said bending down to move his shoulders. A moan escaped his parched lips as he blinked at her. She felt in his vest pockets for his knife but found none.

"His weapon is in my pants, Tessa." Darya spoke with calm as he watched Chase. Tessa hurried to his side, plunging her hand inside his pockets. Before the captain could stop her, she pulled out the blade. It never occurred to her how intimate the gesture was until Chase rammed his weapon into Darya's side to move him away from her. "Zoric?" She dropped the knife when it sprang open but managed to retrieve it in order to release his hands. She rubbed his arms to help him with the stiffness until he stood up.

Shoving her aside he barreled toward Darya like a lopsided toy with some of its wheels missing. Outmaneuvering the Serbian, she wedged herself between the two men and pushed against his chest. "Please. No. The children, Zoric." With a gentle touch to his chest, she felt him step away.

Tessa pointed to the girls so he would turn to see them and understand they were waking. Slipping off their cots, they spotted Darya and gasped, displayed a few yawns. They waited as if they were traveling the road to the Wakhan and knew he would call them to his embrace as he did each day.

Zoric took a step back but his chest rose and fell rapidly.

Little voices called to Tessa then Darya.

"Put your gun down, Chase," Tessa demanded. "You're frightening the children. If Darya wanted you dead, your throat would have been slit during the night. He means us no harm."

Darya spoke in Pashto to the children as Zoric made a quick body search. When the Serbian stepped back, satisfied he didn't carry a weapon, he dropped his hands. "It is good, little ones. Do not be afraid. These men are doing their job."

With several more yawns and a couple of sneezes, the children moved toward the only father they'd ever known. He reached down and patted each one on the head. Even Shirin got a pinch on the cheek, making her lower her eyes in shyness. Arzo yanked on his clothing. Lifting her up into his arms he stroked her tangled hair.

"Your man here was dozing when I came through the door." Darya spoke to Chase but his accusation hooked on Zoric whose nostrils flared like those of a fire-breathing dragon. "It has been a while since you slept." He jerked his chin up toward the captain then continued. "Some protection you offer. I have been here for hours."

Chase lowered his weapon then shoved it into his belt holster.

"How did you get out?"

"Misunderstanding with one of the guards when the government woman came to see me. He didn't even realize I took the key." When Arzo laid rapid kisses on Darya's face then giggled, he turned her upside down then back up, much to her delight. Zoric covered his mouth to hide a possible smile before he turned to leave. Even Chase laughed at the girls who jumped up and down, begging for their turn.

"Why did Bonnie come see you?" Tessa knew this couldn't be a good thing. "What did she promise you?"

"I'm a little curious about that myself." Chase folded his arms across his chest. "The Bonnie Finley I knew in Washington always had a motive when she did something nice."

Tessa and Darya locked knowing glances before diverting their eyes.

"Is there something you two know I don't?" Chase walked up to confront her. "Now's the time, Tessa. You have a history of withholding information from me." She opened her mouth to speak as he continued. "You also have a habit of lying to me."

"I told you everything last night." Tessa squinted her eyes to prevent them from batting. He understood she evaded the question.

Darya raised his brows then gave her a knowing grin. "Everything?" His words came with triumphant amusement.

She bristled. "Shut up, Darya." He clamped his lips together in a frown. "You're just trying to anger him." Her glare bounced from her boss then back at the tribesman. "If Chase and Zoric hadn't come after me, all of us would be in serious trouble with Massoud. Admit it."

Darya stuck out his lip and tilted his head to the side. "This is true. But I won't be jailed like an animal when I'm an American citizen. I will use Bonnie Finley, your CO, and anyone else it takes to remain free. I'm a patriot, not…"

"An outlaw? Deserter? How about drug dealer?" Chase quipped.

"Darya isn't a drug dealer," Tessa lied. "I don't like your implication. He saved us from the Taliban. I told you that. If he hadn't come along"—she turned her softened gaze to him—"we'd be enslaved or dead."

Chase's frown deepened. "We will see. In the meantime, you will have no contact with him."

"You can't tell me what to do," she stormed. "After all he's my…" She stopped herself as both men seemed to hang on her words.

Three broad-shouldered MPs filed through the doorway; weapons drawn. The children cried and fell against Darya and Tessa.

"Put those guns away, you idiots." Chase stepped in front of them.

The tallest MP spoke with an unsure voice. "The colonel said we should drag his ass back to the brig dead or alive, sir."

"And I'm telling you, if you don't put those guns away, I'm going to ram them up your—"

"I'm coming," Darya said, handing Arzo to Shirin then kissing Tessa on the edge of her mouth. "I'll not give you any trouble."

Chase pointed toward the doorway. "Out. I've got this. He's not going anywhere. I'll escort him back to interrogation." One of the soldiers took out a zip tie. "I won't need that. This man is an officer and will be treated as such. If you can't do as I say, then get the hell out of here."

"Yes, sir. I'll wait outside until you're ready, Captain Hunter. I'll lead the way for you."

Chase turned his back on the MP. Tessa now held Arzo against her legs and let her gaze linger on Darya who moved closer to her side.

"Thank you, Chase." Her voice turned raspy, parched from so little humidity. She took the opportunity to run her hand down Darya's forearm.

"I'm going." Darya tapped several of the girls on their heads or pulled their tangled hair as he walked past them. "Be good girls."

Little heads bobbed obedience as they watched him leave with the captain.

"When will we see him again, Miss Melanie?" Shirin wrapped her arms around Tessa.

"I think never."

CHAPTER 31

Sacramento, California

Fall robbed the few oak trees of their leaves when the winter rains moved in earlier than usual in northern California where Tessa lived and worked. She loved this time of year or had until she spent part of it in the Hindu Cush in Northern Afghanistan.

Transitioning into a normal life again took some work on her part. Robert had been fed a line of half-truths, which he chose to believe. Director Clark and the State Department had personally contacted him before Tessa's return, explaining she'd witnessed a fatal helicopter crash. Stranded for days with the threat of Taliban insurgency, she and the Undersecretary of State were left to protect a group of orphan girls until help arrived. They were forced to move several times with the help of some mountain folks who had no love for the Taliban. Special Forces managed to orchestrate a rescue, but she'd witnessed several brutal deaths in the process.

"Your wife showed remarkable courage, Mr. Scott." Director Clark remained calm as he stirred his coffee the day he met with Robert to catch him up to speed.

"I don't understand why she went to Afghanistan. Her job was at a conference in Kyrgyzstan."

The director had made sure Tessa knew his exact story so there would be no confusion if her husband started asking questions. She could imagine the hard resolve in both the director's hawkish grimace and voice as he calmed Robert down. "Yes. The plane experienced some mechanical problems and Undersecretary Finley went with the pilot's recommendations to put down in Kabul."

"That doesn't explain why my wife ended up in the north in some godforsaken hellhole. Why didn't the military take care of this?"

"It was thought to be a safe area with lots of local support. The ambassador needed women to pick up the girls since the helicopter would be flown by men. There was no cause for alarm. Mrs. Scott and Ms. Finley volunteered to go."

"Alarm? For heaven's sake, Director Clark, it's Afghanistan." According to the director, Robert paced, ranted, and raved for a good fifteen minutes before coming up for air. "Was my wife injured in any way?"

"I assure you, Mr. Scott, your wife was never in any real danger. We had her on radio the entire time. Because of a storm, we couldn't get a helicopter to them as fast as first thought. But I will say she has seen the horrors of war up close and personal. You need to give her a chance to acclimate back into the real world as we know it."

"What does that mean exactly?" Tessa could imagine her husband's voice lowering as if he were about to hear some bad news.

"The State Department protocol has any employee who witnesses a tragic event overseas, related to the job, receive some counseling." Tessa could imagine Robert might be concerned about the cost. "It is one of the perks of the job, Mr. Scott."

She had to give it to the director; he knew her husband well. "She has been given a clean bill of health. The possibility of a few nightmares and being—how can I put this—standoffish, is probable. Give her some time. She did slip and bump her head, causing a little confusion for a few days. That appears to have dissipated as well, but you can never be sure. So be patient, understanding, and the caring husband she claims you to be."

Even now, weeks later, when Tessa thought of the conversation between the two, she wanted to chuckle. The gentleness Robert demonstrated upon her arrival with the Afghan girls proved him capable of great love and support. He insisted they come home with them until their host families arrived from different parts of the state. Fortunately, most were within two hours of Grass Valley, assuring her visits with the girls would be manageable.

The fact she remained a little jumpy caused Robert some concern. After being home a month, they still had not become intimate. "Tessa, I love you. No matter what, I love you."

"I know, Robert." The fall of his face when she didn't echo his declaration of love caused a wave of guilt to wash over her. "Maybe we can have a date night this weekend. The boys are going to a Boy Scout campout and Heather is doing a sleep over at the Ervins. Martha promised her a baking marathon. She so loves that child." Tessa reached out and caressed his face with the palm of her hand. When he tried to pull her into his arms, the image of Darya overwhelmed her so suddenly she turned away.

"Tessa, I'm sorry. What did I do?" Robert touched her shoulder.

Forcing a light laugh she waved her hand in a nonchalant fashion then decided to plant a kiss on his mouth. A satisfied look spread across his face as he pulled her close. "I have to catch a flight first thing in the morning. I'll be gone for a few days. I won't be back until Monday night. Sorry, hon. We'll hire a sitter next week. How about I make reservations at a B&B in Nevada City for us. We'll have dinner, cruise the shops, and take a carriage ride."

Somehow, she felt relieved to postpone the promise of intimacy. "Sounds great." Pulling away and picking up her briefcase seemed normal.

The rush out the door always meant she couldn't wait to leave for the safe arms of Enigma. At least they knew how she suffered from the weight of her sins. Dr. Wu would be waiting for her and take her someplace tranquil to talk before letting her go to work. She'd come to depend on him since her return.

"Robert, I do love you. I'm sorry I've been so distant. It has nothing to do with you." Tessa grimaced inside knowing it had everything to do with a Kyrgyz tribesman she owed a debt. She needed to talk to Dr. Wu about feeling guilty in returning to her wifely duties. Why she experienced a sense of betrayal to Darya continued to mystify her.

He opened the front door for her. She thought perhaps the "love" word made her husband happy. "I know, Tessa. I mean"— he puffed out his chest in mock humor—"I'm the total package.

Right?"

"That you are." She pretended to be amused at his attempt at humor. Waving good-bye, she escaped to her car.

Had that conversation really been yesterday?

"Hello, Betty Crocker," came a female voice from the open door of her office. Tessa switched from grading papers to see her trainer, Dr. Samantha Cordova, leaning against the doorframe. The two women failed to make much effort at pretending to like each other. "Isn't this your day to be home baking cookies and cleaning toilets?"

Tessa stacked the graded exams for her college students and clipped them together before shoving them into a file cabinet. "No school today. Had to get the kids off for their weekend activities. Decided to come in and catch up on some work." She leaned back in her chair. "Why are you here? I know it's not because you want to do lunch."

Discovering the way to best deal with the Enigma diva meant confronting her head on and never show fear, not an easy task under any circumstance. Besides being by far the most beautiful and dangerous creature, she'd ever met, Sam had the psychological bite of a Black Mamba. Most of the time, the woman scared the living daylights out of her. Tessa like to refer to the female agent as Satan's spawn.

"Good to see you didn't get your head shot off, Betty Crocker." High praise coming from a trainer with a Vlad the Impaler complex.

Sam had watched the little girls gather around Tessa the day they returned, trying to make sense of the new life they were about to embark upon. Those first few hours at the airport were tough.

She'd said only, "Tell me what I can do to help."

Thunderstruck would have been putting it mildly. Sam went to great lengths to help her reassure the children. Her Pashto, although slow, was almost as good as Tessa's. The girls couldn't stop talking about the beautiful lady. Exhaustion from her ordeal, paired with the long trip home, took a toll on her body. For the first time since they'd met, Tessa saw a caring side of Sam. She did the physical management of things so Tessa could concentrate on the children.

Because she had never met Robert, Sam stayed out of sight. She had a way of drawing too much attention and seemed to understand that Tessa didn't need another distraction or too many questions. In the days that followed, Sam took a rest from the verbal harassment and name calling. Today, she'd switched back into the agent from Hell.

"The director wants to see you."

"He could have called."

Sam shrugged. "I was headed this way. Told him I'd stop in."

Tessa let herself do a once-over of the woman and again thought about joining a gym on her way to Weight Watchers right after she went to the BOGO sale at Victoria's Secret. "Thanks. Be there as soon as I lock up here." The Enigma agent stepped farther into the tiny office and shut the door. She put her hands on Tessa's desk and leaned in, muscles bulging like she could crush a man's neck with one squeeze.

"I'm not sure what happened in Afghanistan—Tessa." Hearing Sam speak her name for the first time rattled her a bit. "You had to do things to survive."

"Are you my therapist now? Did Dr. Wu send you?"

"Humph. That hack?" She straightened to her five-foot-ten-inch frame. "No. You were this naive little toad"—Tessa rolled her eyes feeling the warm and fuzzy moment of being called by her name evaporate—"who thought everything to be rainbows and jellybeans before we met."

"Yeah. Thanks for the wake-up call." Sarcasm directed at Sam could be considered a survival instinct.

"We've had our differences."

Tessa pulled out a drawer to retrieve her purse, pretending not to care what Sam had to say. "I'm sorry. What?"

She dared meet Sam's contemptuous gaze to brace against a new onslaught of insults. "I like this Tessa better. Smart. Hateful. Knows how to survive."

"And doesn't give a rip what you think." Tessa raised her chin in a fictitious show of bravery.

Sam's eyes narrowed. "Listen to me. You came back alive. I now know if I need you to have my back, you'll be there."

Tessa's lips parted in shock, but words failed her.

"I doubted you could handle it. I was wrong. Those kids you saved can make a difference. That's on you." Sam arched a brow.

"Good job."

"Sam, I don't know what to say." Tessa's voice softened as a show of victory toyed at the corners of her mouth.

Sam turned on her heels. "Don't get all gooey on me. It's not like we're going to be girlfriends."

"And just like that, the moment is gone." She swung the door open. "You coming?"

Tessa slipped the strap of her purse over her shoulder and followed like an obedient puppy. Sam had already strolled halfway down the hall by the time Tessa turned off the light and locked up. Several men peeked out their office doors to watch Sam. Knowing the woman reserved the right to do her harm at a later date gave her an almost giddy feeling.

"So, we could do lunch though, right?" The words tumbled out like those of a nervous sixteen-year-old who became acquainted with the prom queen.

"Don't push your luck, Betty Crocker." Sam pushed the elevator button then peered down her sculptured nose at Tessa. "You buying?"

CHAPTER 32

Tessa's desk at Enigma resided in a building blending old and new architecture with that of other university halls of learning. It shared space with the teaching hospital that concentrated on infectious diseases. She learned after signing on, other research went on there that would have DARPA drooling with envy. Some of the country's brightest men and women enrolled in the University of Science and Technology Sacramento. Little did they know Enigma based their operations in universities across the country in hopes of future recruitment.

Like shooting fish in a barrel, Tessa had thought when she learned of the procedure. Most of the faculty had no idea what went on in Dragonwells Hall. The idea the seven-story building had several more floors beneath the ground would shock the board of trustees and university president. Enigma's talent remained stellar at living in the shadows, pretending to be something other than the truth.

"Hi, Mrs. Scott." Vernon, the redheaded heartthrob of nerds everywhere waved to her. "When are you going to bring us more cookies?" He walked beside her toward her desk located near the back of an expansive room bare of ornamentation other than maps. Some were dotted with colored pins; others were on flat screens updated every few seconds. Tessa used to stop and watch them, wondering what the colors signified.

"I put some in the fridge, Vern. Stop calling me Mrs.

Scott." She told him this at least once a week.

"Sure. Sure. Sorry." He touched her elbow. "Come on. The boss moved you." Tessa stopped. "Why?"

Vernon shrugged. "You've got a bigger cube now, closer to the big guy."

"Director Clark? Have I done something wrong?" She let Vernon lead her to her office.

This was more than a cube. Granted, it could be her large walk-in closet at home, but it had a glass wall dividing it from the main room and a window looking out onto the campus mall. Not having to share oxygen with people who memorized the periodic table as if it were bestowed upon mankind by Obi Wan Kenobi was a definite plus. Most of the time, Vernon's geeky computer gurus stole innocent glances at her, unless Sam dropped by for a meeting. Then she became invisible until someone slipped in their drool or ran into a door staring at the Goddess of Condescension.

"Thank you, Vern. I see there's already a pile of folders next to the computer."

"Your new PC is ready to go. I built it myself. I'll do a tutorial with you next week."

"Let's do it now. No classes today." Tessa ran her hand over the glass top of the desk. Considering there was never anything as clear as glass at Enigma gave her a new appreciation for irony.

"Big guy says no." He stole a glance over his shoulder with his usual nervous anticipation. "Be careful, Tessa."

Before she could question him further, he turned and yelled at one of his technical protégés. Vernon was the king of conspiracy theories. Never ask him to go into detail about a wacky tabloid you saw at the checkout line in the grocery store unless you wanted to spend the afternoon listening to his thoughts on the matter. She grabbed a cup of coffee and returned to her office to get a feel for things.

Most Fridays were spent at home catching up on laundry for her family. Sam hadn't been far off in her description of her life since returning home. The window drove her to distraction and beckoned her to gaze at life outside. She set her coffee down to cool.

Clouds had moved in and rain wouldn't be far behind. Shifting her weight to one hip, Tessa crossed her arms across her chest after kicking off her heels. She'd tied her hair up in a ponytail earlier, but the coolness of the office chilled her neck. Reaching up, she removed the hair tie, letting her hair fall over the shoulder of her red sweater.

"I love watching you do that." The male voice sounded deep, edged with a slight accent.

She whirled around and fell back against the windowsill as her hand went to her throat. "Darya!"

He stepped inside her office and closed the door. "Darya," she choked, relief washing through her like a tsunami. "Darya."

"Is that any way to greet your husband?" His warm expression disarmed her so quickly she stumbled toward him with outstretched hands until his arms went around her waist. He lifted her up off the floor so only her toes touched the carpet. Sitting her back down, he turned around to display the new Darya. "What do you think?"

She laughed. "Hmm. Blue jeans, denim shirt, and cowboy boots. And your hair." She reached up and tousled his cropped dark-brown hair. "If I had known you'd clean up so well, I would never have left you with all those nurses in Afghanistan."

He reached out and took her hand, bringing it to his lips. "And you." He twirled her around then pulled her close. "I'm not sure I like you being the eye candy for all those young men outside your office. Are your students in love with you?"

Lighthearted laughter spilled into the room.

"They hate me. They think my tests are too hard and unreasonable. I even had one of their parents contact me to give their son a second chance on a late assignment."

"I knew you were tough." His hand went down her back, sending a chill up her spine. "You are beautiful, Tessa. I didn't know until this very second how much I missed you."

Time stood still as they stared into each other's eyes, remembering days gone by when they were free to roam the Wakhan Valley with nothing but the wind to follow them. She grabbed both his hands and squeezed.

"I didn't think I'd ever see you again. No one would tell me anything." Taking a deep breath, Tessa wrinkled her nose. "I can't smell you."

Darya laughed again. "Probably a good thing. Yak dung smoke would not be so popular in your fancy building."

The memory of him lying half-naked under yak robes with her cradled in the crook of his arm made her heart skip a beat. An embarrassed march of heat crept up her neck then face at her carnal thoughts. "My goodness. I'm blushing like a school girl." She put her hands on her cheeks.

Darya took her hands in his once again. "We have unfinished business." The warmth in his voice did nothing to cool her skin.

"What business would that be, Mr. Petrov?" Director Clark walked into the office, filling up the doorway. Neither had heard him open the door. "And how the hell did you lose your escort?"

Darya dropped Tessa's hands with reluctance as he shifted his now-icy attention to the director. "You mean your guard."

Panic pounded in Tessa's senses. "Guard?" Her voice snapped. "Is Darya under arrest?"

Director Clark peered down his eagle-like nose at her then Darya. "No. He has been cleared of any and all charges, even the one of his involvement in Ambassador Jarvis's death. It seems the ambassador got some extra- strength heroin."

Tessa had learned of the ambassador's death and the missing hours Darya couldn't account for after he'd broken out of his jail before she'd left Afghanistan.

Her sigh of relief drew Darya's full attention back to her. "Not to worry. I will explain everything to you." Without diverting his attention from her, he directed his next question to the director. "Right, Ben?"

No one called the director by his first name, except maybe Chase. Startled at the familiarity, she watched darkness fill the director's face. "Is he free to go?" She lifted her face hopefully at Darya.

Darya narrowed his glare at the director. "As free as one can be when you make a deal with the devil. Am I right, Ben?"

"It's Director Clark," he growled.

Darya smirked and spoke with flippant disregard. "Yes, sir."

"I've arranged a meeting for us in the conference room."

Darya turned his grin from the director to Tessa. "I'd rather go someplace more private."

"I don't give a rat's ass what you'd prefer, Mr. Petrov. You'll do what I say. When I say jump your response is 'how high'? Are we clear?"

"I'm afraid I've forgotten how to take orders…Director."

"Then you'd better let Mrs. Scott inform you of my degree of patience before you think about running."

Tessa could feel the level of intimidation between the two men peaking as Vernon appeared in the door. "Ready, sir."

The three followed Vernon to the elevator and rode down to the first floor. When the doors opened to the sterile foyer leading to their end destination, Tessa still didn't understand why they couldn't continue whatever was so important upstairs. The director's secretary stood waiting with her usual pleasant attitude, at the door with Dr. Wu who made eye contact with Tessa but ignored Darya.

"What is going on, Director Clark? Why are we here?" Tessa watched Glenda open the door and wink at her boss. "Is there an emergency?"

The director stood aside, motioning for them to enter. A large sheet cake in the middle of the conference table with plates, and a punch bowl with icy red liquid sat ready for some sort of a party.

"I don't understand." Small voices giggled and her little orphans popped up from behind the table, clapping and laughing, surprising her. When they saw Darya, their squeals of delight exploded as they scampered around the table to mob him.

He fell to his knees, letting them touch his hair, face, and clothes. They reached for Tessa, toying with her skirt and sweater then switched to trying to win the attention of Darya who laughed, scolded them playfully, and hugged each of them before standing up. Even Shirin stepped forward to give him a hug.

Pulling the young teen aside, Darya twirled her around. Shirin stood in her blue jeans, ankle boots, and long-sleeve sweater waiting for his approval at her American transformation.

He touched the head covering and remembered her past. "You look like an American, Shirin." She dropped her chin to reveal her shyness remained the same. He lifted her head up with one finger. "I had better not hear of American boys coming to win your favor. I will throw them beneath the hooves of my yaks!"

Shirin covered her mouth as a giggle threatened to escape. "You do not have yaks, Darya. You sold them for Miss Melanie."

Tessa hugged the girl. "She's right."

Darya frowned. "Humph! So, I did. Then I will have to buy

more! How much do you think I can get for Miss Melanie?"

"A million dollars," one of the little ones chirped.

"A million!" Darya gasped. He rubbed his chin as she twirled around to show her value. "I think you're right. But I think I will keep her. Shirin, if boys start to come around for you, I will break them into pieces with my bare hands!" He pretended to break something over his knee.

Shirin couldn't stop giggling at his claims. "I have missed you, Father." Her words were in Pashto.

"And I you, Daughter." Darya leaned in and kissed her cheek then patted the back of her head.

"Director, thank you." Tessa felt overcome with joy seeing the little faces that'd changed her life. They were thriving. Their host parents meandered around the room, talking to one another while the girls teased each other and hugged. "I don't know what to say."

"Thank, Dr. Wu. It was his idea." He extended a hand toward the doctor who stood apart observing the mayhem. "He claims your therapy needed a little reward for your hard work."

"Where's Arzo?" Darya turned around for the littlest of the orphans.

The director leaned his ear to Vernon then straightened. "She's coming in now."

Tessa and Darya hurried into the foyer to see Arzo skipping between her new parents. She wore a pink dress and ballet slippers. Her sandy-colored hair was done up in purple ribbons. Surveying the area with the curiosity of a child introduced to Disneyland for the first time, she wiggled with excitement. The Afghan couple who held her hands had lived in America for ten years. They were in the process of adopting her. Their joyful faces spoke of love as they stopped and bent down to say something to Arzo. She jerked her head around to see the tribesman and his wife.

Dropping the couple's hands, she ran as fast as her little legs would carry her with outstretched arms. Tessa couldn't hold back the tears as Darya ran to the child and scooped her up in his arms. Swinging her around until she squealed for him to stop, he laughed out loud. Burying her face in his cheek, she hugged his neck before the onslaught of kisses.

"Father, I'm going to be adopted!" Arzo reached over and

hugged Tessa. She'd seen the little girl at least once a week since the couple worked at the university and had promised to let Tessa remain a part of Arzo's life. Her own daughter, Heather, had even taken the role of big sister to the three-year-old.

"That is wonderful news, Arzo." Darya took the extended hand of the new father and offered congratulations. "You must be as good a daughter for this man as you were for me."

Arzo crossed her heart like an American child, but it looked more like a tic-tac-toe chart. "Promise and zap my heart," she said in English.

Darya kissed her forehead. "I think we need some cake, Tessa. Will there be enough for Arzo?"

Tessa tickled the child and moved back inside the conference room where the others had already begun to take a portion of the chocolate crème delight. "Maybe she should have carrots instead."

In protest, Arzo shook her head and wiggled free to join the others at the table.

"Director, I, too, am grateful to see the children." Darya came alongside him while watching the children enjoy their treat.

"Some of their host families drove several hours to get here. As you can see, they are all thriving. One or both of the host parents is Afghani. All of the girls have been given extended visas. If all goes well, the children will be adopted then granted political asylum in the US. We are aware Americans cannot adopt Afghan children, so we wanted to make sure after the sacrifice of our soldiers, State Department, and our own agency, they be given the opportunities promised."

Darya became still as he watched them. "Knowing they would have been enslaved or killed because they are girls not so long ago…" Tessa heard the catch in his voice. "It was worth it."

"Tessa, aren't you going to introduce me to your friend?" Samantha Cordova entered the room like a queen. Her warm gaze devoured Darya then cast a fleeting smirk Tessa's way. Without waiting for the introduction, she extended her hand toward Darya and stepped closer. "Dr. Cordova. Call me Sam." His hand surrounded hers as she gave her usual killer smile that could melt a glacier in short order. "You must be Roman Darya Petrov. I've read up on you. Tessa hasn't even mentioned you, so I took it upon myself to do a little digging. Now I see why she kept you such a secret." Her hazel-green eyes covered him from head to toe.

Tessa reached in and removed Darya's hand. "Better wash that. Sam has some kind of mysterious rash the doctors haven't been able to identify." She clicked her tongue before batting her eyes at the competition. "Still running a fever?"

Sam pulled back her shoulders. "Such a kidder. She keeps thinking this is clown school. We so love her little jokes."

Both women forced a laugh then sobered at the same time.

"I'd be happy to show you around while you're here," Sam continued.

Darya slipped his arm around Tessa. "I already have plans."

CHAPTER 33

When the party broke up, darkness had already fallen. Much to Tessa's disappointment, Director Clark and Vernon whisked Darya away, said there were some details of his release needing attention. She spent the night in her apartment after being told she needed not to concern herself with his plans for the evening. If she returned in the morning, she could participate in a briefing with the director. She didn't return to Grass Valley since Robert traveled for business and the children were engaged in other activities. Staying at her apartment, not far from the university, continued to be yet another secret she'd managed to keep from her husband.

Although Robert knew she sometimes spent the night in Sacramento, he believed she took a room at the university or a hotel out by the airport, depending on whether the State Department requested an appearance in D.C. As long as he didn't foot the bill for her stays in the city, they didn't raise any suspicions. If he knew Enigma insisted she take an apartment, he might be a little more concerned about her activities.

Chase had screened several places for her to live but, in the end, she'd gone over his objections to purchase an apartment on the second floor of a charming old house once belonging to a wealthy doctor. The opportunity to buy a piece of prime downtown real estate within walking distance of her day job and Old Town Sacramento sealed the deal. The house held four apartments, two on each floor. Her thousand square feet of bliss was the only apartment with a terrace and French doors.

Coming in the front door, you could see the entire apartment, except for the bathroom and walk-in closet. Tessa filled it with flea market finds and online bargains. It felt warm and safe. She purchased things her husband would not appreciate since his style leaned toward modern and clutter free. She had no one to answer to here.

As she slipped toward sleep, later in the evening, her cell phone dinged.

"Chase? Where are you?" Tessa pushed herself up to a sitting position then adjusted her pillows to prop against her back.

"Trying to get home. I'm hoping to be back in a couple of days if not sooner. I take it since you answered your phone you aren't in Grass Valley."

"Robert is out of town and the kids had plans. The director wants me in first thing tomorrow morning."

The silence hung heavy for a few seconds. "Have you seen Darya?"

Even over the phone, Tessa noted coldness. "Yes. He's somewhere at Enigma tonight with the director." She imagined the information he wanted to know would never be asked. "Chase?"

"Yes." He turned back into the distant warrior he could morph into when he hid his feelings.

"It will be good to see you." She scooted deeper under the covers. "Why is Darya here?"

"We'll talk when I get home." He paused before he continued. "About Darya, Tessa, don't do anything you'll regret later. Can you sit tight until I get home?"

She waited a few seconds, hoping he'd explain himself or declare his true feelings for her. The closest he'd ever come to a crumb of intimacy was telling her she saved him. It wasn't enough.

"Good-bye, Chase." By the time she'd spoken his name, the line was dead.

~~~

Waiting became an art form you learned living in the Wakhan Valley. The rooftop of the world with its brutal winters, nomadic
~~~

herding, and lack of amenities for good health gave a man a great deal of time to ponder his position in the world. Time moved at a snail's pace when time had no meaning; the shifting of the wind across mountains shrouded in clouds marked the minutes of each day.

Darya backed himself into a corner and stood without comment as the director spoke in a hushed voice to Tessa. The outside noise, although buffered through thick glass, still distracted him from concentrating on this new life. Both the smells and sounds of a crowded civilization grated against his ability to be at peace.

Watching the woman dressed in jeans and a white blouse helped him focus on his objective. Even from where he stood, her scent touched his nose, sweet but strangely different than the way she'd been in the Pamirs. He'd noticed it the day before when he'd taken her in his arms.

The thought occurred to him maybe Chase might be remembering such a thought as he prepared to come home. Time remained an opponent. Once the captain returned, Darya knew they would be pitted against each other in more ways than one. Tessa caught his attention as he stood statue still and offered a warm gaze as the director continued to talk. The overpowering urge to grab her and run made him drop his hands to his side. It was difficult not to react to the joy on such a delicate face, but he remained outwardly unaffected as she turned back to the director.

"And that's it, Tessa." The director stood, a sign of dismissal. "Darya leaves tomorrow morning on a flight at…" He lifted his watch. "Ten a.m. I'll have my secretary make reservations at a hotel with shuttle service." He turned his skeptical gaze on the former tribesman. "Mr. Petrov, I trust you'll be on time and not deviate from the plan."

Darya pushed away from the corner, moving to Tessa who gathered up her purse and umbrella. "You can trust me, Director Clark."

The director's frown deepened. "We'll see. The only reason you made it this far had to do with Undersecretary Finley speaking to the president on your behalf." He turned to Tessa. "And Tessa, of course."

"Nice to have friends who know people in high places." His tone sounded flippant. "Can we go?"

"Provided you don't leave town." Director Clark leveled a grimace at Tessa who continued to glow in Darya's presence like he was some kind of rock star. "Tessa, do you want to babysit him the rest of the day or should I call someone else? You've been here all week. I'm sure you need a break."

"I'd love to." Her blush failed to hide her excitement. "I mean, I've got nothing else to do. I'll be fine."

Darya opened the door with a jerk. "Darya?" The director took a step closer.

"Yes?"

Director Clark narrowed his eyes a bit before lowering his head enough to stand as an eagle with a dangerous beak poised to rip open his dinner. "Do not mistake my generosity for weakness."

The former tribesman glared at the director. "Do not mistake my compliance for cooperation." He ushered Tessa out into the hall.

~~~

Walking arm and arm through Old Town with a steady drizzle falling against their umbrella, Tessa and Darya spoke in hushed tones through the darkness closing in around them. At first, Tessa worried someone from Grass Valley would recognize her on the arm of another man. But the weather kept people home. They were one of two couples in the restaurant lit by candles and a roaring fire in a stone fireplace. Soft jazz played in the background as the two devoured steaks, potatoes, and salad. They sat for several hours before deciding to brave the rain.

The surprise of seeing him dressed in a nice shirt and sport coat when she picked him up earlier had made her wolf-whistle. His new black jeans had made her wonder if Vernon had taken pity on him and made a quick trip to a we-got-everything kind of store.

She didn't ask why he'd been detained the night before and he didn't volunteer the information. She loved Vernon for showing Darya kindness but wondered if the director hadn't put him up to keeping track of him.

As she retrieved her messages, Darya buckled up in the passenger seat. Tessa froze at the text from her husband.

"Problem?" His accent still came through, causing Tessa to
~~~

touch his face.

"Not sure. Maybe." A little confused she shook her head. "Robert will be flying in tomorrow morning. Guess I'll be staying over after all. The kids won't be home until tomorrow evening, so…" Tessa knew she talked too fast.

"It is late. Do you want me to take a cab to my hotel?" He reached out to her fumbling with the phone. "You are shaking. Why?"

Tessa stared out the windshield. "I called your hotel to confirm while you paid the check. The reservation got canceled so I planned to take you to my apartment and let you stay there. It's just an hour to my home, but in this rain, on mountain roads…"

Darya slipped his hand to the back of her bare neck and massaged it with his thumb. "Stay with me, Tessa. Who knows when we will see each other again?"

Tessa turned her body toward him. Imagining him in a tattered mask, leading his horse to water as he surveyed the vast land before them, a chill racked her body. "You are all that is left of my life in the Wakhan. I don't want to waste another day or night without you."

She closed her eyes as his hand came to her cheek like he'd done so many times in captivity.

Turning the key in the ignition, Tessa pulled away from the curb to rendezvous with a promise.

CHAPTER 34

Darya walked around the apartment with a kind of curiosity that reminded Tessa of how she felt when finding a new antique store to browse. He examined every surface, picture, and knickknack she'd accumulated in a short time.

"What's this?" He flung open the terrace doors and walked outside.

The rain had stopped earlier and droplets falling into the gutters created a soft tapping sound. "This is my favorite spot. I love having coffee out here in the mornings." Her words came out wistful.

"How often do you stay here? Doesn't Robert wonder why you have a place in the city?"

Tessa took a deep breath before stepping up beside him. "He doesn't know anything about Enigma, Darya. He thinks I'm working on my Ph.D. and doing a little goodwill work for the State Department. I never set out to be so deceptive. I'm in over my head now and addicted to the rush."

Darya accepted her answer as he stared up at the sky. "He doesn't know about me, then."

"No. Even the team I'm a part of doesn't know much about you." He turned to her in seriousness forcing her to wink mischievously. "You're my best kept secret."

"Come with me tomorrow." His speech turned to Pashto. "I will take care of you. Leave this pollution and noise behind. We'll go into the mountains."

Tessa faced him. "You have no intention of getting on that plane, do you?" She swallowed hard. "You canceled the hotel reservation."

Darya searched her face as if seeing it for the first time. He put both his hands on each side of her cheeks. "Come with me, Tessa. We will start over."

"Darya, I have children. How can you ask such a thing?" She pushed him away.

"We will take them, too. I would be a good father."

"I know. But I have a husband who needs me."

"You have two husbands." He chuckled and circled her waist. "Have you returned to his bed?" He pulled her tighter against his chest. "You have not gone back to him because of me."

Tessa lowered her eyes. "He's giving me some time."

"So, this Robert is not very smart?"

Tessa stepped out of his embrace, bristling. "Don't be insulting. He is a good man. A good father."

A clap of thunder rolled across the sky, driving Tessa indoors. "Darya, it's dangerous. Come inside."

The skies opened up, rain falling in sheets while Darya stood with outstretched arms, letting the rain pour into his mouth then down his body. He hollered what sounded like a war cry after defeating the enemy in a mythological movie about gods. He laughed.

"Rain! Do you know how long it's been since I could stand in the rain without fear of freezing to death?"

Tessa ran to the bathroom, got several fluffy towels, and returned to the terrace doors. "Come here, Batman, before you catch cold." She motioned for him with the towels.

As she threw her jacket to the kitchen chair, to free up her arms, Darya ran inside, dripping all over her hardwood floors. He removed his sports jacket, leaving the wet shirt clinging to his body. When he stepped closer, he shook his head so the water splashed onto her bare shoulders. Her black dress with the oval neckline exposed a great deal of skin. When he shook his head again like a wet coon dog, Tessa squealed a protest.

"Stop it!" But laughter erupted between them in spite of the mess. "Here. Let me help you out of this shirt." Darya pulled it over his head. Once off, she threw it to the floor. "If you get sick, the director will blame me."

She dried his hair then his neck and dragged the towel slower across his chest before sliding it down to his exposed navel. Memories of how hard his body felt when she'd been under his protection came flooding back to her heightened senses. Every scar, muscle, and breath brought Tessa once again under the spell of her captor.

Taking the towel from her hands, he dropped it to the floor on his clothes. With the care of a surgeon, he removed the clip holding up her hair, letting it cascade to her shoulders. She pressed her body against his chest. Tessa felt his hands run through her hair then down her back until they reached her buttocks. He kissed his way from her neck to her shoulders as his hands explored her body.

"I remember what you like," he whispered as he touched her lips with his.

"Darya," she managed to say as he captured her mouth with his, spilling his passion into her, blocking her ability to think. She felt dangerous and wild as he continued to kiss her almost desperately. He backed her toward the bed as Tessa felt his hands unzip her dress.

CHAPTER 35

It might prove not to be the best idea he'd ever had, but Chase stopped at a convenience store to pick up some flowers. There were two bouquets left at the checkout counter: one with dried sunflowers and the other with half-opened pink roses. He chose the latter, knowing Tessa loved the color pink. He glanced at the clock over the door and wondered if 1:30 a.m. would be too late to stop at her apartment. He pictured her sound asleep or perhaps she might be doing lesson plans for the geography class she taught.

Their relationship, Darya, and working at Enigma, needed to be addressed. Maybe they'd not get past the relationship part and the other two topics wouldn't matter. Keeping work and his feelings for her separate had become impossible. Before he left for Afghanistan, he'd believed they were becoming closer. Neither of them wanted to delve into such tumultuous waters. Surprised to see her in Afghanistan, he might have seduced her if her escort had not met with an untimely death. Later, when he'd gone after her in the Pamirs his fears of never being able to tell her how he felt forced him to realize how much he needed her.

Even when she'd been brought back, he knew their relationship had suffered because of the rogue agent. All the ground he'd gained in the last few months had been wiped out by the daring rescue of Tessa and a bunch of orphans by Darya Petrov. How could a man compete with a guy on a white horse?

"Good, you're still up," he mumbled as he saw a light in her second-story window. He spotted her car in her usual parking place. The building had a secure lock system where you needed to swipe a card to gain access. She didn't know Vernon made him one in case of emergency. He'd never used it until now.

He took the steps two at a time and paused on the landing, wishing he'd shaved and cleaned up a little at the airport before catching a cab into the city. Dropping his backpack under one of the windows, he wondered if he still had time. The hall was filled with dappled light from fixtures installed during a bygone era, part of why Tessa loved the place. She didn't care about the worn carpet or the large drafty windows in the hall.

"I'm not going to be in the hall much, Chase. Besides, the inside has been completely re-done. It'll be warm and toasty."

She'd been so proud of the place. As a gift, he'd bought her a full-size iron bed at a local antique store. He and Zoric put it together before she got home, while Vernon made sure security systems were in place. Remembering how she'd clapped her hands like a little kid still made him glad he'd spent the money.

Two knocks on the door. Hearing footsteps draw near, his chest got the familiar achy feeling again. The doorknob turned and the door pulled open.

"Bet you're surprised to see me here?" Darya smirked, keeping the chain on the door. "What do you want?"

Chase could see into the apartment all the way to the unmade bed and clothes on the floor. He recognized Tessa's jacket and saw another piece of woman's clothing.

"Those flowers sure are pretty, Captain Hunter."

The sound of a shower being turned on in the bathroom drew Darya's satisfied glance for only a second before he turned back to the captain. Chase's temper boiled deep inside as the once tribesman continued to level his own dangerous challenge at him.

"I'd invite you in, but it might be a little awkward." Darya glanced toward the bathroom again. "I'll be sure to let her know you dropped by. Good night, Captain."

He shut the door in Chase's face with a deliberate, slow-motion movement as if to prolong the agony.

Staring at the door for a good thirty seconds before returning to pick up his backpack, Chase hurried down the stairs covered in faded blue carpet. Once out on the street, he headed toward his condo, a good mile away. The rain turned into a heavy mist as he stared straight ahead, trying to ignore the jabbing pain in his chest and the total humiliation welling up inside him. Somewhere along the way, he threw the roses into the street.

The reason he stayed clear of romantic entanglements with married women and Enigma agents pounded his lapse of common sense back into his head. It had been clear in Afghanistan. The Kyrgyz tribesman had managed to captivate Tessa's heart. Even though Dr. Wu said she suffered from Stockholm syndrome, the fact remained she'd chosen him to be her lover, long before tonight.

Stopping in at a liquor store, he bought a bottle of Jack Daniels and wondered how much he'd have to drink before the numbness took over his thoughts. Enough room remained in his backpack for him to shove the bottle inside before crossing the street to his building. The night watchman at the desk never looked up from a rerun of Magnum P.I. as Chase slipped in without notice. He took the elevator to his sixth-floor condo as he let exhaustion finally touch his body.

Entering his foyer, Chase noticed the disabled security system. The time flickered from 2:30 a.m. to the current date. Careful not to make any noise, he propped his backpack against the wall then pulled his gun from under his shirt. His inspection covered the entire room in one sweeping glance as the lights from the city poured in from the floor-to-ceiling windows. Nothing appeared disturbed at first glance. A night-light on the microwave over the stove glowed on high, a setting he never used.

A scooting sound and a sniff came from the other side of the couch. Chase dropped into a crouch. He rushed, weapon held in both hands toward a body curled up on the couch, sound asleep. Returning his gun to his holster, he returned to the security system to watch the feed of the last few hours.

Walking to the sofa, he squatted down next to her. "What the hell are you doing here, Tessa?" he whispered so low it surprised him.

Tessa wore a black dress and pearls, and Chase noticed right off her legs were bare. Black heels lay sideways on the floor next to a file folder with contents half in and out. When he laid his hand on her ankle, the cold of her skin seeped into his fingers. Pulling off the plush white throw from the back of a nearby chair, he spread it across her body. She settled again with a sigh. Waiting for her to warm, he watched as she stretched out her legs then draped her arm down the side of the sofa.

He stared up at the ceiling and took a deep breath.

Dear God in Heaven. Thank you.

~~~

The windows faced west, flooding the room with a cloudy kind of light brought on by more rain. Tessa lay still for a long time, listening to nothing, trying to evaluate again where she'd slept. When her hand touched something hard, her eyes popped open to see Chase sitting on the floor next to her, sound asleep. She wondered how long he'd been there and resisted the impulse to sneak away before he awoke. His unshaven chin down, arms folded across his midsection, and legs outstretched enhanced his statue like beauty which never failed to take her breath away.

Thoughts turning to the night with Darya, she remembered how she almost compromised all she believed in before making desperate promises to escape Afghanistan.

Laying her hand over her face could not remove the vision of Darya's half-naked body pulling her toward ecstasy and betrayal.

"You're trembling," Darya spoke between passionate kisses. "Are you afraid of me?" Taking a moment to pull her into his bare arms he examined the exposed shoulder he'd freed from her dress. "I promise not to hurt you, Tessa."

A heated blush spread up her neck then face as he ran his fingers through her hair. "I'm terrified."

Darya kissed her throat then cheek. "Why? We have been through so much. Do you want me to say 'I love you' because I will a thousand times to have you?"

"I've not been with…" She stuttered and pulled away as he brought her face back to his. "No man besides Robert, my husband."

"And now I am your husband, Tessa." He rubbed his hand up and down her bare back. "Besides, did we not share a kind of passion in the Pamirs? Have you forgotten how we made each other feel?"
~~~

He finished unzipping her dress to her waist. "I owe you. I promised if you got us out of Afghanistan, I would be your wife in every way."

Darya slipped off the bed and pulled her after him. "Yes. I'm afraid I tricked you. My plans were to bring you back all along. I admired your courage and willingness to protect the children at any cost. Taking advantage of that resolve gave me a reason to believe in the goodness of my fellow Americans again." His stroking her arms did nothing to cool the passion which flared up between them.

She wrapped her arms around him; he stood still with his chin resting on top of her head.

"I'm sorry, Darya, I've let you down."

"I'm sorry I didn't find you before Captain Hunter." Pushing back, Tessa wanted to process his words.

"You mean Robert."

"No. Captain Hunter is stalking you for his own."

"You're wrong. He's protective of his team."

Darya ran his hands through her hair then kissed her mouth. "He fears me more than Robert. You are a creature of desire and dreams, a woman not to be contained in the box Robert has put you in. If this were not so, you wouldn't be at Enigma. The captain knows I'm his equal and a great deal more impatient than he in waiting for what I want." Tessa felt bewildered and frightened. "But I will honor your wishes to keep your first marriage sanctified until the time you need me again. Then"— Darya ran his hands over her shoulders then down her sides until they rested on her hips—"I will want my wife to honor her duty to her husband. Your love belongs to two men and Robert is not one of them."

Raising her chin, Tessa let her gaze travel around his angular face. "I know." She took his hand and placed it on her heart. "You are here always."

Taking a deep breath, he handed her the discarded high heels and her handbag. After she took a yellow raincoat from the closet he walked her outside to her car. "Before you go, let me tell you my plans."

Tessa waved good-bye as he went back inside. When she turned to open the car door, a figure loomed in front of her.

"That didn't take long." Sometimes Sam had the uncanny

ability to sound like the wicked witch from Hansel and Gretel. She reached out and rubbed a finger across the corner of Tessa's mouth. "Better clean yourself up, Betty Crocker."

"What are you doing here, Sam?"

"The director thought our tribesman might be planning on running. I volunteered to keep an eye on him after his hotel reservations mysteriously vanished." Sam sought out the second-story window, and Tessa followed her gaze to see Darya watching them. Sam handed Tessa her keys. "Guess someone blocked you in. No way you're getting out. Take my car." Her attention returned to Tessa. "I can watch from your car as good as my own." Sam unlocked the car door and slid inside. "Would it hurt you to vacuum this thing out? Smells like dirty socks." She wrinkled her nose. "I called the librarian; you can stay with her."

"Claudia?" Tessa couldn't imagine Claudia agreeing to the request. Known to be rather eccentric and a neat freak, the only friend she claimed was Chase who indulged her weird behavior. "She said I could come over?"

An exasperated sigh passed through Sam's lips as she shoved her all the way to the car.

But it hadn't been okay. Claudia wouldn't even let Tessa in the door. She lived in the same building as Chase, so she took Tessa to his condo and pushed her through the door then left. She deactivated the alarm system and grumbled as she left, "Chase wouldn't care. He isn't home anyway. He likes you. It's okay. He won't care." Being slightly autistic, the woman tended to repeat the obvious.

She'd arrived hours ago then taken half of an antihistamine tablet she'd found in her purse and dozed off before she could stew much about the events of the evening. Now here she lay next to the man who pretended to find her annoying on most occasions, interesting on others.

Rolling to her side, Tessa suspended her hand over his bent head, deciding whether or not to touch his ebony hair which had grown down over his neck. She'd never seen it so long and thick. Scooting closer, she dared toy with the strands, bringing a few close to her nose to inhale his scent. Resting her hand on his shoulder, she watched his chest rise and fall in a slow rhythm.

Daring to let her hand move to his chest to feel the beat of his heart, Tessa realized she was close enough to inhale his masculine scent causing Darya's words to haunt her. Some of her memories of Chase remained fuzzy on the outskirts of her mind, but touching him made her feel, and it was not the same as Darya.

As she withdrew her hand from his chest, Chase lifted his head from sleep and spoke through a yawn. "Why didn't you get in the bed?"

"Seriously? I didn't want to sleep on the same sheets as your brainy bimbos."

"I don't bring women here. I stay at their places, and they can change the sheets."

"Good to know." Tessa made an effort to sit up as Chase turned to face her. "Guess I was a surprise when you got home. If I'd known you were coming in so soon, I would have found a hotel room. Claudia refused to let me stay with her after saying she would." Tessa swung her legs to the floor and noticed Chase gawking at them before pushing himself to a standing position.

Chase stretched out his arms then yawned again. "Why didn't you go to bed?" Tessa let him pull her to her feet then stepped away to put some distance between them. The realization they'd shared a deep friendship in the past surfaced in the back of her mind.

"I don't like to sleep alone on Saturday nights. Since you took up the whole sofa like a spoiled feline, there wasn't any room for me. I thought about carrying you to the bed but figured I'd get kicked in the crotch or thrown through the plate glass window." He put his hand over his heart. "It would have been totally innocent on my part, of course." His boyish grin gave her goose bumps as Darya's words of warning kept rushing at her.

"You'd best remember that, Captain Hunter." She pointed an accusing finger at him. "I'd better go. Robert is coming home early. His flight arrives at ten."

"Delayed. Snowstorm in Chicago. So, relax."

Tessa wanted to ask how he knew but remembered Enigma knew everything, even pointless details like when someone's husband was snowed in in another city. She moved toward the kitchen.

"Hungry?" he asked, following her on bare feet. "Starved."

"Good. Me, too. Fix us something." He bumped her shoulder

with his. "Coffee, strong. Not like the stuff you drink." She plugged in the coffeepot as he opened the drawer and pulled out some silverware. He grabbed a knife and dropped it on the counter, sending Tessa up against the wall with a gasp.

"Tessa," Chase said reaching for her. "I'm sorry. I'm sorry." He shoved the knife back in the drawer. "Baby, it's okay. I didn't mean to." He stepped closer, careful to slow his speech and movements. "Come here."

Stepping forward, she touched his arms. "I'm still a bit of a mess, Chase. I'm okay. Really."

Chase placed his hand on the back of her head, but she jerked away. "Go. Get a shower. I'll see if there's anything to eat." He didn't move until she shoved at his chest.

"Please, Chase. I need a minute. When I get a cup of coffee, I'll be good as new."

He disappeared into the bedroom, leaving the door ajar. Wondering if he thought she'd call out to him if needed or maybe join him in the shower felt a bit disconcerting.

She found a coffee cake in the freezer and had popped it into the microwave when her phone beeped. Seeing Darya's picture, she slithered farther back into the kitchen for privacy.

"Hello."

"Leaving. Taking your car. I'll leave it in Auburn."

"My car?" Had Sam decided to leave after the lights went out in her apartment?

"Captain Hunter dropped by last night. Said I'd let you know. Wasn't too happy to see me."

"You'll keep your word?" Tessa whispered.

"You know the plan, Tessa, and where I'll be. I'm a phone call away."

The line went dead as Chase came through the bedroom door in clean jeans with a red T-shirt stretched across his chest. "What smells so good?"

She managed to lay her phone down and move to the microwave. "Caramel coffee cake. Found it in the freezer. Coffee is ready, too."

Once she removed the pastry, Chase divided it up onto plates then grabbed some paper towels for napkins. After he carried the food to the bar dividing the kitchen from the living room, Tessa joined him with two mugs of steaming coffee.

"I stopped by your apartment before I came here last night." He funneled in a large piece of cake and talked through his chewing.

Tessa picked up her coffee and let the heat seep into her hands. "Pretty late to be paying me a visit. Sounds like stalking." She set her cup down and pointed a fork at him.

"Someone besides Darya was there." Tessa's fork paused in midair.

"I thought it was you. I could see unmade bed and clothes were everywhere. You can imagine what I thought." He leveled an accusing glare as he continued to chew then gulped his coffee.

"Must have been Agent Nymphomaniac."

"Sam." Chase smirked. "Jealous?"

She shrugged. "Maybe. A little." I'm going to strangle the woman.

"I got the impression something else happened up there in the mountains. Wasn't there a wedding night?"

"Yes. But I bargained my way to freedom."

He cocked his head to the side, brow furrowed. "So, you never slept with him."

"Holy cow. Of course I slept with him," she snapped indignantly. "But we never consummated the marriage. Isn't that what you're asking?" Tessa slid off the barstool and carried her plate to the sink. "It's none of your business, Chase."

Chase joined her and set his plate on top of hers then moved to the coffeepot. "You mean to tell me a man like Darya didn't take advantage of you after paying a handsome sum to marry you?"

"That's exactly what I'm telling you. I've slept with you and we've never had sex." What an irritating insinuation. Besides, what he didn't know wouldn't hurt him.

"I'm a gentleman."

"So is he. We never had sex. Not even last night when..." Chase raised his chin as if anticipating bad news. "When he could have collected on our deal."

"Tessa, you are going to have to stop promising your body to men like me and Darya when times get tough." Her mouth flew open in protest as he laughed. "You promised me the same thing when you thought I was dying in D.C." He repeated word for word what she offered him if he'd fight to stay alive. He leaned back against the counter and folded his arms across his chest, muscles bulging. "How many men am I going to have to kill to stay at the head of the line?"

"You're insufferable." She hurried past him into the living room and grabbed her purse. Hopping on one foot to slip on her shoes slowed her escape. His deep laugh followed her as she headed to the door. As her hand touched the doorknob, Chase put his hand on the door, preventing it from opening.

His breath came next to her ear. "Don't go, Tessa." She turned her head, finding him staring down at her. "Don't go."

"This is a mistake," she whispered as her eyes fell on his mouth.

Her phone beeped from the kitchen counter where she'd left it. "Are you going to get that?"

Tessa hurried to the kitchen and picked up her phone. A picture of Sam tied and gagged in her apartment greeted her. She choked back laughter as she carried it to Chase. "Guess I'm not the only one capable of making mistakes." To her surprise, Chase laughed out loud.

EPILOGUE

Screams burst the silence of the village where large fires burned in deep holes in the ground. Men huddled around the blazes as their backs turned away from the tent where their leader received medical attention. His death had been imminent, yet he had survived his terrible wounds.

A doctor pushed back the flap of the tent and motioned for one of the men to come inside.

"He wants to talk to you. Don't stay long. I had to remove his leg below the knee." He shook his head. "I don't understand how he is still conscious."

The Taliban fighter entered and covered his nose from the smell of rotting flesh. As he moved closer, Massoud coughed then turned his head to acknowledge his presence.

"You have a job," he coughed again then grimaced. After a few seconds, he continued. "They need to die. All of them."

"Who, Massoud?"

"That Kyrgyz pig, the American soldier who helped him, and the woman."

"The woman?"

"The one with the yellow hair and blue eyes. The one they call Tessa. Especially her."

The End

ABOUT THE AUTHOR

Tierney has been in education for over thirty years. She recently stopped teaching World Geography for a nearby college to pursue her writing career. Creating a workshop for beginning writers, speaking at schools and serving as an officer in the writing group Sleuths' Ink, are some of the work she does when not writing. With the creation of *Winds of Deception,* Tierney is working with one of the crew members of USS Liberty in hopes of obtaining the Medal of Honor for him. She is also working with Mission K9 Rescue to create a children's book about four-footed soldiers that save lives.

Besides serving as a Solar System Ambassador for NASA's Jet Propulsion Lab and attending Space Camp for Educators, Tierney has traveled across the world. From the Great Wall of China to floating the Okavango Delta of Botswana, Africa, she ties her unique experiences into other writing projects such as the action thriller, *An Unlikely Hero*, the first in the Enigma Series. *Winds of Deception* is the second in that series. Living on a Native American reservation and in a mining town for many years fuels the kind of characters she never tires of creating.

Besides teaching and writing, Tierney enjoys family, gardening, reading and music. Other pursuits involve learning Hebrew in hopes of incorporating the knowledge in a future Engima Series. She likes to research and sometimes that has involved learning new skills, such as being certified with various weapons.